A Woman's Desire

Beatrice drew a deep breath and dared a glance at her irritable boarder. He was big and solid and his wet shirt revealed entirely too much of—

She didn't dare think of what lay beneath the wet linen. Meeting his eyes was somehow even worse. Mr. MacTavish's glare managed to heat her all over, as if he'd assessed her and found her lacking and was angry at her for it.

She didn't want to ride beside him in the narrow chaise. He smelled of manly perspiration and she could see golden brown hairs curling against the thin linen. She wished he'd don his coat.

He didn't wait for her to find an argument. Without permission, he grabbed her around the waist and set her firmly on the carriage seat. Before she had time to catch her breath, he climbed beside her. She burned through the corset where he'd touched her.

All A Woman Wants

Patricia Rice

A SIGNET BOOK

SIGNET
Published by New American Library, a division of
Penguin Putnam Inc., 375 Hudson Street,
New York, New York 10014, U.S.A.
Penguin Books Ltd, 27 Wrights Lane,
London W8 5TZ, England
Penguin Books Australia Ltd, Ringwood,
Victoria, Australia
Penguin Books Canada Ltd, 10 Alcorn Avenue,
Toronto, Ontario, Canada M4V 3B2
Penguin Books (N.Z.) Ltd, 182–190 Wairau Road,
Auckland 10, New Zealand

Penguin Books Ltd, Registered Offices:
Harmondsworth, Middlesex, England

First published by Signet, an imprint of New American Library,
a division of Penguin Putnam Inc.

First Printing, June 2001
10 9 8 7 6 5 4 3

 REGISTERED TRADEMARK—MARCA REGISTRADA

Printed in the United States of America

PUBLISHER'S NOTE
This is a work of fiction. Names, characters, places, and incidents either
are the product of the author's imagination or are used fictitiously,
and any resemblance to actual persons, living or dead, business
establishments, events, or locales is entirely coincidental.

BOOKS ARE AVAILABLE AT QUANTITY DISCOUNTS WHEN USED TO PROMOTE
PRODUCTS OR SERVICES. FOR INFORMATION PLEASE WRITE TO PREMIUM
MARKETING DIVISION, PENGUIN PUTNAM INC., 375 HUDSON STREET, NEW
YORK, NEW YORK 10014.

For Ellen, who endures a writer's neuroses with grace and patience, and succeeds where others would have smashed pumpkins (or other crushable matter!).

And as always, to Mary Jo and Connie and everyone else who has listened to screams of frustration and made sense out of the incomprehensible, you're my sanity. Thank you.

And forever, to my husband and children, for you are my heart, and I love you.

Prologue

"Not that way, ye keelhaulin' son of a sea serpent!" Lachlan Warwick MacTavish shouted, jumping to the dock ramp to grasp the rigging on a crate of cotton in danger of a watery fall. Holding the heavy crate in position, he waited while one of the crew hastened to right the ropes and swing it to a safer landing.

Below, his father's new London business agent appeared mildly startled by Mac's sudden, ungentlemanly leap into action. The man drew the frill-bedecked maiden who stood at his side to a more appropriate distance while she covered her ears with gloved hands to avert any further depredations on her delicate sensibilities.

Swearing beneath his breath, Mac shifted the heavy crate to show the inexperienced cargo man the ropes, yelled at his first mate to keep a closer watch on the unloading, and, stretching his muscles against the unusual restraint of a coat, grudgingly returned to the elegant pair waiting out of harm's way.

Gulls screeched, men cursed in the rigging as they brought down a storm-battered sail, and Mac thought he would far prefer being on his ship than here, discussing pleasantries with a money counter and his fashionable daughter. He had no use for ladies, and they had no use for him once they had his measure. That seldom took long. This one already wore the look of distaste he generally encountered on feminine features. He'd never quite managed the languid, fastidious elegance of a gentleman.

Brushing at the cargo dirt now smeared across his fancy coat, fingering his one good neckcloth, which was now loose and askew, he hid a grimace as he bowed an apology to the waiting couple. "Beg pardon, but some of the crew are a bit green."

The delicate lady in her many petticoats edged away from his overlarge presence. Impatiently, Mac balled his fists and ignored her, leaning down to hear the prattle of his father's agent as they traversed the dock toward the safety of the street.

His mind, though, took flight to a dock not far from this one, a dock at a shipyard boasting a spanking-new clipper with masts raised, fittings and final coats of paint ready for installation at the new master's command. His command. Finally.

"Your father says you have a canny head on your shoulders when you're inclined to use it," the agent was saying.

"Aye, well, we have a wee bit of disagreement on those uses from time to time." With iron determination, Mac tempered his impatience to see the ship he'd commissioned. He had a dozen duties ahead, and one was humoring this old man. He needed all the goodwill he could summon to obtain the agent's aid in stocking the new vessel Mac would be sailing home.

"Well, you've brought me a fine shipment, from all reports. Have you a list of goods you'll be wanting to take back?"

"And I'd be a fool not to, wouldn't I?" Eyeing the fine horse waiting for him at the curb, Mac paid no heed to the female swaying beside him. Women—ladies, at least—weren't on his current list of priorities.

Later, when he had time, he would divert his restlessness with the company of a tavern wench.

This time next year, it would be his own ship cutting across the ocean, carrying profits to his *own* bank account, rather than his father's. It was all very well and good to know he'd someday inherit his father's wealth, but not if the wealth depended on an enterprise that was expiring of old age and moribund thinking. His father couldn't see that the future of shipping lay in speed.

"You say your sister's here in London?" Cunningham inquired congenially, satisfied that he was dealing with a sensible businessman. "I'd thought you Americans stayed to the other side of the pond."

"We've family up and down the coast on two continents. Safer than keeping all our eggs in one basket." Mac didn't mention that far from being a close-knit family, they were a closemouthed, stubborn, cantankerous lot on the whole. The MacTavishes thought the Warwicks, the maternal side of his family, were a lot of foppish ne'er-do-wells; the Warwicks thought their Scots relations by marriage were mere shopkeepers. And their American relations—well, they'd never been forgiven for the Revolution.

He didn't intend to call on any of them except his sister. Eight years his junior, she'd followed him like a little lamb through childhood, tormenting him in front of his friends, making him laugh like a simpleton in private. He adored the little brat, when she didn't annoy the devil out of him.

The little brat hadn't written in nearly nine months.

As Cunningham and his daughter climbed into their carriage, Mac offered his hand to his father's agent. "It will be a pleasure working with you, sir. Shall we meet tomorrow to discuss purchasing?"

"Aye, and I'll look forward to it."

The lady nodded stiffly and looked away. She had

no doubt come hoping for an aristocratic, wealthy gentleman. She'd found an uncouth, bulky American instead. Accustomed to the reaction, Mac waited to be rid of the pair. He needed to get back to the unloading, try to clean himself up again, and then make his way to Marilee's London town house.

Mac turned and strode back to the dock, shouting a curse at one of the men lollygagging in the rigging. The idea of joining Marilee and her viscount husband for a stifling evening of polite conversation galled him, but family came first.

From the back of his restive mount, Mac eyed the impressive edifice of the viscount's London home with disfavor. No lights lit the upper-story windows. He'd sent word of his arrival, but the family didn't seem to be at home.

Annoyed that he'd donned a fresh dress coat for nothing, Mac easily held the tossing head of his nervous horse while contemplating his next move. He could leave his card—no, he'd burned them one cold night in a fit of drunken amusement. Well, hell, he'd leave his name with a servant. They'd know to look for him at the docks.

Not being a worrier by nature, Mac hadn't thought anything of his sister's lack of communication until his parents had pointed it out before he'd set sail. They'd never forgive him if he didn't at least attempt to check on her. He might love his sister, but at times she could be a damned nuisance, like most women.

Muttering about thoughtless chits with nothing in their heads but fripperies and fashion, Mac tied the horse to a post and took the front stairs two at a time, already feeling confined by the city's tall buildings and narrow streets.

He wasn't built for the boundaries of city life. He needed the ocean around him, or perhaps the grand prairies of the West. Once he had his fortune securely in hand he could explore the possibilities.

His thoughts drifting to the fortunes to be made should railroads ever cut across the American continent, he sounded the door knocker and waited.

A piercing childish scream shattered his complacence. Frowning, he glanced around, seeking the source of the racket. It sounded more like fury than terror. Since he had no offspring and didn't spend time around anyone else's, he couldn't be certain.

The door stayed firmly closed in his face.

Damn and blast it, where were the servants?

The scream shrieked again from overhead. He glanced upward at the windows opened to the warm May evening, although the oppressive stench of coal, horses, and raw sewage that permeated even this fashionable part of London couldn't precisely be called fresh. A child's sobs blended with the shriek, clamoring over the outside noises of clopping horses and the cries of a distant fishmonger.

If Marilee couldn't control her children any better than that, then the servants probably rode roughshod over her as well. Where the devil was her husband? He couldn't expect a gentle soul like Marilee to manage a full household of servants on her own.

Turning the knob and finding the door unbolted, Mac simply strode in. Nervous energy surged through him, but he wouldn't release it by bellowing at the staff. Just because he was large enough to charge through these civilized halls like a raging bull didn't mean he had any need to do it. Moderation, patience, and methodical planning were much better substitutes for irrational emotion. He'd learned his lesson the hard way: sitting in one too many jail cells after a brawl.

Since no one noticed his entrance, he laid his tall beaver hat on the hall table and followed the screams.

He'd had temper tantrums in his youth, but he didn't think they'd been allowed to reach this scale.

Taking the stairs two at a time, he heard the murmur of voices as he reached the third-floor landing. No one appeared to greet or question him, and Mac fought a surge of irritation. Marilee was obviously not at home, and the servants were shirking their duties. He would sack them all if they were his.

A babe's wails joined the screams of outrage, growing louder as he approached a closed door at the back of the hall. Even the babe seemed to be having a tantrum. Why the devil did anyone want children anyway? Screaming nuisances, the lot of them.

Turning the key still in the lock and opening the door, he would have entered, but a grubby gremlin shot through the doorway and bounced off his knee before fleeing down the corridor. He caught sight of a half-naked little savage with overlong curls of a dirty and indeterminate color before the mite scrambled down the banister and slid out of view.

Astonished, he sought the source of the continuing wails. A naked babe sat in the middle of what could politely be termed a potty accident. At his appearance, her wails diminished to a hiccup and a sob as she regarded him hopefully. Wrinkling his nose at the stench, Mac stared into trusting blue eyes beneath a mop of golden curls, and his heart cracked open.

Rage erupted close behind the weaker emotion.

Patience, he reminded himself firmly. Logic. Control. There must be nursemaids to handle this matter.

Not daring to touch so frail a creature as the tiny babe with his big, clumsy hands, Mac backed out— and bumped into a solid, indignant virago.

"And what the devil do you be doin', I ask? This be no place for gen'men. Be you some kind of pervert? Out with ye!"

Though she easily carried two hundred pounds of

fat—half in her jowls, Mac calculated—she didn't
budge him any farther than he cared to be budged.
Calmly balling his fingers into fists instead of grabbing
the front of her filthy apron, he scowled down at her.
"Where are the nursemaids? And when will Lady
Simmons return?"

"A lot ye know," the woman spat. "And hasn't the
lady been dead near this year and you just askin'?
Hmph."

Shocked into immobility, Mac remained blocking
the door as she tried to shove past him and enter
the nursery.

A nasty lump stuck in his throat, paralyzing his ability to speak. Striving for control before he broke into
grief-stricken sobs like those coming from behind him,
he choked.

Marilee couldn't be dead. Not the sweet, sunny sister who sang through his childhood. She was too vivid,
too alive. The hag had to be referring to a different
Lady Simmons.

A neat maid wearing a clean apron and a worried
expression appeared on the back stairs, towing the
half-naked demon who'd raced past him a moment
ago. Mac determinedly fought back the moisture in
his eyes to grasp the moment.

"What the hell is going on here?" he roared, eyeing
the lot of them with disfavor.

The demon, which he now recognized as a boy,
scowled and attempted to tear free of the maid's hand,
but she merely grasped him tighter and twisted a fist
in his shaggy hair.

"I found his lordship in the kitchen," the maid murmured, her gaze darting back and forth between Mac
and the nurse as she pushed the tot ahead of her.

His lordship. Mac's lip curled at the title. Marilee
and his mother coveted titles. If this bundle of rags
and rage was a lord, Mac would pay money not to be

one. "Are you the nurse?" he demanded, deliberately shoving aside thoughts of Marilee to focus on what had to be her children. He wouldn't—couldn't—believe the slut's lies. Where the hell could his sister and her lordling husband be?

"No, my lord." The little maid bobbed a curtsy while keeping a firm hold on the boy's long, frilled shirt. He wasn't wearing trousers. The maid glanced apologetically at the massive woman with hands propped on hips. "Mrs. White is."

"That's right, and this is me territory. Now bugger off. Ye don't belong here."

He most certainly did not. If he were master here, he wouldn't have allowed this mountain of filth into the house. Instead, he pointed toward the back stairs and spoke in his calmest tones. "Out," he ordered. "Leave these premises immediately." He turned to the young maid, ignoring the furious Mrs. White's gasp. "Where are the other servants?"

"Well, I never!" the nurse fumed. "And who do ye think ye be, ordering about a respectable widow?"

The unmistakable scent of gin tainted her breath, and Mac had to clasp his hands behind his back, prop his booted feet apart, and glare down at her as if she were a wayward cabin boy to keep from strangling her. "I am the children's uncle, and if you do not remove yourself at once, I shall heave you out the window. Understood?"

His threat must have finally been communicated. The woman's jowls turned a mottled purple, but she huffed and puffed and finally swung ponderously around, muttering curses. He was under no illusion that she would follow orders, but she'd learn. If he had to bring a cat-o'-nine-tails with him, she would learn.

Two mobcapped heads peered around a nearby door, and Mac pointed at the space vacated by Mrs. White. "You—out here. Explain yourselves."

"They're the undernursemaids," the little kitchen maid whispered. Even the squirming tot in her hand had grown still and wide-eyed as the scene unfolded.

"Why is that babe in there alone and crying?" Mac tried not to shout, though his patience hung on a rapidly unraveling thread.

"She ain't had her milk?" one guessed aloud.

"We's out of laudanum," the other said helpfully.

God, give him strength. As he glanced down and realized the small boy with the grimy face had one arm in a sling and the same blue eyes as Marilee's, the frayed thread snapped.

One

Somehow, all these bills and invoices had to be paid. She'd neatly entered them in her household accounts, tallied them, and placed them on her father's desk, as always.

Except that her father was no longer there to perform whatever magic made the bits of paper go away.

Frowning away tears, wishing she could retreat to the solace of her piano and forget the desk existed, Beatrice Cavendish stared at the stack of sorted bills.

She knew to a ha'penny how many coins remained in the strongbox. It wasn't sufficient for that entire stack. And quarter day was almost upon them, so she owed the servants' wages as well. The desperation that had been building in her for nearly six months threatened to swamp her now.

"You need Mr. Overton, Miss," Cook said gruffly, standing with hands behind her massive back. "The grocer worrit none about what's owed when Mr. Overton was about. A lady shouldn't be worriting over such."

"Papa sacked Mr. Overton." Miserably, Beatrice counted out the coins for the grocer's bill. They had to eat. Surely that bill was a priority. "Mr. Overton wanted to enclose the fields. What would happen to all our tenants if we did that?"

"The lazy no-goods would have to git off their arses—beg pardon, miss. It's not my place to say."

No, Beatrice thought, it wasn't. Mrs. Digby would never have said such a thing, but her former housekeeper and butler had taken the small inheritance Squire Cavendish had left them and set up housekeeping in the inn they'd purchased in town. Bea was relieved she didn't have to worry about the Digbys' large salaries any longer, but the established chain of command had disintegrated with their parting.

The bankers and lawyers had not explained how her father's once vast reserves of cash were to be replenished once they were all dispensed.

Perhaps, if the Earl of Coventry were ever in residence, she might discuss the problem with her father's best friend. But the Earl spent little time here.

"Miss." From the study doorway, Mary wadded up her apron. Something must be wrong for her to intrude. The sole provider for an invalid mother and six younger siblings, she anxiously held to the proprieties of her new position as upper parlor maid, and Mary knew that parlor maids should not be seen or heard by any of the family.

Not that there was any immediate family left besides Beatrice—only Aunt Constance, who swept in once a year, turned life upside down, then absconded for another eleven months. Bea suppressed a momentary lapse into self-pity.

"Where is James?" she asked, referring to the footman who had joined the household shortly before her father's death. James's family connection to her was so distant as to be invisible, but she didn't know what she'd do without his enthusiastic—if somewhat eccentric—support. It was typical of him not to be around when he was needed, rather like a younger, irresponsible brother.

She'd often wondered if her father had suffered

some premonition of his death that he'd brought
James home to help her out, but her father hadn't
been a very imaginative man. No doubt he had
thought just as he said—her cousin wished to earn his
living as a footman, and they could pay better than
the miserly Earl of Coventry, for whom he'd been
working. Though she knew that affluent households
often employed impoverished relatives, she had some
difficulty adjusting to a male servant who was also a
distant relative—especially one who spoke his mind,
and knew her so well that he feared no reprisal.

Her life was filled with many oddities these days.

"James is . . . off to see a man about a dog?" Mary
whispered nervously.

Which meant James was in the privy. Cheeks flam-
ing, Beatrice attempted to assume an air of authority,
knowing she failed miserably. "What is it, then?"

"Mr. Dobbins's goats do be eating the laundry, miss,
and the hounds has got loose again, and they're chasing after the Misses Miller. Jemmie is after them, but
there's none to mend the hole in their pen."

How could any one person do it all? She had a
houseful of servants who performed their duties when
instructed, but someone had to direct them. She'd
never thought to order about gardeners and sta-
blehands and tenants and— She couldn't even think
of all that on top of managing her nonexistent funds.
How had her father done it?

Not very successfully, if the threatening letter from
the bank meant anything at all.

She would sell the silver epergne. No one would
miss such a thoroughly useless piece. The proceeds
would pay the staff, if not the bank.

"Thank you, Mary. Give Jem a hand, would you?"
Remaining seated so as not to tower over her staff,
Bea nodded stiffly, mimicking Mrs. Digby's manner

with the underservants. A lifetime of shyness paralyzed her tongue.

When Mary had curtsied and departed, Beatrice
pushed the small stack of coins across the desk at
Cook. "Give these to the grocer, if you will. And best
have the scullery maid chase the goats out, or they'll
be in the kitchen garden next." She'd said that sensibly and with some degree of authority. She could
learn. Must learn.

"Right you are, miss." Cook hid the coins in her
apron pocket and bobbed an awkward curtsy, then
hesitated. "Miss, is all well? I've got my Robby to
think of, and if anything was to happen to my
position . . ."

"You have a place here for life," Beatrice assured
her. Cook had always been there, like family, for as
long as she could remember, as had most of her servants. She might seldom talk with them, but she knew
Robby was Cook's crippled youngest boy, just as she
knew the twelve-year-old scullery maid was an orphan
with no other home to turn to. This was a small village, and a poor one. Opportunities for employment
were limited, and every one of her servants had some
connection holding them here. If she couldn't pay
them, they and their families would go hungry. Most
of the town depended on her apparently nonexistent
income.

Relieved, Cook nodded. "Speak with Mr. Overton,"
she dared to add, before hurrying back to her usual
haunts.

As the study door closed, Bea shut her eyes, and a
single tear trickled down her cheek. She'd wept until
she couldn't weep anymore these past months after
her father's death, and again with Nanny's passing last
week. She had few tears left in her, and at the moment, they were all for herself.

She'd never thought of herself as a selfish person.

Pulling the embroidered pillow from behind her back, she punched it into shape again. She'd made this for her father the Christmas before last, and he'd sworn she was the best daughter who'd ever lived. He'd died only a few weeks before this past Christmas. She'd never had a chance to give him the matching footstool she'd worked on all year. She'd thought her many gifts and accomplishments were important to him, and that was all that mattered in her world.

Stupid her. The cold, cruel facts of life faced her now. No one had ever pointed out to her that she was an ignorant, overindulged spinster, beyond a prayer of changing. Of course, who was there to point out such things? No one. Her father had liked her just the way she was, so it simply hadn't occurred to her that she was singularly useless.

Like every little girl, she had once entertained passing fancies of being beautiful and desirable, but the fact was, she was twenty-eight years old, tall and ungainly, without hopes of a suitor. She'd never been introduced to society, never been taught the social graces necessary for that introduction. Her mother had died when she was but a toddler. Her father had taught her sums. The former curate's wife had taught her piano and embroidery. Nanny Marrow had taught her letters and reading before taking a position in another household. Despite her lack of schooling, for all intents and purposes, Beatrice was a highly accomplished lady.

As she matured, her father had encouraged her to order the London fashion magazines, and she read his newssheets regularly. Aunt Constance had erratically added to her knowledge. And Nanny Marrow had written letters from all the places she'd stayed.

Nanny Marrow! Grief washed over Bea at the loss of the one friend who had taught her far more of the world than the alphabet. It had been only a year since

Nanny had retired in the village and only a week since the lung inflammation took her. The hole in Bea created by her loss kept growing wider.

Despite Nanny's efforts, Bea's many accomplishments were wholly useless for anything practical, like paying bills and managing tenants.

Tapping her quill pen against the desk, she gazed out on the lawn. The head gardener had turned to drink, and she supposed she ought to sack him. The lawn hadn't been scythed in weeks, and a rainstorm had tumbled the roses from their trellises. They spilled over the walkways.

If only she could find a book that would teach her how to manage an estate, then she might learn more about her father's account books and figure out what was wrong. They'd never had debt collectors at the door when her father was alive. There must be something she wasn't doing right.

Why weren't girls given the same education in estate management that boys were? Had her father really thought a long Meg like his daughter would accidentally stumble across a husband to manage her inheritance? And what if that husband dropped dead as her father had? She'd be in the same predicament. She had to learn for herself. An entire staff and town depended on this estate. On her.

She pulled out the bank letter again, unfolded it for the forty-ninth time since its arrival. The sum mentioned was so enormous, she couldn't fathom it. Her household accounts for the year didn't equal a twentieth of this amount, and she couldn't pay *them*. How ever would she find such a sum? If she sold every piece of silver and bit of furniture in the house, she couldn't pay this bill.

She had searched her father's desk, written to every bank and solicitor represented by crumbling documents dating back decades, with no success. Her father had obviously thought he'd live forever. The estate wasn't entailed, and aside from James's distant connection, her father had no living relatives outside herself, which was the sole reason she'd inherited without question.

Nervously smoothing the heavy fabric of her mourning gown, Beatrice desperately tried to think of another solution. She had tenants. She ought to have income. Surely she owned crops and sheep. Mr. Overton would know. She would have to eat crow and call on him.

No, she had to do this on her own. Life was too uncertain. Even if Mr. Overton got over his pique, he would never willingly teach her to run the estate. He was just like Papa, thinking women were incapable of more than tatting and sewing. And if she objected to his methods, he'd only quit and walk away again, and she'd be right back where she started. Every path she took brought her to the same conclusion.

A man would never believe she could manage an estate on her own.

Heaven only knew, *she* didn't know if she could manage an estate on her own.

Pacing the room, her full skirt rustling as it brushed against the heavy furniture, she prayed for a miracle. She stopped to search her father's shelves for the millionth time, hoping for some inspiration, but most of the books dated back to the turn of the century. Things had changed since then.

Her father hadn't.

Wearily, she pulled out a volume on agricultural production and attempted to make head or tails of the lengthy lists of which counties produced which crops and when, but it was meaningless to her. She felt as if she'd been stranded in a foreign country with no coins and no means of speaking the language.

What she needed was someone to teach her by

doing, as men were taught. Of course, that meant she would require a knowledgeable man who was not only willing to teach her, but also believed she was teachable.

Better to ask for a miracle.

The pounding of the door knocker resounded so loudly in the hall, she jumped and almost dropped the book. No one in the village knocked so forcefully.

Fear clenched her insides as she waited for the servants to answer the door. A bill collector? She should have instructed the servants to say she wasn't at home.

James was in the privy. Mary was helping Jemmie chase the escaped hounds. Had the dogs caused some dire accident in the lane?

The knocker rapped again, with a slamming authority that would not be denied.

Shelving the book with a shaking hand, Beatrice smoothed her skirts again. She wasn't good at talking with strangers. Her brain and her tongue simply didn't connect. Just the angry sound of the knocker immobilized her.

She had to grow a backbone.

When it became obvious that no one would answer, she clenched her teeth to combat terror and swept out of the study as if she were master of all she surveyed.

She *was* master of all she surveyed. That was the problem. She was an incompetent master.

After fumbling with the massive door bolt, she cautiously swung the huge door open on the gloomy, threatening day. Amazingly, a dark green waistcoat and rumpled white neckcloth blocked her usual view of the lawn.

Being as large as she was, she didn't think she'd ever looked a man in the waistcoat before. Gaping, she tilted her head back. Green eyes narrowing in grim resignation studied her as if she were the last thing on this earth that the visitor wanted to see. A lock of golden brown hair fell appealingly over a wide, furrowed brow, and, without thinking, Beatrice took a step backward.

A whimper extracted her from a survey of clenched lips and square jaw, and her gaze dropped to the bundle the man held. A growing wet spot on the green waistcoat and a glimpse of wispy golden curls wrapped in a man's short box coat so startled her, she almost closed the door in their faces. Rain began to pour.

With a whoop and a burst of energy, a small muddy form bolted past her skirts, skidded on the Oriental rug, and raced for the stairs. Tousled curls above a blue velvet coat disappeared around the landing.

"Excuse me, madam." The stunning giant dumped his burden into Bea's arms, shoved the door open, and, taking the steps two at a time, raced up the stairs after his small charge, leaving damp footsteps in his path.

Utterly distracted, Beatrice gazed down at the bundle she held, into beatific blue eyes in a cherub's face, and almost forgot the savages invading her upper story.

She'd never held a baby before.

They stared at each other raptly. The infant popped a thumb into her rosebud mouth, but her gaze never left Bea's. Caught in the study of tiny fingers and chubby cheeks above a lace-bedecked smock, Bea didn't register the dampness spreading across her bodice until shouts overhead intruded upon her reverie.

A man's roar followed by a childish scream of outrage abruptly brought her head up, and she grimaced as moisture sank through the fabric of her bodice and her chemise and chilled her skin. Heavy boots pounded down the stairs, coming into view first, followed by dirt-streaked trousers over massive . . . thighs. Bea gulped, flushed, and tried to look away.

It had never occurred to her to look at a man's . . . limbs . . . before.

Narrow hips, a wide chest beneath an unfastened waistcoat and twisted neckcloth, and a squirming, shrieking toddler clasped under one masculine arm appeared next. The look of mixed resignation and rage on the broad, chiseled features coming into sight as he reached the bottom of the stairs should have sent her fleeing. Instead, curiosity compelled her to remain, clinging to the smelly, sopping child in her arms.

If she did not mistake, a stranger and two children had just arrived on her doorstep on the brink of a rainstorm. In novels, did it not tend to be an abandoned mistress arriving with babes in arms during a howling snowstorm?

"I'm here to speak with Miss Cavendish," the man said peremptorily, heaving the toddler over his shoulder. The boy loosed his bandaged arm from its sling and tried to climb down the man's back, but his captor's big hands firmly wrapped around small ankles, preventing escape.

Dressed as she was, he probably thought she was the housekeeper. She could say Miss Cavendish wasn't at home and send this terrifying apparition away.

She could tell from his stance that he was entirely too certain of himself. His restless energy permeated the room and would stampede right over her if she admitted to her existence. His massive size reduced her elegant foyer to the size of the closet. But he had the most fascinating green eyes, and a bronzed, windswept look that no gentleman crossing these portals had ever possessed. . . .

She could almost feel the hurricane winds of change sweeping through her cloistered walls.

She didn't have a clue as to who he could be.

"My lady!" an effeminate male voice squeaked

from the depths of the interior. "Shall I show this motley lot to the door?"

Bea closed her eyes and sighed as James finally appeared.

The stranger's eyes narrowed again as her bewigged cousin, in a scarlet coat and gold buttons, hovered behind her. A growling terrier would offer more protection.

Donning her haughtiest demeanor, Beatrice raised her eyebrows in the stranger's direction. "I am Miss Cavendish, sir. I believe you have mistaken me for someone else."

Expressively, she held out the child for him to retrieve.

He glowered at her, glowered at her cousin, and holding the squirming boy firmly beneath one muscular arm, refused to take the babe. "I've been told you can tell me of Nanny Marrow."

The bottom dropped out of Beatrice's heart at this mention of her lifelong friend.

"Nanny Marrow passed away last week." To hide a fresh spurt of tears, she swung on her heels and marched into the formal parlor.

Two

Mac stared after the supercilious Englishwoman and tried to comprehend her devastating announcement. Nanny Marrow could not possibly be dead. Fate couldn't be so cruel.

How in the *devil* would he return to London without someone reliable to hide Marilee's children?

He stalked after Miss Cavendish, disregarding the bewigged footman who was holding out his hands in a useless effort to stay him.

"What do you mean, Nanny Marrow has *passed away*?" he roared. He shouldn't roar. He should conquer his temper, his impatience, his frustration. He should grovel politely, and question carefully. He knew that. But dealing with two holy terrors beyond his experience and control had compounded the pressures of Marilee's death and his fury at her husband, and he thought he might explode. He desperately needed answers, right now.

In his haste to follow Miss Cavendish, he nearly tripped over an embroidered ottoman.

The parlor was stuffed with man-sized sofas covered in delicately tatted doilies, massive tables overflowing with fragile figurines, feathery ferns in heavy brass containers, and other rackety contradictions that would have spun his head off had he not fixed his gaze on the tall, curvaceous figure maneuvering the maze with ease, apparently retreating to the support of an enormous piano.

The woman was a target he could sight without complaint. As she swung around, his gaze dropped appreciatively to the splendid bosom against which his niece rested. A man could fill his hands gladly with a woman like that.

He should have had a damned wench before absconding from London so he wouldn't be salivating over a haughty aristocrat like a green lad now.

"Nanny Marrow is dead?" he clarified, since she hadn't responded to his demand. He didn't dare let loose the squirming tot beneath his arm, despite a string of epithets spilling from the brat's dirty mouth. Fortunately, the boy's pronunciation was poor and the words muffled, or the woman would no doubt have them hurled from her hearth.

"She was . . . quite old," the lady said stiffly, looking longingly at the piano.

Was he so far beneath her damned dignity that she couldn't *look* at him? Mac drove his free hand through his rumpled hair. "Why the hell didn't that pompous excuse for an innkeeper tell me that?"

She shot him an accusing look for his language, smothered a quiet exclamation, and, balancing the babe in one arm, caught a kitten in midleap before it tumbled an army of porcelain shepherdesses. With expertise, she flipped the kitten onto an afghan draped over a sofa, where the animal began contentedly shredding the wool.

Beneath Mac's arm, Percy quit cursing and watched the maneuver in apparent awe. Taking advantage of his new interest, Mac flung the boy onto the sofa with the cat.

"Mr. Digby?" the woman asked in dismay. "Mr. Digby sent you?"

He had to concentrate on priorities. Figuring the suspicious footman was still within earshot, he turned and caught him in the doorway. "The babe needs dry cloths. See if the maids can find some."

The fop's look of interest froze. "Miss Cavendish?"

"I'm sure Mary can help," she answered absently, looking down at the growing stain on her black bodice.

"My lady," the man insisted, "it would not be proper—"

The woman shot the red-coated dandy a look that was nearly as impatient and frustrated as Mac's own, and Mac hid a grin of appreciation.

"If Mr. Digby sent him, he can't be too dangerous, and the child is *wet*. Send Mary in here once she finds the cloths. And has Dolly polished the silverware yet?"

The insolent footman drew himself up with hauteur. "Polishing silver is a senseless task. Who could possibly notice?" With that pointed dig, he sashayed out.

"If he wasn't always right, I'd hide him in a closet."

Diverted by the lady's sigh of exasperation, Mac swung back in time to stop Percy from climbing over the sofa back in search of the cat. He had to get out of here before the boy destroyed everything in sight.

The only problem was, he had absolutely nowhere else to go.

"*My* kitty!" the boy screamed in outrage, fighting for release as Mac lifted him by his coat back and removed him from the upholstery.

"Miss Cavendish's kitty," Mac informed him firmly. "You may have one once we're on our way home."

"Don' wanna go home," the boy whined.

Miss Cavendish raised her lovely cinnamon eyebrows, forcing Mac to look past the hideous onyx brooch on her delectable bosom and acknowledge the intelligence in her clear, almond-shaped eyes. She'd braided her reddish brown hair in polished rope circles over her ears, but stray wisps escaped to shiver about her slender throat. He wondered if her skin tasted as creamy as it looked, and coughed nervously to clear his throat. He couldn't remember ever having such a thought about a proper lady. Normally, their stiff manners were as off-putting as their overabundance of petticoats.

How the devil would he explain his predicament without revealing who the children were? Once his drunken brother-in-law recovered from his stupor, he would have men roaring across the countryside in pursuit of his stolen children.

"Umm, the children's mother died, and they were a trifle . . . unhappy . . . until I arrived," Mac contrived uneasily. "I'd hoped to hire Nanny Marrow to look after them. When I found her house boarded up, I inquired at the inn, but they said the rooms were under renovation, and I should inquire here."

A maid appeared carrying a stack of dry cloths, followed by the bewigged footman. The tight-lipped lady surrendered Pamela to the maid. From the smile lines around her eyes, and a glimpse of dimple when she looked at the chirruping baby, Mac decided those rosy lips didn't normally frown. It was just *him* that she disapproved of.

"Do you and the children have a name?" she wondered aloud as she delicately covered her damp bodice with a shawl the footman handed her.

"Mac," he improvised instantly. "Mac Warwick. These two are Bitsy and Bud." He'd have to hide their identities until he developed a clearer plan of action.

"Bitsy?" She wrinkled her patrician nose in distaste. "Bud? Well, then, perhaps Bud would like a biscuit and some milk in the kitchen. Excuse my manners." She gestured toward the glowering footman. "This is James, my cousin. Perhaps you could take the children to the kitchen, James?"

A cousin as footman? Mac had heard of ladies acquiring cicisbeos, but disguising them as servants was a new twist. This bewigged young fop didn't appear masculine enough to interest a woman. "Bud won't go without Bitsy. If your maid would be so kind as to go with them . . ."

Miss Cavendish nodded uncertainly. "Of course. Mary?"

The maid bobbed a curtsy, the footman scowled, and Mac released his grip on Percy. The boy took off like a cannon shot, and, cursing like a seaman under his breath, the bewigged footman loped in pursuit.

As Mary departed in their wake, Beatrice wished she could follow. She'd much rather watch the antics of the children than confront this massive man who vibrated with more energy than she thought the walls could hold. Now that the children had departed, her tongue twisted in knots. She had a dozen questions she didn't dare ask. Was the children's mother his wife? Should she express her condolences? Of course, if she hadn't been his wife . . . One wouldn't wish to question too deeply in such affairs, especially since he didn't seem at all familiar with children. What did the man want of her?

She didn't think she ought to include *man* and *want* in the same thought. The combination did odd things to her insides—like draw her notice to the intensity of his gaze.

"You wouldn't know of any available nursemaids in the area, would you?" he demanded more than asked.

"Those with any sense have left for more populous areas." Nervousness made her angry, and the words were blurted out. "The only babies around here are those of servants. I suppose you might ask at Landingham or the Carstairs estate, but the earl is elderly and never in residence, and the Carstairses visit only during hunting season."

He looked frustrated as he ran his hand through his hair and tumbled it more thoroughly than his son's. She could see the resemblance in the golden brown locks, though the children had blue eyes and not their father's green. His accent was odd and vaguely un-couth, despite his excellent grammar. And his wrin-kled attire was a disgrace.

"I need to take the children to my parents in Vir-ginia. I've a ship leaving in a few weeks." He ground out the words from between clenched teeth.

Virginia. An American. That explained the accent, if nothing else. She had no idea what she was sup-posed to say, so she stood there like a great lump, nervously twitching her fingers against the piano. Was she supposed to make some hospitable offer? She'd caught a glimpse of a carriage in the drive. Surely he had wealth if he knew of Nanny, who had worked in some of the best houses over the years.

He glared at her and began pacing, until he smacked his shin on a low table and nearly stumbled over her writing desk. Her father had sought to please her by buying her things. She'd about run out of places to put them. In any case this man would be too large for any room he entered.

With an exceedingly masculine growl, he retreated to the fireplace, where he leaned against the mantel and all but barked at her.

"I need a place to keep the children while I'm wait-ing for my ship."

Well, he could tarry all he liked—somewhere else. She had enough problems of her own. Beatrice dared to stare at him while she waited for him to realize she had nothing to offer. He had a piercing way of looking at her that made her feel bubbly inside, but she re-fused to let that daunt her. She was safe here, in the protection of her own lovely home. And he was a rude, crude, uncouth stranger who shouldn't expect anything.

"I need a nursemaid," he clarified, with some urgency.

Perhaps . . . if he needed a nursemaid as desperately as she needed . . .

He did, if his look of agitation meant anything. Despite his rumpled appearance, her visitor wore a gentleman's clothes. She recognized the richness of the embroidery on his satin waistcoat and the fashionable cut of London tailoring. Gentlemen should know of estate management. But why would a gentleman be gallivanting about this remote countryside with children and no nursemaids?

Still, one could either let opportunity slide by or seize the moment. Bea took a deep breath and let the notion spill out before she could reconsider. "*I* need a teacher of estate management."

"You're in need of an estate manager?" he asked with polite curiosity, apparently startled by her sudden change of topic.

"A teacher," she said as firmly as she was able.

"A teacher?" he asked, incredulous.

"A teacher of estate management," she confirmed.

"A teacher." He didn't look pleased.

Casting him a sidelong glance, she could tell by the way his jaw muscle twitched that he was appalled at the idea, as any man would be, she supposed. She should know better than to believe in miracles.

He grimaced, ran a hand over his face, then stared back. "I'm not a teacher. I'm a businessman. But I've worked my father's plantation and have some grasp of land management, although you've an entirely different set of circumstances here."

Beatrice pressed her hands against the knot in her stomach and tried not to leap to conclusions. She couldn't pay him, but she didn't dare say that aloud.

Every able-bodied person in the village would pack up and leave if they knew she could not pay her bills. She nodded, as if she understood where he was leading.

He clenched and unclenched one great fist, pounding it impatiently on the mantel. "You're a woman. You should know what the children need. Give us a place to stay, and I'll take a look around, see what I can do, maybe have my agent in London find you an estate manager who can look after things."

"I want a teacher," she said decisively. His assumption that she could deal with his children was laughable. As if she knew any more of babies than she did of estate management.

"I'm not a teacher." He glared at her again. "You can tell me what you want done, and I can tell you how I'd do it. That's the best I can offer."

Her stomach clenched and hope trembled. "In exchange for room and board?"

"And nursemaids for the children."

She'd wanted a miracle, but now that one had walked in her door, she was suspicious of its origins. Why would a man like this—even an uncouth American—offer to help in exchange for room and board?

She was a fool to agree.

She would be a fool not to.

Oh, my. Could she do this? What would the curate say? And the Misses Miller? She would be the talk of the town. He hadn't even promised to teach her.

But he wouldn't stay long, so he couldn't run all over her like another man might.

And his fingers were clenched as tightly as hers, his frown just as anxious.

Taking a deep breath, Bea nodded. "You may have the steward's cottage. Mary has experience with children. She will look after them while we work."

Butterflies danced in her belly, stirred by a dangerous gleam in his eye. So, she was nervous. She squeezed her fingers against the flutter. If he would cut his hair and dress a little more presentably, he would be a truly impressive—and terrifying—sight.

She had the niggling suspicion that she might have just made a deal with the devil.

The bright light of interest in his eyes confirmed it.

Three

With Mr. Warwick and his children duly ensconced in their new abode, Beatrice returned to the task at hand—finding the funds to pay the staff. Hiring someone to haul off her modish furniture would throw the town into spasms of despair and wouldn't pay the bank note, in any case. She ran her fingers lovingly over the piano keys while her cousin waited impatiently. Selling the instrument would be the last thing she would do.

Digby had discreetly sold the best silverware without asking questions. Perhaps she might disguise the disappearance of other pieces, if only to pay the servants. "We must sell the silver epergne, James, or at least the coffee set." Saying the words to the accompaniment of Mozart wasn't quite so difficult.

"Oh, never the epergne," James wailed with a dramatic flinging of his gloved hand to his forehead. "We will be ruined, completely *ruined*!"

Beatrice bit back a smile at his antics. She never knew what role he would play next—he'd just imitated Clara Miller to a fare-thee-well. She wished she could be as . . . as free to emote as James. The lulling melody beneath her fingers turned to a rollicking comedy she'd heard at a Punch and Judy show.

She'd never learned to look at servants as creatures

beneath her dignity. They were people, part of her family, and she was always interested in them, as she'd always been curious about a cousin who insisted on working for wages. But she was too shy to ask for more than he was willing to impart, and James dodged delicate inquiries with the grace of a gazelle.

Now that Nanny was gone, James was the only person in the village to treat her like a friend. He had been the only one audacious enough to offer her a shoulder to cry on the night her father died. They'd wept buckets together. She couldn't part with him despite his absurdities. Of course, a footman would be accepted without question in the household. An unmarried cousin might not.

She supposed she must maintain some semblance of authority in her role. "It's sell the epergne, or sacrifice your allowance and forgo the pleasure of buying more gold buttons this quarter," she said sternly, looking up from the piano keys. James had designed his outrageous coat himself, and he'd insisted on the powdered wig as well. The pretentious ensemble might be all the rage in London, but she thought it seriously out of place here.

He sobered and stiffened his spine and shoulders. "You cannot possibly sell the epergne in the village. It would be a disgrace."

"Not to mention an impossibility," she murmured. The village had no jeweler or silversmith. "You will have to take it into Cheltenham, as Digby did."

"Digby is old and wears black and looks the part of a gentleman. The storekeepers would brand me a thief," James declared. "Besides, I simply cannot wear black," he concluded, as if this were argument enough. He shuddered eloquently. "I would look a carrion crow."

"Thank you very much," she said dryly, glancing down at her own black bombazine.

"Oh, but black becomes you," James insisted. "I do envy you your coloring."

Well, he was the only one. Rusty hair and ghostly skin struck her as exceedingly boring, not to mention unfashionable.

He was diverting the subject. She crossed her hands on top of the keys with a resounding crash. "You must wear black and look dignified and go to Cheltenham, James. We have no choice. Mr. Digby is busy opening the inn, and I cannot impose on him anymore. You must stand in his place."

James quit fussing with his buttons to look at her directly. "No, cousin, it's time *you* learned to go about in the world. You cannot hide away in this backwater forever. If you are to keep this household afloat, you must find a husband, and it cannot be done here, unless you mean to court that uncouth American. Selling the silver won't help."

All the resolution flooded out of her, and Beatrice slumped. At the moment, she couldn't even muster indignation that he thought she couldn't manage on her own. James was *always* right, drat his painted and powdered hide.

She'd never been outside of Broadbury in her life.

Which was worse—the thought of venturing outside her sheltered world, or the thought of courting an uncouth American?

Her mouth going dry as she thought of the scowl on the giant's handsome face, she wondered where she could find the funds to hire a driver for her barouche.

"What the devil do you do with all these horses?" Striding through the towering stone barn after dinner, passing stall after stall of expensive, idle beasts eating their worth in hay, Mac couldn't conceal his disgust at the waste.

"I sold the jumpers," Miss Cavendish answered coldly, her many layers of petticoats stirring the dust.

"Then what the hell are all these pretty things?" he demanded, gesturing toward half a dozen fine-boned mares. "Not plow horses, I wager."

"Carriage horses. My father had the finest in the shire." Pride tinged her normally reticent voice. "And we're here to discuss the leaky roof, not the animals."

Right. This wasn't his estate. He'd just bite his tongue, and not question what wasn't his. Obviously English nobles didn't possess the same frugal instincts as wealthy Americans. He glared upward at the medieval abomination she called a roof. "The damned barn is made of stone," he exclaimed in disgust. "Why the devil does it still have a thatched roof when it can support tile?"

"Your language," she protested, stepping away from him and toward the doors.

He wanted to shout *Damn my language!* and blister her for stupidity as if she were one of his men. With difficulty, he tried to remember: teachers did not berate their students, especially not noble ladies who were too polite to curse back.

He'd better start practicing proper etiquette if he hoped to hide Marilee's children for the next few weeks.

"My apologies," he said gruffly, stalking past stalls of carriage horses, riding horses, and even a plow horse or two. She couldn't fix the roof, but she kept up with her wealthy neighbors. *He* didn't have to live with that hypocrisy. He'd be gone as soon as he could complete his clipper, stock both his ship and his father's, and sail away with the children.

Even in the dusk of the tall barn he could locate the spreading water stain on the inside wall. He'd worked as hard as any hired man on his father's plantation. He could fix a real roof. A thatched roof was

another matter entirely. "I take it you have no interest
in improving the barn with tile or slate." He knew he
sounded grumpy. He didn't mean to, but his hostess
had a damnable way of drawing regally away every
time he barked. After the disasters of this past week,
he derived some satisfaction from making an English
aristocrat jump.

Marilee.

Mac closed his eyes against the gaping hole his sister's death left. Even though he'd confirmed her death
from childbed fever through reliable sources, he
couldn't believe his gentle sister was really gone. He
could still hear her singing nursery rhymes and laughing as she shoved hay from the loft onto his head. She
had been far, far too young to die. And much too
loving to die alone.

Grief surged through him, but he'd learned not to
give in to raw emotion. He had to appease this silly
female so Marilee's children would be safe from their
drunken sot of a father and his ignorant minions.

"I suppose there's someone hereabouts with experience at thatching?" He tried to sound reasonable. He
didn't want to be thrown out on his ear.

"Yes, of course, but . . ." Her voice dragged off
hesitantly. "But I'd hoped you could . . ."

He turned and studied her pale face through the
dusk. "Just tell me who it is. I'll work out a trade and
no coin will come from your pockets."

She looked immensely relieved, and he fought a moment's surprise. She obviously had more wealth than
Croesus had gold. Why didn't she simply hire a
thatcher?

"I . . . Thank you. It won't be too difficult, will it?"
she asked anxiously, inching toward the door.

He strode briskly for the exit. Maybe she thought
all Americans were barbarians who ate ladies for midnight snacks. Or maybe she just thought *he* was the

barbarian. It didn't matter. He need only endure her vapors for a week or two.

"Don't know until we look. What else needs work?"

"Well, oh, dear . . ." She hurried to catch up.

Her soft scent wafted around him as they stepped into the evening air. She stood shoulder high to him, and should he be so inclined, he could comfortably wrap his arm around her waist without bending to accommodate her. Surreptitiously, Mac eyed her waist. Maybe it was some trick of the full skirts that made her look so trim in the middle. His gaze drifted higher. She might be a snob, but she was definitely all woman.

Why the hell hadn't some proper English gentleman come along and claimed a prize like this one? Proved they were all namby-pamby idiots.

"I'm not certain what needs doing most," she said with a helpless gesture. "Father told me my place was in the house, and I needn't worry about such things. And now I—"

Her voice broke, and Mac shoved his hands in his pockets and gazed at the first star appearing on the horizon rather than watch her wipe away a tear. Fine pair they made. They'd both be weeping in a minute.

He used to wipe away Marilee's childish tears.

"I'll take a look around in the morning, all right?" he said gruffly. "Then I'll come talk to you, and we can decide what needs doing."

"Thank you," she whispered. She had rich brown eyes, the kind that could heat a man's heart. "I *can* learn. If you will explain things to me . . ."

"You could hire someone," he pointed out. "That's what most people do."

The warmth left her eyes, and she turned away again. "And then I'd be just as ignorant as I am now. Good night, Mr. Warwick."

Ah, hell, he'd stuck his foot in it again. When would

he learn that he had no place in the company of ladies?

He stared up at the towering mansion on the hill as she hurried toward it. Against the evening sky, it soared majestically in a fantasy of turrets and gables that swept the stars. Lights twinkled in mullioned windows. An oil lamp swung outside, illuminating the half-timbered stone wall of the older block, shadowing the ivy-covered stones of the new.

The house was as lush and provocative and haughty as its owner.

Mac rubbed his forehead and sighed as Percy clambered to the back of what was probably an antique sofa and reached for what was most definitely an antique Black Forest cuckoo clock. Even the steward's cottage in this place came with expensive ornaments.

"Get down, Buddy," he yelled as he dragged his exhausted body into the front room. As time passed, he had more and more sympathy for the nursery maids. He hadn't had a moment's rest since he'd left London.

"My birdie," Percy declared firmly, reaching for the swinging wooden pendulum. The cuckoo warbled one final note and withdrew behind closed door. *Smart bird.*

Mac crossed the room and scooped the boy up before the entire clock fell on his head. Percy screamed in fury. From the floor, Pamela joined in.

"Are you murdering them?" a female voice asked through the open parlor window.

Oh, hell. Holding a wiggling, screaming Percy, Mac glanced out to see his hostess framed by the multi-paned windows. This morning she wore a complicated pin of jet at the throat of her high-necked abomination of a gown. An enormous bonnet covered her hair and hid the better part of her face.

"I'm saving this one from breaking his neck. The other is apparently disturbed that I didn't do the same for her." Mac shoved the kicking, cursing child through the open window. "Here. You shut him up. I'll look to the other."

Holding Percy at arm's length, Miss Beatrice Cavendish of Cavendish Court looked properly appalled at finding herself in possession of a screaming child, but Mac lacked the patience to care.

As he lifted Bitsy from the floor and gingerly tested for wetness, he watched Miss Cavendish wrestle with her unexpected burden. Percy—Buddy—had apparently shut up long enough to inspect his new keeper. His lower lip stuck out, suggesting he'd not be quiet for long.

"Did you have oatmeal for breakfast?" Mac heard her ask as he wrapped a blanket around his niece in preparation for taking her into the chilly morning air.

Buddy nodded suspiciously.

"Then you should have jam for dessert," Miss Cavendish informed him briskly. "Apollo likes apples and sugar cubes after he eats his oats."

Mac briefly contemplated the possibility that he'd handed his nephew to a lunatic, then realized she'd just compared Buddy to her favorite horse. He was beginning to suspect she knew as little about kids as he did.

"Come on, little bit." He swung the now quiescent babe to his shoulder. "We'll feed you sugar cubes and apples, too. Miss C will turn you into a good, strong horsie."

Pamela gurgled happily and yanked on his hair.

Grimacing, Mac joined Miss C in the yard and offered the smaller child in exchange for the rambunctious Buddy. "He'll disappear into the mist if we let him go."

She didn't look at him as they made the exchange,

but defiance tinted her whispery voice. "I wish to accompany you today so that I may learn how to hire a thatcher without giving him money."

Hellfire. He didn't need this woman following him all over the countryside. He'd almost rather haul the brats with him. "I'll barter," he said testily. "It's nothing you need worry your pretty head about."

Her pretty head jerked up as if he'd slapped her. For the first time, she really looked at him, and her eyes spat the fires of damnation. Mac was so surprised that he almost walked into a rhododendron.

"Don't *ever* say that to me again."

She marched up the drive before he could process the warning. He'd seen soldiers with less rigid posture. What the devil had he said now?

Balancing Percy on his shoulder, Mac strolled after her. "Don't ever say *what* again?" he inquired with interest. Obviously she didn't expect gentlemanly flattery.

She didn't turn around as he fell into step with her. "My *father* always told me never to worry my pretty head. And look where that's got me." She gestured at her unscythed lawn and tumbling roses. "I haven't a clue as to what I'm supposed to do about leaky roofs or unplowed fields or sheep in need of shearing. I'm supposed to sit in my parlor and knit while everything falls apart for lack of management, but I mustn't worry about a thing."

That gave him a glimmer of understanding as to why her estate showed such signs of neglect.

"You're supposed to hire a steward or caretaker or some such. Or find a husband." He added that with a hint of spite. His parents had drummed the need for a wife into his head often enough for the words to pop out without much thought.

She glared at him from beneath the bonnet trim. "Oh, very fine. I'll send for Lord Knowles, shall I? I'll tell him he can have my father's hounds in exchange for marriage. Then I can sit and knit while he drives the hounds into the ground and my tenants into penury. And if I'm truly fortunate, he'll break his neck in a drunken jump, and I'll have to start all over."

Beatrice blinked in astonishment that she'd actually uttered such scathing comments. She buried her face in the sweet-smelling neck of the child in her arms, and tried not to look at the tall man who was easily keeping pace with her and watching her with such interest. Perhaps she dared speak her mind because he'd be gone in a week or two. Perhaps she dared because he had no expectations of her.

He didn't seem to be appalled at her vehemence. He actually seemed to be pondering her diatribe. Maybe Americans didn't think women foolish.

"I take your point," he said gravely. "Husbands are a nuisance. Now, explain away a good steward."

"They quit when one disagrees with them." She refused to tell him that she couldn't afford one.

"Of course. If one is disagreeable, stewards would be hard to find."

He was laughing at her. She didn't know whether to weep in frustration or tell him what she thought of his behavior.

No doubt he'd just laugh at her if she tried.

"I'm going with you to the thatcher's," she said firmly as they reached the house.

"You will learn nothing that will be of any use to you," he warned.

Yes, she would. She would learn how to stand up for herself—at least with one man.

It was a long way from confronting the bankers and solicitors who threatened to take away her home, but it was a step in the right direction.

Four

Refusing the offer of the lady's antiquated barouche, Mac harnessed the horse to his rented post chaise. He'd hated leaving his own horse in London, but he'd had to remove the children in haste.

"It is a very small carriage," Miss Cavendish said dubiously. Her fingers trembled as he helped her in, making him extremely aware of how small her hand was.

Odd, how he could forget for even a moment that she was one of those delicate ladies he so despised. Her soft scent of lilacs crept up on him when he least expected it.

"The carriage is light and well-balanced, which is more than that monstrosity of yours can claim." Irritated by his reaction to her, Mac circled the carriage to the driver's side. He'd already determined that everything about her estate was ancient, except the house and its contents. The mansion had been added on to, improved upon, decorated, and embellished until it looked more a fantasy castle than a place to live.

The princess presiding over the fantasy crossed her hands in her lap and haughtily straightened her shoulders. Mac might despise snobbery, but Miss Cavendish came by her regal bearing naturally. A woman of her build and stature could do no less. Now, if he could only persuade her to talk or smile, the next few weeks might be tolerable.

As they drove down the drive and through the hedged lane, the village of Broadbury spilled down the hillside below them. The unusually wide road running between rows of neat two-story cottages identified it as a market town. Built one against the other, each cottage glowed with the warm golden tones of the local stone. Nodding heads of colorful flowers adorned windowsills and yards all up and down the road. He'd come from a country of large brick houses, some with gracious columned porches, but Mac couldn't remember ever seeing a town as charming and picturesque as this one. Or as indolent.

A lone man stood on a ladder in front of one of the wider buildings, removing a tattered wooden sign depicting a faded bull. At the foot of the ladder rested a bright new sign of a golden crown. An idler leaned against the inn wall, apparently directing the placement of the sign, probably to the annoyance of the sign maker.

A few sheep ambled in the green pastures surrounding the village. A brown cow chewed contentedly at a sheet hanging on a line in a backyard. A small boy kicked a stone down the rutted lane. Beyond that, Mac couldn't find a single sign of industriousness. At home, there would be farm wagons and horses traversing the street, men arguing on the tavern steps, women gossiping on the walks as they strolled from shop to shop, and carters and smiths and wheelwrights all going about their business. How in the name of heaven did this backwater survive?

He'd hoped to find someone who could help him with the children when it came time to sail, but he'd be lucky to find someone who remembered what children were.

Frustration gnawed at him as a bell pealed desultorily in the church tower opposite the inn. A black-robed curate, looking too young to be out of school, strolled from the front door of a neighboring cottage in the direction of the crumbling church. The church's wide door sagged open, welcoming any creature who cared to enter. He'd find no protection from the viscount and his men here.

"Oh, there's Mr. Rector on his rounds now," Miss Cavendish said with what sounded like relief.

Owl-eyed behind gold-rimmed spectacles, the curate watched with interest as their carriage approached. Mac had never intended to meet the whole town. He'd meant to hide the children with Nanny Marrow while he rode back to London to see to the purchasing of shipments and the preparation of his clipper. He was at a loss as to how he would accomplish either in this place, but his main concern was concealing his identity.

Not being one to cower behind bushes, Mac resolutely drove Miss Cavendish down the hill into the narrow confines of Broadbury. He'd chosen this hiding place. Now he must live in it.

"Miss Cavendish, it's a pleasure. I see the gentleman found you." A portly, fiftyish man, Mr. Digby appeared very much the butler he once had been as he helped Beatrice from the carriage.

"I don't believe I've had the pleasure." The curate rocked back on his heels and inspected the newcomer with curiosity as he waited for Mac to tie up his horse.

Flustered, Beatrice handled the introductions, although she suspected she flubbed them badly. Mr. Warwick was regarding her with a raised eyebrow, an expression that produced shivers all the way to her toes. He had the most amazingly thick and expressive brows, in a shade of brown darker than his hair.

Rubbing elbows with him all the way into town had made her extremely light-headed. Perhaps she was coming down with something.

"Mr. Warwick is teaching me estate management," she said primly. "We need the name of a thatcher to repair the stable roof."

"Teaching?" the curate asked with amusement. "Is that what it's called these days? And are you an acquaintance of the earl's, or of the Carstairses, Mr. Warwick?"

Beatrice narrowed her eyes at the implication that her neighbors had sent a man more interested in acquiring her property than a nanny. "He's an American, Mr. Rector. He was hoping to find Nanny Marrow to look after his children."

"Nanny Marrow's sister lives in Virginia," Mr. Warwick explained curtly. "She wished me to persuade Nanny to come live with her. It seems I arrived too late."

Mr. Rector clucked his sympathy. "Well, fine thing that you and Miss Cavendish have found each other. Miss Cavendish surely knows all that Nanny Marrow taught her. Fine woman, our dear Miss C."

"Really, sir," Bea demurred, "if we could please have the name of a reputable thatcher, we shall be on our way."

The obstinate American pursued his own goal. "I'm sure the children are in good hands with Miss Cavendish, but my time is limited. I shall see what I can do while I look for a nursemaid."

"A nursemaid," Mr. Digby mused, then abandoned that unprofitable subject. "When will your aunt be arriving for her annual visit, miss? The gypsy circus she brought with her last year has been a constant source of conversation."

Just the thought of the turmoil her aunt always created made Beatrice's mind reel. Of course the villagers

talked about her. The gypsies had sold half the shire
ancient mares painted black to disguise their age, and
her father had had to recompense everyone once they
realized they'd been cheated.

Still, she so desperately needed her aunt's wisdom
right now, she would willingly endure the mischief that
accompanied it. "I've not heard from her yet. I'm sure
you'll know the minute she arrives."

The gleam in her ex-butler's eye spoke his full
agreement on that point. "We'll look forward to
seeing her."

Tortured minutes later, they escaped with the direction of a reputable thatcher.

So far, Mac had seen precious little sign of anyone
capable of handling two demanding children on an
ocean voyage, or one even willing to relocate. Apparently the British thought America a barbaric place
unfit for civilized habitation. Mac heaved a sheaf of
thatch from the ground, then viciously hurled it to the
barn roof. How the hell would he transport the children across an ocean without a competent nursemaid
and governess? He'd have to tie them to the mast.

At the sound of soft laughter, he glanced toward
the stable yard.

He was slaving away on a damned barn, exchanging
his labor for assistance in thatching Miss Cavendish's
stable, and the lady wasn't even paying attention. She
was talking to the thatcher's wife, showing her the
gaudy piece of jewelry she'd been wearing.

The church bell tolled noon, and Mac swiped at the
sweat pouring down his forehead. He contemplated
removing his shirt, but the prim woman enveloped in
yards of silk would no doubt faint from distress at the
sight of a half-dressed man. If he needed to remember
why he spent most of his time in his father's shipyards
where ladies didn't dare trespass, the sweat pouring

down his soaked shirt served as a reminder. Ladies expected men to be like them, never perspiring and always smelling of perfume.

Miss Cavendish ought to be thrilled with her footman.

To his disgust, his "student" chose that moment to trip daintily across the stable yard in his direction.

For the first time since he'd met her, she was actually smiling. Her bonnet had loosened sufficiently to reveal rebellious wisps of russet hair curling around her high forehead, and her beauty caught Mac in the gut. He had the inane urge to shove her bonnet back, loosen the polished ringlets brushing her chin, and frame her smile for safekeeping.

She'd shriek bloody terror if he so much as touched her.

"I made a trade!" she whispered in awe. "She admired my pin, and I offered to teach her to make them in return for her services. She said she could finish helping her husband with the barn, and we'd be even."

Delight danced in her dark eyes, an entrancing smile played upon her lips, and Mac struggled to repress the inappropriate desire to swing her into his arms. Remembering his wish to see her smile, Mac resolved to be more careful what he wished for. Growling, he wiped his face with his sleeve. "Fine. Then I'll check your tenants' fields next. They ought to be planted by this time of year."

Her smile died, and he felt as if he'd kicked a puppy. As her gaze fell, it apparently struck his sopping shirt, and she reddened and turned away. Mac bit back a curse and reached for his coat. He had the rebellious urge to flaunt his state of undress so she would look his way again.

Why the hell did he want to make her notice him?

"I made that pin," she said with a note of defiance. "I have some useful talents."

"You have to know the value of your product before you attempt to market it. Come on. I have work to do."

He'd rather work out some of his frustration on the back of a horse, but if he was to teach his dignified hostess, she would have to sit beside him.

He harnessed the horses himself rather than watch the stable boy botch the job again. He'd wondered why a stable as expensive as hers didn't have a head groom. Some inkling of comprehension emerged—trading gaudy pins wouldn't pay the salary of a good groom.

Could the blamed woman be living the life of Croesus on no money? Was she waiting for a wealthy man to snatch her up and save her from penury?

Mac ground his back teeth at the thought, and waited for her to catch up with him. Her long black skirts trailed in the grass, hindering her progress.

Grimly, he held out his hand to assist her into the carriage.

Instead of taking his hand, she knotted hers together. "I'd rather walk."

"I don't bite," he snapped. Her refusal to acknowledge his physical presence made him feel like an uncivilized ogre.

Beatrice drew a deep breath and dared a glance at her irritable boarder. He was big and solid and his wet shirt revealed entirely too much of—

She didn't dare think of what lay beneath the wet linen. Meeting his eyes was somehow worse. Mr. Warwick's glare managed to heat her all over, as if he'd assessed her and found her lacking and was angry at her for it.

She didn't want to ride beside him in the narrow chaise. He smelled of manly perspiration, and she could see golden brown hairs curling against the thin linen. She wished he'd don his coat.

He didn't wait for her to find an argument. Without permission, he grabbed her around the waist and set her firmly on the carriage seat. Before she had time to catch her breath, he climbed up beside her. She burned through the corset where he'd touched her.

"I'm not a patient man, Miss Cavendish. If there's work to be done, I do it, and I see no sense in dillydallying. Where are your fields?"

"I . . . Why, I suppose we'd best see the ones nearest town first." Seated beside this giant man, she didn't quite know what to do with herself. The only man she'd ever sat this closely to in her life had been her father.

If she could think of him as a servant, she might manage. She'd been dealing with servants all her life. Polite, deferential ones, not ones who exuded raw masculinity and wielded the iron hand of authority. No, Mr. Warwick definitely wasn't a servant.

Briefly, she shut her eyes to recover her wandering thoughts. "If there's work to be done, then we'd best be about it," she said as formally as she could. She would *not* let him have the upper hand.

He shot her an aggravated look, but she ignored it as the horses trotted down the broad main road.

"The fields, Miss Cavendish. Why aren't they planted?" He gestured toward narrow strips of land, some plowed, some planted, some still dense with weeds.

"Widow Black has been in ill health and can't work her rows. Mr. Williams broke his foot and hasn't returned to his field since the plowing. The tenants who worked those other strips left after Father died, and I didn't know how to assign them to someone else."

She could feel the force of his astonishment and refused to meet his gaze.

"You mean each of those damned strips is worked by a different farmer?"

"Your language, Mr. Warwick," she responded primly. He was supposed to be *teaching* her, not yelling at her.

"Damn my language to hell and back!" he shouted. "Language has nothing to do with this. You'll have a whole town of starving people if this is the way you tend your land. What in hell kind of system is this?"

"It's the way things have always been done, and it's always worked quite well." She didn't dare look at him. She could remember the furious arguments her father and Mr. Overton had had over a similar topic. The system had worked for her father. Mr. Warwick didn't have to curse at her as if she were at fault.

"Medieval," he grumbled. "I suppose now you'll tell me that they each have equal strips of fertile and less fertile land."

"That seems fair to me. Why should we favor one tenant over another? The widow deserves the same chance as Mr. Farmingham."

"Don't tell me." He lashed the reins to speed the horses. "Mr. Farmingham is the one whose strips are planted and growing, isn't he?"

She glanced sideways and, noting the grim set of his square jaw with its neatly chiseled chin, glanced away again. "Mr. Farmingham hasn't been ill all winter."

"Mr. Farmingham should be rewarded for not being ill all winter," he shouted. "How the devil can you collect rent from tenants who produce no income?"

"I don't know," she said faintly. She really didn't. She knew her father's journals recorded the rents, but she couldn't fathom the initials and abbreviations he'd used.

"Give me the estate accounts," he said wearily. "We'll start there. Where I come from, women know how to handle such things."

Beatrice turned to him in amazement. "They do?"

He urged the horses faster. "They had to learn or starve. We've come a long way since the land was first settled, but the attitude hasn't changed."

She sat back and marveled at the idea of women working alongside men. In petticoats and skirts? She narrowed her eyes in suspicion. "*You* don't like me working with you."

He grunted. "*You* are a lady. Ladies are pains in the tail end."

Well, she thought hotly, so she was a lady. That wasn't such a bad thing, not nearly as bad as a plain, ugly spinster. Or an irascible, ill-tailored gentleman.

She stuck her nose up in the air and didn't reply. Couldn't. He'd tied her tongue in knots again.

Five

"There, that is Widow Black's house." Bea pointed to a neat thatched cottage with a thin stream of smoke curling from the stone chimney. "We must stop and see if her little boy's croup is better. Cook makes a wonderful syrup for coughs."

Reluctantly, Mac reined in the horse. He'd prefer to examine account books and talk to the men who planted the fields, but he could think of no polite way of refusing the lady.

A young woman of faded prettiness appeared in the doorway with two small children clinging to her limp skirts. Recognizing her guest, she instinctively patted her hair into place and brushed a cowlick back from her little boy's forehead. "Miss Cavendish," she called welcomingly. "How are you today?"

The woman's accent was more educated than Mac had expected. He helped his hostess down from the cart.

"I came to ask you the same thing." Miss Cavendish hastily withdrew her hand from his and glided toward the widow, as if he didn't exist for any purpose but helping her out of carriages. "How is Robert's cough?"

"The syrup and the steam worked just fine." The widow patted her son's blond hair. "We'll be planting the field before you know it."

Mac sauntered up to join the women. Miss Cavendish glanced at him nervously, then offered a curt introduction. "This is Mr. Warwick. He's come to teach me about estate management. Mr. Warwick, the Widow Black. I showed you her rows earlier."

The widow regarded him anxiously. "We've had illness in the family, but I'll begin plowing tomorrow."

"Perhaps your neighbors can help you. Theirs are done and planted." Gritting his teeth, knowing how he sounded to the frail young women, Mac stalked off to examine a loose board in her shed wall.

Behind him, he heard Miss Cavendish murmur reassurances. Give him a sailor to order about or a merchant to yell at, but ladies? Grabbing a hammer and ladder from inside the shed, he applied himself to pounding nails while the women nattered.

He'd ask for the estate account books again. He could read mathematical figures with more ease than he could navigate a conversation with a female.

If we are to progress into a modern age of steamships and railroads and manufactories, we must do so with the wisdom of the best minds, education, and talent this country can provide. How can we know what vast natural resources we possess if we do not educate all our children and not just those of the privileged?

Beatrice sat back and admired her elegant script. When she had started this exchange of letters with Lady Fenimore at Nanny's urging, she had never dreamed the lady's husband would become a member of Parliament. In that first letter, she had timidly asked Nanny's employer about the prevailing attitude toward female education. To her immense surprise, the lady had responded intelligently, as Nanny had predicted.

Since then, Beatrice had broadened her knowledge of the world through her correspondence. Her father would have been appalled, had he known, but what he hadn't known hadn't hurt him. She had derived immense satisfaction from the exchange and from knowing that someone of intelligence thought her opinions valuable.

As she signed her name with a flourish, pounding feet and a cat's terrified meow erupted in the hall.

"Bad kitty! Nasty-noisy-damheathencwyinhorrors!" a childish voice piped.

Bea winced. Had she translated that garbled sing-song correctly?

"Come back here, you little menace! Leave those animals alone."

James. With a sigh, Beatrice laid down her pen and rose from her desk. Why was James minding the children?

Opening the study door in time to catch her cousin flinging a roaring Buddy over his shoulder, she glanced around for some sign of Mary. As the cat skidded out of sight around a corner, James caught her look and scowled.

"Tag, you're it," he said crossly, shoving Buddy at her. "Do something with him before someone throttles him. Cook caught him using her best ladle to dig holes in her herb garden this morning. It's a wonder we aren't having boiled Buddy for dinner."

Gingerly catching the toddler by the middle, Beatrice gazed helplessly at the boy's wide-eyed expression. What did one do with a four-year-old? Especially one with very odd ideas of entertainment?

"Where's Bitsy? And Mary?" she asked in bewilderment.

"Last I saw, the babe had removed her soiled nappies," James grumbled, "and Mary went to fetch hot water to clean her. She asked me to watch the monsters. Never again!"

Buddy puckered up at James's harsh tone. Terrified

he'd cry, Beatrice bounced him as she'd seen Mary bounce Bitsy. She winced as Buddy's hand smacked her nose.

"All right, I'll see what I can do." Beatrice tried to fish the boy's sticky fingers from her chignon. Apparently entranced with the hairpins, he pulled harder.

"Find a husband," James retorted. He flounced off, still muttering.

Find a husband. That was helpful. Husbands who could solve all her problems and grant her fondest desires were as available as genies. Her aunt had sent her a trunkload of enchanting nightdresses to encourage her foolish dreams, but Beatrice had outgrown them as she'd outgrown adolescence.

Beatrice grimaced at another tug on her hair. She couldn't imagine a husband solving the problem of undisciplined hooligans. No doubt a husband would expect *her* to handle the children, while he sat in his study puffing cigars and reading the newspaper—as her father had done.

Wondering if Buddy didn't need more of his father's presence, and if Mr. Warwick's elderly parents could really be the best solution for such an active child, she started for the stairs, then jumped as the front door swung open without a knock.

Mr. Warwick stalked in, carrying the estate account book he'd insisted she give him. She hadn't wanted to reveal the extent of her debt, but her father's books were so incomprehensible, she thought she was safe as long as she didn't give him the bank letter.

As he advanced on her, she noted he'd actually cleaned up and donned a rather nice coat and another green waistcoat that brought out the color of his eyes. He'd washed his sweat-soaked hair, and it gleamed in the sunlight. Somehow he looked a little less gruff and bearlike with a golden halo on his head, although the drawn-down eyebrows warned of his less than angelic mood.

He looked as startled as she at this meeting, but noting Buddy's fierce grasp on her hair, he hastened to the rescue. "The brat has a grip like a vise." More gently than she might have expected for so large a man, he pried the boy's fingers loose.

The proximity of all that masculine height and breadth surprised Beatrice into silence. Her nose practically rubbed his jaw as he untangled his son from her hair. He smelled faintly of exotic spices, and she could barely breathe until he stepped away.

She filled her lungs with air and stared somewhere below his chin. "Thank you. He's apparently a little more than Mary can manage."

"He's a little more than a lion tamer could manage." He shifted the wary child to his wide shoulder as if he were a sack of turnips. "This book is near worthless without the asset pages. All it's showing is a constant drain of cash. Where are the rest of the books?"

Bea picked at an invisible thread on her cuff. "I don't think there are any," she murmured, praying he didn't explode. Her father must have kept the rest in his head.

The intimidating man growled and bounced his son on his shoulder. "I understand your previous steward lives near here. I'm not entirely familiar with your weather or soil, and I'd like to ask him a few questions."

Beatrice tried to keep her breathing even and appear nonchalant. She simply needed practice in talking with men. Practicing with this man was akin to learning to shoot by aiming at lions.

"My father and Mr. Overton didn't see eye-to-eye." She sounded breathy even to herself. She closed her eyes, clasped her hands, and tried to calm her nervousness. "Mr. Overton's modern methods are too expensive for a small estate like this, and they would only upset the villagers by defying tradition."

Those words came from her father's mouth, not her own. Still, her father had known what he was doing, and she didn't. She refused to let this stranger rule her in ignorance as her father had.

"Overton can at least advise me as to which crops are suitable at this time of year and which tenants are best at raising them," he argued.

"I didn't ask you to replace my steward," she snapped, retreating to arrogance by reminding herself he needed her as much as she did him.

She opened her eyes to see Buddy climbing down his father's back. Mr. Warwick held him idly by one foot and glared at her as if she'd turned into a gorgon. She wanted to duck her head and hide, but she couldn't deem a man with a squirming child on his back dangerous. She held her ground and glared back.

"I'm a sight more qualified for the position of steward than carpenter," he informed her with arrogant calm. "You have enough acreage out there to provide a substantial income that could feed the entire village, but the better part of it is lying fallow."

"I should imagine the tenants know what to plant and when," she said, though he had caught her curiosity. Enough income for the whole village? She winced as Buddy grabbed a handful of Mr. Warwick's hair to pull himself up. "I don't know why *you* can't speak with them about it."

"I shall as soon as I know what I'm talking about." He hauled Buddy upright and the boy wiggled to get down.

"Then I will go with you." Some of his brashness must be rubbing off on her for her to say such a thing. She didn't want to see Mr. Overton or ride beside Mr. Warwick. But she *did* want to manage the estate. And that required visiting tenants and fields and other daunting activities. Perhaps it would be easier with this man as a shield.

Her only alternative was to wish for that imaginary man who could provide her every fantasy. She had to be practical.

"Fine," he agreed irritably. "You can hold this imp while I handle the horses." He shoved Buddy back at her.

"Maybe you could harness Buddy, and I could handle the horses," she said dryly, as the boy instantly scrambled from her arms to chase the kitten from under the stairs.

Mr. Warwick's appreciative grin so startled her, she forgot both kitten and Buddy. *My word.* He had a heart-stopping smile when he chose to use it.

"How about I just put a rope on him and tie him to the fence?"

"Leading strings," she suggested. "Teach him to walk before he gallops."

Buddy's high-pitched cries of delight as he shimmied up the stair rail in pursuit of the kitten sent them running.

"The fields must be enclosed," Mr. Overton insisted as they tramped the meadow to reach the top of the hill. "Ye canna do anything with the land all pieced like a crazy quilt."

Hauling her black skirt and petticoats indecorously above her half boots, Beatrice scrambled to follow the two men striding over the furrows. "We'd lose all our tenants," she called after them. "Papa would never allow it."

"Your father is dead," Mr. Warwick replied rudely, stopping long enough to haul her over a fallen tree trunk.

His rough, strong grip almost distracted her until he opened his mouth again.

"Enclose the best fields and rent them to Farmingham," he continued. "If the others can't produce enough profit to pay the rents, then find new tenants."

"That's horrible!" She stopped in dismay. "You can't throw people out of their livelihoods like that." She caught Buddy's arm to prevent him from toppling off the log.

"The world is changing, and they must change with it," Warwick insisted. "We must look to the future if we are to grow and advance."

A young man with a face weathered by years of exposure, Mr. Overton gestured at the fields. "I earned more from these few acres this past year than your father made from his best tenants."

"My father had a care for his tenants. They're like *family*." Beatrice had never argued with anyone in her life, but she couldn't let people like the Widow Black be put out of their homes.

Still, Mr. Warwick's visionary outlook hit a chord of truth. If *she* couldn't live in the past any longer, how could she expect the world around her to remain unchanged?

Beatrice hid her uneasiness by brushing her skirt down, tilting her chin upward, and adopting her best aristocratic manner. "My father managed it," she pointed out.

As they stared each other down, Buddy stomped through the fields as if he were as large as his father and, hands on hips, glared up at a woodpecker in a dead tree.

Impatiently, Mr. Warwick turned his back on her and stepped to the top of a low stone wall to study the view. Hands on hips, massive legs akimbo, he stood like a giant colossus surveying his kingdom. "I've seen children with a more open mind," he called down to her. "Why the hell did you want me to teach you if you won't listen?"

"He's right, Miss Cavendish," Mr. Overton said more gently. "Your father operated on his cash reserves and borrowed at will. The banks are nae likely to lend to a lady, nor to a landowner whose profits are dwindling."

"I can't turn my back on friends," she said desperately.

"They're not your friends, Miss Cavendish. They're your tenants, and they know their duty. If they do nae pay the rents, then they know the consequences."

"Half of them haven't paid the winter or spring quarters," Warwick growled from his kingly position. "If they can't pay you, you can't pay your creditors." Restlessly, he leapt down and strode toward the next field. Buddy ran to follow him.

"Don't make me do this!" she cried after him. "Don't make me be the evil villain that destroys their way of life."

But he wasn't listening. He was relentlessly forcing her to follow or be left behind.

Mac sat uncomfortably on the edge of the carriage's narrow seat as he handled the reins. The woman beside him held her head haughtily erect. Her earlier cry of anguish had scalded him until he figured he'd bear the scars for life. A softhearted woman like this should have a man sheltering her from the hard facts of life.

"You could sell the estate, I suppose," he said awkwardly. He didn't think any new owner would endure these medieval land practices, but he didn't see any benefit in mentioning that.

She shook her head and clutched Buddy like a lifeline. The boy had fallen asleep, cradled contentedly against her breasts. She might pretend a disinterest in the brats, but she had a way with them. Perhaps she reminded them of their mother. Maybe he ought to find a mother for them instead of a nursemaid.

Mac retreated from that thought in a hurry. He had no business becoming involved with the children or Miss Cavendish and her medieval estate. He had a shipping company to build. His mother would care for the children.

Determinedly, he guided the carriage down the leafy lane between stone fences decorated in ferns and primroses, pretending he didn't hear his companion's sniffing.

"How did Father do it?" she finally asked. "Teach me how to read his books."

"I'll show you, but it won't improve matters. You may have cash reserves somewhere, but unless you marry wealth, you won't have enough to continue as you have."

There it was again—her biggest failure. Had she married as expected, her tenants and servants wouldn't be in such a predicament. And now this man knew it, too. She was a failure as a woman, a failure as a mistress of her property. She might dream of a fairy-tale prince to manage things, but she *must* learn to manage on her own.

Could she trust a veritable stranger as her teacher?

Her father had believed women were too fragile to deal with the tribulations of the outside world, and, judging by her own lack of accomplishment, he might have been right.

But then, could it be that his protectiveness had made her the weak creature that she was? If so, in what other ways might her father have been misguided?

Could Mr. Warwick actually be *right*? He and Mr. Overton had agreed on many things. Her father's former steward was prospering while her tenants were not, and from all evidence, Mr. Warwick thrived too. Could her father have been wrong?

Maybe. In which case, maybe he'd also been wrong in claiming women were fragile and helpless.

Six

Mac saw his letter to his London agent off on the evening mail coach, shoved his hands in his pockets, and contemplated the all-male camaraderie of Digby's tavern. Light poured through the ancient mullioned windows, and loud voices and laughter beckoned. The ex-butler had evidently found some means of opening the most profitable part of the inn despite the continuing renovation. Stopping in for a drink or two was infinitely preferable to returning to a household of women and screaming children. Perhaps someone at the inn could help in his search for a nursemaid who was willing to travel.

He had to do something soon. His London agent had reported that the children's father, Viscount Simmons, had come around asking questions of Mac's whereabouts. If the sot thought anything of his children at all, it would be only a matter of time before he set the authorities after him. He must sail before that happened. And he needed a nursemaid before he could sail.

The flames of the tavern fire licked up the chimney as Mac stepped into the smoky room. Everyone turned to watch him enter, but he had no problem with that. He was accustomed to the company of men. They didn't mind if he spoke gruffly or didn't speak at all. They didn't expect flattery or flowers. Unlike women, men expected nothing of him, and he *liked* it that way.

He greeted Digby, ordered an ale, and nodded congenially at the bespectacled curate. The thatcher stopped by to discuss further repairs, and another tankard or two later, someone had introduced him to the brother of some lordling who had stopped in to check on one of his smaller estates. He seemed a convivial sort, and they raised another mug to the caprices of weather and crops and settled into a deep discussion of how railroads and industry were the hope of the future.

Not until he heard the church bell toll eleven did Mac realize how late it was. Miss Cavendish would be impatiently awaiting his return. The children were no doubt turning the house into a barn. Heaving a self-pitying sigh, he made his excuses and stepped into the chilly mist, listing only slightly to starboard as he trod the lane toward the court.

He'd never thought to be burdened with the onerous responsibility of children. If they weren't Marilee's, he'd be off for the coast in the morning.

Instead, he was stuck here in the mud of the distant past. He glared at the candlelit windows of the mansion looming at the end of the drive. No gaslights in this rural outpost. They didn't even have running water. No wonder she had a dozen servants. Half of them must be required for pumping and hauling.

His wayward thoughts leapt to imagining Miss Beatrice Cavendish of Cavendish Court stepping into a steaming hip bath scented with lilacs. He could almost see her creamy complexion heating to a rosy glow in the lapping water. If he imagined those magnificent breasts bobbing on the surface, he'd cripple himself. She might be self-centered and ignorant, but Miss C was one fine figure of a woman.

Mac looked up to see that fine figure flying toward him. He might like to pretend she offered an eager welcome for his return, but even through the pleasant haze of ale, he recognized the onset of disaster. Trying not to stagger, he broke into a run, and promptly tripped on a rut in the road.

"You're drunk!" Appalled, she halted as they met in the drive. "You stink of ale and smoke."

"I don't get drunk," he growled in protest. "And you smell of lilacs and talcum."

Momentarily taken aback, she raised a hand to her splendid bosom. "You, sir, are *inebriated*," she retorted. "And perfectly useless."

As she started to turn back, he caught her waist and lifted her feet off the ground. "I, madam, am slightly tipsy but far more useful than your London fribbles."

She screeched and grabbed his shoulders for balance as Mac swung her into his arms and placidly carried her up the drive. He *liked* having the physical ability to put her where he wanted her. And he wanted her somewhere private, preferably supplied with a bed. Her breasts crushed like feather pillows against his chest. If only he could rid her of the damnable corset . . .

"Put me down, you demented monster!" she shouted loudly enough to shatter his eardrums. "Your daughter needs a physician, not a drunkard."

Mac dropped her like a hot rock. Ignited by alcohol, panic spread with the speed of wildfire. "What's wrong?" he shouted.

She picked up her skirts and headed huffily for the house. "A fat lot of help you'll be. Your daughter could be breathing her last breath, and you would be quaffing a few tankards with the boys."

"Bitsy? Is something wrong with Bitsy?" Fear evaporated any trace of alcohol as he staggered after her. "What? Tell me!"

"I think she's eaten something she shouldn't."
Anger still scorched her voice. "I've sent to the earl's
residence to see if they know of someone to help, but
the nearest physician is in Cheltenham."

Bitsy would eat a toad if someone put it in her
hand. He'd dallied in the tavern, and she'd poisoned
herself. It was all his fault. Mac broke into a run past
his angry hostess.

She scooped up her skirts and stayed apace with his
ground-covering strides. "She's thrown up everything
she's eaten. I can't keep milk down her. She's crying
and acts as if her . . . belly . . . hurts."

His mother had warned him never to mention body
parts around ladies. Another good reason to stay away
from the lot, except Miss C had overcome her squea-
mishness for Bitsy's sake.

"Chamomile?" he suggested as he bounded up the
outside stairs toward the wide front door.

"Won't stay down. Cook suggested a tincture of laudanum and aniseed." She trailed him closely as he ran
into the lamp-lit foyer.

"No laudanum!" he shouted, racing toward the
stairs. "That could be part of the problem. She's been
poisoned with the stuff."

"Don't be ridiculous. Everyone uses laudanum. I
don't know why I'm listening to a sot." She sailed up
the stairs after him.

"I'm not a sot," he shouted. "The more laudanum
a person takes, the more they need." He was nearly
breathless by the time they reached the third-floor
nursery. Panic exploded through his skin at the sight
of Pamela screaming and drawing her knees up to her
aching belly while a maid held her over her shoulder.

"Where's Buddy?" he demanded, reaching for his
niece.

"I put him to sleep in my room, and my maid is

with him." Beatrice swept into the room and brushed her fingers over Bitsy's forehead. "She's still feverish."

Bitsy wept noisily, chewed on her fingers, then held out her arms to Beatrice. The child quieted to choking sobs as Beatrice rocked her against her breasts.

"Could it be constipation? Maybe some mineral oil . . ." Mac's head spun, and he couldn't think clearly.

"Not after what she done up here this morning," the maid answered quickly.

From the shadows in the corner, the tall footman gestured helplessly. "My mother always gave me warm tea with honey and bits of sopping toast."

Mac thoroughly disliked the bewigged weathercock, but he grabbed at any suggestion now. "If she likes warmth, that might work."

James looked grateful and hurried out the door to fetch the requested items.

"Nothing stays down," Beatrice warned him.

He couldn't bear to stand helplessly by and do nothing. "Where does the earl live? Could I go there faster by taking the fields?"

"Landingham is the country estate of the Earl of Coventry. He's seldom in residence, but he often has guests who might know who we could call on."

The Earl of Coventry. Shocked into silence, Mac curled his fingers into fists. The Earl of Coventry, the viscount's father, the children's grandfather. How bad could any one man's luck be? The earl had shown little regard for his grandchildren in the past, but he would no doubt throw Mac into a dungeon if his son had told him who had stolen the children. He should never have let himself get involved in an emotional situation. He *knew* better.

Would Miss Cavendish help him hide the children if the earl showed up? *Not bloody likely.*

Think straight. Now wasn't the time to go off the

edge. "I'll go to Cheltenham, then. A physician should know what to do."

"It took him three days to arrive when my father had his seizure, and then he had nothing to suggest when he arrived. My father died the next day." Bitterness crept into Beatrice's voice, but she cuddled the sobbing infant gently, rubbing her back as she paced up and down the carpet.

The specter of his irresponsibility loomed over Mac. Had he left the children where they belonged, they would have had experienced nursemaids on hand. Bitsy might not have become ill at all.

Or they could have dosed her with laudanum and left her to recover or die as she would. As they had Marilee.

"Tell me what to do," he begged.

"I don't think there is anything either of us can do," Bea answered. "We'll wait and see what happens."

James arrived with the hot tea sweetened with honey. Beatrice sat down and tried to persuade the child to sip, but Bitsy cried frantically, sucked her fist, and turned her head away. James looked as if he would weep.

"I'll go to Cheltenham," her cousin promised. "I'll fetch the doctor and sell the silver to pay him. Or we can take the babe with us?" he asked hopefully.

"Not if he's a quack!" Mac roared. "I'll not have quacks about her. Give her to me then. I'll make her drink."

Beatrice shrank back in her chair as the babe's father suddenly loomed over her, but he looked so miserable, she couldn't fear him. "You can't force tea down her. She'll choke."

"You said heat helps," he said angrily. "Then we must give her heat. If she won't take the tea, where are your warming bricks?"

The man was either mad as a hatter or drunker than

she thought. Beatrice stared at him. "You would have her eat a warming brick?"

"Don't be a fool, woman! I'll have her lie upon one. We'll tie it to my shoulder, and lay her there." Pacing restlessly, he shouted at the hovering servants. "Fetch warm bricks!"

The bewigged footman raised his eyebrows, braced a thoughtful finger aside his nose as if considering the wisdom of this suggestion, then ran as Mac stalked toward him with a thunderous expression and raised fists.

Beatrice bit back a smile. If that was how one made James take orders, she would have to practice growling.

"Miss." Mary intruded tentatively, not flinching as Mac swung in her direction. "Mayhap it's not just her belly hurting. My mam always has a bit of ice when the babes are teething. It seems to soothe them."

"Teething?" Beatrice and Mac asked in unison.

Beatrice didn't dare look at him but watched her maid instead. "How can ice make her stomach better? I can't even persuade tea down her."

"Ice might ease the crying," Mary said carefully, edging away from Mac's menacing size. "When their teeth break through, they turn fretful."

"Where's your ice?" Mac demanded.

Mary bobbed a curtsy. "Icehouse, sir. I'll be right back."

Mary's departure left them alone together. Nervously, Beatrice watched his massive frame stalk back and forth, dodging cradles and child-size furniture.

"I'm not drunk," he growled, as if she'd accused him of it again.

"Mildly inebriated?" she suggested. "Terminally irascible?"

"A man can't die of irascibility," he grumbled. "A man might turn gray and die of worry over screaming brats, or shoot himself in the head in a fit of madness over women, but he can't die of irascibility." He heaved coals on the grate and jabbed them vehemently.

Beatrice's mouth curved upward at this insight into the surly man's head. "Either case sounds like irascibility to me." She'd never dared speak to another person like this, but he seemed to need distracting, and she had a lot of words bottled up inside of her that she'd never been allowed to say.

He shot her a glare that had more pain than anger in it. At sight of the sobbing child on her shoulder, he turned helplessly back to the fire. "I'm not fit to care for them."

"Someone must," she said practically. "And it appears as if you have been appointed. The brick will have to be wrapped carefully or it will burn both of you."

He shrugged. "Wrap Bitsy in blankets. I'll not die of a little heat." He looked up as James raced into the nursery with an armload of bricks. "You'll dirty your pretty gloves," Mac said dryly.

James pursed his lips, glanced at Beatrice, then knelt on the hearth and arranged the bricks under the grate to heat.

Mr. Warwick stared up at a china doll garbed in ruffles and lace sitting on a wall shelf. "You're an only child?" he inquired.

"My mother died when I was less than two, and Papa never remarried."

He grunted and turned to watch the bricks heat. "Had a governess, did you?"

Exhausted, Bitsy sobbed a hiccup on Beatrice's shoulder and sucked harder on her fist. She suspected Mr. Warwick felt as uncomfortable as Bitsy, which was why he was asking awkward questions. It was rather nice understanding why someone did something.

"No, just Nanny Marrow until I was ten. Papa said I'd learned all a girl needed to know." She would have liked to have learned more, but she'd been much too shy to attend boarding school. She'd towered over the other children from her earliest years.

Mr. Warwick's grunt sounded disapproving, but he said nothing as he used the tongs to remove a brick and wrap it in one of Bitsy's cloths. "Let's give it a try." He reached for his daughter.

Bitsy started to wail when he moved her, then settled down with another sob against the heated comfort of his shoulder.

Mary rushed in with a wine bucket half-filled with ice chips. "They'll melt quickly, this small," she said breathlessly, "so I did not make so many."

Mr. Warwick attempted to arrange child and brick and free a hand to reach the ice, but Bitsy squirmed and complained at the shift. He glanced helplessly at Beatrice.

He wouldn't ask. She could see he wouldn't. He'd bend himself into a knot trying to do it all before he asked for help. She ought to let him. She ought to sweep out of the room and leave him to the child he'd so obviously ignored for too long.

He didn't strike her as the type who would neglect his children. Rather than puzzle over the enigma of her guest, Beatrice took the bucket. He was entitled to his secrets as much as she was entitled to hers. "Thank you, Mary. Why don't you catch some rest now? And you too, James. I think you've done all you can."

At her tone of dismissal, they backed uncertainly toward the door, no doubt wary of leaving her alone with a stranger. Surely that was a foolish concern under the circumstances. Turning her back on them, she held a piece of ice between Bitsy's gums. The infant eagerly chewed on it, and for the first time that evening, she quieted.

"Thank God," Mr. Warwick muttered.

Beatrice echoed the sentiment as the child closed her eyes and relaxed.

Without the cries of a distressed child to intrude, the intimacy of her closeness to this overwhelming man struck her. The warm approval in his eyes as he looked on her almost buckled her knees.

She had handled a situation that he couldn't, and he *appreciated* it. Her toes might never touch the ground again.

Seven

"**G**iyyap!"

Gremlin hands jerked at the hairs of Mac's aching head, and a deadweight settled on his shoulders. Moaning, he tried to drag himself awake. Every bone in his body protested as he shifted position. The gremlin emitted a high-pitched squeal that seared his nerves.

"Buddy." He groaned, recognizing the sound now that he was awake. Where was his keeper?

Eyes still clenched against the pounding pain of a hangover, he groped behind his neck to grab the brat, hauling him down from his perch and into his lap. He seemed to be sitting upright, at least.

At the sound of a feminine moan, Mac pried open one eye. He didn't think he'd been in a state last night to induce moans of pleasure.

A mass of crumpled petticoats spilled over the narrow cot beside him. Setting the wriggling toddler loose on the floor, he rubbed his eyes and looked again. Miss C and Bitsy. Morning sunlight illuminated their fair complexions, and he was tempted to rub his fingers over Miss C's cheek to see if it was as silky as it looked. Remembering the roughness of his hands, he refrained.

She'd helped him through last night's terror. In his

mad escape from London, he'd never contemplated
how he would deal with the children if he didn't have
Nanny Marrow. He was paying the price of that
thoughtlessness now.

Rubbing his aching temple, Mac watched as his
hostess blindly located the babe with her hand, reassured herself that all was well, and rolled to her back,
nearly falling off the narrow cot. He snickered, and
she woke instantly.

Buddy crawled onto the pillow beside her. "I gots
a horsie, Missy," he announced, pushing the stuffed
remains of a bedraggled animal in her face. "Pammy's
not cwyin'." He bent approvingly over his sleeping
sister and planted a wet kiss on her cheek.

Missy. Miss C, Mac's addled brain translated as he
reached over to haul his nephew off the bed. Buddy
hadn't learned to use his sister's nickname yet. Maybe
Miss C wouldn't notice. He should be grateful she
hadn't badgered him with questions he couldn't answer. "You'll wake your sister, brat. Play on the
floor."

Miss C's eyes popped open again. Her hair hadn't
entirely come down from its pins and combs, but wisps
curled and fell about her cheeks and neck. With those
wide brown eyes staring up at him, she didn't look
much older than the children.

"How's Bitsy?" he asked, thinking a bit of distraction prudent. He didn't imagine she had much experience waking with a man in the same room.

Her gaze instantly shifted to the squirming babe
sucking her thumb. She tested a padded bottom.
"Wet."

Mac leaned his aching head against the chair and
watched through half-lowered lids as Buddy scooted
about the floor, chasing a toy horse. The prior night
was still too raw in his memory for comfort. "They're

so damned small and helpless," he murmured. "How can I possibly keep them safe?"

"You can only take care of one minute at a time." Her calm appraisal soothed his ragged nerve endings.

He listened to the rustling sound as she sat up and straightened her petticoats. Too bad she wore so many clothes. He'd have liked to have seen her in only a shift. Or less. He scowled instead of following that lustful train of thought. "They have an entire future ahead of them. How can I see only the present?"

"Marry," she said with what he detected as a hint of spite. "Let your wife worry about the present while you fret over a future that hasn't happened yet."

The nursery door softly opened and closed, leaving him alone with the two helpless babes. How the *devil* had he gotten himself into this?

Marilee, he remembered. He was doing this for his sister—who was probably rolling around heaven, laughing at his predicament.

He peered suspiciously out the window to see if any angel feathers floated by. Marilee had always enjoyed a good joke.

Beatrice hid in her room until she heard Mr. Warwick greet James and recognized the sound of the front door opening and closing. He behaved as if he were quite at home.

She couldn't believe she'd fallen asleep in the same room with him.

Her cheeks burned, and she wouldn't look in the mirror as she shook out her fresh skirt and petticoats and prepared to face the questioning eyes of her household. She would simply pretend nothing had happened.

Nothing *had* happened, she reassured herself. They'd merely taken turns walking the floor with Bitsy

until the babe had fallen asleep. Beatrice couldn't precisely remember when that was. Perhaps she'd fallen
asleep first. And Mr. Warwick had laid the babe down
and rested his eyes. That must have been it. Nothing
to be ashamed of. She had more pressing matters to
consider.

Such as quarter-day's fast approach. Did she dare
send Mr. Warwick into Cheltenham to sell the silver?
He must certainly surmise the precarious state of her
finances by now. Of course, with her luck, he'd no
doubt sell the silver, abscond with the funds, and leave
her with his children.

Maybe not. Whatever else she might think of him,
he treated the children with tenderness and fretted
over them with the care of an anxious parent.

Dragging herself down the wide marble staircase,
she didn't see any sign of James, the wretch. She supposed he was hiding in the kitchen, giggling with the
maids over last night's escapades. She really had to
make him go into Cheltenham for her. She simply
didn't have what it took to haggle with shopkeepers.

She entered her father's study prepared to ring the
bell and remind James of his duty. Instead, she
stopped dead at the sight of Mr. Warwick sitting at
her father's desk, his feet propped on the wide surface,
an account book on his knees, while he scribbled notes
with a metal-nibbed pen. She'd thought her father a
large man, but the nape of Mr. Warwick's neck towered over the chair's back, and his booted feet
dwarfed the desk.

He glanced up at her entrance, grunted something
that might have been a greeting, and returned to scrib-
bling notes.

Flabbergasted, she merely stood there, staring. Was
she supposed to meekly retreat to her parlor as she
had done when her father was preoccupied?

By all the saints, this was *her* house. He couldn't

force her to leave. "What are you doing?" That really should have sounded like a demand instead of a squeak.

He impatiently set his pen aside. "Tallying income per tenant. You have only two who seem to pay regularly."

"Mr. Farmingham and the Dubbinses," she responded promptly. She might not be able to read account books, but she knew who paid regularly.

"Overton says your best acreage is in the valley. I'm suggesting you enclose those fields and lease them out to Farmingham and Dubbins."

"I can't pay for fencing," she protested, amazed she could say anything at all. Mr. Warwick sat there like a statue of a Greek god framed in the sunlight pouring through the windows behind him.

If she remembered correctly, Greek gods tended to do rather capricious and quite frequently evil things.

"Let your tenants wall off the fields as they work." He looked up from his notes as if daring her to defy him. "It's to their profit to keep the sheep out."

He had a square-cut jaw and a chiseled chin that stuck out much too far for her comfort. The little dent in it would be appealing if he'd only smile. Instead, it looked as if he was clenching his teeth waiting for her reply.

"Where will the sheep graze?" she asked, hating herself for her ignorance and her lack of protest.

Before he could answer, the front door knocker rapped. He looked at her expectantly, but she wasn't about to let him off the hook. "James can get it."

He swung his feet down from the desk as if suddenly realizing a gentleman should rise upon the entrance of a lady, though he didn't rise. "I sent James into Cheltenham."

Anger seared her cheeks. She wanted to shake the complacent look off this man's face. "Why?"

How would have been a better question. James never did as told.

The knocker rapped again, and feet pattered in the hallway as one of the maids hastened to answer it.

"You didn't give me your cash books, so I didn't know how much capital you had to advance your tenants for seed. I sent James to obtain an accounting from the bank he said your father used. Perhaps there are funds you don't know about."

The voices outside the door grew louder, and his gaze shifted to the entrance.

Beatrice stepped away just as the door flew open to admit a stout matron in a tartan silk gown and an emerald green turban. The newcomer's gaze faltered in surprise at the sight of the man at the desk, but she recovered quickly. "Beatrice, dear!" the apparition exclaimed, holding out her arms. "How good to see you again. Has it been perfectly ghastly these last months? I hurried here just as soon as I could."

"Aunt Constance!" Beatrice barely got out the words before her great-aunt swept her into a powdered embrace.

"You poor, dear child, left alone to fend for yourself all this time." She kissed Bea's cheeks and led her affectionately toward a sofa. "Had I thought your father so careless as to pop off like that without warning, I never would have gone so far from home. It's quite unconscionable for men to die so young. Whatever do they expect us to do?" She hugged her niece effusively and settled her onto the cushions, as if Beatrice were her guest instead of the other way around.

As Mac rose from behind the desk, the whirlwind of silk and scent swung around eagerly. "And who have we here, my dear? You did not write me of any expectations. You know, given your circumstances, you really shouldn't have to wait until your year of mourning is up. A husband is just what you need right now."

If the power of humiliation could only lead to invisibility, Beatrice would disappear from the face of the earth forever. Mac's look of horror must nearly match her own. "Oh, no, Aunt Constance," she corrected hastily. "This is Mr. Warwick. He's helping me to understand Papa's account books. Mr. Warwick, this is Lady Taubee, my great-aunt Constance. She has been traveling on the Continent."

Composing his features, Mr. Warwick nodded tightly and looked as if he would flee out the window if given half a chance. Her aunt often had that effect on people.

Gazing in trepidation and awe at her aunt's resplendent attire, Bea shuddered in anticipation. She'd wished for her company, but she tended to forget between visits that her aunt's taste reflected a far different world from her own.

"My, my, you are a fine figure of a man," the older lady said admiringly. "Did Coventry send you to help out? Are you related to the Gloucestershire Warwicks?"

Beatrice could almost swear that red flushed his cheekbones, but he merely stood stiff and unyielding and answered without inflection, "No, my lady." Turning to Beatrice, he bent his neck enough to acknowledge her. "I'll leave you to your visitor, Miss Cavendish, and see myself out."

"The sheep," Bea called after him. "You haven't told me—"

"I'll handle it." With a warning in his tone, he stalked away.

"Oh, my. Is he an American? Such fine, broad shoulders! And fiery eyes!" Constance swirled to admire her niece. "And you look so fetching, dear. No wonder he can't keep his eyes off you."

Beatrice stifled an inward groan. She remembered all too vividly her aunt's blatant attempts at match-making when Beatrice was but a shy seventeen.

"If he looks at me at all, it is to see if he has ground my bones to ashes yet," Bea complained. "He thinks I'm an addled fool. Have you just come from London? How did you arrive so early?" Rising from the sofa, Beatrice steered her aunt from the subject and the study. Her mother's aunt was everything she would never be, but as long as she wasn't the current object of her managing ways, she was delighted to have her company.

"Missy! Missy!" A boyish voice rang out as they stepped into the hall.

How did the child consistently escape the nursery?

Attempting to climb the banister with one arm still in a sling, Buddy lost his grip in his excitement and landed flat on his rear end, narrowly missing the first stair.

As her aunt's eyes widened in astonishment and Buddy began to wail, Beatrice's heart sank to her feet. She could already hear the cogs whirling in her aunt's overactive brain—children, a widower, and her poor, unmarried niece.

She might as well be seventeen again.

Mac strode hurriedly toward the cottage, mentally locating the children's bags, while attempting to formulate a plan of escape. Any woman wealthy enough to know Coventry, travel the continent, and recognize his mother's Warwick relations must travel in high circles. He didn't fool himself into hoping the right noble Sebastian, Viscount Simmons, hadn't screamed his recriminations all the way to the queen. All London would be rife with rumor. She had only to write the earl. . . . He had to hide the children elsewhere.

Where? How? He didn't know if Cunningham had

stocked the *Virginian* yet. He couldn't very well throw the children on board in the captain's care and let it set sail. They needed, at minimum, a proper nurse-maid to look after them, as last night's incident with Bitsy had proven.

Even if he could find a nanny, he wasn't at all certain that he could smuggle the children onto his father's ship. If the viscount had a single brain in his head, he would have someone watching the *Virginian*. Mac would be much better off waiting for the completion of his own ship. No one but he and Cunningham knew about his ownership of the clipper. He'd never have a chance to oversee the final fittings now, but he'd be content if he could just lock the children on board and set sail immediately.

But he couldn't even reach London. He'd had the post chaise returned to its owner, and stealing Miss C's horses would not be wise, even if he could manage two babes on horseback, which he couldn't.

Besides, he'd promised Miss Cavendish he'd help her, and he didn't take promises lightly.

"Mac! Whoa! Over here. I've been looking for you."

A young man in a top hat riding a stylish gelding hailed him from the cottage drive, and Mac groaned. The brother of Lord Something-or-other, whom he'd met last night at the inn. He must have been drunk last night to introduce himself to the bloody aristocracy.

"I've come to see those hounds you told me about. I've a hunting box less than a day's ride from here, and my gamekeeper swears Cavendish has the best hounds in the field. Do you think Miss Cavendish could be persuaded to part with a few?"

Mac would sell the whole howling pack if they were his, but they weren't. And he couldn't go back to the house to ask. The devil must be laughing up his sleeve by now.

"The hounds are out past the stable," he called back. "But Miss Cavendish has company. Take a look, and I'll ask her later."

Instead of riding his prancing steed toward the stable, the young lordling swung down from his saddle and waited for Mac to catch up. Lean and elegant, he looked the type to court a lady like Miss C. He probably knew how to spout poetry, when to flourish flowers, and which damned flowers to flourish.

"I heard Lady Tawdry came through town. I don't suppose you could persuade fair Bea to introduce me? I've heard her aunt is one of the finest raconteurs in all England."

Lady Tawdry? Mac's eyebrows sailed upward, and the younger man flushed. Carstairs, Mac remembered. Maximus Daventry Carstairs, Dav for short, impoverished younger son or some such.

"Lady Constance Taubee," Carstairs corrected apologetically. "The woman is a living legend. Outlived three husbands, sailed the world, uncovered mummies in Cairo, and danced with Fiji islanders, I understand. She only visits England because of Bea."

And the damned woman had chosen this moment to return. Mac kept the sentiment to himself. "She's just arrived. I imagine Miss Cavendish is settling her in."

Carstairs groaned. "I'd go to the door and leave my card, but Bea won't receive me. I don't think she's ever forgiven me for calling her a long Meg when I was but a lad of nine. She was twelve at the time, and had the most glorious red braids. I didn't know how else to catch her attention."

Reluctantly, Mac grinned at the admission. Carstairs was young, but not as toplofty as some of his peers.

"When was that, last year? She's probably over it by now."

"Very funny. Just because I'm cursed with this youthful mug doesn't mean I'm still in leading strings. She's held that grudge for sixteen years."

Sixteen years? The wide-eyed, lovely Miss C was— twelve plus sixteen and not married? Not possible. Were all the men around here blind as bats?

"I can't imagine she even remembers it," Mac answered gruffly. He'd thought her proud and stiff-necked until last night. Now . . . It didn't matter. Promises or not, the children's safety came first. He had to round them up and run.

Oddly enough, part of him didn't really want to leave.

Eight

"I'm not in the least bit tired, dearest Bea," Lady Taubee assured her as she settled into a parlor chair. "Let me take my tea while you tell me all."

Her redoubtable aunt must be nearly sixty, but Constance refused to admit the weaknesses of age. Beatrice almost wished she would so she might send her off to rest while she ran out to question Mr. Warwick about the sheep. He had seemed decidedly grim when he'd walked out earlier. She didn't think it boded well.

"There is little enough to tell," she admitted, taking her place at the tea table and giving up any hope of speaking with Mr. Warwick soon. "Papa died quickly. I don't think he was in much pain, as I told you in my letter."

Lady Taubee waved away that explanation. "Your father has gone to his just reward, I'm certain. It's the living who concern me. You cannot manage all alone, dear. We must find you a good husband."

"I don't believe that's the solution, Aunt Constance," Bea said tentatively, not yet possessing the knack for argument. "I would rather have someone teach me how to run an estate."

Lady Taubee laughed. "Don't be foolish. Your tenants would take advantage of your soft heart and you would be bankrupt in six months." Her head rose as she noticed Beatrice's silence. "You aren't bankrupt, are you? Your father always seemed well-to-do, but he's spent quite a bit refurbishing, I see."

Beatrice couldn't prevent the color rising to her cheeks. Heaven forbid that her aunt should learn of her dire straits. Constance would haul her off to London and parade her about like a circus elephant until she found someone desperate enough to take Bea off her hands. "I've not learned how to manage yet. You needn't worry. I'm certain there's more than enough to tide me over until I learn."

"Oh, most certainly not!" Lady Taubee said in tones of horror. "I'll not have you lose everything your father worked so hard to gain. We must find you a husband." She brushed away Beatrice's protests. "You were meant for having babies." She cocked her head with interest. "Explain again why you are taking care of that man's children."

"I'm not. Mary is. In return for room and board, he's helping me learn to manage while he waits for his ship to be readied for the journey home."

"Hmmm." Lady Taubee did not seem appeased. "He dresses his children well. He must be a gentleman if he reads account books."

"I did not ask what he does. He said he could help, and I accepted the offer."

An undermaid scratched at the parlor door, and Lady Taubee called for her to enter. Beatrice had learned long ago that her aunt tended to take command wherever she went. It had never bothered her before, but she was becoming a little resentful that no one thought her capable of handling her own life.

"There's a gentleman to call, miss." Darting their redoubtable guest an anxious glance, the maid bobbed a curtsy and held out a tray containing a calling card.

Beatrice didn't bother looking at it. It would be

impolite to weary her aunt with villagers so soon after her arrival. "Tell him I'm not at home."

"Don't be ridiculous, Bea." Lady Taubee picked up the card and nodded approvingly. "Show Mr. Carstairs in, please, and bring us more tea. Tell Cook we'd like some more of those jam tarts."

Escaping as if happy she hadn't been ordered to fill the vases with flower arrangements and invite the village to dinner—as had happened in the past—the maid scampered away.

Resentment didn't begin to describe Beatrice's feelings at this high-handed rearranging of her preferences as well as her household. Cook didn't have enough help to make more jam tarts at this hour, and Molly had better things to do than run back and forth all day. "Dav is a useless bit of work," Bea protested. "Why ever would you wish to see him?"

"I'm certain he does not call on *me*, dear," Lady Taubee replied placidly, sipping her tea. "I would like to examine your potential suitors to see which one we should bring up to snuff."

"Suitors?" At that astounding assessment of her caller, Beatrice could only sink back in her chair and stare. Dav was three years her junior and hadn't a sensible brain in his pretty head. He came here a few months out of the year for foxhunting mostly, and she'd seen him in church, but a suitor? Never. She'd barely even spoken to the man.

Sweeping into the room and gallantly doffing his hat and bowing, Mr. Carstairs freshened the closed parlor with the scent of outdoors and sunlight. His merry smile alighted on Beatrice, then danced to her visitor. Uncovered, his glossy black curls gleamed like polished ebony.

"My ladies, this is a treat! Miss Cavendish, you are looking as charming as ever. And might I have the pleasure . . . ?" His voice trailed off suggestively as he turned to Lady Taubee.

Awkwardly, Bea performed the introductions.

"I was afraid Bea was cooped up and lonely in this rural outpost," her aunt declared, patting the cushion of the love seat beside her. "But I see I shouldn't have worried if she has the company of young gentlemen such as yourself."

Bea scowled as Dav threw her an impudent grin. The man had the attention span of a butterfly. He must truly be bored to call here. Bea was sorely tempted to escape screaming out the front door. She did *not* need another man telling her what to do when she'd much rather learn for herself. And she certainly did not need a flibbertigibbet like Dav, who would run her mad before the day ended. She doubted he knew any more about estate management than she did.

"Miss Cavendish hoards her charms," Dav declared lightly. "But I could not let her hoard you as well, Lady Taubee. You are a rare treasure meant to be shared."

As they exchanged annoying flattery, Beatrice caught a movement at the door. Thinking it was the maid, she gestured for her to enter, only to discover Mr. Warwick standing there, a scowl to match her own on his face.

"I didn't mean to intrude."

Next to Dav's lean, elegant sophistication, Mr. Warwick seemed like a bull in a china shop. He filled the doorway with his old woolen coat and tall, muddy boots. No fancy hat covered his tousled hair, and his neckcloth looked as if he'd torn it apart in a fit of frustration. He wore the same plain green waistcoat he'd worn the other day, and he hadn't bothered fastening it before he'd come in. He looked ready to ride a horse or sail a ship, not enter a lady's parlor. Her heart pounded a little harder as she fully realized how much more masculine Mr. Warwick was than a dandy like Dav.

"It's not an intrusion, Mr. Warwick." And it wasn't. She'd far rather wrangle with him over sheep than listen to Dav's silliness. "Would you like some tea?"

"I've just come to take the children out for a while. Thought they might like to ride in your pony cart, if you don't mind the imposition."

He seemed exceedingly nervous. Odd. He'd never struck her as being the sort to be uncertain about anything.

"Mary asked permission to take them to visit her mother in the village," she replied. "She has a little brother about Buddy's age. I didn't think you'd mind." Beatrice watched with curiosity as his face turned expressionless. He started backing from the room the instant her aunt gestured for him to enter.

"Do come in, Mr. Warwick, and tell us more of yourself. My niece isn't such a taskmistress that she won't allow you time for a sip of tea."

Beatrice saw the flash of alarm in his eyes, but if she was saddled with the tedium of Dav, Warwick could endure a little tea. "Molly's returning with a fresh pot. Have a seat, sir."

He obeyed. Reluctantly, perhaps, with a look that warned of retribution, but he did not ignore her request as others did. Feeling oddly triumphant, Beatrice offered him the plate of cakes. Gingerly, he took one between his thumb and forefinger. The dainty scarcely seemed large enough for a man his size. "I could ask Molly to bring you something more substantial. . . ."

"This is fine," he snarled, disposing of the treat in a single bite while perched on the edge of his seat.

"Ask Miss Cavendish about the hounds," Dav said eagerly. "She'll only bite off my head if I try."

"Don't be absurd, dear boy!" Lady Taubee chuckled. "Bea couldn't snap at a turtle."

"Bea has never seen a turtle to snap at," Beatrice muttered under her breath.

A corner of Mr. Warwick's mouth quirked upward as if he'd heard her, but he nodded politely at Dav's request. "Miss Cavendish, Mr. Carstairs is interested in acquiring several of your foxhounds, if you can spare them."

Spare them? She'd give the lot away just to save the expense of their care, not to mention the relief of freeing the air from their howls. But her father had doted on those dogs. She couldn't give them to just anyone. And Lord Knowles would be furious. He'd been after her for them since her father had died.

"I've had other requests," she said hesitantly. "I must see they have a good home. . . ."

"Knowles," Dav said with disgust. "Don't let him browbeat you. You're quite right to be careful with fine animals like those. Why, you have three bitches out of Foxy Lady that will . . ." He launched into an avid monologue on dog breeding that left even Aunt Constance stupefied.

As Molly returned with fresh tea and cups, Mr. Warwick took one and settled back in his chair with what actually appeared to be a gleam of pleasure, while Dav rhapsodized over past hounds and breeds.

"You haven't told me where you'll put the sheep," Beatrice whispered as she leaned over to offer Mr. Warwick more cakes.

"Shall I give you a lesson on sheep breeding practices?" he murmured, his attention still seemingly on Dav.

"It would be more practical than hounds," she muttered. Seeing her aunt throw her an admonishing look, she sat back.

"Well." Lady Taubee interrupted Dav's discourse.

"It certainly seems as if you should take up the squire's avocation. Beatrice, dear, do you think you could be persuaded to part with those dear dogs?"

"Dav and I will work out the details later," Mr. Warwick said smoothly. "I'm sure you ladies wouldn't wish to be bored with the negotiations."

"I say, old boy, that's splendid. Let us retire to the study and work out—"

Mr. Warwick halted his boyish eagerness. "In good time, Dav. Give Miss Cavendish a chance to adjust to the idea."

"Excellent thought, Mr. Warwick. Where in America are you from, sir?" Lady Taubee diverted her intense concentration to the newcomer.

Beatrice thought he looked startled and wary at the question.

"From Virginia."

Lady Taubee beamed. "I have a good friend there. She's begged me to visit, and perhaps I shall once I see dear Beatrice happily settled. Are you a sailor, sir?"

"I have sailed," he replied evasively.

"Excellent! I do enjoy a good adventure now and again. I've always wished to own my own clipper so I might pursue the waves on my own schedule rather than at someone else's command. I've just returned from Sicily and met the most fascinating people there. There's a hotel with food like . . ." She waved her hand dismissively. "But Beatrice is a homebody and refuses to accompany me. Do you believe a woman's place is in the home, Mr. Warwick?"

He squirmed uncomfortably, and Beatrice felt a twinge of sympathy. Aunt Constance had a way of trapping people into saying things they would not admit otherwise. It didn't seem quite fair to practice on someone who obviously had as little skill at social discourse as Mr. Warwick.

"Aunt Constance, you know perfectly well he must insult one or the other of us if he answers that honestly. Pick on Mr. Carstairs, if you must. He is quite capable of giving you a polite two-faced reply."

Mr. Warwick choked on his tea.

Dav grinned. "Why, Miss Cavendish, I hadn't thought you'd noticed me or my talents. I must have made an impression after all."

"You're a rogue, sir," Lady Taubee said pertly. "Now, I wish to question Mr. Warwick. Why don't you toddle along and admire your new acquisitions."

Warwick was out of his chair faster than Dav. "He hasn't acquired them yet, my lady. If you'll excuse us, we'll leave you ladies to more civil discourse."

He stalked out, practically dragging a blustering Dav—who, unlike Warwick, at least managed a polite bow and farewell.

"Well," Aunt Constance said after the men left. "That was enlightening. Have you more suitors I should interview?"

"They're not suitors, Aunt Constance," Bea said wearily, relaxing with her tea now that the invaders had departed. "Mr. Warwick will be gone within a week or so, and Dav will be gone as soon as he has his hounds."

"Don't be too sure of that. You're an available female with land. Every single male in the shire is bound to be sniffing around. Who is the Lord Knowles they mentioned? Is he married?"

"He's Papa's age and his only interest is in hunting. Don't matchmake, please. The curate has tried for years, without success. I'm quite content as I am."

"Nonsense." Lady Taubee firmly set her teacup down. "All the world can see you're unhappy. You're just too isolated to know better. Now, I think I'll visit with Mary's mother. It should be entertaining to meet Mr. Warwick's children."

Beatrice definitely did not like the way her aunt said that, but she had no means of telling her not to interfere. Aunt Constance was a force of her own, akin to whirlwinds and tidal waves. One was swept helplessly along.

Nine

He had to leave. The old lady was far too sharp, and she was already suspicious. Mac fretted the whole time he discussed the damned dogs with Carstairs. He should never have forgotten how small an island England was. Lady Taubee could probably trace his ancestral tree back to Adam and Eve if she knew his full name. She only needed to trace it to Viscount Simmons.

He had to escape. Now.

"My brother is at the blacksmith's. He can give you a bank note for the balance," Carstairs said as he handed over the coins in his purse. "Are you staying on with Miss Cavendish? You should talk with Hugo. He's been trying to persuade the squire to enclose his fields for eons."

"Hugo?" Mac had lost track of the conversation.

"My older brother, the baron, remember? Father sent him to persuade Overton to take a position on our Somerset estate, but the chap is being stubborn. Can't say as I blame him. If I had a little land of my own, I'd not work for anyone else either."

Mac had heard all this last night and could sympathize, but not right now. He needed to collect the children and find a new hiding place. Thoughts spinning, he fell in with Carstairs's request to accompany him into the village. The bank note for the dogs and the coins in his pocket would give Miss C a little cash to tide her over for a while.

Lord Hugo Carstairs, baron, looked amazingly like an older, more cynical version of jolly Dav. He lifted a pointed dark eyebrow at his introduction to Mac and didn't immediately reach for the bank note his younger brother requested.

"You sold him Miss Cavendish's hounds?" he drawled. "How generous." Crossing his arms, the baron leaned against a wall and watched the blacksmith shoe his restive stallion. "And where do you intend to kennel these hounds, Dav, old boy?"

Holding his high-crowned beaver hat, Dav impatiently brushed at a dirt smudge marring the expensive surface. "We have that whole farm with nothing on it but sheep. It won't hurt to kennel a few hounds for the hunting season."

"The sheep at least earn their way," the baron pointed out. "That's more than can be said of dogs."

That was Mac's opinion on the matter, but he didn't have time to barter with arrogant lordlings. "Sheep are barely earning their weight, from all reports," he said disagreeably. "Until someone has the ambition to install a mill and those new looms, you're stuck with accepting a factor's prices for their wool. Send a draft to Miss Cavendish when you're ready for the hounds. I bid you good day."

He started toward the inn in hopes Digby might know where he could find Mary and the children.

"The squire owned the only mill," the baron called after him. "It's water I lack, not ambition."

Damn. Mac swung around, examined the baron still lounging against the wall, and nodded acknowledgment. Overton had told him the Cavendish land encompassed the main river source, but the mill had closed because of the competition from factories in the north. It wasn't his concern. "Call on Miss Cavendish sometime," he replied curtly.

He strode off, cursing British arrogance. Carstairs was naught but the heir of an earl. Mac's mother was the daughter of an earl. Titles were irrelevant in this day and age. If the baron had any sense at all, he'd be courting Miss C in hopes of acquiring a beautiful wife who owned a useful mill and a lot of valuable land. Mac figured Carstairs was waiting for the daughter of an earl to come along instead. *Stupid.*

He tried not to imagine the cynical baron courting Miss C. She might have a shade too much pride for Mac's taste, but it was obvious she didn't have the sophistication of a man like Carstairs. She needed a protector, not a seducer.

Mac rolled his eyes at his own thoughts. What Miss Cavendish needed or didn't need was none of his concern.

Upon questioning, Digby gave Mac the location of Mary's parents. Mac had no idea how he would hide the brats until he could set sail. He just knew the sleepy little village of Broadbury had suddenly become too populated for comfort.

He growled at Mary's mother when he learned the children had already left. She backed away, and, feeling an oaf, Mac hurried off.

As he returned to the Court, he heard laughter and hurried a little faster up the drive. He would borrow the pony cart. He'd see the cart returned with adequate compensation for its use. He could hide at an inn. . . .

He sprinted past a towering rhododendron and almost stumbled over Miss Cavendish sitting on the grass, her full black skirt spread around her, holding her hands out to an upright Bitsy. Mac held his breath as the babe put one chubby leg before the other, obviously determined to reach the outstretched hand. One step, two . . .

She plumped down on her padded backside, and Mac hastened to pick her up before she cried.

To his amazement, she was giggling, and so was Miss Cavendish.

"She keeps trying to walk, but her bottom is too big." Miss C laughed as the babe waved her hands at her. "I don't think she likes crawling in the grass."

Mac had to stop a moment to readjust his thinking. He'd been worrying and fretting all morning, anxious to spirit the children away, and now she'd confronted him with a bucolic scene contrary to all his fears. Bitsy was laughing proudly as she rose to her tiny bare feet again, undoubtedly staining Miss C's petticoats with grass but undeterred in her quest to reach the first loving arms she'd probably ever known. Had Marilee ever had a chance to hold her daughter, or had she died without seeing her? Mac swallowed a surge of grief at the thought.

"Where's Buddy?" He sounded surly, but Miss Cavendish was concentrating on Bitsy. She had a remarkable way of ignoring him when he was at his worst.

"With Aunt Constance. I left the two of them chattering away. She's never had children of her own, and she dotes on them. I'm sure he's spilling all your secrets by now." Bitsy fell down a little closer, and Beatrice reached over to haul the toddler into her arms, hugging her as she glanced up at him. "Did you sell the hounds?"

Mac dropped the pouch of coins on her skirts. "He still owes a sum he's persuading out of his big brother. Expect a call from Lord Carstairs and don't let the dogs go until he pays up." That sounded too much as if he were planning to leave, and from her puzzled frown, he could tell the question had crossed her mind. Fortunately for him, she wasn't the type to nag or interrogate. If he had time to think about it, he'd appreciate her calm acceptance of his abrupt manners.

But her mention of Lady Taubee prying at secrets increased his anxiety. He prayed four-year-olds didn't know how to tell secrets. "I'll check on Buddy."

"I was about to take Bitsy in. I'll check on him. The thatcher had a question I couldn't answer. Could you . . ." She gestured in the direction of the barn.

Heart thumping oddly out of kilter, Mac reluctantly turned away to see what the thatcher needed. He couldn't let Miss C's soft brown eyes distract him for long. If Lady Taubee knew the Earl of Coventry, she'd report the presence of the children in an instant. He had to count on her not wanting to cause trouble until she had proof that Mac was the kidnapper all London sought.

Hurriedly, he checked at the barn, answered the thatcher's question, verified that the pony cart had working wheels, and retraced his steps to the house. Miss C was nowhere in sight, and with relief, he headed inside. If he could retrieve the children . . .

Hearing Buddy's rambunctious shouts from the nursery as he entered, he started toward the stairs. An icy voice from the hall stopped him in his tracks.

"I think, Mr. *MacTavish,* we might have a word in private."

At this use of his full name, Mac heard the door of a dungeon cell clanging closed. He swung around to face the source of doom.

Lady Taubee stood imperiously outside the study, her dark eyes snapping, daring him to run. He'd never run from adversity in his life, but he considered it now. Unfortunately, the children were upstairs, and he didn't have the cart hitched to the pony. Not that one could outrace pursuers in a pony cart.

He was trapped.

With arrogance, Mac nodded his head and changed direction to follow Lady Taubee into the study.

The aristocratic old woman gestured toward a straight-backed chair across from her. Mac waited until she was seated on the love seat, then usurped the desk chair.

"You don't deny your true name, then?" she demanded.

"Do I stand charged of that? I didn't know it was a crime," he retorted.

Oddly enough, Lady Taubee smiled. "I can remember your mother denying she flirted with my beau on the grounds that she'd kissed him, not flirted with him." The smile disappeared. "My niece is not sophisticated enough to understand such refinements on truth. You have lied to her, Mr. MacTavish."

"For good reason, my lady." Mac waited impatiently for the boom to fall. He needed to know which way to dodge, and so far they only danced around the subject.

Above them, Buddy's shouts escalated into hysterical screams. Mac didn't wait for the lady, but, leaping from his chair, he dashed into the hall, taking the stairs two at a time. Vaguely, he was aware by the first landing that Miss C followed, but he didn't question her appearance. Somehow he'd known a child's cry would bring her running.

As Mac charged into the nursery, panting from his race to the third floor, he looked desperately for spilled blood and broken teeth.

"I was merely teaching them their numbers," Mary cried from the window seat.

Bitsy sat sniffing and hiccuping in the far corner of the room while Buddy stood protectively in front of her, hands on hips and glaring a challenge at the adults invading his territory. He'd freed his arm from its sling and bunched his small fingers into fists, but his bottom lip was quivering. On the floor in front of them lay an assortment of broken sticks.

"Counting sticks," Beatrice said as she entered. "Why on earth should they carry on over the counting sticks?" She bent to retrieve one of the broken toys. "Aunt Constance taught me my numbers with these."

Beatrice watched as Mr. Warwick squatted to lower his large frame to the boy's height. She noted how his shoulders strained at the coat seams, and his boots muddied his trousers, but he paid no notice to his attire. She tried sweeping past him to pick up Bitsy, but he held up his hand to prevent her from passing. "Buddy, what's wrong?" he asked carefully.

Buddy looked uncertainly from Mr. Warwick to Beatrice, then flung himself, sobbing, into his father's arms.

Behind them, Lady Taubee stumbled in, panting with exertion, her turban tilting at a precarious angle as she took stock of the situation.

Not understanding any of this, Bea ignored Warwick's warning, marched past him, and lifted Bitsy. Settling in the rocking chair, she cuddled the little girl in her arms as if she belonged there, and for the first time, she considered what would happen when Mr. Warwick took the children away. Would he find someone who would look after them and hug them and reassure them as they needed?

"Buddy, tell me what's wrong." Mr. Warwick sounded as desperate as the child sobbing in his arms. "Are you hurt?"

"Bad sticks," he said through hiccups. "Bad, bad, bad, sticks."

"I simply spread them on the floor," Mary explained. "Nanny Marrow used to teach us to count with them. Then we'd stick them into potatoes and make dolls of them."

Mr. Warwick picked up one of the slender, pointed

sticks and held it in his palm. "It's a toy, Buddy. Just a toy."

Buddy grabbed the stick in his pudgy fist and jammed it into his father's knee.

Mr. Warwick yelped and hit the floor hard, accompanied by the ominous sound of a tearing trouser seam.

Bea gasped as she caught the implication behind Buddy's action. "Get rid of those sticks at once," she said as softly as she could through her fury. "He learned that from someone. Children imitate what they see."

Bea scarcely heard her aunt's cry of dismay as Mr. Warwick's gaze met hers, and she read his answering anger and helplessness. What kind of parent didn't even know when someone tortured his children?

Not Mr. Warwick. She could tell by his rage that he'd just discovered what the children had suffered, that he understood what she wasn't saying out loud. Maybe it was time she demanded a few explanations. She couldn't believe a man who could walk the floor with his daughter all night would let anything—or anyone—harm his children.

Mr. Warwick removed the stick from his son's hand and snapped it in two. "No more sticks, Buddy. We'll count toes and fingers from now on. And no one will hurt Bitsy, either. Look, she's all wrapped up in Miss C's hair."

Beatrice ignored the sticky fingers pulling the long curls beside her ears into wispy ringlets. Tears welled in her eyes at the thought of what these children must have endured. What satisfaction could anyone achieve from jabbing pointed sticks into tender flesh? It had never even occurred to her that toys could be used in such a fashion.

Aunt Constance and Mary were already gathering up the sticks and systematically breaking them into little pieces. Mr. Warwick carefully rose with Buddy in his arms, promising him a pony ride, and Beatrice closed her eyes at the sight revealed as he turned toward the door. At least he wore underdrawers beneath the split seam.

But oh, my . . . The possibility of what the underdrawers covered tickled fantasies she'd rather not examine, and she hugged Bitsy tighter, ignoring the thumping of interest in her breast.

"Mr. Warwick," she called daringly, "you might want to stop at the cottage before going to the stable."

"Right." He sounded gruff, and she didn't have to peek to know his cheeks were stained with color as he strode out, the hole in his trouser seam gaping.

It seemed that the bluff, giant American embarrassed as easily as she did.

"He's a good man, Bea," Constance said softly from the floor as she gathered up the last of the sticks. "You couldn't do much better than to latch onto a man like that." She sighed wistfully after their guest's departing back. "In another day and time, I would set my cap for him myself, but I'll make the sacrifice and give him up for you."

Beatrice ignored her aunt's wishful thinking. Remembering Mr. Warwick's high-handed manner of taking command of her house, her servants, and her tenants, Beatrice thought maybe he was a good man for anyone but her. She didn't know how to stand up to a man like that, a man who knew far more than she could ever learn, a man who fascinated her far more than she should allow.

Lady Taubee didn't corner Mac again until an hour before dinner. At wit's end after the nursery episode, he'd spent the afternoon calming Buddy, without completing plans for their escape. He figured that if he ran now, the lady would have the authorities after him in a minute. His only hope was to reason with her.

Wearing an exotic dinner gown of what appeared to be Chinese silk embroidered with dragons, Lady Taubee didn't look particularly reasonable now that she held him captive in the parlor. Mac would have faced real dragons and pirates with less trepidation.

"You kidnapped those children, Mr. MacTavish," Lady Taubee said severely, without preliminaries. "Viscount Simmons has men looking for you. There are rumors all over London."

"I'm amazed he dares admit he's lost them," Mac replied callously, stretching out his legs from the wing chair he'd appropriated. "From what he told me, he has no other income but what our fathers provide for their support. If he admits they're gone, the money stops. Hiring men is a dead giveaway to the earl that his grandchildren have disappeared."

Lady Taubee frowned. "I haven't heard Coventry is in town, but it's no matter. Those children are not yours. You cannot just spirit them away."

"I'm their uncle. I can and I have." Donning his boldest demeanor, Mac folded his arms across his chest. "Simmons is a drunkard who hires nursemaids to drug the children into a stupor. They're so careless, they broke Buddy's arm. You saw with your own eyes today proof of what the children have endured. I made Simmons sign over their custody to me, and I have the legal papers to prove it."

"Which is why you're hiding here under an assumed name? I'm too old and too experienced to believe that, sir." The ostrich plume in her hair shook with her vehemence. "I may sympathize with your cause, but not to the extent that I'll allow you to harm my innocent niece with your perfidies. Once the earl discovers what has happened, he'll hunt you to ground and bury a hatchet in your scalp. And he'll run down anyone who stands in his way. Coventry is not always a reasonable man."

Mac had hoped the children's grandfather might be a little more sympathetic. He should have known better. Stomach sinking, he rose. "The children and I will be gone by morning."

"Sit down, young man!" Lady Taubee sternly pointed at the chair he'd just vacated. "You will take those children nowhere, or I'll have every man in the village after you. You can no better care for those children than their father can."

After these latest episodes, Mac knew the truth of that. He knew nothing about raising children, had never thought to learn. He just knew better than to leave these small bits of Marilee in careless hands.

With an aggravated sigh, he lowered himself to the chair again. "You have a better suggestion?" he asked bitterly.

"Yes, though I would have preferred to wait and allow nature to take its course. I am not so blind that I cannot see interest growing between two people, and I can think of no two who are better suited. But your circumstances demand immediate action."

She smiled beatifically at Mac's blank look. "It's the perfect solution. My niece has need of a man to look after her and her interests. You need someone to look after the children. What better arrangement could there be?"

Mac narrowed his eyes in suspicion. "That is what *we* thought, but you seemed to find my presence objectionable."

Lady Taubee laughed. "The *earl* is objectionable. Dear Bea approves of you, and rightly so. You seem to be a man of intelligence and compassion. I know your parents, know you come from good family. I think you will suit her very well."

Squirming uneasily in his chair, wanting to tug at

his suddenly tight collar, Mac clung to the chair arm. "Suit her?"

Lady Taubee leaned over and patted his hand. "A fine young man like you should be wedded by now. That would take care of your wanderlust."

"I have no wish to take care of my wanderlust," Mac growled. He thought he ought to stalk out, but, captured in the woman's odd fantasy, he simply stared.

"Of course you do, dear boy. You would not wish to end up like me, with no home or family to hold you." For a brief moment, loneliness darkened her eyes before they flashed merrily again. "Court my niece, and I will not mention your name to Coventry and his misguided son. Hurt her, and I'll have you spitted and hanged." She beamed as if she'd just offered him the gold at the end of the rainbow.

Mac couldn't believe his ears. He sat there staring at the dotty old witch, waiting to hear something reasonable. She raised her eyebrows and outstared him.

"Court your niece?"

"And marry her." Lady Taubee nodded firmly, plume bouncing.

"Marry her?" He didn't think it was horror lacing his voice so much as disbelief. Miss Cavendish was a fine woman, but he was a traveling man. His home was an ocean away. Perhaps this was some sort of jest.

"Do not take that tone of voice with me, sir," she scolded blithely. "I'm quite right in the head and have far more experience than you do. Beatrice is a wonderful, loving, obedient, beautiful woman who deserves a good man and a good life. She's simply a little shy. If you'd quit barking at her, she'd overcome her shyness."

Shy? The haughty lady with her nose stuck in the air—shy? Even if he believed that, he was not the kind of man a discriminating lady would marry, should he be inclined to marry. "You don't seem to understand," he said cautiously, searching for words to explain. "I live in Virginia. I spend most of my time at sea. I intend to take my niece and nephew home to my parents, where they belong. Miss Cavendish belongs here."

"Of course she does, silly! This is her home, and she loves it. That's of no matter. You have the ability and knowledge to run her estate. Sail the sea, if you must. Do what you like with the children. But marry Beatrice and look after her."

Mac ran his hand over the back of his neck, tangled it in his neckcloth, and shook his head. "Ma'am, you are not making sense," he said as evenly as possible. Surely she didn't want to see Buddy and Bitsy returned to their filthy nursery, although he thought the crafty old witch capable of condemning him to a British dungeon if he refused her. He simply couldn't see what advantage she saw in marrying her niece to an American whose circumstances didn't allow him to stay here and protect her.

The lustful, impulsive part of his brain conjured up the image of Beatrice in his bed and almost sank his argument before it began.

Oblivious to his discomposure, Lady Taubee rose with a rustle of stiff petticoats and a bob of her colored plume. "I'm making perfect sense. You and those children are endangered by any precipitous action you might take if you run from here. My niece is in danger of losing everything she holds dear without the aid of a competent man to help her manage. I should think three weeks sufficient time to court and win her."

She swept from the room with the authority of a queen.

In disbelief, Mac sat there a little longer, hoping she'd return to tell him she jested.

The only sound he heard was that of Bitsy's happy

gurgles as Miss Cavendish carried her through the house.

He'd been taught to respect and defend women from adventurers like him, and Lady Taubee had just offered him the opportunity to possess everything his primitive nature could desire—not only a lovely woman for wife, but one who tolerated his presence with equanimity, and who would be happy to pursue her own course while he followed his.

How the hell could he take the high road of principles and logic when the low road of temptation was so much more appealing?

Ten

"Surely you have something prettier than that to wear to dinner!"

Aunt Constance marched into Beatrice's bedchamber, gave her black gown a dismissive look, and proceeded to her wardrobe. "Now that I am here, I see no reason for you to stay in mourning another day. You're much too young to look like a widow. You must have something more festive for a warm spring evening." She shot Beatrice a mischievous look. "I'm sure that fine young American would enjoy seeing you as you really are."

Alarm raced through Beatrice at her aunt's impish demeanor. She knew to distrust that look. Glancing down at her black gown, she knew it looked frumpy, but who was there to notice? She didn't intend to invite Mr. Warwick to dinner.

She'd always loved fine fabrics and stylish gowns, and her father had indulged her, to the detriment of his bank account. She hadn't felt the urge to dress up lately, and knowing she could not buy new, she'd not stirred herself to think about what she wore. She frowned as her aunt produced a girlish gown several seasons old. Her aunt had been acting oddly all afternoon.

"It's been only six months, Aunt Constance," she protested. "I really don't think—"

"Nonsense, child. Try this on. Such a lovely shade of pink will suit you well."

Given her aunt's preference for gaudy colors, Beatrice didn't think she should rely on her judgment. "Not pink, please. Dark purple, perhaps?"

Lady Taubee puckered her nose, then returned the pink gown to the wardrobe and rummaged for the requested color. "You have an elegant figure that you should show off more often, my dear. I do wish you would come to London for a Season. We could have so much fun together."

Beatrice smiled fondly at this oft-repeated admonition. "I'm a trifle old for a coming-out, Aunt Constance, and I've never possessed the vanity to show myself off." Nor the courage to visit London society, where she would appear a towering giantess among the delicate flowers of the ton, but that was an old argument.

Deciding on a purple silk, her aunt laid the gown over her arm to examine it. "You have the vanity to wear fashionable gowns, so you must know they look good on you."

"I wear gowns for people to look at *instead* of me," Beatrice corrected. "While everyone admires the details of my wardrobe, they do not notice who is wearing it."

Constance shot her a disapproving look. "For an intelligent woman, you say the most foolish things. Now here, put this on, and let's see how it suits."

With a sigh, Beatrice submitted to the unfastening of dozens of tiny buttons, tapes, and hooks, the selection of a strapless petticoat bodice to go under the lower neckline of the evening gown, and the fastening of the purple bodice with its gentle layers of flounces falling below her shoulders in place of sleeves. She wrinkled her nose at the result. "A trifle dressy for a quiet evening at home, isn't it?"

"Don't be silly. A woman can never look too elegant. You have such lovely shoulders, you wear this style well. I think we should have a dinner to show you off. You need jewelry. Where is your box?" Lady Taubee lowered the off-the-shoulder flounce slightly, then bustled off to examine the jewelry box Beatrice's maid produced.

Bea didn't bother examining her mirror to see the results. She'd ordered this gown for a dinner her father had given for some of his hunting companions a year or two ago. The old men had patted her on the back, called her a fine-looking young woman, and spent the evening drinking her father's claret. She'd adorned the table during the meal as expected and disappeared into her parlor after that. Acres of purple silk did not transform her into anything new or interesting, but the silk felt good against her skin, and now that she was out of black, she appreciated the vibrant color. Perhaps it *was* time to look around and see what she could make of this new life of independence.

Provided she didn't go bankrupt beforehand.

Settling on an amethyst-and-crystal necklace and earbobs, her aunt fastened them around Bea's throat, admired her handiwork, patted her niece's polished curls, and smiled. "You are quite the loveliest woman I've seen in some time. It's a shame you insist on depriving London of your presence."

Bea gathered up her skirt and strode toward the door. "Shall I ever need funds, I'll hire out as a dressmaker's display dummy. Cook will be fretting if we don't hurry." She had lived with herself long enough to know what she was, and what she was not. She might learn to be an independent woman, but she knew she could not be a social butterfly.

With an exasperated sigh, her aunt followed.

As she descended the stairs, Beatrice detected James standing at attention in the front hall, his gold buttons gleaming and his scarlet livery immaculate, the wretch. "How could you go to Cheltenham and not take the silver?" she scolded.

James didn't lower his gaze from its lofty position on an ancient portrait well above her head. "I was not instructed to take the silver, Miss Cavendish."

"I *told* you to take the silver, James. I'm the one paying your wages, not Mr. Warwick!"

He lifted a wicked eyebrow, reminding her that she *hadn't* paid the wages.

"James, you are a blessing, and I shall be certain to tell your mother so." Constance patted the footman on his liveried arm and shooed Beatrice toward the parlor.

Stunned by this recognition of her supposedly distant cousin, wanting to question her aunt in private, Beatrice hurried toward the formal parlor.

She halted in midstride at the sight of a tall, elegant gentleman rising to his feet as she entered. *Warwick!* Bea stopped abruptly, and her aunt nearly ran into her.

Stunningly handsome in black tails, frilled shirtfront, and white, low-cut waistcoat, he also looked immensely uncomfortable. A peacock feather from the Grecian urn brushed his broad shoulder. He edged away from the gate-legged table adorned with seashells and porcelain shepherdesses, adroitly avoided the tapestry-embroidered stool, and froze rather than navigate his way around more clutter. Perhaps she'd feathered her nest a little too lavishly, but she'd had twenty-eight years in which to do nothing else.

She thought her guest might strangle on his high neckcloth should he lower his clenched jaw sufficiently to look at her. Instead, he stared pointedly over her head just as James had done and murmured something that might have been a greeting.

Beatrice knew a trap when she saw one. Mr. Warwick would never have invited himself to dinner. She swung on her beaming aunt. "What have you done?"

"The boy cleans up splendidly, does he not?" Lady Taubee said with admiration as she rustled through the room. "Mr. . . . *Warwick*? Does not our Bea look lovely tonight?"

At some undiscerned warning in her aunt's voice, Mr. Warwick glanced down at Beatrice, and she thought he might swallow his tongue before he could speak.

"S-splendid, indeed," he murmured hoarsely, tugging at his neckcloth and fixing his gaze determinedly on her face.

If she were a vain, mean-spirited woman, Beatrice would flaunt her bosom and increase his discomfort, but her embarrassment of riches in that department had always been a cross she bore grudgingly. Had she known Mr. Warwick would dine with them, she would never have agreed to wear this gown. Her aunt was definitely up to her old tricks.

"Aunt Constance did not tell me to expect guests," she said curtly. "Excuse my surprise. It was most unseemly of me."

Something like sympathy flickered across his expression before he curbed it and nodded formally. "Lady Taubee is a woman of many surprises."

"Without surprises, life would be boring," Lady Taubee agreed. "Come along, children; I do believe dinner is waiting."

Resentment seethed just below Beatrice's surface as she placed her gloved hand on Warwick's proffered arm. This was her house and her table, and she had every right to be consulted before a guest was invited to dinner. She loved her aunt dearly, but the old woman took entirely too much upon herself.

"I checked on the children a little while ago, and they seem to have calmed down," Bea said politely, searching for a neutral topic rather than the scathing phrases rising to her tongue. She had a great deal of experience in keeping her opinions to herself.

"This past year has been difficult for them," Mr. Warwick said in the same detached tones that he would use to discuss the weather.

From habit, she took her usual chair at the right of her father's place, jolting slightly at the brush of Warwick's warm hand as he helped her into it. Aunt Constance usurped the seat at the head of the table and gestured for their guest to sit at her left. Aware that Warwick sat directly across, where he could not miss the full display of her bosom, Bea looked anywhere but at the uncouth American. Except that he didn't look so uncouth tonight.

"I believe we ought to invite the charming Carstairs men tomorrow evening," Lady Taubee announced with a smug smile. "And perhaps the curate and his wife. This house has been far too dismal for too long."

"The Carstairses are only passing through," Warwick said stiffly. "They'll be on their way tomorrow."

Beatrice would have sighed with relief except that would necessitate breathing. Her corset seemed to have suddenly tightened, until she thought she might suffocate. She didn't wish to entertain Mr. Warwick two nights in a row, not if it meant watching him watching her all evening.

"Such a pity." Lady Taubee sighed. "Well, I shall call on the curate and see who else is in residence. There are generally a few entertaining sorts at Landingham."

"Aunt Constance," Beatrice said in a hiss, "this is a house of *mourning*. We cannot entertain."

"You mean you don't wish to entertain," her aunt scoffed. "Would you deny your poor old aunt a few meals in good company after she has traveled all this way to see you? Of course not," she answered for her, blithely ignoring Bea's heated look. "It will do you good to see fresh faces."

Equally ignoring the tension of the man on her left, Constance rattled on. "Tell us of the places you've seen, Mr. Warwick, the things you've done. It's always a pleasure to hear from another adventurer like yourself."

Beatrice stole a cautious glance at her dinner companion. He'd trimmed his golden brown hair to a neater length above his already rumpled neckcloth, but no amount of gentlemanly trappings could conceal his ardent desire to be anywhere but here. She thought she almost saw a plea of desperation behind the look he gave her, but he spoke calmly enough, so she must have been mistaken.

"I'm not an adventurer, but a man who seeks the future. My interests happen to lie on both sides of the Atlantic, that is all."

"Very well, then, tell us of your interest," her aunt commanded.

Beatrice didn't know what had possessed her aunt to fasten her attention on an American, or why Mr. Warwick had agreed to the charade. She would have thought he had more resistance than that.

As they talked of steamships and railroads and industrial development, their stiffness was almost forgotten. Mr. Warwick's eyes gleamed with the fire of ambition as he warmed to his subject, and Aunt Constance offered opinions on every topic, some intelligent, some skeptical. With the skill of a practiced hostess, her aunt steered the conversation, learning far more about Mr. Warwick in a single sitting than Beatrice had done in several days.

His restlessness and impatience were not the mark of an uncouth man, she realized, but of one accustomed to wielding power and authority. She should have suspected the like sooner, but the children had distracted her. *He* had distracted her.

She shifted uncomfortably as she wondered why he had chosen to stay here.

"Did you know that Beatrice is an accomplished pianist?" Lady Taubee asked as she rose from the table while the servants cleared the largely untouched pudding.

Aunt Constance had dined with kings and queens, and Mr. Warwick could build railroads and ships, and *she* could play the piano. *How quaint.*

"I am certain Miss Cavendish has many talents," Mr. Warwick said dryly, standing to assist her.

Crawling in a hole or turning invisible would be particularly useful talents, Bea thought. She wished she could erase her entire existence as Mr. Warwick drew back her chair and his powerful arms brushed close to her nearly bare ones, causing goose bumps to rise all up and down her skin. If he noticed her reaction, he did not comment on it.

Oblivious to her niece's discomfort, Constance marched on heedlessly like a company of infantry trampling fields underfoot. "Bea is much too timid to play for guests, but perhaps you could persuade her, Mr. Warwick. The evening is too young to end."

Why didn't the wretched man stop her aunt? He had no inhibition about telling Beatrice what to do. Surely he could find an excuse—

"I would be delighted to hear Miss Cavendish play, if she would be so gracious as to consent."

Bea wanted to kick him squarely on the shin—hard. Did she detect a note of maliciousness in his voice as he offered his arm and cast her a questioning glance?

"Surely you might call her Beatrice by now," Lady

Taubee chided, leading the way into the parlor. "You young people are so stuffy. Why, in my day we would have been flirting and laughing and rolling back the rugs by now. Wouldn't a dance party be lovely? Perhaps I should play while the two of you dance."

That was far more than Bea could tolerate. The presence of the elegant gentleman beside her was too overwhelming as it was without imagining his arms around her in the intimacy of a dance. Her knees weakened at the very thought of fulfilling her fantasy of dancing with a man who was not only taller than she, but also broader and stronger and more irresistible than any she'd ever met. Given encouragement, her childhood dreams of love and marriage would take root and grow. She refused to sustain her aunt's delusions.

"I must plead my aching head," she fabricated. "I'm sure you and Mr. Warwick have much to discuss, Aunt Constance. I'll go up and check on the children before retiring. They seem to have calmed down, but one never knows."

Mr. Warwick caught her hand against his coatsleeve, not releasing her. "You are unfailingly gracious, Miss . . . Beatrice. Might I accompany you to the nursery? I would see the little dev . . . dears safely asleep."

Beatrice bit back a laugh as she recognized Warwick's frustration. So her aunt was pulling his strings as well. She could sympathize. Her aunt was very good at prying information out of people. Beatrice wondered which of Mac's secrets her aunt had uncovered for him to submit to this charade.

"Of course," she said aloud for her aunt's sake. "Let me show you the way. If you will excuse us, Aunt Constance?

"You play the role of gentleman uncommonly

well," she whispered under her breath as they left the parlor. "Are you an actor, perchance?"

He grunted irascibly, more in his usual form, and allowed her to ascend the stairs ahead of him. "At the moment I feel like a blamed stuffed turkey. I will scare Bitsy to death."

Bea chortled. "Nothing scares your daughter. Be careful she does not chew off your pretty stickpin, though."

"I could say something rude, but an evening of politeness has robbed me of the ability," he muttered as they reached the third-floor landing. "I may never be the same."

Beatrice smothered a chuckle. "I doubt it. You are already reverting to type. Please excuse my aunt, Mr. Warwick. She has illusions of transforming the world into what she expects of it." For a brief moment, she felt very much in sympathy with him.

Outside the closed nursery door he halted her with a hand on her bare arm, shattering their moment of ease. In the light of a small lamp, his normally complacent expression took on an air of desperation. "You and I must talk, Miss Cavendish. I cannot trespass on your goodwill any longer."

A knot formed somewhere below her corset as she searched his eyes. She was not accustomed to personal revelations from men, and his plea caught her off guard. "That is a first, I believe," she said nervously. "Even my servants trespass at their leisure." She ought to be afraid. He was a stranger who had already proved he was more than he seemed, one who held secrets she had no right to hear.

But that inexplicable chord of sympathy resonated between them as he released her.

"It's the gentle people of the world who are most often trampled," he acknowledged. "I would not take advantage of your generosity any longer. Your aunt means well, I believe, but she is placing us both in an untenable position. Perhaps, in the morning, if you could spare a few minutes . . ."

He'd called her gentle. And generous. Something was definitely wrong. Stomach knotting, Bea glanced anxiously toward the stairway. Her aunt would expect him to descend shortly and say his farewells. She couldn't keep him here and demand explanations now.

"You will give me a sleepless night," she whispered in anguish. "Tell me it's nothing that need worry me so I don't pace the floor."

"I cannot tell you another lie." He sighed. "But I swear to you that no harm will be done before then."

Oh, fine, and what about after that? she wanted to ask. Instead, she shoved open the nursery door and tried to pretend that all was as usual.

After all, "usual" for her these last months had been all that was unexpected.

Eleven

More out of sorts than usual after an almost sleepless night, Beatrice brushed briskly at wisps of hair that refused to roll up neatly, swiped at the sausage curls lying limp against her cheek, and pulled them up beneath a lacy white cap. Rebelliously, she donned her high-necked black gown. It suited her mood perfectly.

She couldn't imagine what Mr. Warwick wanted to talk to her about. Or worse, she had spent the night imagining all sorts of dreadful things. Maybe he was an escaped criminal, or his wife was alive and looking for the children, or . . . She couldn't think on it. Life was too impossible as it was without imagining worse.

Aunt Constance always took her morning chocolate in bed, so she needn't worry about encountering her for an hour or two more. Yesterday's various excitements had led to vivid nightmares of dancing with large men who twirled her relentlessly across a dance floor that looked remarkably like a path to hell.

She'd actually heard Mr. Warwick's gruff voice whispering seductively in her ear, occasionally taunting her, sometimes repeating words that had her waking in a sweat. She didn't want to know what those words meant. The mixture of emotion and unaccustomed physical yearning he aroused in her confused her enough. Men had always made her aware of her breasts, but only Mr. Warwick had made her wonder what it would be like to be touched there.

Irritated at the path of her thoughts, she swept down the stairs and headed outdoors. She would lay this particular nightmare to rest immediately.

It was still early enough that the grass sparkled with morning dew, and rosy clouds lingered on the horizon. A robin warbled happily over his breakfast worm as she marched toward the steward's cottage, drawing her shawl more firmly around her to ward off the chill. Had she any sense at all, she would have sent someone to command Warwick to the house, where she could wait comfortably by a fire.

He materialized from behind a laurel hedge as if he'd been waiting for her. She nearly took a step backward at the unexpected confrontation, but she was growing used to Mr. Warwick's imposing presence and imperious demands. He didn't hide behind polite words and pleasant expressions as most people did.

He hid behind scowls.

She frowned right back. "Aunt Constance won't be up for an hour or more. The children are sleeping, or were two minutes ago. What did you want to discuss?"

"You're cold. There's a brazier in the stable. Come along." He strode off without any of the polite gestures he'd offered her last night.

Well, that much at least was back to normal. Bea hurried after him.

As he threw open the stable door, he glanced over his shoulder at her. "Didn't anyone ever warn you about going off alone with strange men?"

"It's not as if the opportunity arises with any frequency," she said caustically, sweeping past him, "or that I couldn't knock down most men, should I have need to do so." She'd never said such a thing to anyone in her life, but Warwick's bluntness opened the path for her own.

"I think you underestimate the strength of men if you believe that." He left the stable door open and strode briskly toward the stone wall where the brazier sat. "Don't repeat this behavior with anyone else. You may be safe with me, but not necessarily with other men who might be eager to acquire your wealth by any means available."

"I don't generally associate with desperate men, or any men at all," she said dryly. She shook off a vision of what it might be like to be overpowered by Mr. Warwick. The fleeting notion left her breathless. "Surely you did not bring me out here to warn me about my behavior."

He threw in coal and kindling and carefully struck a friction match before applying the flame to a length of straw. "No, I just don't know how to approach the subject without insulting you. You've been too generous for me to offer you insult, but I fear I have already cost you more than I should."

"Stop dancing around the subject! I've tossed and turned the night away trying to imagine what dreadful thing you have to say. It's not as if I haven't been insulted before. Just say it."

He stood to his full, towering height. His face was in shadow, but some trick of morning sunlight illumined the gold of his hair as he recited his perfidies. "My full name is Lachlan Warwick MacTavish. The children are my niece and nephew, Percy and Pamela Simmons. They have a whole slew of other names as well, but I won't bore you with them. I'll just say they're the children of Sebastian, Viscount Simmons, the grandchildren of the Earl of Coventry, and by now, I daresay, all of London is seeking them."

Bea felt as if the breath had been knocked out of her. She looked around for a place to sit, found an upended log that someone had fashioned into a seat, and dropped down on it. She stared at the man standing beside the brazier, legs akimbo and hands behind his back as if waiting for a firing squad.

"If they're your niece and nephew . . ." She sorted through the trail of names and relations. "They're your sister's children?"

"My late sister's," he said gruffly. "I arrived in London to discover the viscount had not bothered notifying my family of her death. From all reports, the viscount has been drowning himself in brandy and has been incapable of doing anything sensible for months."

"I see." She heard a catch in his tone, a note of grief as well as anger. "So you thought to get even by stealing his children?" She tried to find the sense in that. She didn't think Mr. Warwick a foolish man.

Impatiently, he drew a crate closer to the brazier. "Sit here, where it's warmer. I might be an idiot, but I'm not a dangerous one."

She didn't really think him a dangerous man so much as a troubled one, although she didn't know why. Kidnapping children certainly wasn't the act of a saint.

She transferred to the crate and held her hands out to the heat. The new position placed her much closer to Mr. Lachlan Warwick MacTavish. She would have to start thinking of him as Mr. MacTavish. "Do you often tell lies, Mr. MacTavish? If so, why should I believe any of this?" Somehow it didn't seem reasonable to be civil around this man, and once she set aside the barrier of etiquette, her timidity appeared to dissipate.

"You need only verify it with your aunt. She's just been through London and suspected at once." He dragged the cut-off log to the other side of the brazier and perched on it, looking at his hands. Even sitting, his was an imposing presence. "I occasionally let strong emotion get the better of me, and don't plan things as thoroughly as I should. I can only excuse myself by saying I sought to protect the children. The viscount had so neglected his household that the children were in grave danger."

His proximity did odd things to Bea's breathing. In the best of all possible worlds, she could lean over and pat his hands consolingly, but she hadn't discarded all her reserve. "So, in effect, you rescued them?"

His head jerked up, and his grave expression reassured her.

"That was my intention. I even obtained the viscount's signature on legal papers, but when he changed his mind, I lost patience, broke his beak, and fled with the children. I believe they'll be better off raised by my parents than by a man who has no care for anything but the wealth they represent. Unfortunately, transporting them across an ocean is proving to be a bigger challenge than I imagined."

Trying to imagine Buddy and Bitsy on board a ship, Bea had to agree with him. He'd need an army of nursemaids to keep them safe.

She actually believed his tall tale. She shook her head and rubbed her eyes as if the bear of a man across from her would disappear, and her quiet life would return to normal.

"Unless you know of someone who would be willing to travel to Virginia with me, I suppose I must sail without a nursemaid," he said wearily.

"Are you saying you must leave now? Is Aunt Constance threatening you?" she asked in mystification. She didn't know how all the pieces of this puzzle fit together.

"Yes." He breathed a deep sigh. "She says she will have me thrown in jail and return the children to the viscount if I don't cooperate."

"Cooperate?" A frisson of alarm traveled through

her as Beatrice stared at his massive shoulders bent in resignation. "What on earth does she want you to do?"

He lifted solemn eyes to hers. "Marry you."

Mac thought Miss Cavendish might tumble right off her seat at his announcement. He reached out and caught her arm to steady her. She shook free of his grip, and he detected anger in the way she drew away from him. He could scarcely blame her. "I think your aunt may be a bit of a lunatic," he added helpfully.

She shot him a scathing glare, then lifted her chin and looked beyond him. "Everyone thinks I'm a helpless ornament. I'll not label Aunt Constance for her behavior any more than I would wish to be labeled for mine." She sat silent, twisting her hands in her lap as she absorbed what he'd told her.

"You are what you make of yourself," he said practically. "There's no shame in being beautiful."

"Don't mock me." She refused to look at him. "I know I'm tall and homely and I've accepted that men will never look at me as marriage material, but I really do resent being thought useless."

It was Mac's turn to be shocked. "Tall and *homely*? Are you insane, woman? If you're tall and homely, what in hell does that make me?"

Startled by his vehemence, she actually looked at him for a change. "Men can't be tall and homely."

She actually thought she was homely, he realized. He'd spent the better part of his life feeling like an oversize bull walking through a doll-house world, and the poignancy of her misconception connected with bruised bits of his own pride. Forgetting the topic that had brought them here, he couldn't resist pointing out the silliness of her statement. "I'm taller than you are," he reminded her.

"You're a *man*," she said, as if that mattered. "Tall men are . . . are *masculine*."

Flattered despite himself, Mac bit back a grin. He'd been called a clumsy oaf and a "right bit of rudeness" before, but no gentle female had ever condescended to smooth his ruffled feathers with flattery. "James is masculine?" he inquired innocently, seeking the limits of her definition of masculinity to further assuage his wounded pride.

Flustered, she looked back to her hands. "James isn't homely."

"Bernie the baker is masculine?" he suggested, beginning to enjoy himself. His life must have become a convoluted horror if this bit of nonsense amused him, but he was grateful to this woman for so many things, while resenting her lofty manner at the same time, that this new aspect of her character appealed to him.

"Of course not. Bernie is . . ." She threw up her hands in frustration.

"Pudgy," he rudely supplied. "And the curate?"

"He's not tall. You are making no sense."

"So a man can be short and homely?" He led her on, waiting for her to see the foolishness of her conclusions—or wanting to hear her opinion of him again.

"That's not what I mean. *Women* are homely," she asserted, a trifle uncertainly.

"Perhaps you just don't *think* of me as tall and homely," he offered.

"Of course I don't think of you as tall and homely," she said with indignation.

"Just as I don't think of *you* as tall and homely." His triumphant logic had her eyes flashing ire, and she was the farthest thing from homely that Mac could imagine. He didn't know how she'd arrived at her conclusion, but he was beginning to think less of her father, and entirely too much of himself. He puffed with pride that a lady as striking as this one thought him masculine.

She subsided into an uneasy silence, and he wished he knew what thoughts swirled inside that pretty head. He had come to realize that more thoughts dwelled there than she revealed to the rest of the world. She might be ignorant, but she wasn't stupid.

And her ignorance was the fault of the people who'd raised her and the society that restricted her.

"It's all a matter of opinion," she finally said with a sigh. "I take your point."

Hesitantly, she searched his face, and he could almost read her wishes because they so coincided with his own. "You're not homely," he answered, knowing she would never ask the question. "You're taller than most women, yes, but that's to your advantage. When you enter a room, every man's head turns to watch and admire you. And if I say more, I'll embarrass you as well as myself."

A smile flitted uncertainly across her lips. "I believe we've strayed from the topic, but if it helps . . ." She hesitated, then blurted, "You are not homely either." She shrugged and gestured weakly. "But I cannot contrive the right word. James is *handsome*, so I don't wish to call you that. It's not the same thing at all."

"I'll settle for *masculine*. I like that. Now that we have confirmed our mutual admiration, shall we return to our problem?"

"My aunt wants you to marry me, or she will have you up on kidnapping charges?" She reduced the question to its cruelest form now that she'd recovered some of her equilibrium.

"Old women tend to think they know better than anyone else. I've been told often enough that I should marry and that a good woman would settle me down. Unfortunately, I've never seen the advantage of settling down."

"I can understand that," she said wistfully. "I wish I could be brave enough to do what you do. I don't even have the courage to leave Broadbury, much less sail an ocean."

"You've never had the opportunity, and you're afraid of the unknown." Mac dismissed her fears with a flick of his hand. "I've been on ships since I could walk. Ladies terrify me, but I daresay they don't you." He'd never said such a thing to anyone, but he had an odd need to reassure this curiously vulnerable woman. Of course, she held his future and that of the children in her hands. It was in his best interests to pacify her.

"Ladies terrify you?" she asked doubtfully, raising her delicate eyebrows. Her eyes widened. "Is that why you're always barking at me? You're afraid of me?"

He shrugged. "Just . . . uncomfortable. Let's leave it at that, all right?"

His haughty lady dissolved into an almost blissful smile at discovering this weakness in him. "I have never stopped to think how I must appear to others. This has been most enlightening."

"This discussion has not solved our problem," he corrected. He couldn't have the damned woman thinking he was *afraid* of her, but he certainly couldn't tell her she had him by the balls, either.

"Oh, solving the marriage problem is easy," she said with startling aplomb. "Did she give you a date by which we are to declare our intentions?"

Mac watched her suspiciously. "Three weeks from yesterday."

She nodded. "Aunt Constance is incapable of staying in one place for any length of time. She has no doubt already set some plan in motion for her departure. We will merely play along with her wishes for the next few weeks—" She halted, as if realizing something. "Of course, there must be a few conditions."

"Of course," he said dryly. "Such as?"

She clenched her hands tightly. "You will use this time to teach me what I need to know about managing my estate. I do not wish to be dismissed or humored any longer."

"That seems fair, if you're willing to accept my occasional irascibility. I'm not a patient man." He might as well lay that out clearly right now.

A lovely, shy smile blossomed on her lips. "I've noticed. Fair enough." Then, remembering, she asked, "Your ship? When does that depart?"

Now that they had formed a conspiracy together, Mac didn't wish to disappoint her. He knew his father's ship would set sail any day now, but he still didn't have a nanny to help him. He would write Cunningham to take care of seeing the *Virginian* off. His father wouldn't be happy and would no doubt cut him out of his proposed partnership, but the safety of the children was his priority. "I have a ship of my own," he admitted. "It can sail as soon as it's completed."

She narrowed her eyes. "Is there anything else you wish to tell me?"

He grimaced. "That my family is related to half the aristocracy of Great Britain? That I'm a businessman and don't own any estates?"

"Right." She pulled her gloves on more securely and adjusted her shawl. "Of course. How foolish of me to think otherwise." She stood up.

He rose with her, knowing he'd just placed his future in her hands. Nervously, he awaited her decision.

"Well, then, as I was saying, we'll simply play along with my aunt's wishes until she leaves. You'll pretend to court me, and I'll pretend to be courted. Once she's certain I'm suitably settled, she'll be about her journeys. Then you may take the children and sail away. I'll not report you to a drunkard who neglects his children"

"Suitably settled?" he asked warily.

She looked off into the distance. "Announcing a betrothal should do it. She cannot expect me to actually marry until my year of mourning is ended."

Why did he not feel the least bit relieved as she strode briskly out, leaving him to stew over all the possibilities lurking between "suitably settled" and "sailing away"?

Watching her skirt sway hypnotically with her long-legged stride, Mac wondered if the next few weeks wouldn't be a severe test of his ability to restrain his impulsiveness. He'd almost learned to control his temper, but he'd never had to rein in his lust.

Twelve

"I wish to consult with several of the property owners in the vicinity," Mr. Warwick—nay, MacTavish—said stiffly later that morning, as he stood in the foyer addressing Bea and her aunt, looking somewhat like a beleaguered giant. "Would you care to accompany me into the village while I do so, Miss Cavendish?"

Bea couldn't imagine why she would, but if he thought this a necessary part of the charade they must play, she ought to go along with it. She couldn't believe her child-loving aunt would return the children to their drunken father, but she saw no sense in taking chances either.

She just wished she knew what name to call her "suitor." "You must call me Bea," she said politely, aware that her aunt was listening. She wasn't entirely certain how one went about a courtship, but informality seemed appropriate.

Mr. MacTavish's stern face cracked a smile. "And you must call me Mac. It's a fine day for a brief jaunt."

No man had ever courted her. Perhaps she ought to simply enjoy the experience, knowing that nothing would come of it. She needn't fret if her hair strayed or her gown became dusty or if she said the wrong thing. None of it mattered to this man. "Should I bring the children?"

Aunt Constance immediately intruded. "No, no, of course not, dear. You go on with your young man and have a fine time." She smiled flirtatiously at Mac and patted his arm. "If you won't, I will."

Gazing at the toes of her shoes, Bea bit back a conspiratorial smile. "Of course, Aunt Constance. I'll fetch my bonnet, shall I?"

Stiffening even more beneath her aunt's triumphant smile, Mac caught Bea's arm and all but dragged her toward the door. "The day is too fine for bonnets," he declared, "and your hair serves as crowning glory enough. Time is wasting." As he pulled her outside, he threw over his shoulder, "You are all that is gracious, Lady Taubee."

Bea thought she'd burst out laughing before they reached the carriage. "You are as inept at courting as I am about being courted," she murmured as he helped her in.

"Just be glad I'm not forced to sit in your parlor, sipping tea," he said grimly, climbing up beside her. "I would go mad and probably swing from the chandeliers."

"An excess of energy, Mr. MacTavish?"

"That's one way of putting it." He shook the reins and set the horses into a trot. "Keep in mind that I'm a bachelor, and you're an attractive woman, and don't wear too many of those dresses like the one last night if you expect me to keep my wits about me."

Startled, she glanced over at the grim set of his jaw. "You didn't like my gown?"

He shot her a blunt look that expressed far more than she wished him to put into words. "Don't turn coy on me. Three weeks is a dashed long time, and we've already discussed your appearance. If you need more flattery, find Dav."

"I'm having difficulty separating honesty from impertinence, sir. Perhaps it's best if we lay down a few rules. I won't tell you what to wear if you don't tell me the same."

He huffed an exasperated sigh. "I knew there were reasons why I never tried discussing anything with a woman. I swear you don't even try to understand."

"I would *try*, if you would just *explain*. You tell me not to wear one of my best evening gowns, and I'm supposed to take that as some sort of warning?" Bea wished she had thought to bring her parasol so she might beat him about the head until some intelligence emerged.

He halted the carriage to allow a flock of sheep to saunter across the drive. She thought a flush of red stained his cheekbones as he stared straight ahead.

"I've told you I'm not comfortable around women. Not ladies, anyway. The other kind . . ." He stopped and rearranged his words just as they became interesting. "I'm not about to explain a man's nature to you," he continued gruffly. "Just take my word for it that you will get much more sense out of me if you dress as you are now."

"Since I'm not getting much sense out of you now, I'm quite certain I'd rather not see you completely senseless," Bea agreed pertly. "I will not wear the purple gown again, but Aunt Constance will insist that I wear colors. She berated me quite firmly for going back to blacks."

"Color has nothing to do with it." As the last sheep ambled across, he glanced down at her again. "Wrap yourself in shawls, and I shall strive to keep my mind on more . . . uplifting topics." Tugging on his necktie as if it were strangling him, he reddened and turned away.

His words might be puzzling, but the way his glance had lingered on her bodice was not. Beatrice's breasts tightened against the fabric of her chemise, and she did her best not to look down at herself. She started to straighten her shoulders, thought better of it, and pulled her shawl around her despite the day's warmth. She didn't know whether to die of embarrassment or wallow in the pleasure of knowing she could distract him with her . . . uplifted topics. Her breasts had been more nuisance than pleasure before, but they tingled with expectation now.

Fearing that path, she set her mind firmly on the straight and narrow. "Why are we going into town?"

"Carstairs mentioned you have an unused mill and a source of power, and I want to talk to a few people about what uses they could be put to."

"The river does not always run strong, so the mill cannot operate continuously. I think it was once used for grinding corn, but there are cheaper sources of corn than trying to repair the mill." Bea liked it when he looked at her with approval like that.

"So you do know a thing or two about the estate." It wasn't quite admiration tingeing his voice, but for a man who didn't speak flattery, it was close enough.

"My father talked. I listened. I knitted and embroidered and played the piano, and listened. My opinion wasn't required."

"I see." They reached the summit of the hill before descending into the village, and he slowed the carriage.

Below, a woman in broad homespun skirts and a kerchief chased a boy in breeches and cap into the house with the clip of her hand against his ear. Beyond that, there seemed to be little activity.

"Do you have an opinion on the use of the mill?" he inquired thoughtfully as they began the descent.

Bea drew in a deep breath and wondered if he really expected a reply. It didn't matter, did it? He would be gone in a few weeks, and his opinion had no import on her. "I understand some of Father's sheep were bred for the fine quality of their wool. I've heard of several towns using their mills for spinning wool for carpets, but our wool is apparently too fine for that. I thought . . . well, blankets might be loomed if we could use local wool."

"Blankets? I hadn't thought of that." Skillfully, he handled the brake and the horses until they arrived at the inn. "Do you know anything about wool spinning?"

That easily deflated her burgeoning hopes. "No."

"No matter. There are ways to find out. Our cotton mills are becoming industrialized in Virginia, but wool is tougher and still produced by hand. There may be a process that suits this mill." He climbed from the carriage and came around to help her.

They had industrialized mills in Virginia. She had always thought of that land as being fierce and filled with log cabins. She really must learn more about his home. She accepted his hand without thinking and was startled by his strength as he lifted her down.

Digby appeared in the inn doorway, wiping his hands on an immaculate white apron. "Good morning, Miss Cavendish, Mr. Warwick. Mr. Overton is waiting inside."

"Good morning, Digby. I love the new sign, and the bay window sparkles just like at home. How's Mrs. Digby?" Hurriedly disengaging her hand, Bea smiled at her ex-butler as he offered his arm while Mac fastened the horses. She couldn't blame the Digbys for leaving her and investing their inheritance in the inn. She'd thought it rather romantic that they'd married after all those years of working together.

"Mrs. Digby is in her idea of heaven," Digby responded with pleasure. "The new linens have arrived, and she's sorting and cleaning and stacking and preparing for guests. We'll be fortunate to have a fresh cup of tea out of her."

Mr. Rector and his wife strolled across the street to join the conversation. "There's not a time when Mrs. Digby has failed to have fresh tea brewing," the curate claimed. "Good morning, Miss Cavendish. It's a pleasure to see you here today. We thank your aunt for the dinner invitation. She is all that is gracious."

Dinner invitation?

Smythe hurried over from the dry-goods shop. "Tell your aunt I've ordered the gold filigree and the emerald satin, but I haven't found a source for doves yet. Do you think pigeons might do? I can order some excellent carrier pigeons."

"Pigeons?" Her mind spinning at Smythe's odd questions, Bea absently wondered about the growing number of people in the street. Clara Miller emerged from the milliner's shop with her sister, Jane. After greeting Mrs. White, the brewer's wife, they hurried toward the inn. Whatever on earth was happening to stir the entire village like this?

Not quite catching Smythe's reply as Mr. . . . Mac steered her into the dim interior of the inn, she gazed in surprise at the assorted faces already assembled in the taproom.

Digby had mentioned Mr. Overton's presence, but she counted her tenants, Farmingham and Dubbins and their wives; Mr. Green, the blacksmith; and Lord Carstairs, whom she thought had left for London. What in the name of heaven had Mac done to gather all these people together? And why?

"Why do they all seem to be watching us?" she whispered anxiously.

She jumped as Mac took her arm and led her through the throng. Had Mr. Digby just winked at the curate? Surely, they didn't all really believe . . .

"Perhaps your aunt has been busy," he murmured.

She colored as she considered what her aunt might have said to the townsfolk.

Except for Hugo Carstairs, the baron, these were all people she knew, so she had no need to be nervous. She had just never been in this sort of gathering, unless one counted church. And even with church activities, she usually spoke only with the women over bake sales or the like. Until the Digbys had taken over, the inn had been an unsavory place, and she'd never been inside. She glanced around with interest, trying to take her mind off the crowd and the collective attention.

Ancient timbers framed the ceiling. A massive stone fireplace filled the far wall. She suspected Digby had moved wing chairs near the fireplace for the ladies, and that the benches lining the wall were the usual seating. Sunlight sparkled through the mullioned bay window.

"Have a seat . . . Bea," Mac murmured in her ear as he led her toward one of the chairs. "I think I might come to enjoy being on a familiar basis with the squire's daughter. His lordship is looking at me with much suspicion."

"I am not the one related to half the nobility of Great Britain," she said dryly, undeterred by his nonsense. "You do not think Lord Carstairs or his brother have heard the rumors about the children, do you?"

"They've been in Somerset. Let's hope they don't remember me as any more than your suitor when they reach London." Mac stepped back and shook hands with Overton as she settled into a chair.

Bea nervously tried to remember if Dav had seen the children. She suspected that if he had, they'd been with Mary. Men like the Carstairses didn't bother themselves with children and servants. Mac was right. They might suspect him of being a fortune hunter, but they would not associate him with the viscount's missing offspring.

As Overton led Mac over to talk with Bea's tenants, Clara Miller sidled up to her. "You've done yourself quite proud, Miss Cavendish. These Americans are so much more . . . substantial, don't you agree?"

Substantial? Bea's lips quivered in amusement as she regarded Mac's . . . substantial shoulders. "Yes, quite," she murmured. The petite spinster had always made her nervous by flitting about like a wren, peering and prying into everything. Today she didn't appear so daunting, and Bea didn't feel so much like a giant-ess in her company.

Had Mac's interest in her "bounty" changed her perceptions? Could a man truly be interested in some-one her size?

"Why is your aunt not here?" Miss Miller inquired eagerly. "Surely she hasn't left the village already. You will need a chaperone with a man like that about."

"Aunt Constance has little interest in our doings." The small matter of two urchins didn't need men-tioning, although the warning about a chaperone shot a chill down Bea's spine. She hadn't thought in terms of chaperones, but now that Mac had successfully warned her that he didn't find her unattractive, she ought to. She wasn't certain how she felt about a man thinking of her as desirable.

As people gradually settled into chairs and the unof-ficial meeting came to order, she surreptitiously watched her autocratic boarder maneuver malingerers into seats. If he was telling the truth, and he actually came from a wealthy family, she didn't understand why he would have any interest in her. The Carstairses had never given her a second look.

As a child visiting with his family, Dav had pulled her braids and called her a long Meg. Hugo had been in school most of the time and had seldom deigned to notice her when he visited during the holidays. The rest of the men in town she considered companions of her father's. She knew which ones drank too much, and which ones were inclined to pinch the maids. Familiarity bred contempt, she supposed.

Perhaps she was as much a novelty to Mac as he was to her. That must explain their interest in each other.

Satisfied, she sat back and let the men open the meeting. Her father never would have included women, but now she was the biggest landowner in the area. Of necessity, they must include her. Why hadn't she ever considered that before? She had authority.

Pleased with that idea, wondering how far it might take her, she listened as the curate led a short prayer for the betterment and improvement of Broadbury. Digby stood up and announced the inn would soon open for guests, and that the kitchen would be open for lunch as well as dinner. Mr. Smythe announced a new shipment of muslin, and Clara Miller wanted to know why he couldn't order more lace.

The meeting would have immediately deteriorated from there, Bea surmised, if Mrs. Rector hadn't stood up and asked if there was any support for a cooperative that would allow them to group their purchase needs and buy in quantity from the city, since Mr. Smythe could stock only local products. There weren't enough ladies present to stir that discussion, but Bea made a mental note to investigate it further. She'd never heard of a cooperative, but as the largest purchaser in the area—except when the earl and his retinue were present at Landingham—she thought it a subject she should explore.

She was feeling quite authoritative and important when Mac stood up to address the group, looking handsome, substantial, and respectable.

"I'm sure all of you know by now that Miss Cavendish is enclosing her lower fields and leasing them to Misters Farmingham and Dubbins. Additional seed, equipment, and labor will be needed to put them into full production, which will stir the economy to a small extent. However, the prior tenants will be left adrift unless we stimulate additional production elsewhere."

Mac's casual but decisive attitude as he paced the front of the room held her attention. What in heaven's name was he talking about? Economy? Production? She hadn't authorized setting any tenants adrift. In fact, she couldn't actually remember authorizing the enclosures. They'd discussed it, but he'd never told her where her other tenants would pasture their sheep if they enclosed the valley.

The men in the room were nodding agreement as Mac spoke. Did every one of them know more than she did?

Of course they did; they were *men*. Her resentment built.

"Lord Carstairs has brought it to my attention that Miss Cavendish's property includes a mill that will require some repair to bring it into full production. I am not entirely familiar with the operations here, but Miss Cavendish has suggested that the mill might be converted to spinning wool for blanket making, thereby bringing in additional workers, visitors, and income to the area. With a little help—"

The quiet murmurs produced by Mac's first words erupted into excited questions and a loud din of conversation as everyone talked over and around each other.

No one paid the least attention to Bea, who sat, stunned, wondering when Mr. Lachlan Warwick Mac-Tavish, kidnapper, had become her spokesman.

"What the devil are you doing out here?" Mac demanded from the seat of the carriage, keeping even with her as Bea stalked down the dusty lane toward home. He'd never seen the lady so irate. He didn't have a clue as to why she'd gone into a tizzy, though he could admire the way her chest heaved from the exertion.

"Why ask?" she muttered, lifting her skirt and walking faster. "I'm sure you have an opinion and don't need mine."

"What the hell is that supposed to mean?" he called after her as she crossed into the grassy verge. "You got up and walked out and never said a word. The blanket making was your damned idea." He'd thought to please her. After their conversation earlier, he'd been feeling almighty confident of his place in her thoughts. Where had he gone wrong?

"Your language, sir!" Furiously, she took a break in the hedgerow to step off the road and cross the low stone fence.

"What the hell has my language got to do with it?" he yelled in frustration as he watched her escape into the field where the carriage couldn't follow.

So much for thinking he'd begun to understand at least one female on this planet.

Thirteen

Beatrice glared at R.J.R., esquire's, letter to the editor declaring the education of women and laborers a waste of time and resources, as women were too frail of mind and body, and educating mine workers would only give them ideas above their station.

"Balderdash," she muttered, reaching for her quill to dash off her opinion to Lady Fenimore. Right now, men were lower than pig slop on her list of favorite things. "With Mr. R.J.R. as evidence, I'd say men's minds are too narrow to squeeze in more than the menu for their next meal," she complained, dipping her pen into the inkpot.

"What was that?"

She looked up from her desk and scowled at Mac standing in the study doorway. "Go away. Go far, far away and leave me alone. I am not speaking to you."

"I'm gratified to know that," he said dryly, ignoring her warning and entering to search a shelf of books on agriculture. "I'm not hearing you."

"This is *my* house," she reminded him. "*My* study. You have no right—"

"Must be ghosts," he muttered, pulling a book from the shelf and shaking his head. "I could swear I heard someone speaking to me."

As he strode out with his book, Beatrice flung her

quill at the closing door. She didn't need one more demanding, impossible man in her life. He had no authority here. She would not submit to male tyranny ever again.

Patience, Mac told himself. Patience, caution, and methodical planning would serve him better than shaking Miss Beatrice Cavendish until her curls rattled.

Unable to escape to the usual male sanctuary of the study, where an angry Bea buzzed threateningly, he threw off his coat, grabbed a hammer and nails from the barn, and looked for something to pound. Dav had finally claimed the hounds, so they didn't need the pen any longer. He could use wood from the pen to repair the stable fence.

He had no clue why Bea wasn't speaking to him. He'd thought to please her by introducing her idea of the wool mill. True, he wouldn't be here to see the project through, but he'd set the idea in motion. Her rents would increase with the enclosed acreage, and she might eventually see a tidy profit from the mill. Where was the problem in that?

He'd thought the mill much more practical than flowers, and he'd thought Beatrice a woman to appreciate it. Obviously, he'd been wrong. He slammed a nail into the planking so hard that it splintered.

Cursing, he ripped off the rotten plank and picked up another. All right, so maybe he was being hasty. After all, Beatrice was trying to help him save the children. Another woman would have condemned him for acting so brashly that he had to hide from the law. His own father would have his hide. Mac liked it that Bea accepted that he'd done what he'd done, and there was no point bemoaning it.

He grimaced as Bea's aunt galloped toward him in a whirlwind of dust and trailing scarves. He had a sneaking suspicion the busybody was behind Smythe's questions about doves. Bea had been too furious later to remember the conversation, but Mac had visions of wedding bells pounding in his brain, and doves—or pigeons—seemed to fit in with them. He shot a nail sure and true through the plank as Constance reined to a halt, waving a piece of stationery and laughing.

"Oh, you will appreciate this, Mr. MacTavish!" She gaily accepted his proffered hand to leap down and brandished the letter without releasing it. "Half London believes the viscount has murdered his children, and they're calling for an investigation."

"That must be wearing on his temper," Mac growled, picking up another plank and fitting it to a post.

"They say he has disappeared from public view." She glanced at the letter a little more doubtfully. "Perhaps he drinks only in private now."

"Or perhaps he's sobered up enough to start hunting for me." Mac drove a nail into the plank, wishing he could drive out his guilt so easily. He'd dragged Bea into this mess. He ought to be considering ways of disentangling her rather than embroiling her further.

"I've asked a friend to speak with an employment agency. She said she'd send candidates for nursemaid out on the next mail coach." Lady Taubee's usual good cheer had returned. "Although I'm quite certain Bea would love to keep the children, if you'd just ask."

He wasn't about to explain that Bea had no intention of keeping him or the children. He latched onto the straw she offered. "I'd better meet the coach then. If you'll excuse me." He picked up the planks and stalked away, leaving Bea's aunt to meddle elsewhere.

On her way out the front door to post her letter in the village, Bea almost turned around and fled when she saw Mac approaching, waistcoat open, linen shirt soaked with perspiration, looking determined. Buddy's tug on her hand reminded her that she was mistress here, and she had no need to fear a man who couldn't keep his neckcloth tied.

Heavy skirts swaying, she sailed down the entrance stairs, pretending to ignore him.

"Your aunt's watching from the stable yard," Mac warned as he halted in front of her.

Bea concentrated on the beads of sweat glistening on his forehead instead of the grim set of his mouth. Chin held high, she didn't reply.

"Don't you think she'll wonder at a courtship where the couple doesn't even speak?" he inquired tauntingly.

"Missy says I can have a candy," Buddy declared without any of the circumlocution adults require.

Caught from two different directions, Bea hesitated. She had no desire to entertain the company of this man who exuded sweat and masculinity. But the child releasing her hand to climb trustingly into his uncle's arms reminded her of her duty to protect the innocent.

"We're courting, remember?" Mac said insistently.

"Don't you have anyone else to order around?" Leaving Buddy on his perch, she headed down the drive.

"When did I order you around?" he demanded, swinging his nephew to his shoulders and falling into step beside her.

"When did you ask my opinion?" Smiling falsely, Bea waved at her aunt as they passed the stable, until the towering rhododendrons lining the drive blocked her view. Plunged suddenly into shade, she tried to ignore her "suitor's" proximity, but her wide sleeves kept brushing against him as he wrestled with the boy in the narrow lane.

"When did you have an educated opinion to offer?" He set Buddy down and let him run ahead. Grabbing her arm, Mac forced her to a halt. "All you've ever done is stick your nose in the air and pretend I'm beneath your notice."

Bea's eyes widened, and she gulped air at his intimidating stance. He loomed large and menacing and gave her reason to reconsider her foolishness. At the same time, he set her heart pounding, and she wanted to stumble out an apology for hurting him.

Before she could open her mouth, Mac rolled his eyes and smacked the heel of his hand to his forehead. "I apologize. That was uncalled for. I'm not much good at making polite conversation." He fell into step with her again.

"I noticed." Her jaw snapped shut as she glared straight ahead, hiding behind the shield of her bonnet as she relented enough to say, "Neither am I."

"Fair enough. Let's not be polite. Tell me what's nagging you." Mac grabbed a stick from the hedgerow and called to his nephew. "Here, Buddy, knock that stone like this." He showed the child how to hit a stone with the thick end of the stick and send it wobbling down the lane.

Delighted with the new game, Buddy quit crawling into hedgerows to concentrate on the stick and stone.

All the starch wilted out of her as she watched Buddy gambol in the dirt. "I have to live here after you're gone. I'm the one who has to make the decisions about enclosures and mills and the like. How can I learn to do that if you keep doing it all for me without discussing it first?"

Heaving a sigh of disgruntlement, Mac trudged down the lane in Buddy's wake. He was much too aware of the supple curve of Bea's waist above her swaying skirt, and the full swell of her bodice above that. Women were meant to be gentle and compliant. They had no business asking questions a man couldn't answer.

"I can't teach you everything you need to know," he complained. "You need a steward and a man of business and a damned husband. All I can do is show you what needs doing until you find them."

"I can't pay a steward or a man of business and I don't want a husband," she protested. "I don't want to spend the rest of my life ignorant. I want to *learn*."

A vivid image rose before him of sitting beside this tempting woman on a love seat with only a flickering fire to illuminate the pages of a book they studied. He could wrap his arm around her waist, her breasts would be a hair's breadth from his nose . . . and he would be a doomed man, if the tightening in his groin meant anything at all.

"Then hire a teacher," he said gruffly, striding after the boy running down the lane. Even casting aside politeness, he couldn't explain why men should never teach women. "I am obviously not the man you want," he yelled over his shoulder.

Bea clutched her reticule and fought back childish tears as Mac chased his nephew. She'd thought they'd come to some understanding, but she should have known better.

Perhaps she really should find a husband while she still had an estate worth saving. Could one place a notice in the paper? *Giantess spinster with large, mortgaged estate in need of patient husband willing to educate her in fundamental farming.* It might attract some entertaining replies.

Perhaps she should sell the estate and travel with her aunt. Someone far more competent than she could restore the town to a thriving economy.

Someone more competent than she would dismiss half the servants, enclose the fields, and throw out the tenants to take up sheep breeding and modern agricultural practices. Mac might scorn her father's old-fashioned methods, but they'd held the village together for centuries. Modern methods made money, not communities.

"Missy, Missy, look what I found!"

Smiling fondly at the boy's eagerness as he bent over a butterfly, Bea felt another tug at her over-worked heart as her thoughts wandered another step. A husband could give her children. Would that make up for her lack of knowledge?

No, it would merely present her with a new set of dilemmas. She knew nothing about raising children either. Or having them. She had little idea of how marriage brought about babies. The very idea raised heat in her cheeks.

As she caught up with Mac, she cast a sidelong glance to his big body and wondered what it would be like to actually marry. She'd never been kissed, and she had an odd longing for this man to hold her close. He'd sail away soon enough. What could it hurt? It would be one more lesson under her belt, so to speak.

Unexpectedly, Mac reached out to tuck a straying curl into her bonnet. His hand brushed her cheek, making her shiver with warm anticipation. She looked at him questioningly. Surely he couldn't read her thoughts.

"I'm a lout and a clod." He lifted Buddy to his brawny shoulder as the butterfly flitted away. "I'll try to teach you the account books."

"I'll try not to ask stupid questions," she agreed hesitantly, not understanding why he'd changed his mind, fearful he would change it again.

"Any question you have won't be stupid," he of-fered. "It will just mean I'm a lousy teacher. Don't expect too much of me."

His warning flew right by her head, along with all her other fears. Utter delight chased them away. He would teach her. She would learn to stand on her own.

*   *   *

As the mail coach rumbled to a halt in front of the inn with a blare of horn and wail of brakes, Mac watched eagerly for the nursemaid who would rescue him from the spider's silk slowly winding him in its trap.

A plump young girl with cherries bouncing on her hat stepped down, tugging a toddler with her, and his stomach sank to new lows. Both girl and child wore the vapid expression of contented cows and moved at the gradual pace of ancient galleons.

Buddy would have them walking the plank before the ship left port.

Mischief danced in Bea's fine eyes as she watched their slow progress. "With her as nursemaid, you would have *four* children to watch," she murmured. "Wouldn't that be fun?"

Fine time for the haughty female to develop a sense of humor. Mac shoved his hand in his pocket in search of coins to recompense the candidate for nanny so he could send her back from whence she came.

Fourteen

"The children know Mary, and she's good with them. I fail to see why she can't go with us," Mac said curtly, pacing up and down the dirt lane in front of the Cottles' neat stone cottage.

Several days of mail coaches carrying unsuitable nannies had passed, and he was growing increasingly frustrated.

Crouching to lift Mary's baby sister, Bea smiled apologetically at her maid's mother. "He's like this when he can't have his way. Don't let him frighten you." She'd seldom done more than exchange pleasantries with any of the villagers before Mac's arrival. Lately, she'd been thrust into the position of providing a softening barrier between her tenants and Mac's American tactlessness. Mac didn't even notice.

Mrs. Cottle wound her apron around her hands and nodded uncertainly as she watched Mac study a dead tree limb scratching the cottage's tile roof. "It's not that I don't want better for the lass—" She gasped and stared as Mac reached for a sound limb and swung his large frame into the tree.

Bea sighed with a mixture of appreciation and exasperation as the broad muscles of Mac's back stretched his shirt to the limit. The man was incapable of sitting still and carrying on a civilized conversation, but she had to admit she harbored a fondness for the way all that brawn worked. She winced as he cracked off the dead limb with a powerful twist, then dropped the branch to the ground. His neckcloth and shirt would be grimy with sap when he climbed down.

She tickled the child in her arms and nervously avoided the image of Mac stripping off his dirty shirt. Her mind took the strangest paths these days. "I understand, Mrs. Cottle," she said reassuringly. "With ten young ones at home, you need as many hands as can be spared. Mary's a hard worker. I don't know what I'd do without her."

Mac dropped to the ground, brushed off his hands, and glared at her. "You could live with a little dust for a few months."

"Mrs. Cottle cannot live without her eldest daughter," she retorted. Now that she knew he was all bark and no bite, she could stand up for herself a little better.

"I have a cousin. . . ." Mrs. Cottle offered tentatively, glancing back and forth between them to see if she should proceed. Noting she had drawn their attention, she unwrapped her apron and brushed it down. "She has daughters. I could have Mary write—"

"Do that." Mac snapped the broken branch into pieces and stacked the bits by the gate. "I'll pay well. There's plenty of employment to be had in Virginia."

"Or he'll send them safely home, if they prefer," Bea interceded gently. "He seems to think Virginia is the only place to be." The hint of resentment in her voice surprised her.

Mac apparently didn't hear it. Tugging his coat back on, he seized Bea's elbow and nodded abruptly at Mary's mother. "If you would do that, I'd be most appreciative."

Without a fare-thee-well, he steered Bea bodily

down the side street toward town. "Why the devil is it
so difficult to hire a good nursemaid?" he complained.

"Perhaps because you terrify them? Or because
they don't wish to travel halfway 'round the world. Or
because you declare them incapable of handling two
incorrigible, ill-mannered children and send them
away. Bitsy and Buddy need the love of good
parents."

There, she'd said it. He was always telling her what
to do. It seemed fitting that she should be permitted
to turn the tables.

Mac growled, but before he could speak, his gaze
caught on some sight in the street below. "What is
your blithering footman doing dressed like that?"

"It's his half day off. He's entitled—" Bea glanced
down the hill at a group of elegantly tailored young
men. "Oh." James looked as if he'd just stepped from
a men's expensive fashion plate. She didn't think she
paid him *that* much. The gentlemen with him appeared
a trifle disheveled and dusty from the road.

Abruptly, Mac pushed her down a carriageway between two towering hedges. "Simmons!" he hissed.
"That traitorous wretch James must have summoned
the children's father."

"James wouldn't do that," Bea whispered back,
shaken as much by Mac's hand catching her waist and
hauling her onward as by any perceived threat. The
gentlemen seemed harmless enough, although their
rising voices sounded much like her father and his
friends when in their cups.

Not bothering to argue with what he'd seen with
his own eyes, Mac shoved her into a narrow alleyway
concealed by the overgrowth of the hedge. Biting back
a litany of curses, he tried to think what to do now.
The children were nearly a mile away. How could he
reach them before the viscount did?

"Honestly," Bea said, still protesting. "James wouldn't

betray us, not even for a reward. He's *family*. The children are quite safe."

Mac wanted to believe her, but his own experiences with family weren't reassuring. In this proximity, he was too aware of Bea's disturbingly feminine presence. A hint of lilac easily distracted him when he needed his wits about him.

All he could do was wait and hide and pray Simmons didn't head this way. Resting his back against the wall, he prevented Bea from rushing off by pulling her into his arms. Now that he actually held temptation, he couldn't resist nuzzling her neck just below her earlobe. He needed distraction.

"Mr. MacTavish," she exclaimed breathlessly. "What are you doing?"

"Courting," he muttered. The lure of her bountiful breasts tore at his willpower. He was a man who needed to touch, to grasp, to act. . . .

"We can't . . ." She shuddered and wilted closer as he pressed his tongue to the place he'd kissed. "This isn't . . ."

Amusement rippled through him at her inability to complete a sentence. "Think of this as another lesson, more interesting than account books."

The approaching sound of argumentative male voices halted further exploration.

Mac groped along the stone wall, parting the bushes until he discovered a gate into the next yard. Wincing as the latch creaked, he dragged Bea through the opening, eased the gate shut, and leaned against it while he looked for an escape route.

"This is foolish," she whispered, brushing nervously at the long curls he'd disturbed at the back of her head.

He cocked an eyebrow at her. "Shall I turn myself over to Simmons and free you from my embarrassing presence?"

Her eyes widened in such fear and concern, he could have kissed her there and then. She wanted to protect the children as much as he did. A woman of obviously good sense.

"My father won't part with a farthing," a querulous male voice said in a low tone from the other side of the wall. "When he returns, he'll no doubt disown me. It's in your best interest to help me."

"Simmons," Mac hissed in Bea's ear, pulling her to him again. She nodded, and stood taut against him, not objecting to his possessive hold. If it weren't for his brother-in-law on the other side of the gate, he'd be enjoying this. Miss Cavendish was one handful of a woman.

"You gambled and lost," James said loftily from a distance past the gate. "A gentleman pays his gaming debts."

"To other gentlemen," Simmons said scathingly.

Their voices were traveling farther away. Bea began to wriggle impatiently in Mac's grip. He glanced around the walled garden. Unless they chose to invade the attached cottage, they had no other escape but the gate—nor any way of seeing where the viscount was.

The argument faded down the alley.

Did the damned footman know about the children or not? Maybe he could climb over the wall. . . .

The gate behind them rattled.

"You can come out now!" James's voice was unnaturally cold as he shook the old wooden planks. "They're gone."

Mac cursed and, gently releasing Bea, set her upright. "If he has Simmons out there, they'll have me arrested," Mac said curtly before she could open the gate. "I've left the name of my father's agent on your desk. Order him to do whatever is necessary to protect the children." Reaching past her, he released the gate latch.

Frozen by Mac's alarming warning, Bea held her breath until she saw only James standing there in his city attire. Hand to chest, she gulped deeply while the two men glared at each other.

"The hedge would have hidden you well enough," James declared angrily. "You didn't need to drag Miss Cavendish in here with you."

"If you hadn't called the bloody damned viscount out here—"

"I never did!"

She'd never seen James so angry. In fact, both men had reached explosive limits without any provocation that she could see. Hastily shoving flyaway hairs from her face, Bea brushed between them and the gate. "Where is the viscount now?" she demanded. "If he sees those children—"

"Off to see a prizefight," James said with disgust. "The lot are drunk as lords already. They said they were making inquiries, but they drank more than they questioned."

Elbowing Mac out of the way, James hastily followed Bea as she swept into the lane. Mac snatched James by the collar and lifted him to the side. Bea ignored the byplay. She didn't understand anything right now. She didn't know why James was dressed like a gentleman, or why Mac had held her as he had, or why her heart was pounding as if it would escape her chest. She certainly didn't know how James knew about Viscount Simmons or why the viscount would search for Mac in an out-of-the-way place like Broadbury. Surely he didn't expect Mac to be at his father's estate.

Mac cupped her elbow and firmly slowed her down. She'd almost broken into a run, she realized. How ungenteel.

Letting a near stranger kiss her neck didn't precisely qualify as ladylike either.

"Stop and have tea with Mrs. Cottle," Mac told her.
"I want to have a talk with your fribble. I'll be back
shortly." Without giving her time to question, he
pushed her up the hill.

Perhaps this was why women were called the frailer
sex, Bea mused as she let him shove her away. Feminine
heads rattled when men kissed them, yet Mac's head
didn't seem harmed one bit by the encounter.

"Get back here!" Mac shouted as James sauntered
toward town once Bea was safely tucked away at the
Cottles'. He didn't wait for James to respond, but took
giant strides to catch up with the footman's deliberate
ones. "Now tell me the truth, you maggot." He col-
lared the bastard again, forcing him to halt. "What
the devil are you doing meeting the likes of Simmons
and his cronies?"

"Pardon me, sir," James said haughtily, "I fail to
see in what way my activities are any concern of yours.
I answer only to my cousin."

"If you harm those children or Miss Cavendish, you
will answer to *me*," Mac growled, shaking the flea bait
for good measure. Since James was nearly as tall as
he, if not as large, shaking him wasn't an easy task,
but he had anger enough to do it. "How do you know
Simmons? What kind of inquiries did he make?"

Bea's cousin waited until Mac flung him aside with
disgust before replying. "It's no concern of yours how
I know him. And all London knows he seeks his missing children." He drew himself up haughtily and
brushed at the coat Mac had crushed while waiting
for Mac to finish cursing as fluently as any sailor.

Mac quieted and glared at him, and James continued. "Miss Cavendish has been all that is kind to me.
My one task in life is to see that she comes to no
harm. I consider you the danger here, not me."

"Then consider Simmons the biggest danger and

stay away from him!" Frustrated at not being able to throttle the man, Mac settled for a warning.

James looked down his lofty nose at him in a manner reminiscent of Bea's haughtiness at its worst. "One should always know one's enemy," he said vaguely, before wandering off toward the village.

"Where's your aunt?" Mac whispered as Bea led him into the parlor. It had been days since they'd seen Simmons in the village, but he was continually looking over his shoulder for one reason or the other. At the moment, her aunt's suspicious absence had him nervous. He hadn't been left alone with Bea since those few minutes in the garden.

"Showing Cook how to make Turkish Delights, I believe," Bea responded absently, gesturing for him to take a seat.

Mac deliberately chose the sofa and tugged her down beside him. He tempted the fates—or her aunt—by sitting this close, but one small sample of Bea's proximity had generated a hunger for more. He wanted to hear what quirky idea her earnest expression concealed now, but he hid his anticipation behind blandness. Her ideas were generally good, but he enjoyed her eagerness to convince him.

"I wish to start a consignment shop," she told him boldly, handing him the account books he'd been teaching her to read.

"A consignment shop?" Politely, Mac tried to glance down to see if Bea's shawl had slipped from her bare shoulders yet.

Shaken by his close encounter with Simmons, frustrated by his inability to escape this trap Bea's aunt had set, he felt like a sitting duck on a pond surrounded by hunters.

Could any man blame him for clinging to Bea's mundane problems like a lifeline to sanity and to Bea's calm as a poultice for panic?

"A shop, yes," Bea said eagerly. "I don't know what 'consignment' means."

He squirmed to create a little more space between them while trying to remember her question. "Consignments are goods a storekeeper offers to sell for a percentage of the price. If they don't sell, he doesn't owe for them. But you'd need a shopkeeper."

"The Miller sisters," she declared. Then she frowned. "But if nothing sold, they would be paid nothing. And Broadbury doesn't have very many visitors."

She might be ignorant of the bookkeeping aspect of business, but Mac could see that she possessed an astute grasp of the practical elements. "Digby's inn will attract a few travelers," he said carefully. "The mill will draw more. And there seem to be quite a few great houses hereabouts that must entertain their owners and guests upon occasion. If they had some reason to visit town, I'm sure they would. A shop might offer a reason."

She regarded him with unconcealed pleasure, and before Mac could anticipate her action, she leaned over and brushed his cheek with a kiss. "Thank you!"

Unable to endure temptation any longer, Mac trapped her neatly rounded chin before she could pull away, and relished the silky texture beneath his rough fingers. Her eyes widened, and he thought she stopped breathing. Hell, he knew he had. Her pale lips parted, and her gaze darted nervously to his mouth, which he seemed to be lowering quite irrationally toward hers.

"The two of you seem to be in fine fettle this evening." Lady Taubee launched into the room in time to catch the touching scene. "Beatrice, dear, it's much too warm to be wearing that shawl."

The old bat must have been standing outside the

doorway, waiting for the moment, Mac thought grimly as he retreated. He ought to be grateful for the intrusion.

To Mac's relief, Bea ignored her aunt's admonition about the shawl. The shimmery rust color of her gown didn't affect him one way or another. What held his fascination was the way her sleeves barely clung to her shoulders, leaving him avidly anticipating the moment when they would slip further. As it was, the gown's design revealed soft slopes and swells of creamy skin and a smattering of freckles in a place he'd get down on his knees and beg to explore. Every so often her shawl would shift, and he had to wish for blinders until she adjusted it.

"We're discussing a consignment shop, Aunt Constance. What things do you think might sell in a place like Broadbury?"

"Such romantic conversation," Constance said dryly, lowering herself to a wing chair. "All this younger generation thinks about is money."

"Bea and I aren't poetry readers." In frustration, Mac resigned himself to jousting with the old tartar.

"I see that." Lady Taubee gifted him with a sardonic lift of her eyebrows. "Well, at least you have interests in common. A consignment store, indeed. We're turning into a nation of shopkeepers."

"You would prefer being known as a nation of idlers and do-nothings?" he challenged her. "At least Americans are interested in progress."

"Mac," Bea protested, "Aunt Constance didn't mean anything by that. Things change so fast, it's hard to know what to expect. Have you ever been on a train, Aunt?"

Mac noticed that Bea shifted to leave a space between them, but her fingers toyed with a loose thread in one of her flounces, so she wasn't quite as calm as she sounded.

"Of course, child. I took one to Evesham on the way here. Smelly, horrible machines, but much quicker than a coach. I've never liked hiring chaises." Lady Taubee retrieved her watercolors from the easel she'd set up in the midst of the cluttered parlor. "I think we ought to have a dinner party to discuss your plans, dear."

Bea frowned. "We would have to invite Lord Knowles, and he'd hate the idea. And then he'd find out I've sold the dogs to Dav, and I'd never hear the end of it."

Mac had his own reasons for not wishing to hobnob with the local aristocracy, and he shot Lady Taubee a telling look. She was baiting him for some reason. Was that some sort of threat?

"Well," Constance said with a sigh, frowning at her exotic painting of colorful tents and waving palm trees and ignoring his glare, "I daresay you're right, dear, but it seems a shame not to have a teeny tiny little dinner while I'm here."

The conniving old tyrant had tenderhearted Bea wrapped around her little finger, Mac thought. He wanted to snap and growl and warn her away, but he didn't have that right. He could almost imagine the old woman chuckling over his inability to control the situation. Now, if Bea were really his wife . . .

That thought brought him to an abrupt halt. They actually had him thinking of Bea and *wife* in the same sentence. Heart pounding as if he'd just stepped back from a cliff's edge, Mac desperately sought distraction.

"We could invite the curate and his wife," Bea suggested. "That would be proper and wouldn't require inviting everyone else."

She rose and retreated to the piano, leaving a gaping emptiness beside him.

"As you wish, dear. I suppose those charming Carstairs men have departed?"

"Days ago," Mac agreed with a measure of triumph at winning a round. No longer confined to the love seat, he stood to restlessly prowl the room. "The Season is in full swing, you know. They're gallivanting about ballrooms as we speak."

"Ahh, yes." Constance gave a forlorn sigh. "London is so entertaining at this time of year. I'm sure dear Bea would be snatched up by any number of discerning gentlemen if only I could persuade her out of this mausoleum. But I understand. The children are much more important."

Mac knew a moment of guilt until Bea's gentle fingering of the piano keys crashed discordantly.

"I would be the gawk of the season," she exclaimed. "I'm *happy* here, Aunt Constance. I would not have you forfeit your fun for me. Go to London if you wish."

Mac reverently wished the old lady would obey. He drifted in the direction of the piano. He liked the way soft wisps of hair curled enticingly around Bea's vulnerable nape, brushing the slight mark he'd placed upon her. The thick heaviness behind his trouser buttons warned him of the danger of that possessive thought.

"I would be negligent in my duties to my niece's only daughter should I leave you unchaperoned, dear," Constance declared. "Let's speak no more about it. Invite the charming curate and his lovely wife and we will have a delightful evening, I'm sure."

Fifteen

He needed to talk to Bea—alone. But they were never alone.

Swinging around in the desk chair and gazing out the window to watch her playing on the lawn with the children, Mac dug his fingers into his hair in frustration. If he sent a servant out to collect the children, her aunt would gallop into their path in a cloud of dust, or a maid would run out with word of some new disaster, or that smirking fribble of a footman would trail along to keep them company. Simmons's idle pass through the village had jangled Mac's nerve endings.

His only opportunity to catch Bea alone was in the evening, and Mac knew perfectly well her aunt left them for only a few minutes at a time in hopes of catching them at something foolish again. And he *would* do something foolish. It was much too easy to forget a drunkard like Simmons while imagining Bea's kisses.

He turned back to the desk and the letter from his London agent. Talking to Bea alone was wishful thinking, but he couldn't delay his decision any longer. The *Virginian* was stocked and ready to sail. Every instinct told him he needed to be on board, fleeing with the children to the safety of home.

He turned back to watch the children again. Bitsy

was clapping her hands and Buddy was dancing to some nonsense Bea sang for them. He was fascinated enough to wish she were the kind of woman who would marry him for the sake of the children and run off to Virginia with him, but he knew she was not. Bea's roots were sunk deep in the soil of this village.

Grimly, Mac picked up his pen to write the letter sealing his fate. The *Virginian* would have to sail without him. Besides, Cunningham had reported suspicious men watching the ship. He'd never smuggle two noisy children past the viscount's spies.

With more penstrokes, he ordered Cunningham to oversee the final fittings of the clipper and stock it, as well.

Setting his jaw, Mac finished his response to his agent's inquiries. And in a letter that took much longer, he explained to his father why he was not on the ship as expected. Telling his parents of Marilee's death brought tears to his eyes all over again, but explaining to them why he'd kidnapped her children was twice as difficult.

Mac sealed the letters, gave them to James to deliver, and to assuage his lingering guilt and despondency, wandered out to the front lawn to watch the children.

Bea looked up in surprise as he lowered himself beside her on the blanket she'd spread across the grass. "I thought you had gone with the carpenters to the mill."

"I had some correspondence to answer." Awkwardly, he leaned back on one hand and dangled the other over his bent knee. It was almost peaceful in Bea's company. She allowed a man calm in which to think, to relax, and to admire the beauty around him.

"You are very kind to help me while my aunt holds you hostage," she murmured without looking up from the ribbon she smoothed into Bitsy's sparse curls.

He grunted and looked away from the tender scene to watch Buddy crawling on hands and knees beneath a bush. "You're harboring a wanted kidnapper whom all of London is after, and showing the children more kindness than they've known since their mother died. I'd declare us even."

"It's awkward," she said, from out of the blue.

He waited, but she didn't explain. Glancing over at her, he saw that she was watching her aunt directing a caravan of servants and boxes toward the kitchens while speaking earnestly with a scarlet-liveried James. *Awkward* didn't begin to describe the position the old lady had put them in. "Well, it gives me some practice at courting," he said to lift her spirits, "though I suspect I'm going about it all wrong."

She turned her smile in his direction. "I've never been courted, so I couldn't say. I suspect if you appeared at the front door, candy and flowers in hand, I'd faint dead away, so you must be doing something right."

"Umm," he said noncommittally. "I can fix that. I've already started telling your tenants they'll have to pay up their rents or begin looking for work elsewhere."

"What?" she cried in distress. "I gave you no permission to say any such thing. How could you?" She plopped Bitsy down on his chest and started to rise. "I'll have to go see the widow. She'll be in hysterics."

Mac collapsed backward under the weight of the burbling infant, who immediately leaned over to smack his nose with her plump fingers. "Oww," he protested as she dug tiny fingernails into him. "Bea, get back here this instant!"

She was already off toward the drive, leaving him with the drooling babe. Pushing upward while trying not to drop Bitsy, Mac hollered after her, "I haven't told the widow yet!"

She halted and turned to glare at him before heading back toward him. By all that was holy, the woman could spit fire with just her eyes. And her aunt thought her timid. *A lot she knew.*

"Then why did you tell me you had?"

Damned if he could answer that. He shrugged and tried to hand her the bouncing babe. She was having none of it. With a sigh, Mac sat Bitsy on the blanket and crouched down to look under the bushes for Bud.

When he didn't answer her question, Bea rolled her eyes, planted her booted foot on his backside, and shoved. As Mac sprawled headfirst into the shrubbery, she whirled around and marched off.

Warily, Bea watched the hallway as she descended the stairs to her aunt's dinner party. She'd managed to stay out of Mac's way for most of the day by visiting her tenants and reassuring them that no matter what happened, they would have a roof over their heads. The widow had sent her away with a jar of jam and instructions on how to make a hair brooch. Bea would like to wrap Mr. MacTavish into a brooch and pin him on a donkey.

This feigned courtship was becoming insufferable. She'd thought it would be simple to smile and pretend all was well while her aunt watched, then go about her business. But, no, Mr. King-of-it-all couldn't be satisfied with merely teaching her how to run the estate. He had to meddle in all her affairs.

Remembering those stolen moments in the garden, Bea cringed. She had actually *wanted* the miserable man to kiss her.

Mac had wanted to kiss her, too. That knowledge filled her dreams.

She heard the low murmur of voices from the best parlor and stopped to straighten the bodice of her evening gown. Aunt Constance had chosen the rich green figured silk with the dashing décolleté for her. Bea had always worn it with a lace mantelet to disguise the neckline, but her aunt had scoffed at that. Without the mantelet, she felt terribly naked, especially for a dinner with the curate.

Aunt Constance had said other women flaunted their assets, but Bea didn't think she could. She would much rather hide them, especially when Mac stared at her as if she were a rich pudding he'd like to devour, and she started wondering if she would like being devoured.

"Bea, dear! What are you doing lurking in the hallway? Come along, come along, and join our guests." Sweeping up behind Bea, Lady Taubee all but shoved her through the double doors and into the parlor.

Mac stood beside the fireplace, his big hands curled around a crystal wineglass, his glossy hair trimmed and curled in some semblance of fashion. His black evening coat molded his broad shoulders like a second skin, and the fall of linen at his throat would look at home in the best ballrooms of London. Bea tried not to breathe too deeply at the sight of his long legs encased in tight black trousers.

Then she saw the way he looked at her, and she thought she might catch fire and burn into smoldering ash.

Taking a deep breath, Bea turned awkwardly to greet their guests. From the corner of her eye, she saw Mac throw back a large swallow of wine. This had the markings of a very long evening.

Mr. Rector didn't seem in the least disturbed by the cut of her gown. He patted her hand, told her she was looking well, and passed her on to his wife. Mrs. Rector exclaimed over the lovely rosettes attached to Bea's sleeves, wondered if she might order something similar, then launched into a discussion of the cooperative.

Perhaps she just imagined that Mac heated the room more than the fire he stood beside. She wouldn't turn to see.

"My dear, you are neglecting your other guest," Mrs. Rector eventually whispered. "He looks much too lordly to play the part of steward, doesn't he?"

"Well, he's not actually." Bea tried to think what she could call him, but she feared revealing his true identity. James's arrival to announce dinner saved her from explanation.

"Mr. . . . *Warwick*, you really must take Beatrice in. I'll bring up the rear," Aunt Constance commanded.

Bea couldn't understand her agitation in taking his arm. By now she ought to know him well enough to feel comfortable around him. She knew he hated kidney pudding and adored lemon tarts. He thought Broadbury ridiculously primitive and crippled by tradition, and that Americans were much more progressive. He wanted to own railroads. She'd seen him nearly weep in fear over his niece. Why on earth should she be holding her breath now when he towered over her and offered his arm?

"Don't breathe," he muttered as she gingerly placed her fingers over his coatsleeve. "Not until I'm safely seated under the tablecloth. And don't ask," he warned as she started to do just that. "I am facing the fact that I'm far too crude to sit at the table of a lady as stunning as you are."

Heat flushed her cheeks, and Bea not only didn't breathe, she wouldn't look at him as he pulled out a chair for her and her aunt and took his own seat. His tone had sounded more like accusation than flattery. She couldn't reconcile the inconsistency.

"Now tell me, Mr. Rector," Aunt Constance said as soon as they were seated. "What have you heard from my dear friend, the Earl of Coventry?"

Distracted by her wayward thoughts, Bea was slow

to grasp the significance of her aunt's conversational turn until Mac uncharacteristically knocked over his wineglass and hastily sought to sop it up with his napkin. His evident irritation at more than the spilled wine reminded her—the earl was the children's grandfather.

As she signaled James to bring fresh wine and linen, Bea glared warningly at her aunt. Constance ignored her.

Oblivious to the undercurrents, the curate flashed a small smile. "As Miss Cavendish knows, the earl and his family seldom visit his estate. We've frequently tried to solicit funds for the church roof, but our only response is from the steward, who is a most . . . How shall I say this without seeming uncharitable?"

"He is a most disagreeable man," Bea answered bluntly. "He would not let Papa extend the hunting field through their woods. It's not as if anything grows there but trees." Nervously, she sipped the wine her aunt had brought from the Continent. She usually preferred water, but perhaps the wine would get her through this dinner.

"Of course, dear." Aunt Constance patted her hand. "The earl is simply a busy man with more important concerns. I shall remind him of his obligations as soon as I see him. I do hope he isn't off on another of his jaunts."

"Apples don't fall far from trees, particularly winesaps," Mac muttered, setting down his newly refilled glass after taking a large swallow.

Ignoring his reference to the earl's drunken son and the implication that the earl was also a drunkard, Constance waited until the soup was served before returning to her previous thought. "Why, I can remember the time the earl was so furious with a horse thief that he tracked him all the way to France and brought him back to England to be hanged. Dreadful temper, but I suppose he was within his rights. Justice must be served."

Across the table, Mac choked on another swallow of wine. Bea watched him with concern.

"It must have been a very valuable horse," the curate said politely.

"On the contrary, Mr. Rector." Aunt Constance smiled. "The horse had been placed out to pasture. The earl simply detests losing anything that is his."

Oh, my. Bea returned her gaze to her soup. If the earl would chase a horse thief to France, how far would he chase a child thief?

Across from her, Mac nearly inhaled the remainder of his wine. Thinking that an excellent idea, Bea did the same.

Sixteen

"Dear Bea is so modest. She cannot see that her beauty would take London by storm." Lady Taubee laughed at her niece's foolishness. "Why, she need only sit quietly in a corner and men would flutter toward her like moths to a flame."

And get their wings charred, Mac thought grimly, sipping his wine. The damned footman was constantly hovering, filling their glasses, and he'd lost track of how much he'd consumed. Obviously not enough, since he could still see the lovely woman with long, glossy curls brushing her creamy shoulders sitting across from him, pretending he didn't exist. She'd not said one word to him all evening.

"We would hate to lose Miss Cavendish to the city," the curate protested. "Miss Cavendish is Broadbury's biggest asset." Hearing himself, he stumbled to correct his phrasing. "Our *finest* asset. We could not do without her. Why, just last week Mr. Daventry Carstairs said he must come back more often if he could be assured of Miss Cavendish's charming company."

Cynically, Mac thought Dav more inclined to visit his hounds than Bea. She was too fine for either of the Carstairses. She needed someone strong to keep her from bankrupting herself with generosity.

He couldn't imagine where she'd find such a paragon, but that wasn't his problem. His problem was surviving the evening while staring across the table at the most perfect breasts designed by God. High, full, and firm, they strained at the thin silk of her gown until he'd become obsessed with watching for the moment a ruffle slipped. He was a clod. A drunken one, to boot.

A flush rose from Bea's throat to her cheeks, and Mac knew she was aware of his stare, but he couldn't help himself. Leaning back in his chair to stretch his legs and ease the uncomfortable tightness of his trousers, he gave up on food and settled in for a long evening of drinking. He smiled wickedly as she reached for her glass as well.

"Bea would make someone a wonderfully obedient wife," Lady Taubee rhapsodized.

Obedient, his ass. Mac tilted his glass in salute to Bea, who tried to pretend she didn't see. The woman would undermine anything a man did if she thought him in the wrong. He knew her sort— smile pleasantly to his face, then do exactly as she pleased behind his back. He'd watched his mother and countless other women manipulate their husbands that way. No women for him, no sirree. *Independence* was his motto.

He was definitely sloshed. He'd be maudlin soon if he didn't watch out.

"If it wasn't for Miss Cavendish, the parish would have to establish a poorhouse," Mrs. Rector confided. "Because of her and her father, there's not a woman or child in the village without a roof over their heads."

But Miss Damned Cavendish would be without a roof over *her* head if the silly chit didn't change her ways.

"What do you think, Mr. Warwick? Wouldn't Beatrice make a wonderful mother?"

Mac had to jerk back to the conversation to realize

Lady Taubee was addressing him. He wanted to scowl at the meddlesome witch, but big, brown eyes just like Bea's beamed at him from behind wrinkled, rouged cheeks, and he let the wine mellow him.

"Aye, that she would," he agreed with a slight slur. *For someone else's kids*, he added mentally. "She's a bonny lass designed to bear a man's babes."

From beside him, Mrs. Rector giggled, and Mac figured he'd committed some faux pas, but for once, he agreed with the old hag. Bea could inspire even a man like him to want brats. Getting them on her would be worth every minute of walking the floor later.

He hoped he hadn't said that aloud. What the devil had turned his thoughts in that direction?

Bea turned bright red, and Lady Taubee stood up to lead the ladies from the table. *Good. Let them go.* Now he could sit here and quietly drink himself under the table.

"Son, if you need some guidance, I'm here to help," the curate offered after the women left, and the elusive footman had produced a decanter of port and disappeared.

Mac raised an eyebrow in the curate's direction. "I'm one and thirty. What are you, twenty-five?"

The curate's smooth round cheeks flushed. "Age is not the measure of experience. I have six sisters. I've watched their suitors languish at our door since I was knee high."

Mac reached for his port. "I had a sister, and she died after bearing her sot of a husband's second child. Men will never understand women, no matter how many they know."

The curate grimaced in sympathy. "It is difficult to understand why they like us. I believe the fairer sex is more inclined to follow their hearts than their heads."

"And we follow our pricks instead of our hearts?"

Mac couldn't believe he'd said that to a man of the cloth, but he was entirely too aware of the part of him hidden by the table linen. He'd not been in this embarrassing predicament since he'd been a green stripling. And it was all that witch's fault for pointing out Bea's most attractive qualities.

The curate coughed and choked and reached for a glass of water. Helpfully, Mac pitched him a leftover roll. "Bread's best to stop that." He patted his coat pocket and located a cigar. "Mind if I smoke?" He'd had to refrain these last nights, since the ladies had insisted he accompany them rather than leave him sitting alone.

Biting doubtfully into the roll, the curate shook his head.

"My theory is that men and women possess only one thing they can share equally," Mac declared, "and that need be done only in a bed behind closed doors. The rest of the time they ought to steer clear of each other."

The curate nearly turned purple. Mac wondered if he ought to pound him on the back. When the man reached for his water glass again, he decided the curate was probably more woman than man, and he shouldn't have confided in him. Well, it really didn't matter much. The curate wasn't the sort who would dare mention such a subject to the ladies.

Putting his foot up on the chair Bea had vacated, Mac took another good swallow of port. If he could just stay here at the table, a good wine in one hand, a cigar in the other, he'd be a reasonably happy man. The idea of encroaching on the spiderweb of females beyond the drawing room door gave him cold shivers.

Now, if it were just Bea alone . . .

He closed his eyes against that temptation. She was a woman. She would trap him with her soft scents and beguiling eyes and phenomenal . . . Hell, he couldn't even hide behind his eyelids without her lurking there in vivid color and glorious dimension. That he even needed to hide from temptation irritated the hell out of him.

"The ladies civilize our weaker impulses," the curate said, intruding upon his thoughts.

Mac peered from beneath his lowered lids to watch the man nervously crumbling his bread. "How so?" he demanded. He'd just like to see a woman who could have prevented him from stealing Marilee's children. If that hadn't been a weak impulse, he didn't know what was.

"Men are . . . Men are inclined to act on the physical passions of lust and anger." The curate stumbled over his words but seemed to be thinking furiously. "If a physical action is available, they'll take it rather than think it through logically."

"Sheep dip," Mac declared, crushing his cigar in the tray. "I'm far more inclined toward logic than Miss Cavendish is. Her soft heart will lead her to ruin."

The curate shook his round head vehemently. "No, that's not what I mean. Women do let their tender feelings guide them more often than men do, but their actions are more apt to lead to good than evil. Men, on the other hand, are led by their stormier passions. An action taken in anger or lust is more generally a hurtful action."

As Mac attempted to interrupt, the curate waved his hand to signal he wasn't finished. "I believe the ladies can soften us, drawn away some of our more violent tempers, and lead us down more rational paths. You are a blunt man, Mr. Warwick. Are you inclined toward rash, destructive actions after you've . . . uh, spent time in a lady's company?"

Mac snorted. "If you mean bedded a woman, I suppose you have a point. I'm not likely to pop anyone in the jaw after a good bedding. But I don't need 'ladies' for that."

The curate sighed and reached for his port. "Well, no, I suppose not, but that's such a risky business. I've never really understood fornication outside the marriage bed. There's the risk of disease and unwanted children, and there cannot be the same pleasure as sharing something beautiful with one you love. No, I can't think it's the same at all. A wife can be a soothing presence when the rest of the world is out of kilter."

Mac figured he'd had just enough port for that to make sense. Of course, in his version, that soothing presence lay in bed behind closed doors. In any other room of the house, a woman was an intrusion. Except maybe in the kitchen. In bed, though . . . The vision was even clearer. The woman he saw sprawled across his pillow had polished curls and a wide, tempting mouth, and eyes that lit with interesting fires as he approached. Not to mention her more . . . uplifting assets.

The hot poker in his pants heartily agreed with the curate.

The curate coughed politely. "Um, perhaps we should join the ladies?"

Sure, sometime in the next decade or two.

With a determined effort, Mac conjured up Bitsy in dirty nappies and Buddy heaving up the morning's mush, and he was soon in a fine state for confronting the ladies. Nothing like imagining an army of children to take the wind out of a man's sails.

Of course, thinking about the children spawned new doubts. He couldn't remember his parents ever playing on the lawn with Marilee, as Bea had done with Bitsy and Bud. He hadn't really noticed their stiffness until he compared it with Bea's spontaneous ease. He grimaced. Well, that thought certainly had diminished temptation.

As they entered the drawing room, a maid stood with eyes downcast, apparently awaiting a reply to the missive the curate's wife was perusing. At their entrance, Mrs. Rector looked up with relief.

"There you are, Fred. It seems poor Mrs. White is in a terrible way and wishes your presence. I daresay she's overeaten again. Perhaps you could persuade her to stay away from those rhubarb tarts."

With little or no interest in Mrs. White or rhubarb tarts, Mac let his gaze drift across the room until it encountered Bea at the piano. She blushed at his look and hastily turned a page of music, but he'd caught her. She'd been watching him.

She thought him masculine.

He could have her in his bed, beneath him.

That stunning realization blazed a fiery trail across his sodden brain. Sometimes it took a little alcohol to make a man see what was right before his eyes.

She was everything he could want in a woman, and she was his for the asking. The aunt and the curate and half the town had agreed to that. And Bea had admitted her admiration. She didn't think him awkward or loutish. She thought him masculine.

If Lady Taubee could be believed, with a little effort he could have full possession of heaven for the rest of his life. Beneath her proper exterior, Bea possessed a soft and generous heart that would accept him as he was and let him live his life as he chose.

That rapturous notion so mesmerized Mac that he scarcely noticed as the Rectors said their farewells. Soft music tinkled from the piano keys, and he gravitated toward the sound. At just the right angle, he could see how naturally Bea filled out her bodice. Not a false plumper anywhere. He loved the way pink colored her cream skin when he stared at her. She was as aware of him as he was of her. He'd never experienced anything similar. Usually ladies became nervous and shied away when he showed interest, or they looked at him with scorn, as if his awkwardness were the mark of an addled simpleton. Not Bea. His size and awkwardness didn't bother her.

He knew he was bordering on drunk as he took the bench beside her without any encouragement from her aunt. This close, he could inhale her delicious scent— lilies tonight. Yes, he could see her as a tall, voluptuous lily with creamy petals tinged in pink.

He'd lost his sodden mind.

Stiffly, he sat back and tried to arrange his wayward thoughts. He ought to find an account book or something equally deadening before he did something rash. Strong emotion apparently paralyzed his brain.

"Bea has such gentle fingers on the keys, don't you agree?"

Lady Taubee appeared in his peripheral vision, and Mac wished her to hell. Tonight she wore a shawl as prismatic as a peacock's feathers. Her turban sported a glittering diamond in the center. She completely destroyed his illusions. Or delusions.

But the idea of Bea's gentle fingers on him instead of the keys insinuated itself into his paralyzed brain and wouldn't be removed.

"Lovely fingers," he agreed with a fervor that surprised him.

Lady Taubee dimpled playfully and patted his arm with her fan. "Dearest Bea, if you don't want this gentleman, I'll be happy to take him. I've not seen so ardent a suitor since the sheik and I . . ." She laughed. "Well, never mind that." She yawned delicately. "I think I shall retire early. Don't you two stay up too late or do anything I would do!"

Mac didn't notice her departure. He was discovering the advantage of sitting a head taller than Miss Cavendish. If he didn't slump, he could see the way her creamy breasts sloped delightfully into a mysterious valley dotted with faint freckles. He wondered where else he might find freckles on her, and didn't think he could bear not knowing. He was in serious trouble.

"My home is in Virginia." Even he knew it was an inane thing to say, but she didn't blink.

"I know." Her fingers trembled on the piano keys. "Do you think perhaps you shouldn't sit so close?"

"Depends." He inhaled deeper of her exotic scent. "Will you slap me if I kiss you?"

The keys crashed, and she looked so startled as she turned to him that Mac really couldn't resist. She had lush lips meant for kissing, but he thought perhaps he was the only man masculine enough to do so.

Taking her silence for acquiescence, he cautiously lowered his head and sampled the heady moisture of her mouth.

She inhaled slightly in surprise, then inexpertly met his pressure with a tentative pressure of her own. Mac thought he'd expire of happiness as their lips met perfectly.

She didn't slap him.

Steadying her with one hand on her rigidly held spine, he slowly deepened the kiss. She followed his lead hesitantly, exploring this wonder with caution.

She tasted of sweet, heady wine, and he couldn't drink enough. All too conscious of her breasts a hair's breadth from his waistcoat, Mac desperately tried not to rush her, but he needed to know so much more. . . .

He needed to know if she felt his spiraling heat, if she tasted of honey beneath her earlobe, if he was the only man who had ever produced that sensual moan from her throat. He traced her jaw with his fingertips and wondered at the fragility of it. He caught a polished curl and wished he could loose them all and draw his fingers through her hair.

By the time he persuaded her lips to part beneath his, he knew he'd dived off the cliff of no return, but all the logic, reason, and organization in the world couldn't save him now. Once he'd laid claim to the sweet recesses of her mouth, he knew it would never be enough. She responded so vibrantly, so innocent of his carnal lust, that he had to protect her—from himself, from other men who would take advantage of her gentle, giving soul . . . from life, if he must.

He was the wrong man for her, but from all evidence, he was the only one available. He savored the trembling touch of her tongue before reluctantly withdrawing.

Releasing her curls, stroking her soft cheek, and gently, very gently brushing a knuckle over the side of her breast until he heard her swift intake of breath, Mac pulled back enough to gaze down into her wondering eyes.

"Will you marry me?"

From the vast distance of his alcohol-soaked brain, he heard the whispered question bounce and echo around the cavernous room, and knew it must have been him who'd said it.

Seventeen

Marry him?

Perhaps she hadn't heard right. Beatrice blinked as if that would wake her from the spell this extraordinary man had woven around her.

Her lips tingled and burned. Her breasts felt full and achy. Her breath had caught in her lungs and couldn't find release.

She studied the square face above his loosened neckcloth, but Mac's expression hadn't lost its intensity. She thought she might be in deadly danger of being devoured.

She *wanted* to be devoured.

"Oh." The air left her lungs, and she turned hastily away before she did something truly foolish. He'd somehow insinuated his arm around her waist and drawn her so close that their hips touched. She could feel the hard length of his thigh even through her layered petticoats and his elegant trousers. She didn't think he had a soft place on him, and her fingers shook with the need to explore and find out.

He wanted to marry her. He was definitely drunk.

"I didn't mean to startle you." Looking all that was fashionable and gentlemanly for a change, he stroked her cheek and tilted her chin until she faced him again. She thought she read sincerity in the eyes beneath thick, drawn-down brows, but what did she know about men? He didn't sound drunk. He sounded confident . . . and sincere.

"Why?" she asked in bewilderment.

"Why?" Puzzled, he traced rough fingers over her lips, and she shivered with the need for his kiss again. She'd felt so very sure of herself when he'd kissed her. It had been a potent feeling of joy and triumph and passion.

"Why would you want to marry me?" Her question forced logic to shred the veil of illusion he'd woven. Her land could be the only reason for a man to marry her. She really shouldn't have asked. The illusion of love and desire was so lovely while it lasted.

Mac studied her sadly, as if amazed she had to ask, or uncertain of how to answer. "Because you're a beautiful woman, and I want you very much. I'm sure there are many logical reasons, but can't that one be enough?"

It was. Her lonely heart wept with joy at his declaration. She knew she had drunk far too much wine and that her head was spinning as giddily as any schoolgirl's, but she wasn't too befuddled to understand what she'd just been given.

For a blunt man like Lachlan MacTavish to utter the perfect words at a moment like this was a gift, a miracle beyond comprehension. Had he said he loved her dearly, she would have laughed in his face. Had he given her any of those "logical reasons," she would have been strong enough to turn him away.

To tell her she was beautiful in the face of all evidence otherwise, and to admit his desire for her while the proof of it was still warm upon her lips, shattered all her defenses. Every ounce of her hungry soul craved to be thought feminine and desirable.

She had absolutely no clue where these needs led,

but for once in her life, she had the courage to find out. "Are you sure?" she whispered.

He smiled then, and brushed her cheek with his callused fingers. "Aye, and I've never been more certain of anything in my life. Say yes, then run to the safety of your bed before I ravish you in an excess of gratitude."

"You're drunk." She said it with a smile of understanding that he'd never say such things had he not imbibed too well.

"Aye, most likely." He shrugged, but his eyes sparkled. "But not so befuddled that I don't know a good bargain when I see one. I'm not worth the ground you walk on, but if others are too blind to see your value, I'm man enough to ask for it. It's up to you to decide if you'll accept what little I have to offer."

He was offering her far more than she'd ever known, or dreamed. He was offering her a chance to be a woman and a wife. She'd never thought to see the day.

Before she could voice logical objections, she let her dreams answer for her. "I accept," she whispered, not believing her ears even as she said the words.

Then, heeding his wise advice, she gathered up her skirts and fled the room.

In her hurry, she didn't see James waiting behind the door, grinning hugely.

In the morning, waking with an aching head, Bea had plenty of time to repent. What on earth had she done?

Perhaps her memory was faulty, or the scene she remembered was a vivid drunken dream. She'd never consumed so much wine in her life. She could no more imagine a worldly man like Mac offering her marriage than she could imagine accepting him.

Yet the memory of his kiss still burned across her lips.

Hastily, she rose and dressed in a loose gown without the aid of a maid. The sun had barely reached the horizon, and shadows spread across the landscape outside her window, but she needed to correct any wrong impression immediately. She might have imagined Mac's proposal, but she certainly hadn't imagined that heated kiss.

She had to find out for certain what she had done and put a halt to it. She wouldn't have everyone thinking she was a spinster so desperate for a man that she would accept one who had no intention of actually living with her.

If she thought about it, a man who wasn't around to trample her developing independence would probably be the best sort of husband, though she couldn't believe Mac had actually offered that. And she didn't wish to be tied to a man who'd acted under the influence.

All her life she'd been told she must marry, that it was her duty to marry and submit to a husband's will, as she had submitted to her father's for twenty-eight years. She had accepted her father's domination because she'd had no choice. Suddenly she had freedom, and if she hadn't dreamed it, she'd thrown it away— on a man who would ruthlessly evict her tenants and rearrange her life to his way of thinking. Never. It had taken her six months to develop a backbone, and she wouldn't give it up now.

Her heart pounded a little harder as she released the front door latch and escaped into the early morning dew. He'd kissed her. Not a polite peck on the cheek, but a kiss that scorched her memory. Had anyone seen what they'd done, they'd be thoroughly compromised.

This wasn't *possible*, she raged as she ran down the

drive. She wasn't a feminine, desirable sort of woman.
She was an Amazon. She drove men away. If she
began craving their touch, she'd lose her mind. It had
never occurred to her that men would touch her in such
a way. Or that she would want them to. It was heathen.
Wanton. Wonderful.

She spotted Mac leaning on the railing of the stable
yard and swerved across the wet grass in his direction.
She didn't question why he was up at this hour. If he
was as confused as she was . . .

When she leaned against the fence beside him, he
turned to search her face, but she wouldn't look at
him. She didn't think he was smiling. He certainly
didn't greet her in a loving fashion. She didn't know
what to say now that she was here to say it. She was
a little too conscious of his proximity.

"Does your head hurt as much as mine?" was all
she could think to say.

"More." He grunted the word, then offered her the
steaming mug in his hand.

It smelled of coffee, and she shook her head.

He sipped his coffee, and she sensed he still watched
her. Goose bumps prickled her skin, and she had a
decided need for his strong arm around her again.

That was a terrible thought, indeed.

"Have you come to take back your acceptance of
my proposal?" he finally asked, in a voice completely
devoid of expression.

She shot him a startled look. "I should think you
would be taking back the *proposal*."

His smile was slow and awe-inspiring, and she shivered as he brushed her cheek with his broad fingers.
His touch made her crave more.

"I meant every bit of the proposal," he said firmly.
"I've had naught else to do but think about it these
last hours, and I haven't changed my mind. If I must
marry, you'd be the wife I'd have."

She offered him a wry smile for his honesty. "I never thought to marry, so never thought what manner of husband I'd have. I've simply been told that any decent man is better than none at all. I'm quite certain you're a decent man."

He warmed his hands on his mug and shook his head. "People are fools, but the point is, I belong in Virginia and you belong here."

"Well, that's part of the point," she conceded. "And please do not take this personally, since I think you would be a very good husband, but I really don't wish to have another man in my life telling me what I can or cannot do. I'm just starting to discover that I'm more capable than I thought."

He laughed, a warm and satisfying chuckle. She hadn't offended him, she realized with relief. If there had been any possible way to make a marriage between them, she would have liked to try. But morning had returned her to her senses.

"I wish I could be the one to teach you all that you're capable of," he said with an unmistakable leer over the top of his coffee cup.

She smacked his arm and inched away, but she felt the heat of his voice deep inside her. If she must live alone, she was better off not learning what he could teach her.

"But you're right," he added. "I wouldn't be here to tell you what to do. You either need to learn on your own, or hire someone to handle the place." He returned to staring at the empty stable yard. "From my perspective, a marriage between us would work," he said calmly. "I've commissioned my own ship, and if all goes well, it should have the capability of crossing the ocean in less than six weeks' time. I could be over here every three months in good weather, if I concentrated on shipping and forgot the railroad."

His words warmed places inside her that Bea had

thought frozen solid. A husband. It would take a while for her mind to grasp the thought as a real possibility— a man who would teach her to be a woman, then go about his own business so she might conduct hers. They would be safely within the parameters of all society's boundaries, and still lead their own lives. It was tempting. "As terrifying as it sounds, the idea has merits," she agreed cautiously.

He slanted her a teasing look. "Shall I kiss you again to make certain last night wasn't a fluke? I'm always willing to experiment."

Bea's mouth grew dry as the heat in his eyes warmed her. Perhaps his skin was more weather-darkened than most, and he didn't possess the grace of men like the Carstairses, but his strength was far more appealing than elegance, and the stubborn squareness of his jaw testified to his determination to protect what was his.

"Could we try kissing . . . carefully?" She couldn't believe she'd said that, but just watching the chiseled curve of his lips simmered her blood.

"Kind of a trial run?" he asked, setting his mug aside. "I can try, but be prepared if I go too far. I'm not too good at rational thought once my blood boils."

He'd put her own thoughts into words. He really, truly wanted to kiss her. Bea stared up at him, wondering how to entice him to do so. He wasn't wearing a neckcloth, and she was intensely aware of his powerful throat. He seemed to be waiting for some sign from her. Cautiously, she lifted her hand to his bristly cheek. He hadn't shaved yet this morning, and her fingers explored the sensation of his whiskers.

That seemed to be all the signal he required. Wordlessly he leaned over, and Bea closed her eyes as his mouth brushed hers.

In disappointment, she knew this wasn't what she remembered. This tingled, but didn't burn. She wanted more. Placing her hands on either side of his face, she sought what she remembered. He didn't object, and let her press her lips into his until the fire kindled and slowly caught and the space between them became too much to bear.

He grabbed her then, wrapping his arm around her waist and hauling her against his chest as if she were as weightless as wheat chaff. With the warmth of his chest crushing against her, she was entirely too aware that she wore only the briefest of undergarments. She clung to his linen-covered shoulders, and he pressed his kiss deeper. Once more she experienced the overwhelming sensation of being swept out of herself and into something dark and dangerous and more tempting than any whirlwind. Her hips arched into him, and the strangest urges tugged at her insides. He seemed to sense her need and he flattened her one petticoat until they snuggled closer. She felt shocking heat in places she didn't dare name. Then his tongue led hers on a merry dance that taught her more than she ought to know, and, gasping, she gathered the strength to push away.

Dizzy, Bea kept her balance by leaning back against the fence, one hand still pressed to Mac's chest. He was hot and breathing hard. He growled a protest but released her when she continued pushing away, although his hand wandered to her face and hair, exploring intimately as only a husband should do.

"I think we have a positive answer to that experiment," he muttered, pulling a loose comb from her hastily arranged hair. "I'm not in any condition to consider logical arguments on the subject of marriage right now." Succeeding in unraveling her hair so that it blew in the morning breeze, Mac crushed the back of her skirt against the fence and propped a hand on either side of her so she couldn't escape. "Tell me not to kiss you again, or we'll be in that marriage bed before you realize it."

With his hard body pressed down the length of her, Bea had some understanding of what he meant, and she shivered at the force of his erotic pull. She concentrated on watching his face, the way his skin stretched taut over his jaw as he waited for a word from her. She wanted to retreat, to run before her life ran away with her. Instead, she admired the way one golden brown curl insisted on falling across his tanned forehead. She lightly stroked his jaw to be certain he was real.

"I think we had better take some time to think about this," she said slowly. "I . . . don't know a lot about this sort of behavior. It isn't quite . . . sensible, is it?"

"Not in the least sensible," he agreed, his gaze dropping to where her bosom lifted and fell.

Bea felt the tips of her breasts harden, and she stopped breathing again.

As if he knew that, Mac returned his gaze to her face. "All right, we'll think about this some more. You'd better stay a good arm's length out of my reach, because I'm not likely to think clearly if you're any closer."

"All right, I can do that." *I think*, she told herself as he allowed her freedom to escape. She didn't want to move. "I'd better go in. I'm not properly clothed."

His mouth quirked upward at one corner. "I noticed, and don't think I didn't appreciate it. Tuck your hair up, or they'll assume the worst and we won't have any choices left."

Heat flushed her cheeks as she tucked her hair up in the combs he held out to her. She must look a proper hoyden with her hair tangled about her shoulders, and her gown clinging to her skin, and no support whatsoever to hide her shape. She'd never striven for a fashionable eighteen-inch waist. She wasn't that much of a fool, given her size. But she felt as if she'd just stepped from her bath and wore no more than a robe.

And Mac didn't seem to mind in the least. She stole one last look at his hungry expression and started hastily for the drive.

"I'll come with you," he said calmly. "If you're caught looking like that, your aunt will know you've been thoroughly kissed."

"She's still in bed," she whispered, trying to ignore the erratic beat of her heart.

"Good, then invite me in to breakfast, because I'm not ready to let you out of my sight." He grabbed his coat from the fence rail and pulled it on as he caught up with her.

He was already telling her what to do, and she hadn't even agreed to marry him.

Eighteen

"Good morning, miss, sir." A maid bobbed a curtsy as they entered the front doors. "And congratulations." She scurried out of sight with a delighted smile.

Mac tightened his mouth as she scampered away, then dared a quick glance at his companion. Bea looked a little stunned, but then, she'd looked a little stunned ever since he'd kissed her. A man could get used to a sight like that.

If he'd read the maid's message correctly, Bea might not have time to come to the same conclusion he had. "Could we have been seen from the house windows?" he murmured, guiding her toward the stairs.

She shook her head vigorously. "No, I'm quite certain. She must have meant something else."

Instinct warned she was indulging in wishful thinking, but he didn't pop her illusions immediately. Instinct could be wrong. "Go put on one of those high-necked black things, then. Wear a veil. And smear yourself with camphor oil or something."

She looked at him as if he were crazed, caught his meaning from his expression, and hastened out of his reach and up the stairs. Being a man, and a horny one at that, Mac watched her go all the way up. Her hips swayed like a daffodil in the breeze, and he knew he was daft enough to do anything she told him.

He was in *way* over his head, but he was a man who liked a challenge, and he had no regrets.

Rubbing his bristly cheek, he decided he'd better meet trouble looking his best. Even the simplest of women took half an hour or more to dress. He had time.

Returning to the house shaved and wearing his good morning coat, Mac swept off his hat and handed it to James as he entered through the front doors. The footman led him to the empty dining parlor, where silver chafing pans steamed, and mouthwatering aromas chased away any remaining headache.

He took the seat James offered, shook open the neatly pressed newspaper laid beside his plate, and accepted a cup of coffee as if he'd been breakfasting here all his life. Not until he'd sipped his coffee and the footman had returned with a plateful of eggs and bacon did Mac comprehend the enormity of his position.

He was sitting at the head of the table.

He was sitting where his father always sat at home, reading the paper as his father always did, expecting the servants to wait on him as they waited on his father, and all as if the role were second nature to him.

He stared over his cup at the long length of sparkling white table linen before him. A silver piece spilling over with spring flowers prevented a clear view of the far end of the table. Two additional places were set on either side of him. The delicate pink china and glittering silverware shouted loudly of feminine expectations.

He'd been trapped, fairly and squarely.

Breathlessly, Bea hurried in, still tucking pins into her upswept hair, her heavy skirts rustling as they brushed the chairs. She smiled uncertainly at Mac, and blinked when she noted his position. Before she could say a word, a suddenly stern and respectful James bowed and pulled out a chair for her, even as Mac stood up to do it.

"Best wishes, my lady," James said proudly. Then looking at Mac, who had returned to his seat, he nodded his approval. "And congratulations to you, sir," he said formally, with the respect of a good butler— or the obsequious politeness of a leech.

The noose tightened. They'd *both* been trapped. Before Bea had been given a chance to review the pros and cons, to make any kind of informed decision, the knot had been tied around their throats.

Mac regarded Bea cautiously over his coffee cup. She looked startled and a little frightened, but before either of them could recover their tongues, a loud voice echoed down the hall.

"We'll settle the date shortly. Send into town to see if they have any good card stock for the invitations. The supply in the desk is quite old and yellowed. And tell Mrs. Digby we'll need her yeast rolls for the breakfast. No one can make them as she does."

As the voice boomed closer, Mac and Bea exchanged helpless glances. Aunt Constance certainly seemed prepared for a festive event.

Reading the resignation on Bea's face, Mac calmly turned over a thousand excuses why—for her sake— he ought to pack his bags and run, but he simply didn't want to do it.

He understood perfectly well what he'd done. One did not place one's tongue in a proper lady's mouth without paying the consequences, even if that proper lady had asked for it. He'd known this had been Lady Taubee's intention from the first, and he hadn't avoided the temptation. He hated giving the old witch exactly what she wanted at Bea's expense, but he really couldn't find any serious objection to sharing a bed with the lovely woman who was turning pink beside him. If marriage was the only way he could have her, well, so be it. He'd marry her.

He just wouldn't hang around long enough for them to get in each other's way.

He greeted Lady Taubee with a sardonic lift of his eyebrows as she swept into the room. He bit into his toast as she smiled broadly at both of them.

"I'm so happy for you!" she exclaimed. "I could just cry. This is too wonderful for words." She then proved herself wrong by indulging in a stream of words, beginning with Bea's dear, sainted father and working her way through the wedding preparations.

As the tidal wave of arrangements spilled over their heads, Bea lost her color and sipped her tea silently. Mac wanted to feel sorry for her, but his own roiling emotions hampered him.

Married. He was about to be married. To a woman who didn't want to be married.

Impulse had ruled him again, and this time he'd caught this lovely, generous woman in the downfall with him. He regretted any pain he'd caused her, but a part of him was screaming in jubilation. The wrong part, obviously.

He could tell that behind her pale mask, Bea was thinking hard. He didn't think she could find any way out of this trap, but he thought she might have some clue as to how it had been sprung.

Bea's lips tightened as her cousin bent over the table to serve her aunt's tea, and Mac watched with interest as her thoughts betrayed her. He, too, turned to watch her smiling cousin. He'd known he couldn't trust the fribble. They'd been spied upon.

"James, I'd have a word with you after we're done," Bea said coldly, overriding her aunt's excited chatter.

James beamed expectantly. "I know. It's all too

wonderful. A wedding!" He flitted away, leaving the diners at the table to stare at each other in silence.

"Well, Mr. MacTavish, we can't pretend you're still a Warwick under the circumstances, can we?" Lady Taubee all but cheered. "All will be perfectly well, I'm certain. Coventry can't complain of you when you've made such a splendid connection. You'll see, it shall all turn out for the best."

Bea muttered something under her breath, and Mac seriously contemplated pounding his coffee cup over the old bat's head, but he didn't think the fragile china would have much effect. "I can't think Coventry will be any happier no matter what connection I make. I still must see the children to Virginia."

"You fret too much." Lady Taubee waved her fork dismissively.

Mac snorted.

"We take care of our own here," the old lady warbled on. "Now, when shall we set the date? I'm sure the curate can send for a special license. We must do this with all due pomp and circumstance, you know. Bea ought to have a new gown. The queen was married in the loveliest white gown. I'd love to see you wear white, Bea. And if only Smythe could find those doves, I'm certain—"

"I would look a freak in white, Aunt," Bea murmured.

"Nonsense, child! It's all the fashion, and you shall look charming. How long do you think it would take to send to London for some patterns? We could have it made up here and save time. Instead of doves, perhaps we could—"

"It's Bea's wedding. I think she should be given full choice in what she wishes to wear," Mac said with just enough menace to garner the attention of both women. Bea looked startled, and he smiled reassuringly at her. "I know nothing of fashion, but I've been told you have a marvelous sense of it. Send for whatever your heart desires."

Lady Taubee *hmph*ed her disapproval, but Bea was looking at him with such wide-eyed wonder that Mac couldn't tear his gaze away.

"I like blue," she said with a trace of defiance, watching him. "Silver-blue, with a minimum of lace to here." She recklessly pointed to a place on her high-necked bodice that indicated a décolletage that would have him following her about like a lovesick calf.

He grinned in ecstasy at the image. "That sounds perfect to me."

At the blatant look of hunger he bestowed on her, she blushed and returned to picking at the mangled food on her plate. Mac decided he would enjoy being married to a woman with the same wickedness pouring through her veins as poured through his.

He was fortunate indeed to find the only woman in all England who was so fresh and unspoiled that she didn't even know she should be outraged at his uncouth behavior. Better yet, she *enjoyed* it.

All misgivings fled before brash desire as he turned and winked at Lady Taubee. "Set the date, my lady, but make it soon."

A week after that humiliating discussion, Bea's nerves had frayed to tatters, and her head spun in so many circles she despaired of ever thinking straight again. Pacing the fading carpet of her bedchamber, she tried to pull herself together enough to go down and listen to her aunt and Mrs. Digby plan her wedding breakfast, but she still couldn't accept the enormity of the fact that she was actually *having* a wedding breakfast.

In two days' time, she would be married.

She wrung her hands and paced some more. It was all happening too fast.

She glanced out her double-wide window to the courtyard below, where Mac played with his niece and nephew. Buddy was climbing a tree, and Bitsy was sitting on Mac's shoulders, doing her best to rip his hair out by the fistful. Bea's heart twisted in agony at the scene. He would make a wonderful father.

Except that he wouldn't be here to make a wonderful father. He would be in Virginia. Or on his ship. Or anywhere but here. She tried to tell herself it was no different from being married to a sailor, but she knew better.

She was out of her mind. She'd received a second ominous letter from the bank inquiring about immediate payment, and she didn't know what to do about it. If she showed it to Mac, would the extent of her debt horrify him? Would he demand that she sell the estate?

She had to learn to deal with the estate on her own. The only reason Mac had agreed to this ridiculous farce was because he thought he'd be free to come and go as he pleased, and that she would be happy to see the back of him when he went.

She'd be even happier if he'd go now.

He'd treated her with all due respect this past week, keeping a proper distance, not teasing her with any more kisses. They both knew what happened when they kissed. It was far too dangerous an activity under these uncertain circumstances. It was far too dangerous under *any* circumstances.

She paced away from the window and the view of Mac's broad back and golden brown hair. In two days' time, he would be her husband. He'd have expectations. And then he would leave to cross the ocean, and she might never see him again.

No, she couldn't marry him. It would be quite cruel and unfair to learn the duties of a wife, only to be abandoned. She was far better off not knowing what she would miss.

Below, a cart rumbled up the drive. They hadn't invited anyone but the closest neighbors to the wedding, so they didn't expect company. It must be one of the many deliveries her aunt had ordered. Bea stared at the magnificent icy blue bridal gown hanging on her wardrobe door. The Miller sisters and the seamstress had spent the week working on that gown. It had arrived just this morning, made of silk that Mr. Smythe had already had in his shop. It was the loveliest thing she'd ever seen in her life. Even she might look beautiful in a gown that shimmered with tiny pearls and a delicate flowered net special-ordered from London.

She swung back to the window at the sound of Mr. Digby's voice coming from below. Mr. Digby was so enraptured with his inn that he could scarcely be persuaded into church on Sunday. What was he doing out here?

She watched as her former butler said something that made Mac's expression go grim. *Oh, dear. Not now. Please don't let anything happen to those children now.* She could think of no other reason for Mac to look as if he might turn and flee at this very moment. He'd been remarkably easygoing about the wedding preparations. He hadn't even complained of being trapped into marriage, although he'd looked a trifle hunted upon occasion, when her aunt tried to pin him down on details.

Without thinking what she did, Bea picked up her skirt and raced down the hall and stairs. People still called him Mr. Warwick, but sooner or later everyone would know that wasn't his real name. He'd had to tell the curate his full name for the special license. What if the earl had returned? The viscount would tell him who had stolen his grandchildren. The coincidence of a MacTavish appearing here with two small children in tow would be too much to overlook. They were an isolated village, and news of London didn't travel through frequently, but anything was possible. *The Carstairses!* The Carstairses had gone to London. They hadn't known Mac as MacTavish, though.

As she raced out the front door, Mac gave her a tight facsimile of a smile, and Digby looked relieved. Sweeping off his hat, he bowed as much as his portly stomach would allow and murmured something about checking on his wife.

As Digby departed, Mac dropped Bitsy into Bea's arms. "The viscount apparently has men posting flyers in the village and across the countryside, offering a reward for my whereabouts. The flyer doesn't mention the children or why I'm wanted, and uses the name MacTavish and not Warwick, but the description was sufficient for Digby to report it to me. There aren't many men my size hereabouts."

"Oh, my." Bea hugged the babe and let Bitsy pat her cheeks as she stared up at Mac. "What shall we do now? Why didn't the viscount mention the children?"

"To keep his father from knowing they've gone missing, I suspect." Mac shoved his hand through his hair, further tousling his already tousled curls. Despair haunted his eyes. "I could pack them up and leave right now, take them to the train station in Evesham and be gone before anyone knows it."

"And where would you go?" she demanded. "If you run, everyone will know you're the man they're hunting."

Returning his attention to her, he nodded as if he'd already reached that conclusion. His expression grave, he drew his knuckle down her cheek. "If I stay, there'll be no escaping this marriage. Are you certain it's what you want?"

Here was her chance to say no. He'd just made it

clear she would be marrying a wanted criminal, one
who would have to flee sooner or later. She buried
her face in Bitsy's sweet-smelling neck and tried to
imagine returning to the bleak, gray life she'd led before Mac and the children had arrived. Arguing with
James and worrying over coins had been the high
points of her week.

She couldn't turn back time. Shaking her head, she
met his gaze. "Our wedding will be the event of the
season. No one will give a mind to those silly flyers.
They'll laugh and speculate and throw them out and
drink to our health. We don't have much opportunity
for celebration around here. You'll see. Our wedding
will be all that's on anyone's tongues for weeks."

Mac nodded and solemnly accepted her assessment.
"Then I'll do my best to make you and everyone else
proud. I may do all the wrong things upon occasion,
but I try to do them for all the right reasons."

Amusement welled up in her. "I'm sure it's all the
right reasons that have you marrying me," she agreed.
"Obviously you're marrying me because you're generous, honorable, and noble and would not let a plain
spinster waste away for naught."

Laughter danced in his eyes. "Aye, and far from
ravishing you to show you what you've been missing,
I'll generously, honorably, and nobly make a respectable woman of you first. And *then* I'll—"

"Don't you say it; don't you dare say it!" Cheeks
burning, she shoved Bitsy into his arms and fled, Mac's
laughter following her as she ran.

Oh, my. She'd done it this time. In two days she
would marry a man she hardly even knew. Papa had
been right: she was bungling everything terribly, just
as he'd always said a woman would.

Nineteen

The organ groaned to life and began a solemn march Mac had been told had been played at the queen's wedding. They could be playing "Hail to the Queen" for all he knew.

He nervously crumpled the brim of his top hat as he stood at the altar and waited for his bride to walk down the aisle. The vicar had arrived from Evesham, and Mac thought his smile looked sympathetic, as it would be for a man who was condemned to hang. How had a simple business trip turned into a wedding ceremony?

He definitely *wanted* Bea. But marriage? How the hell would he tell his family he'd leaped before he looked again, and married a bride who lived an ocean away?

Bitsy and Buddy bounced from one lap to the other in the front pew. All the ladies of the village were taking turns watching the little hooligans. They were dressed in all their finery, Bitsy in white lace and Buddy in blue satin, with lace and bows and their angelic smiles and curls to adorn them. Bitsy had already ripped the white ribbons off her lacy cap, and Buddy had lost a button off his jacket.

Would Bea still want him when he returned from

Virginia without the children? That thought preyed constantly on his mind.

As did an even deeper concern—would Bea still want him once she understood the bestial nature of men? She'd been raised without the benefit of an understanding mother, and he wondered if she had any idea what to expect from him tonight.

He was terrified that one way or another, he'd make her cry. He didn't want to hurt her at all, but he didn't see how he could help it. Ladies expected things he didn't have in him. He couldn't give her poetry or soft words, or even dance, should the occasion rise.

As the church doors opened, Mac handed his hat to Overton, who'd agreed to stand up with him. His heart or his lungs or some vital organ hung in his throat as Bea entered. She was so beautiful, he couldn't breathe for awe. Gleaming russet braids rolled up and decked with tiny white roses framed her pink cheeks and shining brown eyes. A spill of frail lace covered the curls piled on top of her head. And the gown . . .

Mac took a deep breath before he expired on the spot. She'd promised to cut the neckline down to there, and she had. The glorious curve of her breasts rose high and full above the shimmering blue bodice. How would he survive until tonight? What imp of hell had enforced laws requiring a man to marry in the morning? Why hadn't he thought to arrange a carriage to the next town and an inn where neither of them were known?

Actually, he had thought of that, but Bea hadn't wanted to leave home.

The delicate scent of lilacs engulfed him as she arrived at the altar, and he took her hand into the crook of his arm. She felt perfect beside him. He needn't bend to hear her words, nor fear he'd break her in two with his rough hugs. She didn't shy away from his crude kisses. Physically, they were a perfect match. And since the physical was all he wanted of this marriage, and all she seemed to expect, he told himself that he had no real reason to fear the vows he was about to make.

He listened patiently to the vicar's drone, responding firmly when called upon, and heard with pleasure the musical tones of Bea's replies. She had a lovely voice when she chose to use it. Tonight he would hear her soft cries of pleasure for his ears alone. He would willingly delay his departure for months, with this woman to keep him company in bed.

He'd had to ride to Cheltenham to obtain the ring he slid on her finger now. As Bea placed a matching band on him, Mac felt the familiar sensation of a noose tightening, and he fought to keep from tugging at his neckcloth. Still, the ring didn't look too bad there, and the smile she bestowed on him was worth every minute of terror. He couldn't remember any other woman ever looking at him with such happiness.

The vicar had informed him that sealing the marriage with a kiss was not part of the traditional service, but when the moment came, Mac couldn't resist. How could he vow "till death do us part" without sampling what he vowed to keep? Bea smiled blissfully when he bent to brush her lips with his, and he would have dived in way over his head if she hadn't tugged at his sleeve.

He looked up blindly as a disturbance broke out in the front pew.

Buddy scrambled from his captors and raced up the aisle to haul on the long skirt of Bea's gown. "My Missy," he announced firmly.

Tears rimmed Bea's eyes, but Mac thought they might be a woman's tears over nothing, because she was smiling. Whisking the boy into his arms and hugging him, Mac whispered reassuringly in his nephew's ear, "We'll share, all right?"

Beaming, making him feel he'd done the right thing, Bea hastened to rescue Bitsy from the arms of Mrs. Rector. The babe burbled happily and slobbered over the delicate lace of the wedding gown. Mac didn't know whether to laugh or cry as they proceeded down the aisle to stately organ music with two giggling children in their arms.

Hell of a way to start married life. It was a damned good thing he was getting rid of the wretched monsters, or he'd be lucky to ever see his marriage bed. He looked down at Buddy's defiant expression and over to his bride's blissful one, and surrendered his grumpy thoughts. Somehow he'd made them all happy—for the moment.

"Didn't those posters mention some Scots name?" Bea overheard Clara Miller asking her sister. "And didn't the vicar just call Mr. Warwick by some outlandish heathen name?" The spinster threw a look over her shoulder in Mac's direction. "I'm certain it wasn't Warwick."

Bea's stomach did an uneasy dance, but she approached the women calmly. Anger and protectiveness overcame her natural timidity. "He's an American, Miss Miller," she said as she helped herself to a tea cake. "His father is the descendant of a Scots laird, but his family has owned property in Virginia for a hundred years or more. And his mother is a relation to the Gloucestershire Warwicks, a very respectable family, I'm told. Have you tried one of Mrs. Digby's yeast rolls? They absolutely melt in the mouth."

She sauntered off, leaving the two spinster ladies eagerly filling their plates. She should feel sorry for them. They were in their late thirties and had never married. She'd thought she'd end up like them with

nothing better to do than gossip. As she cast a glance
to where Mac entertained a circle of men, happiness
exploded inside her. No matter what else could be
said about her husband, he was a fine figure of a man,
and he cared for his niece and nephew. When all was
said and done, the ability to love small children said
a great deal about a man.

He looked up, caught her eye, and winked. She
blushed and hastily stepped into a curtained alcove,
any worries over gossip evaporating in the heat of her
thoughts. She might be ready for the night to come,
but she wished she knew more of what to expect. Aunt
Constance had simply told her to follow her husband's
wishes, and she would be fine.

"I hadn't realized he had two children already," she
heard Mrs. Smythe murmur to someone on the other
side of the drapery. "Why, our dear Miss Cavendish
could be breeding before summer's end. She won't
have time for this cooperative Mrs. Rector proses on
about."

Bea blushed to her hair roots but couldn't break
away at the sound of Mrs. White's earthy chuckle ac-
companying this hushed statement. "Dear Miss Cavendish is too much a lady to allow her husband those
kinds of liberties," the brewer's wife said with certainty. "Ladies do things differently. You don't see
any of them at Landingham with big bellies swollen
with child. No, they have separate beds and most
likely only share one at holiday times or some such,
or the country would be overrun with nobility."

Mrs. Smythe snorted loudly. "Well, we're half overrun with the nobility's bastards, so the gentlemen
don't think the same as the ladies then. Of course, if
their ladies don't allow them in their beds, I can see
the reason for that. Men are no better than beasts in the
fields, as I see it, doing indecent things to a woman

until they get us with child, then roaming to the next female in heat. It's a sin, it is."

Bea crumpled to the cushioned window seat, her face aflame. Even though the women wandered off, she doubted she could confront her guests anytime soon. *Beasts in the field?* She'd taken a broom to a pair of cats once that—

Children. What men did to women in bed produced children. She had never given the details much consideration. Now that she'd experienced the unsettling feelings Mac's kisses had introduced, she rather thought they might be just the beginning. She'd known that women who had children out of wedlock had done indecent things, but she hadn't thought about married women doing them. Just exactly what indecent things would her husband expect her to do? Did such acts always produce children?

And did she want children?

That was a sobering thought, one she hadn't given much consideration. Her thoughts wandered back to Mac's tongue touching hers, and she shivered at the implication.

Bea held a hand to her flat abdomen. How was it possible? Aunt Constance really should have told her more. Did she dare ask Mrs. Rector? But Mrs. Rector had no children and probably didn't know either.

She couldn't believe the depth of her ignorance. It wasn't just her father who had protected her from the facts of life. The whole village was guilty. People had children all the time, but she'd seen them only after the babes were born. She'd always been discouraged from visiting when people whispered a woman was "breeding." It must be awful to look upon.

She didn't want to look worse than she already did, and she wasn't at all certain that she wanted children, especially if they grew in her belly. She didn't even want to begin to know how they got there.

When Mac came to find her, she stared at him as if he'd turned into a ram with horns and was about to leap upon her. If that was what he thought he'd do to her—

"Bea?" he asked, a quizzical expression replacing his earlier smile. "Are you all right? You look as if you've eaten something that disagrees with you."

Shame and shyness burned inside her, and she turned away rather than take his hands. His big hands, with which he'd already touched her breast once. Her cheeks flamed as she imagined what else he might do with them. "Too much excitement," she whispered.

"You're not used to it," he said sympathetically. "Did your father never entertain?"

"Once each year, in the fall." Grateful for a familiar subject, she grasped it eagerly. "He'd ask his hunting friends over for dinner before the hunt. This is not the same at all."

"Well, your aunt is having the time of her life. Perhaps she will go away and leave us alone after this."

Alone. Panic loomed large. She clasped her fingers into fists. "Most likely. She likes the Season in London. Perhaps she can help you find a nanny." She was amazed she could say anything so sensible with him looming over her.

"I think I'll go suggest it to her and see how soon I can persuade her to leave."

Bea nodded helplessly, and let Mac slip away without a word.

He wanted her. He was pleased with their marriage. But she wasn't at all certain that she knew what *she* wanted.

She'd been pushed into this marriage just as she'd been manipulated by the wishes of others all her life. The biggest decision of her life, and she'd let others make it.

She had better think quickly about whether or not

she wanted children, then. She had a strong feeling that Mac hadn't given children a thought one way or another. He just meant to have what he wanted of her; then he'd sail away and leave her to the consequences—just as a ram planted little lambs all over the field and ignored them thereafter.

Oh, my. If only she could count on a big, gaping hole opening up and swallowing her, she might survive this day.

Twenty

He didn't know where his wife was.

Nervously, Mac paced up and down the floor of the room he'd been assigned. No one expected him to sleep in the steward's cottage on his wedding night, but he hadn't considered all the ramifications of sleeping in the mansion either.

He pulled a face as he glanced down at the silky robe with its tasseled belt that someone had left on his bed. He hadn't known what he was supposed to wear under it. He'd much rather doff everything, as he usually did. But he was a married man now. He couldn't offend feminine sensibilities by walking around in the bare skin God gave him.

He listened for some sound of the children overhead in the nursery, but the wedding had worn them out. They'd been sound asleep when he'd checked on them.

Grabbing the wine bottle he'd had waiting in anticipation of Bea's arrival, he eased into the darkened hallway, checking for lurking servants. He groped his way down the hall, thinking of how quiet Bea had been since the wedding. Did second thoughts have her cowering in her room?

Why the devil hadn't she told him where her room was? The mahogany staircase split the mansion into

two halves. Glancing down the west wing, he saw no
sign of light beneath any doors. Taking a deep breath,
he tiptoed back the way he'd come, past the door to
his room, and beyond to a statue of some dead
Roman, in the direction of the east wing. About mid-
way down, a faint light from beneath a door illuminated the floorboards and carpet of the hall.

Praying the aunt had a room in the farthest corner
of hell, Mac strode down the hall and knocked. If he
startled the old lady, so be it. She could give him
directions.

He might have imagined Bea's call, but he was too
wound up to care. He'd spent the day—hell, the last
week—imagining Bea in his bed. He wasn't about to
give up now that the moment was at hand.

A flame flickered in a bedside lamp as he opened
the door to find Bea sitting up against her pillows,
reading a book, in a good-sized bed with heavy wine-
colored draperies. A quick glance revealed a few solid
pieces of furniture and none of the fragile frivolity he
feared he would break. A man his size needed a solid
bed under him—particularly for the activity he had
in mind.

His gaze drifted back to the women in the bed.
Wearing some kind of high-necked gown stitched all
over with ruffles and lace and whatnot, Bea waited
patiently while he oriented himself. She wore her hair
in a long thick braid down her back. He wanted to
undo that braid and wrap his hands in all those lus-
trous tresses.

"I didn't know where to find you," he said gruffly.

Dark circles shadowed her eyes, and he wondered
if she'd been crying. The thought made him feel more
than ever a lout. What did ladies expect of the marriage bed? With no one to ask, he had to rely on her,
and Bea wasn't inclined toward expressing her feelings.

Setting down the wine, he could see she'd pulled

the lace-trimmed sheets up to her neck. He dearly wanted to see her naked and sprawled wantonly across those sheets, but he supposed he couldn't expect everything at once. Beneath his tight trousers, his pole was already so rigid he could mount a flag and fly it.

Easing down onto the bed, he leaned on one hand and pressed a kiss to her brow. Without all her acres of skirts and petticoats, she seemed much smaller and more vulnerable. She had such soft skin, Mac's hand trembled as he touched it. "I don't think the world has ever seen so lovely a bride as you," he murmured. He'd memorized that line, but it was from his heart. He'd never forget how she looked as he'd placed his ring on her finger and claimed her in the eyes of all.

"I've been told all brides are lovely," she said flatly, not setting aside her book.

He tried to remove the volume from her fingers, but she gripped it firmly. Growing worried, he studied her face. This wasn't the warm welcome he'd expected. "Is there anything else you've been told that I should know about?"

Her lip quivered, but she drew herself up straight. "I don't think we ought to have children."

Warning bells clamored in his head, but Mac had practice in remaining calm in the face of adversity. "I think that's one of those things God controls," he said evenly.

"It is?"

He heard her surprise and wondered what in hell she'd been told. "The curate and his wife have not been blessed with children, have they?"

She wrinkled her forehead and pondered that before working it out in her decidedly intricate brain. "That's probably because they don't do anything indecent."

Mac wanted to laugh out loud, but he didn't dare. He stood on a precipice right now, and one wrong move would tumble him over. "I don't think it's considered indecent if we're married."

Her mouth straightened into a stubborn line he'd not noticed before.

"But if it can lead to babies, I don't think we ought to do it. You will go away shortly, and I can barely manage things on my own as it is." She watched him cautiously. "Kissing doesn't lead to babies, does it? Couldn't we just kiss?"

His patience frayed as he sought a path through the treacherous swamp of her ignorance. "Bea, I could tell you that kissing is safe, but it would be a lie." He saw her eyes widen in panic and hastened to reassure her. "We've not gone too far, but we would."

Daringly, he tugged gently at the sheet. Apparently unable to decide whether to hold the book or grab the linen, she lost both. He uncovered a nightgown huge enough to serve as a second sheet. She tried to cover herself, but Mac stayed her hand, slipped beneath her defenses, and boldly conquered a malleable, cotton-covered peak. She gasped when he rolled the tip of her breast beneath his palm. As aroused as he was, it was a foolish thing to do, but he had to make her understand how their bodies reacted to each other. Pink tinged her cheeks as she pushed back into the pillows, but he wasn't about to let go now that he finally had the right to touch her. By all that was holy, she felt magnificent in his hands. He wanted to see all of her, touch all of her—inside as well as out.

But she was his wife, and she was terrified. He had to teach her—so many things.

"Feel what happens when I do this?" he asked, caressing her through the linen with amazing restraint for a man who was about to explode. "Touching you like this affects me the same way it does you. And if we kiss, I'll want to do this and a great deal more. That's how God made us. That's why the world is populated with children. It's not because they're such a joy to have around," he added dryly.

Bea thought she'd melt of embarrassment when Mac did not immediately release her breast but used his fingers to create rivers of desire that flowed far lower than he touched. No one but Mac had ever touched her like that. It was *indecent.*

It was wonderful. Her insides were turning to hot jelly and settling in a place below her belly that began to ache.

He was no longer her friend, but her husband. Terror stole along her veins in accompaniment with the shiver of desire he created.

His thumb thrummed a tune across her breast, and she wanted to cry out with the need of it, or shout at him to stop. She didn't know how to do either.

"Don't, Mac," she whimpered, staring woodenly at the bedpost. "I *can't.*"

"You can," he said determinedly. "Just let me kiss you, and it will be easy." He leaned over to do just that.

Grabbing the sheet, Bea rolled to the far side of the bed and clambered out, glaring at him as he sat on her bed, bewildered.

"You already have everything your way," she cried, not knowing where the words were coming from but letting them escape as they willed. "Under law, my land is yours. My tenants are yours. You can do anything you like, and I'll have no say in the matter. It's like living with my father all over again, only worse. At least my father wouldn't force babies on me and then leave."

He seemed in some kind of pain, but she couldn't relent. She'd never stood up to anyone in her life, never refused anyone anything. If she backed down now, she would turn into a spineless jellyfish. Or a fat cow, belly swollen with child. She'd probably have udders spilling with milk. That's why he wanted to touch her there. She almost panicked as she wondered if just that touch would lead to a baby, but she couldn't see how. Surely he wouldn't have tricked her like that.

"I should certainly hope your father wouldn't force babies on you," he said grimly, rising from the bed. "Now, *that* would be indecent." He didn't advance on her but seemed to be seeking reassurances. "If it's what you want, I can have a contract drawn settling the entire estate on you. I don't need your land."

She backed away, refusing to fall for that bemused look on his face or his fancy promises. He'd talked her into this insane marriage. She couldn't remember why she'd let him. The children, she decided. She hadn't wanted her aunt to tell the earl about the children, and now everything was just fine, and Mac could sail away whenever he liked.

"Do you have any idea what happens between a man and a woman?" he asked carefully, when she didn't respond to his offer.

"They make babies," she answered stoutly. "That's all I need to know."

Terror filled her as he narrowed his eyes and started around the bed. Mac was bigger and stronger than any man she'd known. He could throw her on the bed and hold her down and do anything he liked. He could touch her breasts and kiss her and make her all hot, and then he'd do whatever it was that men did, and she'd swell up and everyone would know they'd done it.

When she shrank away from him, Mac lifted his hand in surrender. "For heaven's sake, Bea, I won't rape you. I don't want to steal your damned land, and I don't want to force a child on you if you don't want one. I just wish you'd told me your feelings *before* we got married."

"I didn't realize we'd make babies before this," she whispered.

His face fell and he ran his hand through his rumpled hair. He stood there in little more than a dressing robe, his bare chest looking so manly and powerful she had to swallow twice before she could breathe, and he was still the perfect picture of confusion.

"Oh, hell, you're twenty-eight years old, Bea. Where've you been all your life?"

She didn't know. She'd just been existing, she supposed, and he was forcing her to do more than exist. He was forcing her to look at him as another human being, one who embarrassed as easily as she did, and who got as frustrated. He was frustrated now, she could tell, yet he hadn't offered her any harm.

"I'm sorry," she murmured consolingly. "I'm trying to learn, but no one will teach me. I don't think I ought to have babies, or they'll grow up as ignorant as I am."

He scowled and headed for the bottle of wine. Apparently thinking better of it, he swung around again. "I can teach you a wife's duty to her husband, but I won't have time to teach you all you want to know about the estate, or even babies, before I sail."

Disappointment washed through her, but she stuck her chin out in defiance. Perhaps it was time to tell him about the bank letter, but she didn't have that much nerve. "You may teach me a wife's duty when you have time to teach me what I *want* to know."

Mac stalked closer, backing her up against the washstand. "You'd *want* to know about wifely duties if you'd just let me perform my husbandly ones."

She crossed her arms, but that only drew his gaze downward. "I don't want to have children by myself," she repeated firmly.

He looked even more grim, but backed slightly away. "You're my wife, for better or worse. We'll have to learn to deal with that. In the meantime, I want you to move into the second room in the suite you've given me. Is that too much to ask?"

Distrustfully, Bea held the sheet higher to her chin. "That was my father's suite."

The rumble issuing from his chest was almost a growl, but he kept his voice pitched low. "I'm not your father. Unless you want me to move in here with you, I suggest you start moving your things there in the morning. I'll not have your servants thinking I'm a poor excuse for a husband."

Warily, she nodded. "The other room needs airing, but I'll take care of it."

"Good. Then tomorrow we'll start your lessons on what it means to be a wife."

He strode out, leaving her horror-struck and staring at the door as it closed.

Twenty-one

"If the Ladies' Aid Society will operate the Cooperative and Consignment Shop," Bea said, "they can charge a small percentage for every item sold, and we can save a considerable sum with which to buy textbooks for the children. Someone really must see to their education, and who better than us?"

If the other ladies wondered why Bea appeared at the meeting the day after taking her marriage vows, none expressed their curiosity. Bonnets bobbed in agreement all about the rectory parlor. Bea had never actually attended one of the society meetings before. Her father had said ladies of her position did not attend functions so far below their stations. Ladies didn't marry uncouth Americans, either, but she had. So what was one more transgression in the cause of what was right?

She'd contemplated fortifying herself with wine before standing up before the meeting, but the opportunity hadn't presented itself. Deciding it would be no worse than standing up before the entire town on her wedding day, she'd bolstered her courage and done her duty. It certainly outdid staying home and watching the maids move all her belongings into the chamber next to Mac's. For twenty-eight years her life had been no more variable than the gradual changing of the seasons. Mac had thrown her entire world into turmoil and chaos.

"All children should be given the benefit of knowledge," Mrs. Rector agreed. "I think you have an excellent plan, Miss . . . Mrs. MacTavish."

Mrs. MacTavish. She'd even lost her identity. She didn't feel like a Mrs. She certainly didn't feel like a MacTavish.

Hands trembling, Bea gathered up the notes in front of her, nodded, and stepped away from the library table. She was shaking all over by the time she returned to her seat, but she had done it. She had spoken her mind.

Mrs. Rector stood and addressed the crowd. "Such a project would entail each of us choosing set hours to man the store so that there's always someone in charge. Does everyone agree to that?"

Bea could barely focus on the discussion. She'd done her duty, led the charge, proved she wasn't a hopeless imbecile. She thought Mac might argue with that assessment.

She had disappointed him dreadfully, and she had no idea what to do about it.

If this was the best of all possible worlds, the children would stay with her, and she wouldn't have to bear any of her own. She could easily love Buddy and Bitsy. She could teach them their letters and numbers as she'd been taught. And if the estate ever made money again, she could hire a governess to teach them everything she'd never learned. And just in case she couldn't afford private teachers, the village would have a school.

She had to pry the notion of keeping the children out of her head. Surely the earl knew his grandchildren well enough to recognize them. Mac really did have to take them across the ocean before the viscount returned.

That would mean she would never have children of her own. That was what she wanted, wasn't it? Or was it just the process of . . . getting children that she feared?

She had to stop thinking like that. Holding her chin high, she listened to the other ladies discuss her idea. Because it came from her, they favored it, she realized. They really did think of her as above them. That was silly, but if it worked to the children's benefit, she wouldn't question their attitude.

Clara Miller stood and the group quieted. "Won't we need a teacher?"

From the back of the room the widow spoke quietly. "I have a sister who teaches in a ladies' boarding school. I could ask her."

Bea nodded in agreement. It would be wonderful for the widow to have someone to help her about the house. If she had the funds, she'd hire the sister now.

She wouldn't have any funds until she learned to work the estate.

How could she persuade Mac to teach her what she needed to know if he wasn't speaking to her? It was bad enough that he'd spent this last week in the masculine occupations of repairing the outbuildings and rearranging the tenant shares while she was trapped by the feminine details of the wedding. She'd not had time to learn a thing.

How much longer would Mac be with her? Could he help if she showed him the bank letter? Or would he sell the estate to pay the loan? Despair cloaked her like a fog as the meeting ended.

"Miss . . . Mrs. MacTavish," the Widow Black murmured at Bea's elbow as they stepped into the mist of early afternoon.

Bea halted out of the way of the steady stream of departing ladies. She'd exhausted all her courage for the morning, but the widow was younger than she, and frail and careworn, and she needn't fear her in the least.

"How are your children today?" Bea asked with concern.

"Much better, thank you. Granny Elder looks after them when I go out. I don't know what I'd do without her." Mrs. Black hesitated, as if arranging her words, and Bea let her take her time. She knew what it was like to be stumble-tongued.

"A school is such a wonderful idea," the widow said in a rush of words. "If my children could have a better education than I have—" She halted and rethought her sentence before continuing. "I married young and did not pay heed when I was taught. My sister is much smarter and more educated. If only there were some way . . ." Anguish wrote itself across her fair face as she turned it up to Bea. "She's so unhappy where she is, Mrs. MacTavish. If only I could bring her here, I know we would be fine again. She's a hard worker, much healthier than I. Between us, we could produce a crop so I could pay the rent. I can't lose my house. We have nowhere else to go."

Bea knew that the Widow Black had come here as a bride, that she and her husband were said to be related to some wealthy family but had defied their wishes, and that Mr. Black had died of the influenza a winter or so ago. The widow's family could not be especially wealthy if her sister was teaching school, though.

"I will not let him turn you out," Bea said with the fire of determination burning in her heart. "Mr. MacTavish is trying to bring more wealth into this area, but men don't always see both sides of the coin. I wish I could say we could bring your sister here, but without textbooks or funds for the school, I cannot see how. We cannot even persuade the Earl of Coventry to give funds for the church roof."

The widow bowed her head. "I understand. It is more than kind of you to promise me the cottage. I will work as many hours as I can to help earn the textbook money. And I already have several pieces of jewelry made up to sell when the shop is ready."

"Perhaps by summer's end we will have a school for your sister," Bea said kindly, wishing she could offer more. It was a terrible burden wondering if she ought to cut her staff and hurt their families in exchange for the extra coin to fund a school so she could help someone else's.

Walking home, she nervously clasped and unclasped her hands. She could almost wish Coventry would visit so she might give him a piece of her mind. The gentry had responsibility for the people in their care, and he was shirking his. Of course, any man who would neglect his grandchildren didn't have a care for anyone but himself, so she was wasting her energy thinking otherwise.

Perhaps she ought to ask the Widow Black's sister to become governess for the children and sail to America with them. Then Mac could leave immediately, and everything would return to the way it had been before he arrived.

She regarded such a future with trepidation.

Fingers stained with ink from his new fountain pen, Mac stared in frustration at the scratched-out sentences of the letter before him. Now that the community knew his name, it was only a matter of time before the inhabitants of Landingham heard it. There was no sense in delaying the inevitable. He had to tell the Earl of Coventry why he was taking the children to his parents. But the letter would not write itself. Why?

Because he was afraid the earl would take the children away.

Mac dropped his head in his hands and buried his

fingers in his hair. This was ridiculous. The earl had as much right to the children as his own parents did. In all good conscience, he ought to let the man know what was happening.

He couldn't think straight anymore.

He leaned back in the desk chair and stared out the window at the front lawn. He really needed to write this letter to the earl and another to Cunningham telling him to send out the candidates for steward that he'd found. He would feel much better if he could leave Bea in good hands.

No, he wouldn't.

Hell, he'd never been so confused in all his damned life.

He needed physical activity, not introspection.

Abandoning the letter, he strode into the bustle of activity in the hall. He'd almost forgotten—the maids were moving Bea's belongings into the room next to his. It had taken very little for his bag to be carried in, but apparently moving Bea was a major undertaking. Feather dusters and mops and brooms trailed in a steady stream up and down the stairs. Feather bedding and carpets were carried out to be aired.

As he watched a mattress pass by, Mac admitted the real source of his problems. His wife.

Hastily escaping the activity on the stairs, he strode into the damp air outside, with no particular place to go. He had men with more experience than he had working on the mill. Bea's better tenants were busily plowing the valley fields. He had nothing else to occupy his mind except his wife, his lovely, unpredictable, ignorant wife.

He grabbed a scythe from the stable and began whacking at the weeds around the outbuildings. He'd set the gardeners to tilling fields. Which left only him to tend the lawn.

Bea didn't want children. He'd never given children

a thought beyond thinking of them as a necessary by-product of marriage.

Whack. A line of tall grass crumpled gracefully to the ground. A field mouse scampered off to hide elsewhere.

He'd walked into this marriage blindfolded, operating on lust rather than logic. He always got himself into trouble that way.

Whack. A tangle of weeds crashed to the ground, along with a briar cane that narrowly missed his nose. Jumping backward, Mac shook his head and eyed the fallen roses with disfavor. He would bring order out of this mess if it took him all day.

He wasn't sorry he'd married Bea. He'd never met a woman more suited to his needs. It was his damned needs that were the problem.

Bea was a lady, and he obviously needed a whore. What in hell had he been thinking?

More rose canes swept past his nose. He grabbed a wire and began tugging the canes back to their trellis. The place would go to hell in a handbasket without an influx of cash. He'd better start locating her father's bank accounts.

He owned this place now.

Startled at that realization, Mac leaned on the scythe handle to study the rolling hills and fields, hedgerows and trees dotting the landscape as far as his eye could see. This was all his—the land where Bea had sunk her roots deep. Bea had gifted him with everything she owned, everything except the one thing he wanted—herself.

She didn't want children. Hell, he didn't know if *he* wanted children. Did he?

If it meant having Bea in his bed, there was no question about it. He'd gladly take as many as came. He'd have a passel of rusty-mopped, brown-eyed scamps racing around his feet, tumbling from trees and sliding down banisters.

But Bea would be the one to bear his children, the one who would stay here with them, the one who would walk the floors at night while he ventured far and wide.

He was a damned selfish bastard, but then, so was every other man of his acquaintance. Women had children. Men provided for the children they created. He could provide for his extremely well. He could turn this estate around and make it profitable again. He could give Bea and their children everything their hearts desired.

All he had to do was convince his wife of that.

He needed a plan.

She liked kisses. He would start there.

Twenty-two

"Well, children, it's obvious I'm odd man out around you lovebirds," Aunt Constance trilled as she paraded into the parlor that evening in a filmy shawl that dragged the ground, kissed Bea's cheeks, and turned to a taciturn Mac leaning against the mantel. "Now that everything is suitably arranged, you won't need me anymore."

Nerves already worn to a frazzle, Bea didn't respond, and continued seeking a tune at the piano. An uncharacteristically idle Mac picked up a brass statuette on the mantel and put it down again. Every once in a while, she caught him looking at her, but she remained bent over the piano, not meeting his gaze. His dark blue tailed coat molded to his shoulders. In combination with his black velvet waistcoat, it made him look exceedingly elegant, not to mention dangerously masculine—even if Bitsy had chewed a wet spot into his cravat.

"Bea would be devastated without your company," Mac said politely, bowing.

The courteous argument continued throughout dinner, but all concerned knew how it would end. Aunt Constance was ready for London. Her duty there had been done.

"I shall find out what Coventry knows," she declared as she prepared to leave them alone after dinner. "I doubt that rascal son of his has told him the truth. And I'll seek a proper governess for the children. Just you see, I'll be quite useful to you, and I'll be back before you know it."

"Actually, my lady," Mac interjected, "I've been writing a letter to the earl. Perhaps if you learn his location, you could post it for me."

"I knew you would come around to seeing the sense of the situation." She patted his cheek, kissed Bea, and swept from the room.

He was writing to the earl, Bea thought. What did that signify?

She looked up from her music questioningly, but her husband was pacing the room. He'd memorized the location of her father's card table, the tripod stand with the Chinese vase, and the side table with her Wedgwood collection, dodging them without visible notice. Even the heavily ornate velvet chairs her father had ordered last spring seemed dwarfed by her husband's size. He was like a hawk beating his wings against a beautifully designed canary cage.

He belonged on a sailing ship

She bit her lip and turned to the next page. She'd left the cage door open. He could fly away anytime he liked. "I know of a—"

"Bea, I've—"

Their gazes met and held. He looked so very worried. And frustrated. Bea tried to ignore the pounding of her heart, but just thinking of anything remotely in the vicinity of her chest returned the memory of last night, and her cheeks flushed. He had touched her breasts, done things to them that she had never imagined could be done. And now they ached to feel his touch again. She should have spoken to her aunt, and asked if her feelings were normal.

If she didn't look at him, her mind's eye conjured

him in dressing robe and little else, as he had been last night. She'd seen glimpses of his bare chest. She couldn't even look at his waistcoat without wondering what it would be like to touch him, to feel the muscles hidden there, to know the heat of his skin against hers.

"Bea, look at me, please," he pleaded. "I cannot carry on a conversation with an ostrich."

Cheeks pink, she darted a glance in his direction. He was leaning against the piano beside her. She could reach out and touch his knee. The tops of his . . . limbs . . . were twice the size of hers. She started to look away, but he reached over and caught her hand.

"Bea, I'm not your father."

No, he most certainly was not. She had never been aware that her father had . . . limbs. Never even thought about it. And now she couldn't look away from Mac's.

She tried to pry loose the lump clogging her throat, but she managed only a strangled sound. She stared at their clasped hands. His had faint golden hairs on the back. His hands were large and hard and brown— and they held hers very gently.

"Look at me, Bea." He sounded less patient than before.

Obediently, she raised her gaze again. He had amazingly green eyes, and they swallowed her whole. Even though he kept his gaze on her face, she knew that wasn't all he saw. She'd worn a high-necked gown this evening, but she couldn't hide the way it curved outward, practically offering her to his touch. She'd never thought about how women's clothes were designed, but she understood them better now. She rather felt like a goose that Cook had browned and trimmed and presented for his delectation.

"Bea, I've thought about it. I've done nothing else but think about it all day."

She didn't even have to ask what he'd meant. She'd done nothing else but think about it all day as well.

"I want children."

She froze. She studied his serious expression. He looked almost as panicky as she felt, but his jaw had set with determination. She knew that look. Her heart pounded a little louder. Surely he must hear it.

"I . . ." Her tongue seemed too big for her mouth. She had to say something. "I don't know what to say," she finally whispered. That was brilliantly useful and intelligent.

He looked weary but accepting. "I know. I've bungled this badly. I'm sorry. I knew what I wanted, but I didn't even think about what you might want. I'm completely confident that I can make you a good husband, that I can return your estate to a profit, that I won't be here to embarrass you or tell you what to do, just as you planned. But I thought you understood what marriage entailed."

She tried to shrink away, but he held her hand too firmly. She'd said all she could last night and had no courage left to say it again.

He stroked her hand with his thumb, and faint tingles shivered up her arm.

"I've seen you with Bitsy and Bud—"

"Percy and Pamela," she corrected stiffly.

"I'll not call the poor kid Percy," he objected, then plowed on before she could argue. "That's not the point. You're good with children. You would be a wonderful mother. I hadn't thought about it, I know, because I had other things on my mind."

She knew what other things. She tried to pull her hand away, but he wasn't having any of it. "I think I may have found a governess," she said curtly, hoping to distract him.

She succeeded. He looked eager. "Where?"

"The Widow Black's sister is a teacher. She's unhappy with her current situation. I don't know if she's willing to sail to America, though."

"You'll write to her?" he asked anxiously. "I'd rather have them on board ship before the earl shows up on our doorstep."

She nodded in understanding. This was a topic she could handle. "He doesn't sound as if he'd be a good parent, and if he's not married, he'll hand the children over to nursemaids." She hesitated, not certain she ought to broach the subject that played at the back of her mind. "If he would . . . I mean, I could . . ." Flustered, she tried to find her tongue. "I would keep them, if I could," she blurted out hastily.

"Even knowing they're unabashed rascals and that you know nothing of raising children?" he asked.

She ducked her head again. "You're right. I'd need nursemaids and—"

He stroked her cheek and lifted her chin until she looked at him again. "I would give you all the nurse-maids and governesses you would need, but my mother would be devastated if I left them here. I've already told her I'm bringing them. Now I'll have to return and tell her I have a wife she'll never see unless she crosses an ocean. Unless you're willing to sail with me. . . ?"

She shook her head sadly. "I'm being selfish."

"You don't know the meaning of selfish, Bea. I'm the one who bears that blame. If you don't mind caring for my sister's brats, then children aren't the problem, are they?"

No, she supposed they weren't, not the loving of them anyway. The getting and having of them, however . . .

He didn't release her, and she met his gaze without answering.

He stroked her jaw with his thumb, and nodded. "When the time comes, I'll give you nursemaids. For the rest—I'll teach you to want what I want. Now go on up to bed. I'll be up shortly."

He let her go, and, quivering, Bea hastily escaped.

Shaking, she undressed, washed, and donned her nightgown and a robe. She sat before the mirror she'd used as a girl, stroking her hair with the silver-backed brush her father had given her on her twelfth birthday. The familiar objects didn't soothe her.

She was in her mother's room. Her husband had a room on the other side of that door. Her husband. She'd been mad to agree to this. What had she been thinking?

That she liked his kisses. That he made her feel as no man ever had. That she didn't want him to lose those lovely children to a drunken father and an indifferent grandfather.

So at least one reason had been sensible and altruistic. The others were quite insane. Or ignorant. She hadn't realized that warm looks and warmer kisses led to the fires of hell.

She started to braid her hair, but the door beside her dressing table opened, and she could only stare as Mac walked through.

"Don't," he said quietly, reaching for the brush. "Leave it down."

She froze as he lifted her hair off her nape and carefully unwrapped the braid she'd started. His dressing robe hung to the ground, but she could tell he wore trousers and slippers. She wondered what he would look like without them.

He pulled the brush through her hair, then arranged it over the front of her robe. Cautiously, she looked in the mirror. The tanned column of his throat rose above the broad expanse of his equally brown chest. He brushed his knuckles over her cheeks as if he, too, were looking in the mirror.

"You're afraid of what you don't know, Bea."

Of course she was. Any sensible person would be.

"You didn't know about kissing until I taught you, did you?"

She could see where this was heading. She scooted to the edge of her bench and stood up, hoping to find some escape. Mac stepped into the path between bed and wall, blocking her way. Her gaze fell to the satin collar of his partially open robe. She could see a golden brown curl there. Men had hair on their chests.

What else did they have that she didn't know about?

She looked up rather than consider that question. His broad shoulders filled her field of vision.

He smiled grimly. "I'm not any good at courtship, Bea. I'm not much better at pretty words. I don't know how to persuade you, and I won't force you. But I want a real marriage, and I think you will, too, once you understand what that means."

She would almost rather he forced her. Then it would be over, and she'd know what to expect. Taking a deep breath, regretting it the moment his glance dipped to the neckline of her robe, she sought a sensible reply.

"I don't think there can be a real marriage if you're not here most of the time. And I don't think children ought to be left without a father. I'm sorry if I misunderstood what you had in mind. Please, could we not go back to the way things were? And when you're ready, you can sail away and forget this ever happened."

Mac's mouth took on a devilish curve she'd not noticed before, and he shook his head. "Uh-uh, Bea. Now that I have you, I don't want any other woman. I like having a wife who fits in my arms, and melts at my kisses, and makes funny moans in her throat when I touch her."

She stared at him warily, even as her insides ignited like dry tinder at his words. She bumped into the bench as she tried to back away when he reached for her.

"We'll start with kisses, Bea," he murmured, hauling her up against him, "just as you requested."

She closed her eyes when his head lowered and his mouth seared across hers. His strong arm trapped her waist, and her breasts pushed against the unyielding muscles of his chest. She parted her lips for his kiss and sighed in bliss as he accepted the invitation. This much, she dearly adored.

Only when his free hand invaded her robe and cupped her cotton-shrouded breast did she panic and push away. A fire burned in her lower belly, stoked by the big hand that refused to release her.

"One thing at a time, Bea," he murmured, while his fingers pressed the strangely puckered, sensitive peak of her breast. "I'll not sail away until I have you, but I can wait until you no longer fear me." He grinned wickedly. "I shall enjoy the lessons."

With that warning, he released her, belted his robe tighter, and strode out.

Leaving Bea with an ache in her heart as stubborn as the one he'd aroused in her breast.

Twenty-three

"I'm so happy for you, my dear." Aunt Constance enthusiastically hugged Bea. "I know you'll have a happy life with a man like Mr. MacTavish." Catching her swooping hat adorned with peacock plumes, she turned to the large American lingering in the background. "And I know you'll do what is right, sir. I shall write your mother and explain all. Perhaps I shall visit her and explain in person. I've not been to Virginia."

She enveloped a squirming Buddy in her perfumed embrace, shouted at her hired driver not to drop the satchel with her mirrors, then gestured imperiously at James, who hovered just out of reach. "I shall see your mother shortly. Write to her!" she commanded.

James frowned, but Aunt Constance took no notice. Bea cursed herself for forgetting to question her aunt about James. So many things had happened in so short a time that she'd failed to pay attention to her cousin's problems. Bea decided she would write her aunt once she reached town and ask about James. She was much better at writing than questioning in person anyway.

The bank! She'd meant to ask her aunt to find out who the officers were and see if she might persuade them to wait on the loan. She'd have to write about that as well.

"Perhaps I shall rent a London house and you may all come to visit," Constance called cheerfully, stepping into the carriage with the assistance of her driver.

She hung out the window and waved all the way down the drive, until she was out of sight. Bea lifted a sleepy Pamela from Mary's arms and hugged her to her bosom to keep from weeping as fear and loneliness crept in again.

Mac placed a broad, reassuring hand on her shoulder. "We'll be all right, I promise," he murmured. "We can learn together."

She ought to be shouting in joy at his avowal, but at the moment, emptiness blew through her at her aunt's departure. She was on her own now.

The house echoed with silence. The servants retreated to invisibility. No unexpected guests appeared on the doorstep. No last-minute dinner invitations stirred excitement. Standing in the high-ceilinged hallway, glancing from parlor door to study, Bea heard the silence warning her that Mac's departure would be next.

Trying to ignore the aching hollow created by that apprehension, she stopped in the doorway of the stuffy parlor, tilted her head, and gazed at the litter of ornaments with which her father had feathered her nest. It was time to do something about the clutter.

Reaching for the bellpull, she stuck out her chin in determination. This was *her* house now. She didn't need her aunt or Mac to turn things upside down for her. It was high time *she* disturbed things, for a change.

When James appeared, she pointed at the parlor interior. "As the maids have time, I want everything except the furniture hauled to the attics. I want room to move in here." The thought of so much space produced another idea, and she glanced with interest to the heavily draped windows. "And have them start taking down the draperies. I'm certain they're due for airing." She smiled at the thought of the light that would pour in. Perhaps she wouldn't have them re-hung. The lace undercurtains would do just as nicely.

She liked taking charge of things.

Following that discovery, she heard the unmistakable sound of her husband on the stairs. He was a very large part of her life over which she had no control.

Holding his grinning nephew on his shoulders, Mac skidded to a halt in front of her. "I need to take Buddy into Cheltenham so the physician can see if his arm has healed. He doesn't seem to favor it anymore. Want to go with us?"

"To Cheltenham?" Seized by panic at this unanticipated request, she tried not to reveal her fear. "What if someone recognizes you?" Even more than her trepidation at venturing beyond the familiar, she lived in terror that the viscount's men would return and throw Mac into a dungeon.

"I'll call myself Warwick," Mac said. "Even if there are posters with my description, no one will notice me. I'll buy you a pretty bonnet, and we can have a picnic."

He looked so wonderfully certain of himself and his place in the world. Bea sighed at the hopelessness of explaining. Buddy had rumpled Mac's golden brown locks until they half stood on end, and the irresistible cowlick above his forehead fell forward. Her husband's eyes crinkled beneath the curl, and his beguiling grin revealed a flash of strong white teeth—teeth that had nibbled at her lips the night before.

Oh, my. She ought to look away before he discerned her thoughts, but he seemed captivated by his current plan and didn't notice her blush.

"I'll stay and keep Pamela company," she demurred.

Eyes narrowing, Mac swung Buddy down and sent him scampering up the stairs. Straightening, he pinned Bea with a look. "When was the last time you ventured outside Broadbury?"

Bea straightened a wrinkle on her sash. "I've had no need to leave Broadbury."

Her apparent calm didn't impress him. "You've never in your life been outside Broadbury?" At her nod, he pressed his interrogation. "Before I arrived, did you ever leave the damned house?"

She straightened her shoulders and scowled at him. "Your language, sir!" She could see another curse curling his tongue, so she indignantly hastened to explain. "I go to church every Sunday."

"And . . . ?" He lifted his eyebrows.

"I visit the tenants." She straightened her shoulders and glared back.

Mac made a rude noise. "You've scarcely been off your estate, have you?"

She fumbled with her sash again. "There's not much reason to," she muttered, feeling like an idiot. He'd sailed halfway around the world, and she seldom left her property. "I love it here. Why should I go elsewhere?"

He looked disappointed. "Is it that you're happy here, or afraid to go elsewhere?" Before she could answer, he disarmed her by wrapping one of her long side curls around his finger. "Bea, you're an intelligent woman, but you have a damned narrow view of the world. Come with me. I won't let anything happen to you."

She set her chin stubbornly. "I'll be here, looking after Pamela, should the authorities fling you in jail. Perhaps you ought to take James with you to rescue Buddy, should that happen."

Exasperated, he released her. "The day I take that fribble with me will be the day I drown him. I suppose he's just the kind of man you're most comfortable with. Excuse me; I have to change."

He stalked off, leaving Bea near tears. Mac kept pushing her in directions she didn't want to go, and it was easier arguing with him than doing what he wanted.

She sat outside teaching Pamela how to play pat-a-cake as Mac drove the carriage away. She hadn't thought about it, but he might have some difficulty managing the horse and Buddy, too. But the wretched man wouldn't admit to any weakness, curse him.

Gazing over her favorite view of rhododendrons and nodding willow trees, seeing the field where the rabbits played in the evenings, and the lilac where the robin had its nest, she stubbornly saw no reason why she should go beyond all she knew and loved. Why would anyone want to look at a blank ocean for weeks on end?

Of course, she didn't know what an ocean looked like. She returned to patting her fingers against Pamela's chubby hands.

Carrying a sleeping Buddy—sans splint—Mac saw the study lamp burning and stopped to see if Bea was waiting for them. A stack of letters rested on the corner of the desk, ready for James to post them in the morning, but no Bea smiled from the desk.

He wondered who she could be writing to, but he had his hands full and didn't stop to investigate. He couldn't believe lust had led him into marriage with a woman who was so terrified of her own shadow that she would scarcely leave the house. Still, he supposed he didn't need a wife crusading about the countryside.

He'd be satisfied if he could get her into his bed.

Gently curling the sleeping tot over his shoulder, feeling Buddy's moist breath on his neck, Mac climbed the staircase as confused as when he'd last come down it. What did one do with a wife who didn't behave in any fashion that made sense to him?

The sight of Bea tucking in a sweetly sleeping Pamela wrenched what remained of Mac's heart. His wife was absolutely perfect in every way he could imagine—glossy ringlets swinging seductively against pink cheeks as she leaned forward, creamy swells meant for touching barely hidden by her scarf, a curvy waist a man could grasp firmly—

She turned and smiled at him.

"The doctor removed Buddy's splint," she noted in satisfaction, holding out her arms to take Mac's sleeping charge.

Mac was oddly reluctant to release his burden. This might be the only time he'd ever see the rascal holding still, he told himself. "An untrained monkey would be better behaved," he grumbled, grudgingly releasing his nephew into Bea's arms.

"He just needs love and attention," she whispered, loosening the boy's neckcloth as she lowered him to his bed. "I imagine he loved having you to himself all day."

Mac swelled with pride at her recognition of his efforts, and with something else entirely as he watched the deft way she removed the boy's clothes. He imagined those fingers doing the same for him. She'd learned to deal with the children easily these past weeks. How long would it take for her to learn to deal with him as well?

"I can't understand how his father could give him up," he admitted. If he were entirely truthful with himself, he didn't know how *he* would give the boy up. How could he divide his time between the children and Bea and his business and still get anything done? It was a mystery he'd yet to resolve, but he had confidence that a little planning and organization would do it.

Bea shook her head. "The poor tykes, losing their mother and father at the same time, for all practical purposes. He ought to be ashamed."

If he had children of his own . . . Mac eyed the curve of his wife's bosom, the swing of her skirts, and tried to imagine his child growing in her belly, but he couldn't get past the image of planting one.

"I've some work to do," he said gruffly. "I'll join you a little later."

Work to do, his foot and eye. He needed to find an icy stream.

Bea waited nervously in her new bedroom as the time came and passed when Mac usually said good night. Had she truly irritated him with her refusal to go with him today?

She shied away from her usual habit of thinking herself a coward. She'd stood up to him, hadn't she? She was trying to manage her life for once. That wasn't cowardice.

Pacing the room, clutching her robe tighter, she resolved to blow out the lamp and go to bed without waiting for him. What did it matter if they had scarcely seen each other all day, and she'd like to hear about his visit to Cheltenham? She might as well become used to hearing nothing from him.

The door to the hall flew open and Mac marched in, waving her letters in his fist. He wasn't dressed for bed. He'd gone to the study. He'd found her letters.

Folding her fingers into her palms so she wouldn't look guilty, she turned her back on him. Why on earth had she left those there for anyone to see?

"What are these?" he asked without inflection, as if they were of no interest at all. Of course, if they weren't of any interest, he wouldn't have carried them up here.

Bea sat down at her dressing table and picked up

her brush. "They look like letters to me." Deception didn't come naturally to her. The courage to argue or fight didn't come at all. She just wanted it all to go away so he would kiss her and leave her alone.

She desperately wanted him to kiss her and not yell at her.

"To the Bank of London? And Lady Fenimore? Isn't her husband a member of Parliament? For someone who never leaves the house, you certainly have an interesting circle of acquaintances."

He paced up and down like an angry tiger. What on earth did he *think* was in those letters? "One needn't *know* a person to correspond with them," she said cautiously.

"One must know something to correspond *about*," he replied mockingly. "I cannot imagine you're corresponding with the Bank of London about flower posies for the Sunday service. If you know where your father's accounts are, why haven't you told me?"

"Am I not allowed to write letters without arousing your suspicions?" she demanded. "Must I show all my correspondence to you like a child before I post it?"

"Did I say that?" he barked loudly enough to take the roof off. "I just want to know where your father's damned accounts are and why you haven't told me! There are things I could be doing while I'm stuck out here watching the sun rise and set."

"Oh, heaven forbid that you should be bored, or idle your time on such foolishness as family or a lowly estate in the back of nowhere," she shouted back. "Why don't you hurry back to your London business and forget about the children?"

Wide-eyed in horror that she'd said such a thing in such a manner, she swung on the bench to see how Mac reacted. He stood with hands on hips, legs akimbo, staring at her in disbelief. And then his gaze dropped to her dressing gown, and he seemed to mentally shake his head.

Bea glanced down. Her robe had loosened, revealing the filmy lace of her gown. She didn't think the lace revealed more than her morning gown would, but she hastily tightened the sash. She refused to let him distract her that way. "Stop that," she said irritably.

He grinned and swept an appreciative look up and down her length. "Why?"

Insulted, she stood and held out her hand for the letters still in his grasp. "Those are mine. You have no business with them."

He immediately held them behind his back. "What will you give me for them?"

She stomped her foot and blew a stray hair off her cheek. "Nothing. I will simply write them again."

"And what will you say to them, Bea? That you have a dastardly husband who has usurped your estate and will run away with your inheritance as soon as he finds it? Is that what you think of me?"

"Usurped?" Bea clutched her robe closed as she tried to understand this impossible man that she'd married. "You think I'm telling them to hide my accounts?" If it wasn't so awful, it would be laughable.

"I cannot think of any other reason why you would correspond with a bank behind my back. I thought we were partners. Pardon me if I misunderstood my place in the scheme of things." He thrust the letters at her. "It doesn't matter to me what you do with them. I have my own interests and don't need yours."

She wrapped her fingers in the satin folds of her robe and pulled the lapels up to hide her neck. She didn't want the letters. They would scald her fingers if she touched them. She had *hurt* him with her reticence. She would hurt him worse when he discovered the truth: that he married a bankrupt coward.

"I didn't want to scare you away," she whispered.

"I thought maybe I could fix it myself. You'll be gone in a few weeks, and I wanted you to come back." There, she'd said it. She didn't want him to sail out of her life.

He looked poleaxed. He glanced at the letters in his hand, then back at her. "You thought *I wouldn't come back?*"

Hesitantly, she nodded, searching his expression. He looked at her as if she were crazed. That wasn't a good sign.

He threw the letters at the vanity and didn't notice when they slid off. He ran his hands through his already rumpled hair and looked as if he would strangle on the words caught in his throat.

"Let me get this clear," he finally said. "You thought I'd sail away and never come back if I knew what was in those letters? That I'd forget my vows, forget I had a wife, forget any child we might make, and go on merrily without you?"

Put that way . . . Reluctantly, she nodded again. "I'm not much of a prize," she murmured. "I know my limitations. But I thought . . . if I knew you would come back . . ."

"I think, my dear wife, it's time we came to an understanding."

Without warning, he hauled her up against his chest, and while Bea was still gasping from the startlement, he tumbled them both onto the bed, rolled her on her back, and trapped her between his arms, with the wide expanse of his shirt filling her vision.

Bea thought her heart surely stopped beating as she slowly absorbed the full size and strength of her husband. He'd *lifted* her from the floor! He wasn't even breathing hard. His expression looked very determined, and her heart instantly pounded as the weight of his hips pressed into hers.

"You are my *wife*," he said before she could think

of a plea of protest. "The only wife I mean to have. I may be a rotten excuse for a husband. I may be gone six months out of the year. I may not do as you wish or even as I'm told. Sometimes I'm impulsive. But I always, *always*"—Mac leaned on his forearms and brushed the whisper of a kiss across her cheek— "keep my promises."

Bea searched his face uncertainly. He looked more grim than loving.

Certain he held her attention, he finished his declaration. "I *promise* that I will act in all ways as your husband, that you need never question my devotion to our vows. I *will* return, Bea. I may not always be here to see our children born, and I regret that heartily. I'd never meant to have a wife and haven't planned wisely for one, but that doesn't mean I don't want you. You may not like the idea, but you'd best get used to it."

Bea stared up into the determined face of the man she'd married, the man she'd promised to share the rest of her life with, a man who could kidnap children and sail the seas without qualm, and her heart turned over inside her chest. She didn't doubt him in the least. He would come back.

Twenty-four

"My father owed the bank money," Bea whispered. "I wrote to ask them to search again for any other accounts besides the loan."

Mac thought he ought to be paying attention to what she was saying, but he had a voluptuous woman trapped beneath him, and his body wanted to do other things. He supposed he ought to yell at her for not telling him about the debt sooner, but that was obviously what she expected.

His gaze drifted to the full pout of her pink lips. She licked them nervously, and he thought his trousers caught fire. She breathed deeper, and soft ivory curves lifted to push open her robe. If he froze in this position, maybe the robe would come apart before his eyes and he could at long last see all of the woman he'd married.

"You should have told me," he muttered. *Good job, MacTavish*, he chastised himself. *Offend her.* "I could have had my man of business check on it. You needn't worry your—" *Whoops. Better not go down that road.* "We'll work it out together."

That was better. She looked relieved instead of suspicious. She also tried to pry free from his weight, but he wasn't having any of it. They were on a bed together at last. "Is that all you were worried about?

You weren't writing to Parliament to tell them you have a monster in the house?"

She smiled, and his blood heated. He loved it when she smiled at him. She didn't complain that he crushed her, that he was an oaf and a lummox. She looked at him as if he were the only man in the world for her. She was just *shy*. She had a figure men would go down on their knees and weep to possess, and she thought she was ungainly and unlovable. He didn't know whether to shout his good fortune to the sky, or keep the secret to himself. She was his, and no one else could have her now.

"You'll laugh if I tell you," she murmured in embarrassment. "Or you'll yell at me some more. I don't like it when you yell at me."

Mac touched his forehead to hers and tried not to yell at her any more. "I yell; become accustomed to it," he muttered unfeelingly. "I'm not around women much and haven't learned to curb my tongue, so let me apologize in advance for all the times I'll shout and bellow and behave like a raging bull."

She wiggled and tried to escape again, but her breasts were brushing against his coat, and he wasn't about to let her go.

"I don't like being yelled at," she protested, giving up the struggle. "Maybe you ought to become accustomed to not yelling."

Mac grinned and pushed up so he could see her irate expression. "I adore you, you know." He grinned wider as she blinked in surprise. "You don't twitter and flutter, but tell me just what you're thinking, even when you're scared half to death I'll take your head off. I won't, you know."

She watched him warily. "Won't take my head off? How generous."

"I like your head just where it is." He still didn't have the answers he wanted, but he couldn't resist any longer. Lowering his head, he kissed her until her lips parted and she took him deep inside. Here was the stairway to heaven, the golden rungs to the treasure he craved. She kissed him as if she meant it, wrapping her arms around his shoulders, running her hands into his hair, pressing upward as if she craved the feel of him as much as he did her. Groaning against her mouth, Mac stroked her tongue with a swift, sure intimacy.

She accepted his possessive kiss without protest, taking as well as giving, and, daringly, he pressed further, cupping the full weight of her breast. Desperately needing to explore, fearful of her freezing up again, he nipped at the corner of her lip to keep her occupied while he invaded her robe. She inhaled sharply as he located the pointed peak straining against her nightdress, but she didn't jerk away.

"Are you still afraid of me?" he asked, propping himself up to better see her face. She watched him cautiously, but he thought he saw her eyes darken with the same desire that was spilling through him like hot, thick molasses.

"Yes," she whispered. "No," she corrected. Then, "Maybe."

"Or are you afraid of what happens when I touch you like this?" He gathered her breast in his hand and tormented the peak until she squirmed beneath him.

"I'm afraid of where this leads," she admitted softly.

"Because you don't know what will happen, and ignorance leads to fear." He was beginning to understand her a little better now. His Bea did things cautiously, without the impulsive haste he often employed. If he could only learn patience . . .

She nodded uncertainly, biting the lip Mac wanted to taste again. He wanted to pull up her gown and have at her and put an end to her fear right now, but if he wanted her warm and willing when he returned from Virginia, he'd better play this slowly. This game of advance and retreat was not without its challenges— it was certainly teaching him patience.

"I can tell you what will happen," he offered, "but it won't help. It's better if you let yourself feel it happen." He released her breast and slid his hand down to test the curve of her waist, cupping the splendor of her hip and buttock. Warily, she froze beneath his touch, and he sighed in defeat.

"Tell me," she demanded. "I want to know. I don't understand how babies get there. I don't want to look like Mrs. White."

He bit back a desperate chuckle and shook his head. "Dear heart, there is no chance of that. Is that what you're worried about? How you'll look?"

She shrugged awkwardly and looked away. "I don't know *anything*."

Hell, he'd never thought to give a course on where babies came from, but if that was what it took to get where he wanted to go . . .

"All right," he agreed grudgingly. "If I try to explain, I don't want you laughing in my face or weeping or running away. I'm not good at teaching, and I'd much rather show you, but if it's an education you want first, I'll attempt it."

The look on her face was priceless—as if he'd offered her all the world's gold.

Doggedly, he sought a metaphor she'd understand. "Babies grow from a man's seed," he said slowly. At her look of disbelief, he tried harder. "A man plows and plants his seed and babies grow inside a woman's . . ." He didn't know the right words. He covered her abdomen with his hand to show her. She wiggled and stared down where his hand rested. His groin swelled until he thought his trousers would cut off all blood flow.

She wasn't helping him any. She wiggled her hips

beneath his to see better, and he had visions of spreading those long legs she kept hidden and plowing her field right now. He was about to lose control again.

He slid his hand lower, rubbing her where they both needed his touch. She made a strangled sound as his fingers pressed there. Even through the linen, he could tell she was wet. "You have a hole," he said crudely, rubbing until she shifted her legs apart and gasped at the discovery he showed her. "And I have a pole." He caught her hand and pressed it to the bulge in his pants.

She giggled nervously and tried to jerk away, but he wouldn't allow it. If he had to explain, she had to listen. He rolled onto his side, and rubbed her hand up and down the length of his "pole," pleasuring himself as best as he could under the circumstances. She made funny little sounds and resisted, but at his groans, her gaze snapped up to his face.

"Does it hurt?" she asked in anguish.

"Does it hurt when I touch you?" he asked more savagely than he'd intended. He was beginning to feel like a bloody fool, but she watched him as if he were the answer to her prayers.

"It . . . it feels . . . funny," she admitted.

"It will feel even funnier when I put my pole inside you," he grumbled. "And if you'd just let me do it instead of talk about it, this lesson would go much faster."

She transferred her hand from him to herself, and he buried his face in her shoulder and almost moaned rather than watch her self-discovery.

"We're made to fit together?" she asked in wonder.

"Want me to show you?" Hopefully, he raised his head. Now she was looking at him in doubt. *Ah, hell.* He began unfastening the buttons of her nightgown. He wanted some reward for this torture.

She didn't even seem to notice what he was doing. "And that's how you plant a baby?" she asked, as if he'd just told her babies sprang from cabbage leaves.

"Yup." The last button popped open and, without a by-your-leave, he slid his hand across the creamy silk of her breast. He felt her inhale and not exhale again. Figuring she'd remember to breathe eventually, he leaned over and took her nipple in his mouth.

She screamed—a tinkling, breathless half scream of awe and protest. Mac was beyond caring. She was all cream with raspberry and cinnamon on top, and he'd wanted this for so long, he couldn't stop if the devil paid him to.

"Mac! Wait, you can't . . . We can't . . ."

"I damned well can. And so can you." He spread the bodice open and cupped both mounds into handfuls of sin and tongued his way around both until she was writhing and shoving them in his face and fighting him at the same time. Without a qualm, he rolled onto his back and carried her on top of him. Now she spilled from the lacy linen so he could mold her to his hands, suck deeply, and never let her go.

Bea shivered and shook and tried to prop herself off Mac but she was melting in too many places and couldn't fight him as well as herself. He drew on her breast and her hips pressed downward without her consent. He cupped her . . . her bottom . . . and she lifted her breast to the breathtaking pleasures of his mouth. She had no control over her own person.

Emptiness yawned inside her, driving her to do things she couldn't believe she'd ever dream of doing. Mac urged her to do them. He caught her hips and pushed them against his . . . his *pole*. And she opened her legs as if in invitation, and if it weren't for all the layers of their clothes, he could—

She couldn't bear to think about it. She understood part of it now. He would put . . . himself . . . inside

her. Somehow he would fit inside her, and he would
spill his seed there, and a baby would start to grow.
Panic came with knowledge.

"How does it get *out*?" she cried, pushing away
from hands that touched her everywhere, hands that
multiplied until they plied her breasts and tugged her
hips and rode her gown upward until her legs were
practically . . . *naked*. She gasped and shoved away
and tried to pull her gown down while rolling breathlessly out of his reach. She was all wet and aching
where he'd touched her.

Quickly rolling to his side, Mac stopped her frantic
tugs, catching her flying hands and holding them still
while he caught his breath and admired what he'd
uncovered. Bea shivered at the avidity of his gaze as
he lingered on the expanse of . . . limb . . . uncovered.
No man had ever seen her . . . limbs. They quivered,
and the place between them throbbed and grew wetter
beneath his stare. She thought she might die of shame.
Or need.

She needed to be touched there.

She was a wanton woman. She wanted the bestial
coupling the other women spoke of with such disgust.
She wanted him to touch her, to do what he'd done
earlier, to—

"Get what out?" he asked, looking as dazed as she
felt now that she'd quit fighting.

She couldn't remember her question. Her gown
barely covered the place he'd touched, and she could
swear he was seeing right through the fabric. Her bodice still gaped open, and she lay as exposed as a
Roman statue.

He looked as if he might devour her if she didn't
answer immediately. She must have torn open his
neckcloth in their struggles, and she could see the
tanned, smooth skin revealed by his open shirt. A curl
of hair wrapped around the placket, and she longed

to reach out and touch it. She wanted his shirt off. She wanted to see what he looked like.

She wanted to see what he looked like all over.

Mortified, she nervously tried to turn away. "Babies," she whispered. "They're *big*. How do they get out? It sounds . . . it sounds horribly painful."

That silenced him. His hand released hers, and she hastily brushed her gown down as far as she could reach. She was afraid to look at him as she buttoned her bodice.

He rolled over onto his back and stared at the ceiling.

Afraid she'd gone too far this time, Bea warily turned her head to watch him. His big chest rose and fell as if he slept, but his eyes were wide open. She wasn't at all certain that she wanted to end the lesson here. There seemed to be so much more to learn. . . .

"They come out the same way they go in, Bea," he said wearily. "And yes, they say it hurts. And if I'm being perfectly honest—and I don't want to be, so give me some credit here—sometimes women die of it. My sister did."

They both fell silent and stared at the ceiling. The lamp oil burned low and the flame flickered uneasily into shadows.

He would be here for the planting, but not necessarily for the harvest.

Twenty-five

In a decidedly subdued humor, Mac took breakfast with Bea the next morning. She didn't seem to be any more chipper than he was.

Stabbing his ham, he concluded that when he leapt without thinking, he always did it from the tallest cliffs available. He should have found a mindless wife who was willing to rut and breed without a second thought.

But he didn't want a mindless wife. He loved the way Bea took a subject and methodically studied it inside and out. He loved the way she lit up like fireworks when she grasped the lesson. Of course, last night's lesson hadn't led to the fireworks he'd hoped.

"I had James post your letters," he said, to break the silence. "You still haven't told me what the letter to Lady Fenimore was about."

She paled even more, if that was possible. "I won't yell, I promise," he assured her. It wasn't a difficult promise. After leaving her room, he'd found a bottle of brandy and worked his way through a good portion of it. His head pounded like the very devil.

"There was this awful man . . ." she began haltingly, reaching for her teacup and sipping while she gathered her courage.

Mac immediately felt outrage building at any man

daring to be awful to his shy wife, but he pressed it down, and forced himself to listen patiently.

She didn't look at him. "He wrote terrible letters to the *Times* saying women were too stupid and their minds too fragile to learn, and that they'd only cause trouble if they were given books."

Mac relaxed a fraction. He'd have to remember that truly "awful" men didn't inhabit Bea's world. Except him, of course. How did Lady Fenimore fit in?

"And then some other man wrote and complained about do-gooder preachers who wanted to teach the miners' children when everyone knew the lower classes had no need of education." She set down her cup and poked idly at her eggs.

He could see where this was going now, and he settled back with his coffee to enjoy a good tale. He admired his wife's profile as she spoke. She had a lovely, narrow nose, a wide forehead, and gently rounded cheekbones that softened her features into a beautiful whole. Perhaps she wasn't a modern perfection of beauty, but he saw intelligence and caring, and her gentleness soothed his restlessness.

"I . . . Well, I was upset," she continued carefully, "and I was feeling particularly put-upon because Papa wouldn't allow me to order a book I wanted, and I sat down and wrote exactly what I thought of such a narrow attitude. I sent the letter to Nanny Marrow, because I knew she'd understand. She wrote back to tell me her employer had said the very same things and that perhaps we should correspond."

Mac smiled. So she wasn't entirely timid inside her head—just cowed by circumstances. "Her employer was Lady Fenimore, and she actually listened?"

She darted a glance in his direction and, apparently satisfied that he didn't mean to rant and rave, she smiled and returned to her eggs. "She not only listened, but showed my letters to her husband. He quotes from them in his speeches to Parliament."

Bea's intelligence and eagerness to learn had given her the ability to see and write far more sensibly than most educated men. What might she have been had she been properly trained?

Mac let the realization sink in as he stared over the top of his coffee cup at the gentle woman with head bent demurely, her delicate ringlets gracing a slender neck some men would readily snap for the defiance hidden behind her civility. Her anxious sideways glance reminded him he hadn't spoken.

"I think I'm grateful you're too shy to tell me all your opinions," he said dryly. "You might tell me what you really think of me."

She blinked in astonishment, and he felt worse than a heel. What did she think he would do, scold her like her father? He groaned and rolled his eyes at her inability to see the difference. "The town has no school, does it?"

"Mr. and Mrs. Rector sometimes give private lessons," she said slowly, "but mostly in deportment and religion. We'd hoped to earn money for textbooks with the consignment shop, and possibly hire the widow's sister, but that's as far as we've planned."

Mac nodded his aching head. He could definitely see the advantages of having an educated wife. He wondered if he could find a teacher who taught sex. Not a wise idea.

Before he could open his mouth, James hurtled through the door, a vision in scarlet and gold. "The earl's men are at the inn!" he yelled in panic.

Mac ground his teeth together and tried not to react hastily. He lifted his cup and regarded the footman casually. "And your meaning is . . . ?"

Bea's dark eyes were wide with fear, but she continued staring at her plate as if nothing unusual had been said. He'd give her credit for reacting with much better caution and patience than he did.

"They're looking for a Lachlan MacTavish," her cousin said accusingly. "And they don't appear to be in a good humor about it."

"No, I don't imagine they are," he answered, reaching for his newspaper. "Are you sure they're Coventry's menials, or would the viscount happen to be swinging his weight around in his father's name?"

James glanced at Bea, who sat calmly sipping her tea, then with a little more caution than earlier, straightened his posture and awarded Mac his attention. "I can ask Digby. He'll know the difference."

Mac nodded. "Thank you, I'd appreciate that."

As soon as James disappeared, Bea turned to him with an anxious gaze. "What now? Is your ship ready?"

"There are a few unfinished details, and it's not loaded. I'd rather not make a voyage without a profit if possible." Emulating Bea's calm in the face of danger, Mac didn't immediately heave the children into a carriage and flee, as he had the first time. "I might take a chance on reasoning with the earl, but if those are Simmons's men down there, we'd be wasting our time. How honest are your neighbors when confronted with questions from strangers?"

Bea considered the question. "I cannot say for certain, but they tend to be closemouthed on the whole. Since they think you're helping me, they won't reveal your presence should they believe the men mean you harm."

Mac nodded. "It's like that at home. Digby will steer them away, if I ask. It's just a matter of how stubborn the men are. I think we should take the children away for a few days, as a precaution, and to make the townspeople easier."

Bea stared at him as if he'd gained a second head. "Go away? Where?"

"The Carstairses offered me the use of their hunting box. If you don't think we can handle the children on our own, we could take Mary with us." He waited to see how she accepted that. He couldn't believe she was unwilling ever to leave home. Surely it had just been a matter of lack of opportunity.

She looked a little sick. Her cheeks lost color, and her eyes grew wide and panicky. Still, she didn't immediately object. "Perhaps James is fussing over nothing."

"He may be a fribble, but I don't think he's a moron. We'd better start packing. I have no idea what kind of amenities a hunting box affords." He stood up and threw his napkin on the table, his mind already leaping to the children and their requirements. If worse came to worse, he could leave Bea and the children hidden and ride off in the opposite direction to lead his brother-in-law astray.

Bea rose slowly, her knuckles whitening with the tightness of her grip as he assisted her from the chair. "I'll have the stable boy bring a trunk down from the attic. I think one will fit in the carriage."

She sounded terrified. Mac tilted her chin until she looked up at him. "Trust me," he ordered. "I won't let anything happen to you or the children."

She studied him as if he were all that stood between her and the devil. Then, swallowing hard, she nodded. "How many days?" she asked nervously.

"Pack for a week, and then we will be more than prepared."

"A . . . week," she replied faintly and without the least assurance. "I'll try."

He left the problem to her. He had to send instructions about the mill and the plowing of the lower fields, write Cunningham of this new development, and talk to Digby without the strangers noticing. Mind already dancing three steps ahead, Mac allowed his wife to escape without further question.

Striding into the parlor to look for a pen he'd left on the writing desk, he blinked in puzzlement when he veered his path around an ottoman that wasn't there, and opened the desk without juggling three porcelain shepherdesses. *Odd.* But he didn't have time to question. Finding the pen, he hurried to the study.

A week. In a hunting box. She could do it, Bea told herself firmly. People did it all the time. Just because her father had warned her of all the dangers in the wide world beyond the protection of her own didn't mean she had to believe him. Not any longer.

If she kept her mind on the hustle and bustle of preparation, she might not panic over leaving Broadbury for the first time in her life.

She might fret about highwaymen or broken carriage wheels or the earl's men or if she'd brought enough food and who could cook it, but she wouldn't worry about the stares of strangers or carrying on conversations with people she didn't know.

Her abysmal shyness really was the least of her concern, she realized as Pamela wailed at the commotion, and Buddy escaped the nursery to take a ride on the banister and disappear. It was impossible to concentrate on oneself when surrounded with the chaos of an entire household.

Rounding up Buddy as he tried to follow Mac to the stable, promising him a horsie ride if he behaved, Bea handed both children fresh biscuits from the kitchen, then hurried into her chamber, where her maid railed and heaved gowns all over the bed. Mac had absolutely no idea of the turmoil he'd created.

"Simple gowns, for a country holiday," Bea tried to explain, as if she had any notion of what that might entail.

"This *is* the country, madam," Letty reminded her in the haughty tones she'd assumed since being raised to the position of personal maid. "One needs morning gowns and dinner gowns and riding habits and—"

"Don't be silly. I don't ride. Dinner will be a picnic, and a walking gown will suffice. Be certain to pack enough lingerie, and a few gowns will do."

"But madam, if I do not come with you, who will brush and press them? And who will polish your shoes? And fix your hair? And—"

"Perhaps there will be a skeleton staff there. We can't worry about it now. Mr. MacTavish wishes us to leave immediately, and we cannot disappoint him."

Letty looked at her shrewdly. "Aye, and it's Mr. MacTavish who will be the death or the saving of us all. You've never left this place before."

Bea mustn't think about that. The safety of Mac and the children must come first.

Mac looked grim as he found his wife up to her ankles in petticoats and linen, with Pamela clinging to her neck. "They're the viscount's minions, all right," he said. "Digby's giving them his bland butler's face, but I don't know how long he can hold them off. Are you ready yet?"

Was she ready yet? The children were in a state of hysteria, the servants were rapidly reaching that condition, and he wanted to know if they were ready yet.

"If we take only the barouche, we cannot take Cook or staff," she warned. "Unless the hunting box has servants, we will be all but living like gypsies."

He shrugged that off without any notion of the calamity facing him. "We'll manage. Is this the trunk? I'll take it down."

Bea gaped as he shouldered the heavy trunk and proceeded out the door as if he hadn't thrown an entire household into complete turmoil and terrified her into a shivering ninny. *We'll manage?* Was the man insane?

Or was she insane for following him?

By now, it seemed a moot point. She'd married a total stranger, an American accustomed to roaming vast open spaces, and she might as well accept her fate. From here on out, she must give up any notion of peace or tranquillity and allow the rapids to carry her where they would.

She only wished she knew if hunting boxes had separate bedrooms.

Twenty-six

A leather trace broke before they were two miles down the road. Bea bounced Pamela in her arms and tried to ignore Mac muttering unpleasantries about untrained stable boys as he patched the leather to hold until they reached the next town.

She eyed the field of unfamiliar crops in the valley spreading below the road. What did they grow there? If she thought about things like that, she wouldn't spend all her time looking over her shoulder for the viscount's men or worrying about leaving the safety of the home she knew and loved. A curiosity disloyal to her father's memory blossomed at this first glimpse of the world outside her beloved one.

Pamela threw her small silver cup out of the carriage, and no one noticed until Bea tried to find it when the child whined for her milk. She had to unpack one of the stoneware mugs in the picnic basket and persuade Pamela she could sip from a big cup just as easily.

"Giyyap," Buddy yelled, bouncing up and down on the seat. "Are we there? I want my pony." His biscuit dropped on the floor, and he dived under Bea's skirts to locate it.

"I swear, I shall be rich again and I'll own two

broughams, hire a driver, and burn this rackety barouche," Bea vowed.

Mac threw an exasperated glance over his shoulder as Buddy crawled under the seat. "Can't you make them behave?" He hauled the boy up by the back of his coat while hanging on to the reins with one hand.

"Animal training and child rearing are not among my accomplishments," Bea muttered in a fit of temper.

"Piano playing and ornamenting your castle are, I know." Disgruntled, Mac returned to the reins in time to avoid hitting a large rock in the stream they crossed.

Figuring she had the choice of dumping the picnic basket over her husband's head, ordering the carriage to halt and walking home, or finding some diversion for Buddy, she remembered the wooden pull toy she'd packed in another basket. If these were the adventures of world travel, she'd rather stay home, thank you very much.

As the shadows of evening grew longer, they reached the rutted path Mac thought might lead to the hunting box, and Bea was reduced to praying for a skeleton staff. She wouldn't worry about viscounts in the woods or bogeymen around any corner, if only she could have a maid or a cook.

She and the children remained in the carriage as Mac grimly stalked up to the front door of the square stone cottage at the end of the drive. She could see a light in a window toward the rear, so someone had to be home. She prayed they were patient, kindly people.

If they had to stay at a public inn this night, the viscount would hear of them of a certainty. No one could hide two children like Buddy and Pamela. And she and Mac weren't exactly invisible.

The front door opened. Through the dusk of fading day, Bea could discern a stooped old man dressed in black. Surely this was the right place. A cook, at least, *Please, let there be a cook*. She couldn't boil water if her life depended on it.

Mac returned, his expression unreadable as he helped her down. "It's the right place, but they only have a retired couple here as caretakers. Dav brought the damned dogs here, so they know who we are. I believe we're expected to go out and admire their new abode come morning."

"I shall fawn all over the dogs if I might just have a moment's peace." Bea lifted a sniveling Pamela to her shoulder and waited for Mac to fish Buddy from the floor.

A smidgen of pride lodged in her heart as Mac looked down at her with something akin to admiration instead of the grim expression he'd been wearing all day.

"You've been a saint," he murmured, settling Buddy in one arm and wrapping the other around Bea's shoulders. "I had considered giving them to the gypsies the first day I dealt with them."

Before she knew what he intended, he brushed a heated kiss across her lips that scorched straight down her spine and all the way to her toes. As if he had done nothing unusual, not to mention totally unnerving, he proceeded up the walk to the house.

Wearily, Bea allowed an elderly woman to escort her and the children up the stairs to a dark-paneled bedchamber while Mac unloaded baskets and trunks. The candle the woman carried did nothing to illuminate the heavy draperies and old walnut furniture, but Bea was interested only in feeding the children and tucking them into bed. At her request, the woman showed her a small dressing room where Buddy could use a servant's cot and Pamela could be settled into a makeshift cradle fashioned from a huge dresser drawer.

By now, the children were hungry, irritable, and anxious about their new surroundings. Bea spread a cloth on the rug, settled the children onto it, and handed them bits of bread and cheese while she set out the rest of the food. Their hostess offered to bring up fresh ale and milk, promising to do better in the morning.

By the time Mac unhooked the traces, fed and groomed the horses, and carried the massive trunk up the stairs, Bea was softly singing nursery rhymes to a contented Pamela in her arms, while Buddy pushed his new toy horse around the carpet. Candlelight illumined the golden locks of the children, but it was the serenity of Bea's expression that caught Mac's breath and nearly brought him to his knees. He'd married an angel.

It wasn't lust collapsing his lungs at her beatific smile. She'd had a horrific day. She'd been driven from her home, trapped for hours with hysterical children, with no idea of where she was going or what they'd find when they got there. She had to be as exhausted, mentally and physically, as he was. And despite the storm clouds hovering over them, she smiled at him as if he had just delivered the world's treasures to her feet.

"They really are good children," she said, innocent of the path of his thoughts.

"Just like Napoleon was a good little soldier," he agreed, hauling Buddy off the dresser drawer he was using as the first step in his mountain-climbing expedition to the top.

She chuckled at his comparison, then took Buddy and carried him off to a side room. The children had their own room. Mac grasped that fact swiftly and with appreciation. He would have his wife to himself, in one bed.

Elation and terror followed that thought. With Marilee's children as a forceful reminder of what childbirth wrought, he could no longer go back to thinking of a lusty romp in the hay without considering the consequences.

As Pamela woke and held her chubby arms out to him, Mac succumbed to the onslaught of emotion he'd attempted to avoid since the first day he'd seen his sister's babes. Wrapping his niece in his arms, nuzzling her neck until she cooed in delight, he vowed silently to defend her against all harm, whatever it took. These children—and his wife—came before all else.

His whole world shifted, and the ground seemed to crumble under him at this revelation. He really did want a family of his own. It was no longer a notion, but a need.

A need that brought its own problems. Mac knew he must think twice about dealing with children on a regular basis. He not only had to consider risking Bea's life in childbirth, at a time when he could possibly be at sea, but he had to consider the endless costs of hiring a houseful of servants to raise and teach children in his absence.

The news that Bea's estate was mortgaged worried him. He knew he could make the estate profitable. He didn't know if he could pay for all Bea's servants and the improvements he wanted to make, still pay a mortgage, and keep his shipping investment. He didn't dare tell Bea that. He didn't think selling her home would be an acceptable alternative in her mind.

Bea returned to take Pamela off to bed, interrupting his thoughts. Stripping off his coat and throwing it over a chair back, Mac watched horror etch her features when she returned to catch him stripped to his shirtsleeves.

He threw his waistcoat to join his coat and bent to help her with the dishes. "There's a dressing screen, and I brought up hot water. You can wash while I finish here."

She glanced frantically to the huge curtained bed, to him, and to the door. Mac figured she was calculating the likelihood of escape. Folding the blanket, he shook his head. "Don't, Bea. I'm sorry I've brought you into this mess, but running won't help. We have a lifetime to live together, so we might as well work out some way of doing it."

Her mouth opened and shut in that helpless manner he remembered from the first day they'd met. Bea would never leap without looking, as he did. She'd think everything over three times first. Maybe together they could find some balance.

"I . . ." She threw a nervous glance to the bed again. "Isn't there another room?"

"They're not prepared for guests, Bea. We can manage." He wasn't at all certain of that. He'd not been with a woman in a very long time, and to have the woman he desired above all others beside him . . .

Muttering imprecations at his lofty sentiments about family, Mac left her to undress on her own while he hauled the basket down to the kitchen. How the hell did he persuade his recalcitrant wife that the marriage bed was the best part of living together?

He couldn't. He'd have to rely on the attraction between them, the one that nice big bed would enhance. Hope rising, he hurried back to the bedchamber where Bea waited—

Asleep, curled in a cocoon of exhaustion and enveloping nightclothes.

Resigned, Mac undressed and climbed in beside her. Crossing his arms behind his head, he stared at the darkness of the ceiling. All he needed to do now was convince himself that this baby stuff wasn't an insurmountable obstacle, that he could defend three innocents and a village, and maybe bring down a few temples with his bare hands, all in the space of a few weeks, and he'd be just fine.

Twenty-seven

Bea scrambled from the bed at dawn at the first sound from the children's room. She tried to pretend she didn't see the large man denting the pillow on the other side of the bed, but he was a little too spectacular to ignore. In the early light, Mac's unshaven jaw looked so male she thought her knees would melt into jelly. She didn't remember him coming to bed. She grabbed a dressing robe and ran to Pamela.

She'd spent a night in her husband's bed, and nothing had happened. Marveling, she changed Pamela's cloths and lifted the burbling infant from her crib. Buddy slept as soundly as his uncle.

Or as soundly as she thought his uncle slept. When she returned to the bedroom, Mac was up and looking like a surly bear as he sleepily fastened trousers over his nightshirt. She would have to stop thinking how glorious he looked with the muscles of his chest rippling just below the thin linen and his hair tumbling onto his forehead—and remember what he meant to do to her if she let him.

He smiled slowly at the sight of Pamela waving her chubby fists, demanding to be lifted into his arms. It was so simple at that age, Bea thought wistfully as Mac picked up his niece and tossed her lightly. Hugs and kisses meant love and affection to a child. Hugs and kisses between adults seemed to mean carnal lust and pain and childbirth.

Mac leaned over and kissed Bea's cheek, and heat flooded through her. Well, maybe kisses weren't all bad.

"I bet you would look lovely with a baby at your breast," he whispered wickedly in her ear as Pamela pulled at his hair.

Bea's breasts jutted against her robe, and she became uncomfortably aware of the way the peaks pearled into aching knobs at the image he inspired. *She* might not want a baby, but her breasts did. So much for her theory of the innocence of kisses. Even words could be carnal.

"You're unseemly," she retorted, before grabbing a dress and fleeing for the screen. Seizing her corset, she hooked it defiantly, not bothering to relace it.

"And you're a virgin angel with eyes of flashing passion," Mac murmured as Bea emerged from behind the screen. He dropped Pamela into her arms.

She'd have to remember not to give him time to think up outrageous comments like that. *Eyes of flashing passion, indeed.* Setting Pamela down on the rug, Bea tried to brush her thick hair into some semblance of neatness, but she couldn't help checking her eyes to see if they were any different from the ones she remembered.

All she could see were the black circles under them from lack of sleep.

Wearing a clean shirt and still fumbling with his rumpled neckcloth, Mac ambled from behind the screen and immediately leaned over to press a kiss to the top of Bea's head. "I think I shall insist that we share a chamber when we return. I like watching you brush your hair." He checked her mirror to straighten the knot in his tie and grinned at her reflection. "And

I like being behind closed doors with you so I can kiss you whenever I like." This time he tilted her face to his and kissed her more thoroughly.

Gasping in surprise and outrage, then heating rapidly beneath the fire of his kiss, Bea could no more fight him than she could fight herself. She grabbed his arm to steady her balance as he pressed her backward, and the surge of muscle beneath his shirt at her touch nearly shocked her into releasing him. He was so warm and hard and . . . *Oh, my.*

He looked nearly as stunned as she felt when he stepped away. His eyes lit with satisfaction as he noted the way her breasts heaved. Her hand flew to her waist in hopes of catching her breath beneath her tight corset.

"I'm going down to tell the caretakers I'll pay for more staff," Mac announced. "Since we're here with no other demands on our time, I want you to myself for a while."

He strode out, pulling on his coat and waistcoat. He'd sizzled any working part of her brain, and the only parts of her left functioning didn't seem to recognize the danger he represented. She had the terrifying notion he'd just burned the last bridge between them.

Not waiting for Mac to return, Bea dragged Buddy from bed, wrestled both children into clothes, re-straightening her clothing and hair, then steered Buddy and carried Pamela downstairs. She still had fruit and bread and assorted foods in the baskets, but the children needed milk for their breakfasts. She'd have to see what the kitchen could produce.

The housekeeper bustled out at the sound of them coming down the stairs. Chirping excitedly, she showed them the dining room, proclaimed "Mr. Warwick" to be an exceptional man, and began carrying in plates of food and pitchers of milk and pots of tea.

Mac arrived just as Pamela slapped a spoon in her

oatmeal and splattered it all over Bea and herself. "Heathen Indians behave better than that," he scolded gently, removing the spoon from her sticky hand as she giggled and tried to plant her fingers where the spoon had been.

"Nurse hit her for that," Buddy said pragmatically, scooping up eggs on his toast as if he'd never been taught table manners. "She's a bad girl."

"You're both inveterate brats, but you aren't bad," Mac corrected, holding Pamela's hands until Bea could remove the bowl and wipe them both clean. "And if you'd listen to Miss Bea once in a while, you would learn some manners."

"Pammy calls her Mama," Buddy said through a mouthful of toast, watching them with suspicious eyes.

"Well, she's really your aunt, but Pamela doesn't know better. What would you like to call her?" Freeing his niece once she was clean again, Mac tousled his nephew's hair. "She's not Miss C anymore, so we can't call her that."

Bea held her breath as the little boy turned his gaze in her direction. She was desperately trying not to get too attached, but she feared that if Mac didn't take them away soon, she'd cry her heart out once they were gone.

"She doesn't look like Mama," Buddy answered with a slight quiver of his lips.

Mac sat down beside him and smeared some jam on another piece of toast. "Nope. Your mama had hair like mine, and she was small and smiled all the time. I can remember her laughing and singing up and down the halls at home."

Tears gathered in Bea's eyes at his recitation of a precious memory. It had to pain him, but the boy needed these memories to replace the bad ones.

Buddy nodded solemnly. "She sang me to sleep.

And called me baby doll." He grimaced at the recollection.

"She loved you very much, and I know she was sorry she had to go away, but sometimes God needs more angels," Mac said quietly. "Your mama would make a lovely angel, don't you think?"

Bea pulled a handkerchief from her sleeve and wiped her eyes. How could a man so thickheaded and sure of himself also be so gentle and understanding?

Pamela reached over to tug the lacy hankie from Bea's hands and, laughing, flung it at her oatmeal bowl. Bea rescued it with a watery smile and blew the babe a kiss.

"Won't I ever see Mama again?" Buddy asked, fighting a sob.

Bea had never thought to ask the child what he thought of events; she'd been too busy trying to stay ahead of them herself. Perhaps they'd all needed this time away to sort things out instead of letting the river of life carry them mindlessly on its current. Bless Mac for making the best of what they were given.

"She's watching you from heaven," Mac told Buddy, "and you'll be with her someday. But there are a lot of things to do down here first. Do you think she'd like to watch you go fishing today?"

That successfully ended the tears. Shouting with excitement, Buddy tore out of the room to fetch his new toy horse. When he was gone, Mac met Bea's eyes. "I should have spoken to him sooner, shouldn't I?"

"He might not have been ready sooner," she suggested. "He's been uprooted and transplanted and needed time to settle in a little."

"There will be more uprooting and transplanting ahead," Mac said worriedly, reaching for the coffeepot.

"Not if you're with them. You're their security now." She wanted to sound reassuring, but she knew nothing of children. She simply recognized his concern. And admired it.

The children weren't the only ones she'd miss when he was gone.

That was a terribly unsettling thought. She wouldn't think about the hollow it left in her middle. Life without Mac's shouting and blustering didn't bear consideration.

She gently wiped Pamela's mouth and handed her a small strip of buttered toast to mash in her fingers. She'd watched Mary, and thought she might have grasped the basics of feeding infants. Give them something small and sticky and mushable and eventually it reached their mouths.

"That's a problem," Mac replied gloomily to her earlier comment. "I'll have to go back to desk duty in my father's business if I want to be around when they need me."

"They'll adjust to your mother and father," she suggested. When he didn't reply, she cast a glance in his direction. He didn't seem to be happy with the thought. "You have to make your own life," she said gingerly. "If you're not happy, how can they be?"

He saluted her with his cup and a wry smile. "That's a good argument. I'll remember it." He quickly sobered. "What about you, Bea? Are you happy?"

"I always thought so." She helped herself to toast. "I have everything a woman could want. My only disappointment is not having any real education. I've always wondered what books have been written besides the musty tomes in my father's study."

"I thought women wanted balls and society and men to flirt with."

She shrugged. "I've never had balls and society, so I've never missed them. And I've seen men, and they've not impressed me greatly." She swept him a quick glance. "Present company excluded, of course."

He grinned and poured a fresh cup of coffee. "Of course. Are you still afraid of me?"

"I'm not afraid of you," she said indignantly. *Not anymore, at least.*

But she was afraid of what he could do to her, afraid of what would happen when he left her, afraid of . . . living.

"Good, because I won't do anything you don't want," he said with deliberation. "I'll simply have to make you want what I want."

Buddy rattled in then, and it was a good thing, Bea thought, because she had no idea how to reply to that outrageous pronouncement.

"The cavalry arrived in the nick of time." Mac dropped down on the blanket beside Bea. A small stream flowed lazily at their feet—fortunately a shallow stream. "A maid is stripping Buddy from his wet clothes, and Pamela is sound asleep in the nursery. The housekeeper assures me the maid has a dozen siblings and that she's perfectly qualified to keep the urchins where they belong. We shall see."

Bea reluctantly lifted her gaze from the pages of the novel he'd found for her, and Mac decided he loved her eyes. They were so gentle and understanding, and sometimes wickedly mischievous. He'd found the book moldering on a shelf in the parlor. Maybe he should have read it before he gave it to her.

"I think children belong in streams," she said with a smile. "I think they should stay naked and happy and splash in streams and roll in cowpies all they want."

He grinned, pushed her book aside, and leaned over her until she rolled flat on her back to escape him. He liked having her under him. He'd like it even more if she'd smile seductively, curve her hand around his neck, and kiss him. "I think novels are already turning you into a revolutionary, and I'd better never give you another one."

"Then I shall take up stealing books as a profession," she declared.

"Kiss me, and I'll let you read another page." He nuzzled her neck.

"You don't want to just kiss," she said accusingly. "And we're in broad daylight. After a hectic morning like the one we've just had, I should think you would want a nap."

"I didn't sleep a wink last night knowing I had only to reach over, and you'd be there, all soft and warm and tempting." He curled a straying strand of her hair around his finger and kissed her temple. She wriggled uneasily beneath him, but didn't push him away. "Do you have any idea what just the thought of you does to me?"

"Something bestial, no doubt," she answered tartly. "Shouldn't you be worrying that the viscount's men will come riding up the lane at any moment?"

"No. Overton promised to stop in at the tavern and let slip that an American with two children in tow was last seen at the train station in Evesham. The housekeeper here has a grandson who will go into Broadbury tomorrow and check to see if the men have gone."

"You act as if you have had some practice eluding the law." She didn't lift a hand to touch him, but her gaze never left his face.

Mac liked having her full feminine attention. It made him feel . . . *masculine.* "I've dodged a few scrapes, got caught in others. Sometimes a man just asks to have his block knocked off, and I've obliged on an occasion or two."

She regarded his jaw thoughtfully. "Pity no one is big enough to knock yours off."

"Wicked woman." He couldn't resist any longer.

Bending down, he pressed his mouth to hers, shuddered when she responded with alacrity, and settled in to take the kiss as far as it would go.

A plop of cold rain splashed against the back of his neck.

Mac ignored it. It had been cloudy all morning, but England was always cloudy. Bea parted her lips and slanted her head so he could more comfortably take advantage of her welcoming tongue. Heat shot straight through him, and he didn't notice the next few drops of rain. Or if they hit, they turned to steam.

The deluge that opened a moment later was a little harder to ignore. Bea screamed and pushed at his chest. Mac grabbed a corner of the blanket and tried to yank it over her without twisting them both into knots. Glancing up at the heavy sky and hearing the roll of thunder, he decided a blanket would never suffice.

"Come on. There's a barn just over the hill." Tugging her to her feet, cursing England and its clammy weather, Mac half carried, half pushed Bea over the stile and toward the barn before her skirts accumulated too much water for her to move.

He never did have any luck seducing proper ladies.

Twenty-eight

Skirts soaked and dripping, Bea gasped as Mac pushed her through the barn doors into the filtered light of the interior. Rain beat upon the thatched roof, shaking loose bits of dust and hay, but it was mercifully dry inside.

"I was so absorbed in that book, I didn't see this coming," she confessed, shaking off the wet blanket and looking for a place to hang it.

"Here's a length of rope. Let me string it up so you can hang the blanket and your petticoats. You'll catch your death like that."

Yards of cambric and flannel petticoats clung wetly to Bea's stockings. Removing her petticoats would leave her uncomfortably exposed to the damp of her skirt, unless she took that off as well.

"I don't think anything short of a fire will help," she said hesitantly. "Perhaps the storm will let up soon."

"What are the chances?" Mac asked prosaically, stringing the rope from timber to timber. "If we can find something to burn, I have a flint."

He looked so competent as he knotted rope and tested the line and checked the dirt floor for a likely hearth that Bea didn't have the heart to argue. And no matter how much she was enjoying learning to rebel and think for herself, she had to agree that her petticoats were hideously uncomfortable.

While Mac looked for debris to burn, she stepped behind the blanket to untie the knots at her waist.

"There's a broken barrow here, and some straw. It won't make much of a fire, but we can give it a try," Mac called as Bea wriggled out of one layer after anther. The sodden cloth fell in puddles at her feet, and she shed her wet shoes and stockings as well.

As she threw the first of the flannel petticoats over the line, she felt a tug on the other side, and heat stained her cheeks as she realized that Mac was helping her. If she'd known she would be showing her underthings to her husband, she would have worn her finest embroidered ones.

She was suddenly very aware of her near nakedness. *Thank goodness for drawers.*

"How many of these things do you wear?" he asked in disbelief as she tried to settle the third petticoat over the line. "It's a wonder you don't collapse under the weight."

Bea held up a dainty cambric and lace petticoat and dryly contemplated where she might hang it now that she'd literally run out of rope. "I've heard in France they have something called a crinoline that holds the skirts better."

"I can take you to Paris, you know." He peered over the impromptu clothesline and held out his hand for the last petticoat.

"Paris?" Irresolutely, she lifted the lacy cambric within his reach, and watched as it disappeared on the other side of the line. "I don't speak French. They would think me an utter ninny." She didn't speak French, didn't eat French, and had no notion of how one traveled such a distance, but she was certain it involved a great many strange people and places and was well beyond her ability to attempt. Still, Mac and

Aunt Constance had stirred her curiosity about what lay beyond her small world.

"What does it matter what strangers think?" he called back to her. "The color of one's coin speaks the same in any language."

Bea glanced down at the wet lengths of skirt clinging to her legs and wondered how Mac could be so casual about all that terrified her. Perhaps they didn't think in the same language.

"The fire is burning nicely. Come out and get warm."

The fire was a definite temptation. Telling herself he'd seen her in less, Bea stepped from behind her dressing screen.

Mac stood silhouetted by the flames, arms akimbo, broad shoulders narrowing to lean hips and well-muscled thighs, the image of a powerful man in absolute control. She gulped and almost fled back behind the blanket. He'd removed his wet coat and waistcoat, but maintained the semidecency of his damp trousers.

Knowing that scarlet stained her cheeks, she hurried to warm her fingers and toes. If she didn't look at him . . . If they could just converse intelligently . . .

"I take back what I said about your being an angel."

Eyebrows lifting in surprise, she glanced at him. He was watching her with an intensity that was almost unbearable.

"Angels surely can't be built like goddesses."

"You embarrass me when you talk like that," she said softly, wishing he would find some civil conversation so she could be comfortable again.

"I don't mean to. I told you I'm not much on plying ladies with flattery. How should I go about telling you how lovely you are?"

His plaintive plea drew her gaze back to him again, and she was lost, truly lost. He didn't look nearly as confident as usual, but the raw need in his eyes connected with the desire in her breast and some spark leapt between them—they might as well have been standing in the middle of the fire.

This time she saw the kiss coming. His arm circled her waist, giving her time to run if she wished, but she didn't. He ran his hand up her cheek, pushing the damp strands behind her ears. She saw the question in his eyes but didn't know how to respond. They were in a barn. In broad daylight. Nothing could happen, could it? Kisses would be safe here. And she desperately wanted his mouth on hers.

He obliged. Bea sank into the wonder of this merging of lips and tongues, of heat, and of need beyond her understanding. Her body aligned with his, bending where he held her, pressing intimately in places she wouldn't name even if she could. She just knew the touching felt right, that the strength of his muscled arm kept her from falling, that the press of his hard chest was necessary for reasons beyond her comprehension.

Even the caress of his hand on her breast didn't dismay her as it had in the past. His fingers molded naturally to her curves, as if they were made just for that. She quivered when he found the edge of her corset beneath her bodice and stroked the sensitive crest she'd scarcely known existed until he'd shown her. The sensations stirring inside at the intimate touch still frightened her, but . . .

She trusted Mac.

The wonder of that discovery overpowered all else. Mac wouldn't hurt her. She had seen the lengths to which he would go to protect the children. She knew he would do the same for her. He would shelter her as she stepped into the world outside her own, as no one had ever offered to do before. It was a liberating experience.

"Bea," he murmured, nibbling a path across her cheek

to her earlobe. "I can't take you here, not in a barn, but I want to touch you. Will you let me touch you?"

As if she were in any state to say no to anything he asked. He didn't wait for a reply, but turned her gently to unfasten the myriad hooks of her gown and bodice lining, until the fabric fell free, revealing the delicate frill of her chemise. She felt the heated exhalation of his breath on her nape as he smoothed the muslin bodice from her shoulders and down her arms. The straps of her light summer chemise scarcely covered anything.

Kisses feathered across her nape, and her breasts ached for the same freedom as her arms. She'd never realized how confining clothes could be until Mac's hands brushed her skin in tantalizing places, and his kisses heated fires that required the air to cool them.

He reached around her to untie her chemise ribbons and release the straps, until her breasts strained upward and unfettered above her corset. Still, he didn't touch her there, where she needed him.

"You are so perfect, I'm almost afraid to touch you," he whispered.

The look in his eyes shattered everything she'd believed about herself. She'd always thought herself large and plain. But not to Mac. She believed the truth in his eyes.

With far more daring than she actually possessed, Bea covered his hands where they rested on her shoulders, and drew them downward. "Please," she whispered.

Mac didn't need further invitation. Unknotting her corset, he opened the daintily embroidered garment and slid his hands inside, lifting her free until his palms supported her and his thumbs played erotic tunes on a part of her that thrummed with sensation.

She leaned back against his powerful shoulder, giving him freer access, and offered no protest as little

by little her gown and corset fell away, leaving her
bare to the waist. She felt no chill, only the flicker of
flames near her feet, and the compelling heat of her
husband's touch as he reverently stroked her everywhere he could reach.

He swung her around then, bent to suckle her
breast, and her knees crumpled. Mac caught her and
lowered her to the coat he'd laid beside the fire. He
kept his heavy weight from her, but she knew his
strength and sturdiness in the way his legs pressed
hers closed when all instinct cried for her to part them.

She registered the sudden chill as her skirt slid upward, but Mac played a game with her tongue that
drew all her breath. She spread her hands across his
chest, absorbing the tactile sensations of heat and
damp and muscle. When she couldn't pry open the
tiny buttons of his shirt, he growled and tore it open
for her. Rapt with the discovery of the crisp curls beneath the linen, she forgot the chill of her legs until
Mac's hand slid along her drawers and discovered the
fastening at her waistband.

"Mac," she whispered in horror as his mouth deserted her breast and his attention wandered south-
ward.

"Not here," he murmured, returning his attention
to her mouth. "I won't take you here. I'll wait until
we have that big soft bed and a roaring fire and a hot
bath to warm us."

In her current frame of mind that sounded exceedingly pleasant. She didn't even object as he flattened
his hand across her bare abdomen and explored there.
Everything he did was new and exciting and produced
explosions of sensation. He seemed to like it when she
returned the favor, so she explored the flat ripples of
his chest with fascination and played with them as he
had hers, until he groaned and smothered her with
urgent kisses.

He made her feel beautiful. Powerful. As if she were the only woman in the world.

She arched into his hand when he touched her where it should be forbidden to touch. Her body did as it wished, trusting him to know what she needed.

"This is how I want it to be when we come together, Bea," he whispered near her ear. "I want you all soft and warm and damp and ready for me."

She cried out as his finger entered her, and she fought the invasion without any real will to do so. It just seemed foreign and forbidden and dangerous . . . and wonderful. All the beauty and pleasure he'd taught her found a center and built into a pressure she couldn't deny, until she wept to part her legs and give him entrance, to take him where a hollow opened and hungered and she understood what she lacked and he possessed.

With gentle strokes, he shattered the pressure, exploded all her beliefs and fears and reservations in wave after wave of glorious surrender. Awed, overwhelmed, uncertain of what had just happened, Bea sought shelter within her husband's strong embrace.

"Tonight," he vowed. "Tonight we'll learn what it is like to be truly husband and wife."

Tonight he would make her feel beautiful again. Refusing to let him get away so easily, Bea reached for his neck and pulled him down to her once again.

He growled in pleasure at her boldness, and her heart grew a little braver.

Twenty-nine

"They're sound sleep." Mac closed the bedchamber door and let his eyes adjust to the light of a single candle and the flicker of coals on the hearth. With the bribe of a few coins, the housekeeper had eagerly cleared a separate room for the new maid and the children, guaranteeing privacy for the night.

Bea sat in front of a mirror, brush in hand, watching him. Blood rushed straight from Mac's brain to his groin, but he could still function enough to cross the room and take the brush from her hand. He could tolerate the pulsing heat behind his trouser flap for a while in anticipation of all the pleasure she was about to grant him.

"I love your hair." He pulled the brush through the thick silken strands, imagining her hair wrapped around him. The lace of her nightgown exposed more than covered the full globes of her breasts. If he looked closely enough, he could see the darker crests pressed against the thin fabric. His Bea was a handful in more ways than one.

An inexplicable burst of pride filled him at knowing this woman was his. He'd wanted to conquer new lands, but possessing Bea had far more appeal.

"Are you certain we should do this?" she murmured as his hand wandered with his attention, his thumb fondling a peak pouting to be taken. He loved how she let him do whatever he wished. Bea was innocent of the precepts of the rest of society.

"I'm sure," he said decisively. "I can't imagine God gave us these cravings and told us to go forth and multiply with the intent that we suffer. Our union is expected of us."

She leaned into him so naturally that it almost took his breath away. Without waiting, Mac drew her up and into his arms. He sensed the anxiety in her kiss as he stroked downward, cupping the firm curves below her waist.

"You're mine, Bea," he murmured into her lilac-scented hair, "to have and to hold, for better or worse. The time has come to prove it."

He could feel her nod where her head rested against his shoulder. "We can pretend this is our honeymoon, and we're like any married couple," he heard her say.

"We *are* any married couple." He kissed her long, yielding throat and confirmed the voluptuous length of her curves against him one more time. "Do not ever think otherwise. I married you because I wanted to, because you're the perfect woman for me, because I can no longer imagine life without you. We may neither of us have expected marriage, but we'll learn as we go on."

He knew she needed more reassurance than most, that her shyness prevented her seeing what a treasure she was, but he didn't have glib words to offer. He had only his hands to teach her how he felt, and he used them now.

She shuddered with desire beneath his caress, and he smiled as he pressed more kisses against her nape. "Into bed with you," he murmured, loving the vibration of his lips against her skin as he smoothed her hair across her shoulder and her breast. "Shall I blow out the candle before I undress?"

She lifted her head and gazed at him uncertainly; then, to Mac's delight, she shook her head. If she climbed into the bed with a slight air of martyrdom, he didn't mind. He'd teach her differently in the next hour. For now, he was satisfied that his Bea wanted to see him as much as he wanted to see her. He pulled his shirt over his head and flung it at the nearest chair.

Bea smothered a cry of appreciation as her husband's chest emerged from the chrysalis of clothing. He was sculpted more beautifully than any statue, with muscled curves in his upper chest and washboard ridges on his abdomen, and shoulders that rippled with every movement as he . . .

Unfastened his trousers. She gulped and thought to close her eyes, but fascination overtook her as the buttons slowly fell open. He didn't seem aware of her captivation as he shed shoes, stockings, and trousers as unself-consciously as if he were alone in the room. He wore thin linen drawers, but they scarcely disguised the immensity of the . . . of the . . . *pole* poking outward.

She nearly dived beneath the pillows as he climbed onto the bed beside her.

But she could believe the heat and strength of his muscled flesh as he gathered her into his arms, quelled her fear.

She had no power against her attraction to him. Even knowing what he could do to her, she slid her hands over his broad shoulders and delighted in the ripple of muscle and slide of flesh against flesh as he captured her waist and pulled her into him.

"I'll never let you regret this, Bea," he whispered.

His hand cupped her bottom and pressed her against his hips as he had earlier, but this time only thin linen protected them, and she could feel the rigidity like steel pressing against her thigh. She ought to be more frightened, but she lay back against the pil-

lows where he placed her and relished the sight of her
husband's hungry gaze drinking her in as if she were
manna from heaven.

For the first time in her life, she felt dainty and
desirable and all the things men wanted in a woman,
and the power was heady. She even helped him unfasten the ties on the front of her gown. She liked knowing her breasts gave him as much pleasure as they did
her, now that he'd taught her their purpose.

The bed gave way beneath her as his weight pressed
her downward. She'd not quite grasped how much different a feather bed made as he seduced her softly,
tenderly, and with gentle reverence. Shadows flickered
along his broad frame, making him even larger and
more mysterious, delineating all the places where he
was different from her. He was hard where she was
soft, broad where she was curved.

She learned he could be rough in his haste. He
bruised her lips with urgency when she dug her nails
into his neck and pulled him closer. His hand clutched
her breast too tightly, and she cried a protest. He instantly caressed her, soothing the ache into something
more demanding, so that she pressed him for a repeat.

She whimpered in fear as Mac pulled up her gown,
but he did no more than run his hand up and down
her bare leg, absorbing the sensation of skin polishing
skin just as she did when she ran her hands over the
bulge of his arms. They were together in this. It wasn't
a matter of what he did to her, but what they did
together.

Delight mixed with pleasure as she helped him tug
the gown over her head. He looked at her with such
pleasure and amazement that she wanted to preen
with pride and lift herself closer so he could do as he
willed with her. As he did do with her.

With lips and tongue and caressing fingers, he set
her on fire. It was amazing, wanton, surely immoral,

yet she writhed in anticipation of his next touch, his next kiss, and hurried him onward when he lingered too long. He touched her *there,* and she cried out in relief, then flushed when he chuckled. When he *kissed* her there, she grabbed his hair and yanked him upward.

"Some other time, perhaps," he murmured wickedly, chuckling as he soothed her lips with more kisses.

He'd left her burning and feverish and with a desperate need she couldn't quench on her own. Without a trace of delicacy, she reached for the tie of his drawers and slid her hands beneath the loosened band.

He rolled over and stripped them off, and rolled over her again without an instant's hesitation. Only this time, he positioned his knees between hers, parting her legs until, exposed to the open air, she radiated heat.

Mac's hands bracketed her head, the iron bars of his arms preventing escape as he lowered his weight *there,* where he'd taught her to want him.

Bea knew a moment's fear, a hasty urge to flee before it was too late, but she looked up, saw the hunger and determination in his eyes give way to something tender and yearning, and without a qualm, she arched upward to accept him.

She cried out as he shoved deeply, cutting into her with the first thrust, but she bit her lip as he stilled and his foreign thickness stretched her slowly. Mac leaned over and kissed the lip she had bitten, soothing it with his tongue.

"Aye, and the worst is over, love. From here, it's smooth sailing. Will ye fly with me?"

She wanted to. She desperately wanted to. She wanted to fly and soar and conquer the waves and the clouds. She wept as he plied her nipples with his tongue, and the longing returned, enhanced by the . . .

pole he'd inserted inside her. It felt strange and awkward and wonderful, and her body wanted more of whatever he offered.

"That's my darling," he murmured as she moved hesitantly against him. "That's my wonderful wanton. Take me in, love, take me as deep as you can, and we'll steer a course for the stars."

With his wicked murmurs encouraging her, his hands tweaking and caressing and urging her into greater torment, Bea writhed and squirmed and tried to do as he said, until she was weeping from need, and he wonderfully, marvelously met it.

Her breath flew out of her lungs as he pushed deeper, drew back, and plunged again, mastering her with consummate skill. She could not stop him had she wanted. Wantonly, she surrendered her independence, even as he told her with his hands and mouth and body that he could never have enough of her, that she had won him in some manner she had not yet comprehended.

The pressure built until she could have no thought other than of release, of forcing the pain and pleasure through the place where they were joined until it killed her, if that was what it took. It didn't. It took only the brush of his hand, the thrust of his body so deep inside that she could feel it touch some unyielding part of her. The pressure burst and spun, and she soared and reached and arched against him again and again, as he held her and helped her and let her take as much as she liked of him, until she was breathless and limp in his arms.

"Yes," he breathed in relief. "That's the way I wanted it to be."

And then he took her again, seeking his own pleasure, and she matched him thrust for thrust, delighting in making him groan, and accepting in wonder the powerful plunge that found her center and released the living fluid of his own seed into her womb.

So this was what being married was all about.

Bea lay limp and damp beneath her husband's heavy weight, trying to absorb the fullness of the moment. Married people joined in body as well as soul, and together, they had the power to create new life. The thought was frightening as well as exciting in its immensity. "Does that mean I'll have your baby now?" she whispered nervously.

With a moan, he rolled back to the mattress, pulling her with him. He brushed the hair from her eyes and snuggled her against his side. "It can take many tries, Bea." He sounded as nervous as she did. "It takes years for some people."

She relaxed. Anything could happen in years. She had finally given herself to a man, and he had taken her, and someday they might have a child of their own.

In its own way, that seemed fair. And if a child didn't happen, then the pleasure they brought each other could be enough. It joined them in some fundamental way.

Mac supplied the backbone she didn't have. She offered him . . . what? The gentleness his life lacked? She caressed the soft hair of the arm holding her, and he buried his face against her throat and kissed her there. "There's a first time for everything," he murmured senselessly, before grabbing her waist and rolling over with her on top of him.

Bea sprawled across his chest, her hair falling over her shoulder into a pool against the soft whorls of hair on his chest. She folded her arms across him and rested her head, comfortable with his arm wrapped around her waist. "I think I shall like being married," she murmured sleepily.

"Good." He stroked her hair, pulling the strands

together and smoothing them into some pattern that suited him. "And you'll try not to be too afraid if I catch you with child, and I'm not there immediately to help you?"

She closed her eyes and listened to his heartbeat. "I don't want you to leave." She was surprised at the words as they left her mouth, but she meant them. "And yes, I'll be afraid. I'll worry that something will happen to you. But I'll trust you to return, and I'll be happy, because I want to have your baby. I think you have softened my brain somehow."

He chuckled, a rumble deep inside his chest.

"Aye, but there are parts of me hard enough to remedy the lack, dear heart. And it's a beautiful mush-brain you'll be when you grow big and round with my babe."

She ought to retaliate somehow, but she was too content. She licked at his nipple, and he growled. She could grow accustomed to his growls. And barks. And thunders.

She wondered how soon they could do this again, and how long it would take for a babe to swell her belly, and if this was love warming her insides, as he adjusted her more carefully against his shoulder, and how she would know the answers to anything if he insisted on falling asleep and snoring in her ear.

She would learn. Mac would teach her.

The silly, timid girl she'd been had finally become a woman, but she was no less frightened by the change.

Thirty

They had two days of wedded bliss before the caretaker's grandson returned to tell them that the viscount's men had galloped off to Evesham, and Broadbury was safe.

Bea felt as if she glowed from the inside out. She blushed every time Mac threw her a knowing look. He'd taught her where his thoughts traveled, and hers often strayed down the same path. He'd caught her stealing looks as he dressed, and the male part of him that so captured her fancy stiffened at just her glance, teaching her how he felt when he watched her breasts press above her bodice. He'd tossed her back upon the bed this morning and taken her with an ardency that had left her half afraid to look at him ever since.

She hadn't known she could feel and think such wanton thoughts. There was a different person hiding inside her that she didn't recognize.

That reckless person reached out to straighten Mac's cravat as they prepared to depart their honeymoon cottage. She smoothed the cotton over his broad chest, lingered to absorb the pounding of his heart, then glanced shyly to see if she'd stepped too far out of bounds. They weren't behind closed doors. Perhaps she had been too forward.

Mac grinned wickedly down at her. "You'll not

make a gentleman of me with a few soft touches, you know."

"I don't suppose I have much use for a gentleman," she replied with giddy boldness. She'd never flirted with a man, argued with one, or insulted one until Mac had come along. He took her remarks in stride, without thinking less of her.

A smile of deep appreciation crossed his rugged features. "No, I suppose you don't. You'll not be after me to trip across dance floors and make polite conversation and remember to hold my damned gloves and whatever silliness society demands, will you?"

"I'll ask that you mind your language," she reminded him pertly. "You've the children to think about."

"Balderdash," he whispered in her ear as he caught her waist and drew her out the front door. "Posh-tosh and poppycock."

Bea laughed and a slow heat crept into her heart. Nervous butterflies beat their wings against her corset as she admired the handsome man helping her into the carriage. He inspired in her a confidence she'd never known. She very much feared this was the love that books spoke of, and she didn't know where it would go when he went away, but for now she reveled in it.

She took Pamela as Mac handed her over, smoothed her wispy curls, and gave her a cloth doll to chew. Buddy clambered into the carriage on his own, boldly claiming the seat beside Bea. He immediately scrambled to the carriage floor to inspect the box at her feet, knowing it would contain treats to idle away the hours.

Rather than climb to the front driver's bench, Mac leaned over the door and tickled Pamela's nose. She grinned and gurgled an incomprehensible chain of noises.

"Have you noticed these two are behaving with more civility since they've been with us?" he asked as Buddy bounced back to his seat with a toy horse in hand.

"Children aren't civil," Bea scoffed. "But they do seem to have settled down a little. I think it must be important for them to feel secure, and you've given them that."

He'd given them that and more, she realized as Mac climbed into the front seat. The children were not only content, but happy, as she was. It was something of an eye-opening experience to realize that she was happy. Nervous, perhaps, still occasionally fearful, but happy. She could remember being vaguely content in the past, but never truly happy. Now even the sun shone brighter. Perhaps it was the same for the children.

Things had changed for the better. And it had all started with her first step out of her cloistered world and into the immensity of Mac's. It was frightening—and exhilarating—to think of how one person could turn her entire life inside out.

"I've been thinking," Mac announced as he took up the reins. "We are already a good day's ride toward London."

A cloud covered her sunshine as he tilted her world once again. Hugging Pamela, Bea glanced with alarm at the back of her husband's head. She'd never been this far from home, and she longed to return. She missed her roses and watching how the baby rabbits grew, and she wanted to hear what Digby had done to the inn in her their absence. But Mac was an adventurer. Why had she forgotten that?

"Surely London is several days away," she murmured uneasily.

"Less," he said with assurance. "We can do it. Simmons and his men don't even know about you and won't think to look for us there. We'll just be a happy family shopping in the city before sailing off to America."

Terror took root in her heart and agitated Bea so badly that Pamela swung her doll in distress. America? She couldn't even face the idea of London. They had fires and runaway horses and thieves in London.

"Don't be silly." She tried to sound calm, as if he were reciting an elaborate jest. "We need to discuss the consignment shop at the Ladies' Aid Society to-morrow."

Mac blithely urged the horses down the lane. "They'll survive without you. You can send them a letter. I'll obtain a draft from my bank, and we can fund the store and textbooks. Between the two of us, we should be able to manage the children without need of a nanny, don't you think? As you said, they seem to mind us, most of the time."

She thought no such thing. Panic welled, and she clutched Pamela even tighter, until the child squirmed and whimpered. Buddy glanced at her with suspicion. Loosening her hold, Bea tried to find an even tone that wouldn't frighten the children, when what she wanted to do was scream her terror. "I think you are out of your mind," she said quite firmly. If nothing else, she would learn to argue. "I cannot leave the town and my estate to take off on some harebrained impulse to America."

She could almost see his scowl from the way he hunched his broad shoulders.

"It solves everything," he insisted, "I can have the ship loaded and gone before Simmons knows we're on it. You'll see how much more freedom you'll have in America. Marilee attended a woman's school there. You could, too, if you wished. You can meet my parents, and we can be together instead of apart. The children need you."

He was ripping her into little pieces. A tear crawled

down Bea's cheek as she sought a reply. She knew she couldn't do it. It wasn't just fear holding her back, but love for her home and the people in it. How could she persuade a man like her husband of that?

If she meant to keep her freedom, to learn to stand on her own, she had to force him to listen to her wishes instead of his own. It might be nice if she were strong enough to sail away without a qualm, to be a woman of the world and a partner in his life, but she wasn't. Not yet. She must take one step at a time, at her own pace.

She didn't know how to do it, and frustration sent another tear down her cheek. Pamela patted her face in sympathy, which made everything worse. She didn't want to be parted from the children.

Nor did she want to be parted from Mac, she realized unhappily. She just had the common sense to know that no matter where they lived, Mac would roam, and unless she followed at his heels, she'd be left behind. If she was to live alone, she would much rather do it here, where her roots reached deeply into the soil.

"No," she said with as much firmness as she could muster. She wished she had pen and paper in hand. She was much more articulate in writing.

Mac threw her a puzzled look over his shoulder. "No?"

"No, I won't go with you. I belong here. You are the adventurer, not me."

He halted the horses at the end of the lane leading onto the main road. To the left lay the road to London. To the right, the road wound into the Cotswold hills around Broadbury. He turned in his seat and regarded her tearstained face in bewilderment. "You'll be with me," he said, as if that were all that mattered. "I'll take care of everything."

"I don't *want* you to take care of everything," she

cried. "*I* want to take care of me. And I can't, not in London, not on a ship, not in America. Not if you do it for me. You *promised,*" she reminded him. "You said you would sail off and let me be who I am."

Mac looked astounded, bemused, hurt, and angry, all at the same time. "You're my *wife,* that's who you are," he shouted with his usual bluster. "I don't want to leave you here alone, possibly carrying my child. We can return in the fall, and you'll see that the place hasn't fallen apart without you."

"The village needs me more than the children do. The children have you and your parents. Give me one good reason why I should give up all I know and love to follow you to a strange place and strange people." She glared at him, praying he would understand, knowing he wouldn't. He was being perfectly reasonable. She was not.

Or maybe she was being reasonable, and he was not. Surely she had as much right to her beliefs as he did. *What a stunning idea!* Her thoughts and wishes might be as valid as any man's. *My heavens.* She ought to write that down and publish it.

"This is stupid, Bea." He glanced down at Buddy, who was following their argument with a worried expression. Controlling his voice, he continued, "I could simply turn toward London and there would be nothing you could do about it."

"I would take the first opportunity to catch a coach home," she insisted. "I won't go, Mac. I swear I won't. And if you have decided you don't wish for me to bear a child while you're gone, there is an obvious means of preventing that."

She thought her barely concealed threat of sleeping apart might be an unfair tactic, but she had no other. This time he glared at her with fury. He'd understood.

"Fine. Then we won't make babies." He picked up the reins and turned the horses toward Broadbury.

"You can sit and rot in your mansion, for all I care. I'll ask Mary if she'll be the children's nursemaid and go with me."

"You know Mary is the sole support of her family. She won't leave them," Bea answered with more confidence now that he'd turned in the right direction. Her heart might be breaking at his cruelty but she had never expected less. This was why she had to stand on her own. "Why don't you take the Widow Black and her two children?" she finished wickedly.

"Why not two more?" he muttered, urging the horses faster. "Why not the whole damned town? I'll never load cargo at this rate, so I may as well take passengers."

She didn't say anything. She had *won* the argument. Sitting back, bouncing Pamela, she savored the moment, even if it meant the end of the pleasant fantasy she'd woven these past few days. A man like Mac wouldn't let a little thing like an argument stand in the way of his pleasures, once he calmed down. He'd still want her, even if he would never love the contrary woman she was becoming.

The first doubt crept into Bea's mind when they arrived home and wearily packed the children off to the nursery under Mary's eager guardianship. Bea asked for a cold supper to be sent up to their suite, soaked away her exhaustion in a warm tub, then dressed in her best nightdress and waited for Mac. She wanted to make up to him for her stubbornness, make him understand why she couldn't go with him. She didn't know if she had any better words than before, but in bed she didn't need words.

Only he didn't arrive to eat his supper or to see her new nightdress.

Fear ate at her insides, but she refused to acknowledge it. She could not go back to the days when she waited on a man hand and foot, catering to his every need and whim, while ignoring her own.

She went to bed and shut down the lamp. To . . . *the devil* with him.

With that daring curse in her mind, she tossed and turned the rest of the night.

At breakfast, Mac hid behind the newspaper, just as her father had always done. Bea wanted to throw a roll at him, but she demurely buttered it instead. "Any mention of the viscount's missing children?" she asked with feigned innocence, ignoring James hovering at her elbow with the teapot.

"No, but there's a letter in that stack from your aunt. Perhaps she has news," Mac answered curtly, lifting his coffee cup behind the paper.

Bea sorted through the mail and retrieved the scented letter with her aunt's handwriting. Using a letter opener, she pried up the seal, trying to pretend her stomach wasn't fluttering nervously. If her aunt had found a nursemaid, Mac could leave at once.

She scanned the spiderweb scrawl quickly, then read more thoroughly. Her aunt wrote of balls and soirees and the latest gossip. She made no mention of nursemaids or missing children, or banks, or James. If she could, Bea would reach through the paper and strangle her beloved aunt.

She ought to be delighted that a nursemaid hadn't been found, but she was terrified for Mac and the children. Perhaps she had been hasty in not agreeing to accompany them to America.

No. Even Mary would be better for the children under the conditions of shipboard life. Mary wouldn't be a quivering lump of terrorized jelly. If Bea had the coins to do so, she'd bribe the maid to go with Mac and take care of the children. Except that would be as unfair to Mary and her family as it would be to herself.

"Nothing pertinent at all, not even decent gossip." She slapped the letter down on the table for Mac to peruse at will. He wouldn't believe her without seeing it for himself.

"The latest gossip is that the Earl of Coventry has run off to France with an actress," James said cheerfully, pouring her a fresh cup of tea.

"How do you know that?" Bea demanded. Even her aunt hadn't mentioned it.

James cocked an eyebrow. "I am not without resources."

"And I don't suppose you'd care to reveal those sources," Mac asked dryly, lowering the newspaper and lifting a questioning eyebrow.

"One doesn't." With a sniff, James carried the tea tray back to the kitchen.

"Remind me to dock his pay for insolence." Mac lifted his cup and retreated again.

Bea wondered what would happen if she smacked the paper from his hand, but she wasn't brave enough or foolish enough to try. She'd already pushed him as far as she dared. She supposed it was up to her to make amends.

"You could take the train into London from Evesham," she suggested. "Perhaps with the earl gone, the children would be safe here while you finish your business."

"And what happens if the viscount's men return to the village?" he asked coldly. "What happens when they learn Mrs. Lachlan MacTavish lives here?"

Bea hadn't thought of that. Her throat went dry as she realized for the first time that she could be in as much trouble as he was.

Mac slammed the paper down and rose to tower above her. "Think beyond yourself sometime, my dear, and you'll discover the world is a fearsome place that makes your troubles look small." He stalked out without waiting for a reply.

Bea couldn't swallow the roll stuck in her throat. She didn't want him to *hate* her. But they approached life from such opposite directions that he might as well be across the ocean for all the chance she had of reaching him.

She picked up her aunt's letter and read it again, but it was James's news that went round and round in her head. The earl had gone to France, with an actress. Well, she supposed the children couldn't hope for much help from him. He might not even know the children were missing. In the back of her mind, she'd hoped he would come riding to the rescue, promising that she could take care of his grandchildren since his son was so obviously unqualified. Then Mac could stay for as long as he liked.

It seemed as if he didn't like staying at all.

She frowned as James cleared Mac's plate and deliberately took her aunt's letter with him, leaving the rest of the post on the table.

James never cleared the table.

Well, he wasn't the only one who was behaving strangely these days.

Thirty-one

Bea watched as the maids took down the last of the parlor draperies, exposing the newly cleared room to the fresh air and sunlight of the floor-to-ceiling windows. The porcelain figurines, ostrich feathers, crocheted arm covers, and the maze of folderol her father had thought would make her happy had all vanished into the attics during their absence, as she'd ordered.

The result was a breathtaking space immense with possibilities. She could move her piano into the bay window and enjoy the sun while playing, and place chairs beside the fireplace for warmth and reading in the winter. Her imagination tingled with anticipation.

Pleased with the result, Bea glanced out the newly naked windows to see Mac striding down the lane in heated discussion with Mr. Overton, leaving her behind. Again.

She'd known irritation when her father had ordered still another piece of furniture or bric-a-brac but failed to inform her of the day's news or give her the book she'd asked for. She'd learned to conceal that irritation behind the production of acres of knitted afghans and crocheted doilies and embroidered tapestries.

What she felt now wasn't even close to irritation,

and she'd hang before she knitted another afghan while men ran her life.

Grabbing up a shawl, she started for the door, only to discover Buddy darting into the shadows behind the horsehair divan. She wasn't small enough and her petticoats didn't compress enough to go in after him. She'd noticed he'd been particularly pensive during his supper last night. Could children worry as adults did?

"I think I shall take a walk," she said aloud, drifting slowly toward the door. "I wonder if Buddy would like to go with me? Perhaps I should go upstairs and ask."

His hesitation was so apparent, she could almost hear it.

"Well, perhaps he's enjoying himself too much and doesn't want to be disturbed. I should go on without him." She made a production of opening the parlor door wide.

"No, Miss Bea! I wanna go wif you." He shot out from behind the divan and raced toward the front door, leaving her behind in his rush to struggle with the huge door handle.

"Well, my, my, it's a good thing you were near enough to hear me." She smiled at the boy's antics. It must be hard for a child to understand why he'd been torn from his home and all that was familiar.

Still angry, she opened the door and strode after the men as quickly as only a woman of her height could do. Buddy still outpaced her.

Ahead, Mac halted to gaze upward and shout at his nephew as Buddy scrambled up an apple tree. Seeing Bea approach, he nodded in relief. "I'll get the brat down for you."

"Not for my sake," she answered coolly, before turning to her former steward. "Good day to you, Mr. Overton. Have you noticed if the bottom fields were plowed in our absence? Mac told me he had given the tenants permission to go ahead."

Without waiting for Mac, she continued walking down the lane, all but forcing the confused steward to follow her.

"They have at that, Miss . . . Mrs. MacTavish." He glanced worriedly over his shoulder as Mac beat the branches in search of his nephew.

"And have the seeds arrived to begin planting? I believe we ordered the ones you recommended. It is the right time for planting them, isn't it?"

"Umm, yes, Miss . . . ma'am, it is." He tried to halt at the end of the lane to wait for Mac, but Bea would have none of it.

She took the road toward town, one long stride at a time, forcing him to follow. "Mac says I must increase the rents this fall to cover the improvements we need. Do you think the new crop will be profitable enough that the tenants can afford the increase?"

"Without a doubt, Mrs. MacTavish." With a sigh of resignation, Overton kept pace with her. "With new equipment, you could plow twice the acreage. Your more experienced tenants understand that."

Buddy's shouts of triumph drew near. Bea assumed Mac had captured him and was now hauling him down the lane, but she wouldn't turn around. Let *him* see what it was like to be left behind as if he were of no more importance than a nursery maid.

"Are there crops the less experienced tenants could grow that would enhance their income?" She hadn't thought about that much while enjoying the mindless pleasures of the last few days, but she had noticed that the Carstairses' caretaker grew an assortment of vegetables and took milk and eggs into town from their cow and chickens. She didn't know how much expensive equipment that might require.

"Of course." With a bit more excitement than earlier, Overton launched into a treatise on small-crop farming.

Bea knew the instant Mac approached. She could feel the heat of him, his vibrations of impatience and irritation, and his awareness of her. She supposed one couldn't spend days doing what they had done without experiencing that invisible connection. He probably wanted to wring her neck, but that wasn't all he wanted to do. And it made him angry. She liked upsetting his world as easily as he upset hers.

As he reached her side, Mac held out his giggling, protesting nephew. "Here. Why did you let him out of the nursery?"

She smiled condescendingly at her husband. "He's afraid he'll lose you if you're out of sight. Children need the security of the familiar."

Mac growled but placed the boy on his shoulders, where Buddy grabbed his hair and made himself at home. "Overton has agreed to a share in the profits for looking after the place while I am gone. You don't need to worry about crops and tenants."

Beatrice wondered what it would be like to smack someone. She'd never had the opportunity or the incentive, but she thought she might enjoy it right now. It was either that, or burst into tears and have a tantrum. "Since I'm the one who must hear complaints, then I think I should have some understanding of why we're doing what we are," she said sweetly. "And since you and Mr. Overton know even less about women and children than I do, perhaps I should be the one to decide if Widow Black and her children should take care of a cow and chickens instead of plowing a field."

"Widow Black can't afford a cow and chickens," Mac protested. "She can't even pay her rent."

"She could pay her rent if she had a cow and chickens," Bea countered.

"She needs a place to sell eggs and milk," Mac shouted.

"Then I will provide one," she shouted back, with absolutely no idea how she would do any such thing. She wiped at the tears of fury springing to her eyes, as angry at herself as at Mac.

"Don't make Missy cwy!" Buddy screamed, beating on Mac's head with his fists. "Mama cwied and she went away. I hate you!"

He did his best to scramble down Mac's back, but Mac caught him and hauled him into his arms so he couldn't escape. Overton looked stunned and embarrassed and distanced himself from the family argument, but it was the tears spilling from Bea's eyes that wrenched Mac's heart.

He hugged Buddy hard, even though the boy continued to beat him. "I'm not hurting Miss Bea," he said calmly. "I yell when I don't understand something, and I don't understand your aunt at all, but I won't hurt her. Do you hear me?"

"Papa yelled." Buddy hiccuped and sought frantically for Bea. Reassured that she hadn't gone anywhere, he wiped his nose on Mac's coat. "Papa yelled and Mama cwied and then Mama went with the angels. I don' want Miss Bea to go with the angels."

Bea rumpled the boy's hair, and when he turned to her, she gently scooped him into her arms. "Papas and mamas argue, love, just like sometimes we yell at you because you scare us or make us angry. It means we love you, not that we'll go away."

Mac fought the moisture in his eyes. He knew Marilee. She would have adored her son, cosseted him fiercely, sung him songs, and laughed with him. She would never have yelled in front of Buddy as Mac had, and she wouldn't have been able to hold back tears any better than the boy could.

"Your mama didn't want to leave you." Mac sought

desperately for words he didn't possess. He sent Bea a pleading glance, but she didn't know what to say any more than he did. She hugged his hiccuping nephew. Mac took a deep breath and sought for patience. "But sometimes the angels need people more than we do. They knew you had me and your daddy and Pammy, but they didn't have anyone like your mama. So your mama sent Aunt Bea to keep you company. When I or Aunt Bea holds your hands, that's your mama holding you. Understand?"

Buddy wiped a teary eye and nodded solemnly. "Aunt Bea is Mama holding me?"

Well, that made as much sense as anything he'd said. "Yes. And if I take you to see your grandmama, she will sing to you just like your mama did, and that's like your mama singing to you. If I yell and shout, it doesn't mean anything except I'm angry and impatient and shouldn't be yelling and shouting."

"Say 'Bad Uncle Mac' when he yells," Bea whispered in his ear, loud enough for Mac to hear her.

Buddy grinned. "Bad Unca Mac!" he shouted.

Mac winced and tried to glare at his rebellious wife, but she looked so tempting with her uncovered hair gleaming red in the sun and her curls pulled all askew by Buddy's clinging fingers that he could barely manage not to kiss her.

He had to avoid kissing her. He might be sailing within a week, and he could no longer bear the thought of Bea carrying his child without him near. That realization had crystallized the day she'd refused to accompany him to Virginia. He hadn't decided what to do about it yet, but he knew he cared for her too much to let her suffer that travail alone.

She was smiling sunnily at him now, driving all his responsible notions clean out of his head. They might as well be little butterflies flitting through his brain, in one ear and out the other.

"Give me the brat. I'll take him back to the nursery, and you talk to Overton. But you'd better find money to buy the damned cow before you promise the widow anything."

He marched off, feeling better for having asserted his authoritative, much more knowledgeable rights. He had taken money that he needed for his ship to buy the seed. He wasn't buying any damned cow too.

Mac set Buddy down and engaged him in a game of kick-the-rock for the rest of the way up the lane. He needed to kick something, and rocks seemed safest.

He hadn't known that making love with a lady like Bea could be so wonderfully, immensely different from anything he'd ever experienced. If he thought about the way her eyes watched him with pleasure and admiration or the way her nipples tightened when he reached for them, he'd be in agony before he reached the house. He'd missed her last night. He'd wanted to throw away all his resolve and take her in that damned virginal bed of hers. But she was the one who had thrown the gauntlet in his face. A man could bend only so far and still be a man.

She wanted a *teacher,* not a lover or a husband. Far be it from him to give her any less—or any more—than she wanted.

He opened the front door to let Buddy in and watched his nephew scamper into the now amazingly spacious parlor. Bea had thrown out all the stuffy old gewgaws and furbelows, leaving an open slate—as it were—to write on.

Mac didn't want to read the meaning in that.

Thirty-two

"James, why isn't there a place for Mr. MacTav-ish?" Bea frowned at the single dinner setting.

"He asked to be served in the study, Madam," her cousin said with hauteur.

"Oh, stop that." Glaring at the empty table, Bea refused to sit. She would have months to sit here alone. She didn't want to start now. She glanced at James, who was giving her his disapproving over-her-head stare. "James, sometime you'll have to tell me why on earth you came here to plague me instead of staying with your family."

Impatiently, she started for the dining room door. She'd never dared ask her cousin any of the questions that had bothered her since his arrival. She didn't know why she had said anything now, except that Mac had taught her to say what she thought.

"Actually, my family is from here," James replied, much to her surprise.

And to his own, from what Bea could tell as she glanced back at him. "I *know* everyone from around here. Did you spring up under a cabbage leaf?"

"My mother is from Broadbury,' he said stiffly, not looking at her.

She halted in the doorway, frowning. "And where is she now?"

"She moved to London, where I was born. She often spoke of returning here, but never did. Shall I serve your dinner in the study also?"

She detected an undercurrent in his voice that she ought to explore, but she hadn't totally overcome her reluctance to pry. She nodded. "Yes, please, if you would."

Her father had introduced her cousin as James when he'd hired him, but all footmen were called James. Bea knew from the initials in her father's account books that his initials were JMC, so maybe it was his name. And the *C*? Should she ask? Perhaps Mac could.

Mac and James were like oil and water. Sighing, she proceeded to the study. If her husband thought he could escape by hiding in here, he'd best think again. She had nothing to lose by irritating him, and everything to gain by staying at his side.

"This is now your house as well as mine. You need not dress for dinner if you prefer," she announced as she swept into the study. Since Mac was still wearing his afternoon clothes, that was the only reason she could see for his absence at the table.

He frowned as James appeared with the tea table. "I wasn't hungry. I thought I'd set up a new set of account books for you before I leave."

"Wouldn't it be better if you asked me what I wanted in those books?" She took the wing chair next to the desk and allowed James to arrange the tray before her. "I'd like to have people's names instead of initials, for instance." Since that was on her mind at the moment, she turned to her footman. "Is your real name James?"

"It's of no moment, madam." He poured Bea's wine and refilled Mac's glass. "Will Mr. MacTavish be leaving us?"

"It's of no moment, cousin," she mocked.

James lingered. "The gentleman from the bank was here while you were gone, sir. I thought perhaps—"

"What gentleman?" Bea cried, nearly upsetting her tray to stare at her contrary, anarchic excuse for a footman. "Why wasn't I told?"

"Out!" Mac shouted. "Get out now, you blight upon the face of the earth!"

Bowing formally, James sauntered out, his mission accomplished.

"What bank?" Bea demanded. "About what? Tell me!"

Mac groaned and plowed his hand through his hair. "I don't have time for this, Bea. My ship is almost ready, and I have to figure some way of getting the children out of here, while keeping this damned place afloat until I come back, plus a thousand details in between. There is no reason for you to worry. You have your Ladies Aid Society and your consignment shop and the household to look after. Let me do my share."

"What bank?" Bea shouted, shoving the tray aside and starting to rise.

"From his card, I'd say the bank carrying the estate loan." He gestured at her chair. "Sit down. And if I'm not allowed to shout, neither are you."

Terror rippling through her, Bea sat. "What did he want?" she whispered. Had he come to assess the estate's worth? To give them final notice? What did bank people do?

"I wasn't here. I don't know what he wanted. But I assume from the letter waiting on the desk that he wants to know when we'll repay the loan." Mac lifted an official-looking document.

"Oh, dear." With no further interest in her dinner, Bea clasped her hands and looked pleadingly at the man who now held her future in his hands. "What will we do?"

Any man with any sense at all would sell this ridiculous house with all its ridiculous ornaments and get the hell out of here, Mac thought. Had Bea sold the . . . ? "What happened to the parlor?" he asked cautiously.

"I had it cleaned out," she replied in puzzlement at this diversion. "It's all in the attic. Why?"

Had she done it for him—made space in her life for him? He wouldn't ask. "I thought perhaps you'd sold them." He gestured dismissively. "The parlor looks good," he admitted, as if he knew anything of decorating. His shins appreciated the difference.

She smiled. "It does, doesn't it? I'd hoped you'd like it." Her expression returned to worried. "Could I sell them? Would that help?"

He shook his head. She looked so scared, he wanted to assure her everything would be just fine, and that she needn't worry her pretty head.

She'd take off *his* head if he said any such thing.

Mac rubbed his forehead. "I don't think selling things will pay this loan, Bea. Let me see if we can persuade the bank to extend it for another year."

She sat silently for a minute, staring at her hands—or at the ring he had given her on their wedding day. He very much wanted to make things right, to give her everything her father had given her and more, but he had just sunk all his cash into his new shipping venture. He wasn't destitute, by any means, but Bea's debts were larger than he could manage. It would be months before he recouped his shipping investment.

He'd made an extremely expensive choice in marrying Bea. His father would berate him of a certainty.

But when she lifted her head and met his gaze, he didn't regret his marriage for a minute. This was the woman he wanted, come hell or high water.

"I don't think the bank will extend the loan," she said quietly.

Mac raised his eyebrows in query.

She sighed and produced a crumpled letter from her pocket. "I asked Aunt Constance if she had any influence over the officers of the bank. I received this in the afternoon's post."

Mac thought his breath had formed a solid mass blocking his throat. He took the crumpled paper she handed him, but waited for her to explain rather than read it.

"The principal officer is the Earl of Coventry. He was a friend of my father's."

Mac groaned. The children's grandfather. All was lost. Bea couldn't hide the fact that she'd married a kidnapper. The earl would want revenge.

Bea nervously smoothed the folds of her silk nightgown. Aunt Constance had amused herself over the years by sending items to tuck away in her wedding chest, and she had a selection of nearly indecent nightgowns she'd never thought to wear. This one made her feel awkward and self-conscious, but when she looked in the cheval glass, she saw a woman who knew what a man liked. What *her* man liked.

The heart-shaped lace bodice scarcely covered her breasts. The clinging beige silk draped her waist and hips like a second skin. And her toes . . . She wiggled them against the carpet and let the ache of desire flow through her. Mac had even taken indecent liberties with her toes until she could no longer think of them without blushing.

Mac hadn't come to her room. Again.

She glanced at the clock on her bedroom mantel as it chimed midnight. She'd heard the floorboards squeak in the hall an hour ago. She'd hoped he would wash and disrobe and come to her, but he hadn't.

She wouldn't cry in disappointment. That was childish. She had to make up her mind what to do about it, and act on it. She was a grown woman, after all.

What could she do for a man who had just learned he'd married a bankrupt wife who owed a fortune to his worst enemy?

Tell him to sell the estate? That was what he really wanted, she knew. But then she and all her servants would be homeless. And if the person who bought the estate was like the earl, the village would wither away from neglect.

She couldn't bear it. She might dream of the places Mac had seen, the people he'd met, but this was her home, and she didn't wish to abandon it. She was just learning the courage to be herself here, and until she learned independence, she'd be lost anywhere else.

She supposed it would be equally difficult for Mac to be anyone but himself. He belonged on the open sea, or building railroads, or living in exciting places with people who got things done. She couldn't expect him to give all that up to become a farmer, even if he managed to hide from the earl long enough to do so.

She had no answers to their overwhelming problems. The only thing she knew with any confidence was that Mac liked having her in his bed. She still blushed at the thought that she could think such things, but she also thought she could come to love a man like Mac, even if he sometimes was the most irritating, arrogant, selfish man alive.

Because he was likewise the kindest, most compassionate, most thoughtful man she'd ever known. He was as worried about her as he was worried about the children. He thought he had to take care of them all.

She'd have to show him differently.

Using the suite's interior doors, wearing only her gossamer gown, she swept through their joint sitting room and, without knocking, threw open the door to her husband's bedchamber.

Mac sat in a chair by the cold grate, reading a book by the light of a single lamp. He'd removed his boots, coat, and waistcoat, and thrown off his cravat, creating an image of casual indolence in his stocking feet and shirtsleeves. But Mac was never indolent.

He looked up in surprise at Bea's entrance, and she thought his jaw dropped just a little as he caught sight of her in the light of the single candle she carried. He slammed the book closed and sat up straight. "Is something wrong?" he inquired politely.

Screaming and flinging things at his obtuseness seemed an excellent alternative to smiling seductively, but she didn't think it would be a constructive one. "I want to be a wife," she announced.

"A wife goes where her husband goes," he said impatiently. "You don't want to be a wife. You want to be a student."

Well, that was true. Bea bit her lip and sought a different approach. "Well, then, don't men have women that they don't marry? Mistresses? Could I be yours?"

He rubbed his forehead and shook his head, but she thought she caught just a bit of a gleam in his eye as he absorbed the impact of her gown.

"You're a lady. I can't treat you that way. Your father would come back to haunt me. Your servants would poison me."

"It's essentially what you wanted when we agreed to this marriage." She thought. She wasn't entirely certain of anything, but her tongue had come unleashed.

Crossing his hands over his chest, Mac sprawled his legs across the carpet and studied her with an intensity that heated her blood.

"Men don't marry mistresses. I wanted a wife. I didn't know that you were averse to ever leaving this damned place. I thought we'd have children together, work together. You are the one who doesn't wish to be married." He grimaced. "Not to me, at least."

"That's not true," she protested. "You are the only man I would ever consider marrying." She simply wanted to share his bed again, and he was being obstinate, denying what they both wanted.

He wanted her. She could see it by the way his hands tightened, and the place behind his trouser buttons swelled, and his gaze couldn't tear away from her. He'd granted her the power of being a woman. She need only learn to wield it. Tension rippled through her midsection, but she held the candle steady as she waited for his reply.

"Maybe so, but we're in no position to act on it now. Go back to bed, Bea. We'll work this out somehow, but not now."

She'd spent twenty-eight years of her life waiting. She refused to wait any longer. Slamming the candle down on his bedside table, she swung around and locked the key in the door. Then, with a smile, she dropped it to the floor and kicked it under the door, into the sitting room.

Before Mac could quite grasp what she had done, she repeated the action with the hall door, locking them in. Turning triumphantly as he fell back into his chair, cursing, she tugged her nightgown up. "I won't let you sleep in the chair, you know," she said much more calmly than she felt as the gown slipped over her head and tumbled to the floor.

He stared at her nakedness in the candlelight. She was so entranced by her power to captivate him that she forgot to blush.

"How will you stop me?" he asked, his gaze not lifting from what she'd revealed.

"Like this." Bea crossed the carpet and, with a determination she'd never known, straddled his lap.

"Bea," he groaned in what very much sounded like anguish as she began unfastening his shirt buttons.

She wouldn't look at him looking at her, but at the buttons she poked through their holes, one by one. "I am a very good student," she said firmly. "Do you wish to see if I can pass the final exam?"

Thirty-three

"Bea, we can't do this," Mac muttered, but already the reason why was fading into the red haze of lust. He was an experienced man. He'd seen and done many things. He'd never stared directly at the most voluptuous bosom a man could ever hope to see, and watch as rosebud crests puckered and all but begged to be ravished right before his eyes.

And then there were all the other temptations distracting him. His fingers clenched chair arms a hand's breadth from the firm curve of ivory waist and hips, and there, on the gentle slope in between, beckoned the most beguiling navel he'd ever longed to sip from.

He tried to freeze in place, to control his instant response to the pressure of heat and woman over his crotch, but that was one part of him over which he had never possessed any restraint. The swelling strained his trouser buttons, threatening to pop their last thread if Bea so much as moved.

"Bea, get in bed." He aimed for an authoritative tone.

"No," she said calmly, spreading his shirt open and rubbing her hands over his chest. Waves of glorious hair spilled forward, covering some of the temptation, but then he watched the fullness of her parted lips, and every bone in his body weakened.

No? His timid, shy Bea had told him *no*? For the second time. He must be dreaming. Mac groaned and nearly bucked out of the chair when she tweaked his nipples.

He was definitely dreaming. She lowered herself more securely until only his clothes prevented penetration. He raised his hips in a desperate bid to dislodge her, or to seek the tight inner cave she offered him. He was beyond telling which.

"I want to show you I can learn. How am I progressing so far?"

She pressed that lovely mouth to his. Mac gasped at the sudden ecstasy of her naked breasts firing his skin, and she took advantage by thrusting her tongue between his lips. As her hands and breasts teased his chest, she rotated in an erotic circle on his lap until he rose straight out of the chair.

She immediately wrapped her long legs around his waist and wouldn't let go. Clutching her soft bottom, Mac dropped her back on the bed. He would not be taken for a ride like some green lad. He was the master here, the one who dictated—

Bea popped his trouser buttons through their buttonholes as he pressed her down. Her legs held him trapped, but Mac was beyond noticing as the buttons fell free, and he leaned forward to take advantage of the rosy crests he'd denied himself earlier.

Her squeal of delight as she melted beneath him only increased his ardor. Seizing one tight petal with his teeth, he caressed the other until she was the one bucking for a closer connection.

Mac knew in the back of his mind that he'd lost the battle. He'd had some purpose in resisting that had dissipated with his uncontrollable lust, but the only thing that mattered now was removing the placket of material preventing him from having what he wanted.

Bea's determined fingers took care of the problem for him. Stepping out of the constraint of his trousers, Mac nibbled her lip and thrust his tongue between her teeth; then, catching her thighs, he splayed them wide, and held them pinned until she wriggled and moaned her need and desperately tried to tilt her hips to meet his arousal.

He hadn't removed his shirt, and it hung open, tenting Bea in its folds as he forced her to look up at him, to *see* him, to know this wasn't just some mindless game they played. Perhaps this was all he'd had on his mind when he married her, but they had gone far beyond that since then.

"Mac?" she asked uncertainly as he finally released her mouth.

"You are my *wife,* not my student." He had no clear idea of the source of this declaration, but he thought it was something they needed to clarify. "If I'm making babies inside you, then I have some say in how those babies are raised."

"You *want* to help raise them?" she asked in disbelief.

"Not only want, but will. I'll not have namby-pamby Percys and browbeaten Pamelas or holy terrors who know naught of their father." That much he did know.

"All right," she said hesitantly, watching his expression at first but distracted by parts lower as he drew his thumbs up her thighs.

He loved the way her eyes widened in surprise at each new sensation. "My children will go wherever I go," he warned. He didn't remember thinking about that. It was one of those emotional eruptions that took over his tongue without warning, and it seemed to make sense as he said it. He wouldn't neglect any child of his as Simmons had.

"That's absurd." She gasped as his thumb reached the apex of her thighs and brushed aside tight curls. "You can't possibly—"

She emitted a shaky little cry as his finger penetrated her. "Mac—"

"You started this." He leaned over again, running his hands beneath her curved buttocks, teasing her mouth with his kisses as he positioned his erection at the point of no return. "Now you must reap what you have sown."

She cried out in dismay and eagerness as he cupped and lifted her, then drove so deeply he felt huge enough to batter walls.

He should have stopped and apologized right there, when she whimpered and drew herself higher to ease his entrance, but then she wrapped her legs around his thighs and pulled him closer, and he lost thought of anything at all but the muscles clenching sensitive parts of his anatomy and the release he needed to claim her.

She clamped her legs, rolled her hips, and before he knew how she'd done it, his timid wife sat astride him, riding him so hard and fast Mac could only grab her hips, drive higher, and, with no control whatsoever, erupt with a force that would shatter a volcano.

Her muscles held him deep while the spasms of her release rocked through them, dissipating whatever barrier had kept them separate. Mac felt the dissolution as a physical thing, a melting and merging of their flesh until their blood flowed as one, and he was as much a part of her as she was of him.

Frightening in its immensity, their joining shook his soul as little else had. Gently rolling Bea back to the bed and resting his weight on his elbows, Mac stayed within her.

Bea gazed back at him in wonder. "I think we rocked the world."

"My world, of a certainty," he agreed dryly, too shaken to find logic. "And should anyone ever dare call you timid again, I'll laugh until my sides ache."

He wanted her again. After all that, he was still partially erect and growing. He could tell by the way her eyes widened that she knew it, too. He wasn't precisely a small man, and she was still tight as a virgin. Reluctantly he slid away and helped her to slip beneath the covers.

"It's only with you that I'm not timid," she murmured as he took her in his arms and ran slow kisses down her throat.

"And with the children," he reminded her. "Life changes us. You haven't experienced life yet, but soon you may have more life than your own." He stroked her belly to prove his point. Many more nights like this, and he would catch her with his child, if he hadn't already.

"I can do it," she said bravely, although her lip trembled at his frown. "I want you to think of me with eagerness, so you'll come back soon. I don't want some dainty little female to distract you."

How could he answer that? He wanted her in his bed every night of his life, and she still thought he wouldn't return.

He saw no sense in arguing. Suckling her nipple and teasing her to readiness with his fingers, he eased his anxiety in the only manner they had learned together.

Tomorrow he would make her understand. Tonight he had a delectable tigress in his bed, and he intended to train her to do his bidding.

The future wasn't always clear, but he'd stake anything that his had a wanton tigress in it.

Awakening to late-morning sunshine, Mac smiled sleepily at the spill of dazzling russet hair before his eyes and reached to snuggle his wife against his morning arousal. She purred deep in her throat, nestled into his embrace, and promptly fell asleep again.

Gradually becoming more aware of the sounds that had awoken him, Mac lay still. Voices. In the sitting room between his chamber and Bea's. Childish voices.

Frowning, he eased away from Bea, but his movement woke her. She looked at him questioningly; then she, too, heard the children, followed by a tap at the hall door.

"Wanta see Unca Mac!" a small voice demanded from the sitting room door.

"Mr. MacTavish, sir," a male voice called from the hall. Some urgency seemed attached to the inquiry.

"James," Bea whispered, groping for her nightgown on the floor with her toes.

"Stay there." Mac crawled out of the bed and located last night's trousers. They were a mass of wrinkles, but he didn't have patience with clothing at the best of times.

"Bea, Bea, Bea," a fairy voice chanted from the sitting room. "Mama Bea, Bea."

Mac threw Bea's nightgown at her. The children would be coming in, will they, nil they. Looking enchantingly confused and flushed, she pulled the gown over her head. While she groped to braid her hair into some semblance of order, Mac jerked on his shirt and fastened a few buttons. The knock at the other door was becoming louder. Even he knew something wasn't right.

He threw Bea his robe. "The key is on your side," he shouted at the hall door.

The door cracked open to reveal James looking distressed. "Viscount Simmons is downstairs with an officer of the law," he murmured. "I told them that you are not here and Mrs. MacTavish does not rise until noon. They don't believe me and won't leave."

Mac uttered a litany of curses. "Fetch Overton and

the others. They have their orders." Then, closing the hall door, he turned to watch the children rush in from the sitting room to engulf Bea, their nursemaid trailing worriedly behind them.

He didn't know how Simmons had found him, but he knew enough about English prisons to know an American didn't have much chance in one. And he couldn't desert the children. He had to take them and flee, as he'd always known he would.

He'd made preparations to safeguard Bea should this day ever arrive, but he had never fully realized how painful their parting would be. He watched as Bea hugged and kissed the children and accepted their slobbery kisses in return. Her eyes glistened with tears, so the nursemaid must have told her what was happening. Over their heads, Bea threw him a helpless look. Her distress tore at his heart. He was confident he could elude Simmons on his own, but carrying two children . . . Suddenly the likes of Digby and Overton didn't seem enough. He needed an army.

"I've packed their bags, miss. Ma'am." Mary held out the two satchels with which Mac had arrived. The maid pressed her lips together tightly, then glanced to Mac. "I'll go with you, if you wish. My mam needs me, but she'll understand if I go for a little while."

Heart crumbling to dust as he watched Bea's face, Mac nodded curtly. He wanted his wife with him, but even he realized why she could not go. Not so soon. It would take her time. And the estate was in dire trouble. She wouldn't run away from the responsibility. He needed more time to set things right, but fate was against them.

He caressed her cheek, wiping the moisture there with his thumb. "The ship is ready enough. Perhaps your aunt has found a governess. If not, I'll borrow Mary, if you don't mind. The children need someone familiar."

She nodded as she fastened his shirt buttons, but more tears poured to replace the ones he'd wiped away. "Pack your things," she said. "Let me hold them while I can."

He wanted to hold *her*, but he could see that last night was all he would have for months. Mac glanced at the clock—scarcely half an hour left before noon. He had to get the children and Mary into the carriage and away before Simmons barged up the stairs.

"Thank you, love, for everything," he whispered, caressing her cheek, prevented by the squirming children from saying more. Ten thousand worries swept through his mind. He didn't know how he could take the children to his parents when they so obviously belonged here, or how he could leave them in Virginia when he sailed back to Bea. And he could see all those same doubts rising in Bea's eyes as the inevitable finally arrived, despite all their efforts to pretend it wouldn't.

"I've made arrangements with my agent to advance you any money you need," he said hurriedly, trying to think of all the details he'd planned these last nights. "I'm having the estate set in trust for you, so no one can intervene should anything happen to me."

Her tear-moistened eyes widened in comprehension, but as he'd known, she wouldn't argue in front of the children. He wanted to show her he trusted her abilities, but the gaping loss facing them robbed him of words. He wasn't ready to go.

He had no choice.

Quickly stuffing his limited wardrobe into a bag, Mac donned his coat and waistcoat and boots while Bea bounced the children on the bed. He sent Mary to have the horses hitched to the carriage. He would drive to Evesham, take the train, and be in London before day's end. He'd ordered food, clothing, and toys for the children to be stocked on board, so that wasn't a concern. He'd need to find some way of communicating with Lady Taubee to see if a governess or another nursemaid had been found.

But he wouldn't be here to help if the old earl chose to wreak his vengeance on Bea. Shooting her a searching look, Mac let the pain and confusion overwhelm him for a moment. She was determinedly playing with the children and not looking at him. If he was a morass of doubt, she had to be in holy terror. And there wasn't a thing he could do. She'd given him the children's safety and some of the best days—and nights—of his life, and he was deserting her like a rotten cad.

Which was exactly what she expected of him.

Damn it all to hell. Heaving the remainder of his clothes into the bag, he snapped it shut. They'd both known this day would come. They were mature adults. They'd handle it. He'd slip back here before harvest. He didn't know how long he could stay then, either, but that was what they'd agreed on.

He leaned over and kissed her hair. "Overton will help. My father's agent will look into the mortgage. His address is on the desk, remember. If you need anything, anything at all, you're to call on him. Will you do that?"

She nodded, not speaking or looking at him but hugging the children as if she would never see them again.

She probably never *would* see the children again. When he'd first started on this venture, he hadn't thought that a problem. He knew better now.

His heart cracking at his wife's sobs, knowing he had done this to her, Mac gathered his niece and nephew into his arms, and let Bea straighten his cravat. He desperately wished he could stay just one more day, one more night, so he could find all the words he hadn't said.

He couldn't let Simmons have the children.

Handing his bag to James, Mac crept down the hall and the servant stairs, away from the home he'd realized too late was his—and ought to be the children's.

Thirty-four

Wanting nothing more than to collapse in tears, pound the bed, and kick her feet in terror and anguish, Bea watched out the upper-story window until Mac and the children vanished into the stable. Then she turned away, scrubbing at tearstains.

The tears kept coming—tears of fear as well as grief.

This was no time to give in to hysterics, she told herself sternly. She'd done that the day her father died, and it hadn't helped in the least. Mac's life depended on her. And so did the children's. She had to be strong.

She would not cry. Could not. Not yet.

Calling for her maid, she steadied her careening emotions by choosing the most elaborate morning gown in her wardrobe, a vibrant apple green silk with ruffles down the skirt front and sleeves, and an expensive lace mantelet to cover the bodice.

Mac would have loved the neckline of this bodice. She touched the place revealed above her breasts as he had done so many—not enough—times before.

No, she couldn't think like that or the tears would fall again. No matter how the idea terrified her, she had to delay the dangerously unpredictable viscount.

She had her maid heat her hair into shiny ringlets that peeped from beneath a tight lace cap. It was all last year's fashion, but far above anything one would expect in the rural countryside. She knew how to keep up appearances.

A maid knocked at her door a few minutes past noon. Bea had dressed at record speed, but she fully intended to delay as long as possible.

If it were the earl, she would not be so frightened. No matter what her aunt said of the earl, he had been a friend of her father's. But she'd never met his son and knew nothing of him beyond his neglect of the children. Any man capable of allowing his children to be mistreated to such an extent would not hesitate to harm an adult.

"They're threatening to come up the stairs," the maid murmured.

"Balderdash," Bea replied. "Tell them I am not satisfied with my shoes and will come down as soon as I find a suitable pair," she added in imperious tones.

The maid nodded and scurried away. Irascibility was a wonderful, marvelous thing for hiding emotion, Bea discovered as she wondered where the devil James had gotten to. The aristocratic tones of the irate shouting below as her maid delivered the message caused a momentary frisson of alarm. The low rumble of a second man whose tone she could not discern pacified the shouts. She trembled at the thought of facing either man, but for love of Mac and the children, she would be strong.

Her impossible husband had left without whispering a single word of love or comfort, just a casual mention of his gratitude. She'd known it had to be that way, but her heart was bleeding in so many places, she didn't think it would survive. Men were a different breed, she told herself. They operated on an even keel, full speed ahead, without thought to anything in their way. While her heart was pouring with tears, he would be checking navigational charts.

She would survive. Somehow. Mac had taught her she could stand on her own.

When the impatient bellows grew louder, Bea stiffened her spine, lifted her chin, and soared down the stairs in the same manner as she'd seen her aunt descend. Except she knew she was far more fashionably garbed and far grander in stature than her aunt would ever be. Mac had given her that much confidence.

As she sailed into the visitors' parlor, the jaw of the shorter man dropped to his chest. He was quite some inches below her, although he probably outweighed her by several stone. She assumed from his lack of tailoring and rough looks that he must be the "law officer" the viscount had brought with him. An ex–Bow Street Runner was more likely. Casting him a haughty, condescending look that had him twitching his hat in his hands, she didn't soften her stance as she turned to the enemy.

Viscount Simmons was a handsome blond man of average height who carried himself as if he owned the world. He wore an expensive high-crowned beaver hat, knee boots that no doubt revealed his reflection, and sported a useless gold-handled cane. His cravat was immaculate, his waistcoat ribbed with gold embroidery, and he had not seen fit to replace his fashionable London tailcoat for the tweed of the country. Puffiness about his eyes suggested the dissolution of his life, but other than some softness about the jaw, he appeared hale, hearty, and furious.

"Where is that damned MacTavish? I will not be stalled a minute longer."

Bea nodded regally. "If my husband's company is all you require, I believe London is the closest port. You could start there. Good day to you, sir."

She turned around and swept out again, every nerve in her body quivering as heavy boots followed her.

"Dammit, woman! Get back here. I want my children. Where are they?"

She drew herself up to her full height, whirled in a rustle of petticoats, and glared down her nose at him. "*Your* children?" She sniffed haughtily. "I should hope not. No decent man would claim to be father to those poor abused hoydens. If I cannot be of help to you, then James will show you out."

She looked up to discover Digby waiting at the front door. Her eyebrows soared, but she didn't let the viscount see. "Escort these gentlemen out, please."

"Gentlemen," her ex-butler intoned, bowing and opening the door as Bea turned her back on them and entered her dining parlor.

She couldn't hope that she'd be rid of them that easily. Ignoring Digby, both men followed her. She helped herself to a plate and began filling it.

"Doesn't it even matter to you that your husband is a kidnapper?" the viscount roared, shivering the chandelier.

Bea held a tight grip on her terror by gazing down her nose at him. "My husband is a man of integrity who cares for those weaker than he. But I am certain you would prefer taking this argument to him rather than browbeat a mere woman. I have no idea how often ships sail to Virginia, but I am told he can be easily found there." Bea prayed her hands didn't shake as she set the heaping plate on the table. She had no idea at all what food she'd piled onto it. The mere smell made her nauseous.

Digby arrived to pull back her chair, and she took the seat gracefully, arranging her skirts as if she had all the time in the world. She hoped her visitors were good and hungry. She had no intention of inviting them to the table. She had never been so daring and obnoxious in her entire life. She had Mac to thank for that.

"He is here, I tell you!" the viscount shouted. "Bobbins watched the house all night. He could not have gotten away. And I know he has my children."

Raising her eyebrows in his direction, Bea gently patted her lips with her napkin. "You have been reduced to spying on our household? For shame. It would have been much simpler to knock on the door."

"I *did* knock on the door. And then I've cooled my heels—"

The "officer" tapped the viscount's arm. "He probably took off the back way. I'll take a look around. He's not likely to get far with them two brats."

"That depends on how far you think Virginia is," Bea said serenely, although her heart skipped two beats. "I believe his ship sailed last night, but I cannot say for certain." She glanced at Digby, who hovered between her and the outraged viscount. "I don't think there is anything more I can tell the gentleman, Digby, and I would prefer to dine in peace. If you would . . ." She gestured toward the door.

She rather thought the burly officer would like to grab her by the neck and throttle her, but she reeked of society. He didn't dare touch her.

The viscount, on the other hand, was a different story. He seemed prepared to explode. Had she been a frail, fainting sort, he would have threatened her within an inch of her life. Had she wrung her hands and displayed any hint of fear, he would have been down her throat. She imagined he'd never encountered someone like her before.

She almost smiled at that. Almost. She certainly hoped Marilee hadn't been a frail and fainting sort, but she rather thought Marilee might have tried placating the beast, as most women had been taught to do.

"Search the upper stories," the viscount commanded

his henchman. "Even MacTavish can't spirit away those brats without a train of servants and trunks."

Bea had no desire to see these men stomping through the privacy of her home, but she couldn't ask an old man like Digby to stop them. She sent him a questioning gaze, and he nodded even more regally than she could.

"If madam does not mind, I shall show these gentlemen the door."

The viscount ignored him, shoving past to the hall, followed by his lackey. Bea watched anxiously as Digby followed them out. Where in *hell* was James? He was at least large enough to be intimidating.

At the sound of a new voice and even angrier tones from the hall, she couldn't bear the suspense. Slipping from her chair, she peeked through the space between the doors.

Overton waited just inside the wide front portals, a shotgun cradled in his arms. On the other side of him, the curate in full dress robes waited nervously. Digby blocked the bottom stairs, and as Bea watched, the hall gradually filled from the rear.

Cook's massive round form waddled to center place. Bea's maid stood righteously on her right. The scullery maid, clinging to Cook's apron, stood proudly on the left. Behind and around Cook and Digby, upper and lower servants formed a block of humanity protecting the household from invasion. Trapped between the servants at the stairs and the steward and curate at the door, the viscount could only vent his outrage in curses.

"They're my children!" he shouted. "Percy is my heir. You cannot steal him away. I will call the magistrate!"

"Your father is our local magistrate now that Squire Cavendish is gone," the curate said kindly. "We would greatly appreciate the earl's return. There are quite a few matters awaiting his counsel. I can assure you, the children are well cared for, far better than in the past, if the evidence of my eyes is to be believed. Please, if you would, fetch the earl."

Defeated by reason, the viscount swung around and located Bea shoving the dining parlor doors open. "You! You will pay for this," he shouted. "My father won't let you get away with it. Return my children or this land will be mine."

Satisfied he'd had the last word, he spun on his boot heel and stalked past Overton and the curate. The law officer lingered, throwing a speculative glance to the stairs, but Cook's menacing glare and kitchen cleaver deterred him. He, too, stomped out.

Bea's lips trembled as Overton and the curate followed, shutting the doors behind them. Tearfully, she glanced at Digby, then to her servants as they returned to their places. She'd always thought of them as her family, but she'd never known they felt the same for her. A tear spilled from her eye, and she hastily wiped it away.

"I cannot thank all of you enough," she whispered to Digby as he gently offered his arm and guided her back to the table. She knew he would pass on the message to the others. That was the way it had always been before her father died. She spoke to Digby, and he spoke to the others. She didn't know if she wanted that distance anymore, but she wasn't quite up to calling a meeting to express her gratitude.

"We know what you've done for us," he said with dignity. "You've stepped into your father's shoes far better than we could have hoped. You've married a good man in expectation of saving our positions and the village. You cannot be blamed if a spoiled little boy like the one who just left throws a tantrum and ruins it for everyone. As your husband would be the first to tell you, you cannot do it all."

Digby had never spoken to her in such a manner. Of course, Digby was an innkeeper and no longer her butler, but . . . she thought he might also be a friend.

"If only the earl were a reasonable man . . ." Her voice quavered, and she couldn't complete the sentence. She wanted to lay her arms on the table and bury her face and weep in terror, but she didn't have time for self-indulgence. Everything her father had left in her care would be lost if the viscount had some means of demanding that the loan be repaid. He could force all her friends from their homes.

The viscount could travel faster than Mac. What if the viscount suspected Mac had just left? He'd hunt him down and throw him in prison. She hadn't caused enough delay.

Only the earl could stop his son. If her aunt trusted him, surely the man couldn't be a complete cad. Bea stared at the epergne filled with flowers, her thoughts racing. She turned to Digby. "Where is James?"

Digby cleared his throat. "Ah, hmm, I believe he went with your husband."

Bea thought her eyes might fall out of her head. "With Mac? James went with Mac? Why ever for? They'll kill each other."

"I cannot say as to all his reasons, but I believe he had some notion of speaking with the earl."

"The earl?" Astounded, Bea pushed up from the table, staring at her former butler. "How? Why?"— and more importantly—*"Where is the earl?"* She had a dozen other questions, but this one was imperative. She'd thought the earl in Paris.

Digby looked worried. "I don't know that it matters, madam. There is naught any of us can do. He's not likely to see James. He'll certainly not see the rest of us."

"He'll see me." Bea knew the instant she said it that she should have bitten her tongue and thought three times, but she would not take it back now. She hadn't seen the earl since adolescence, but he'd know her name. She'd plead Mac's case, the children's plight, and fight for her home. He might laugh in her face, but she could leave no stone unturned, and the earl was the only stone in sight.

He'd once called himself her father's friend. "Is he at Landingham?"

Digby coughed and looked at her skeptically. "James said he's just returned to London, madam. Perhaps Mr. MacTavish will see him."

London! "Will James tell Mac where to find the earl?" she asked anxiously.

Digby had the grace to look guilty. "I don't believe so. He has some notion of a confrontation. I tried to persuade him—"

She didn't know what bee had invaded her cousin's bonnet, but he and Mac weren't likely to speak. She'd like to smack their heads together, but to do that, she'd have to follow them to London. *London.* She had to be insane even to think she could.

If she went to London . . . Perhaps if she explained, Mac wouldn't have to run. Perhaps the earl would stop his son and the children could be safe. . . .

She would not let her hopes run away with her. Mac might have sailed before she found the earl.

Swallowing fear, she considered it. She could reach London before a letter could reach Mac. Would James tell Mac about the earl's arrival? Probably not. Her cousin was up to something, which was all the more reason she must go to London. She firmly believed James had the capacity to turn London into a circus should he apply his lazy mind to it, but a circus wouldn't save her home and the children.

"I'll need someone to take me to Evesham," she said as firmly as her shaking soul would allow. She'd never seen a train. She had no idea how to get around London. She had lost her mind.

Evidently thinking the same thing, Digby looked at her doubtfully. "You cannot go alone, madam. It is impossible."

"My aunt does it." She hadn't known she possessed a stubborn streak, but she felt one forming now.

He sighed deeply, but whether with resignation or exasperation, she could not tell. "I will inform Mrs. Digby, and we will join you shortly." With a stiff bow, he turned on his heel and departed.

Bea stared after him in astonishment. He *hated* to leave his inn unattended.

Tears of gratitude welled in her eyes, but she still did not have time for them. She was going to *London*.

Maybe she could catch the same train as Mac.

Heart soaring at the thought, she raced up the stairs as fast as her skirts allowed.

She didn't want to stay behind any longer. Her world was no longer her house, but wherever her husband was.

Thirty-five

"**W**ould you care to tell me *now* what the devil you are doing here?" Mac growled, not for the first time, as the garish footman carried his luggage into the train station.

"Cutting my own throat," James replied airily, striding down the rough wooden platform ahead of Mary and the children.

"I'll gladly slit it for you," Mac muttered as he lowered the bags at the ticket booth and pulled out his purse, "but if you don't tell me what you're doing, you'll have to buy your own ticket."

He would damned well throttle the footman if he did not receive some answers soon. With the children, their nursemaid, and the luggage to carry, he'd been forced to use Bea's ancient barouche. The blamed footman had climbed onto the servants' rumble seat as it pulled out of the stable, and Mac hadn't had time to argue. But he wasn't taking the man to London without good reason. Several good reasons.

"I can buy my own ticket," James said loftily. "I needn't be obliged to you."

"I counted on your helping Bea!" Mac shouted, beyond frustration as he heard Pamela whining and, from the corner of his eye, watched Buddy straining at Mary's hand, ready to escape at the first opportunity.

"It's about time you thought of her," James answered acidly.

Mac didn't have to put up with this. Grabbing the tickets from the seller's hand, picking up the bags, Mac stalked back to help Mary. He wished with every ounce of his life that it was Bea standing there, babe in arms.

He didn't have enough damned hands. Setting down the bags again, he lifted Buddy onto his shoulders and bounced him. His first journey on his new ship would be a horror; he could see that now. If he could find an alternative, he would, but his prospects looked increasingly dim. The damned carriage had been so slow, he'd spent the last hour frantically looking over his shoulder, certain Simmons had to be on his heels.

"The train will be here in a few minutes," he reassured the nervous maid. "We'll feed them then and maybe they'll fall asleep."

She nodded and watched with curiosity as James appeared, ticket in hand. Mac didn't think punching the fop a wise idea, but it would certainly make him feel better.

"If we stand over there, we can catch the first car and avoid most of the smoke." Tucking one of Mac's bags beneath his arms, James lifted two others, leaving Mac free to balance Buddy with one hand and carry a fourth.

All right, so he'd wait until they were on the train to punch him, which was probably what the coward hoped. "You left Bea alone with Simmons," Mac griped as he used his size to shove his way to the spot indicated. Arguing with James gave him an excuse not to think of the trembling of Bea's lip, or the tears on her cheek. Yelling covered a whole range of emotions.

"I did not. I left her in Digby's hands," James said, staring at the rails ahead. "You are the one who deserted her."

Mac refused to be bullied into that argument. Bea knew why he had left. The target the footman's garish scarlet coat offered galled him, but the powdered wig was the outside of enough. "You stand out like a sore thumb!" he shouted in frustration. "Everyone in the shire will know we've been here and when."

James frowned fiercely. "They'll know anyway. Your only hope is to be on board ship and on the tide before the viscount realizes where you've gone."

The hiss, roar, and wail as the train clattered down the track rendered conversation impossible. Mac would have taken time to admire the magnificent machine's speed and beauty, to compare it to the American version in hopes of noting improvements, but he was too furious with the footman and too concerned about the children—and too devastated at leaving Bea—for either.

On his shoulders, Buddy screamed in terror at the noise and yanked Mac's hair. "It's all right, Bud. That's a train. It goes faster than horses."

That shut him up. Buddy loved horses better than anything.

"Giyyap, horsie," Buddy shouted over the roar of the steam engine pulling into the station. "Giyyap!" He pounded Mac's hatless head, dug his small fingers into Mac's hair, and tugged mercilessly.

With malice aforethought, Mac shuffled closer to the footman. They were almost of a height. Shifting slightly to the right, he put Buddy's busy hands within arm's reach of a certain haughty, bewigged head.

"Jemmy, horsie!" Buddy whooped, grabbing for the familiar servant and trying to grapple his way to a new set of shoulders. "Be my horsie!" With his small fingers digging into the powdered wig, he tried to lift himself forward, but Mac held him too tightly.

The wig slipped, and Mac straightened.

Buddy crowed at the new toy flapping in his fist.

James screeched, the train belched coal smoke, its brakes hissed and squealed as it pulled into the station, and, joyfully, Buddy flung the wig as far as he could.

Iron wheels crushed fragile white hairs into dust as the wig landed on the tracks.

Grinning broadly, Mac tried not to stare at the footman's shorn red hair. A man that tall and square-jawed really ought to have masculine black hair, not that feminine reddish stuff that looked just like Bea's—

Mac blinked and took a better look. Just like Bea's.

James glared at him defiantly, clutched his assortment of bags tighter, and shoved his way onto the first car as other passengers descended.

Ten thousand reasons for that red hair ran through Mac's head as he waited for the stairs to clear so he could guide Mary and the children aboard. He could just have Bea on his mind. The maid had giggled at the footman's new look but hadn't seemed to notice anything else odd. After all, James was purported to be a distant cousin. How distant?

It took at least a thousand years to elbow past porters and passengers to the seats James had claimed, juggle baggage and children, retrieve lost toys and ribbons, and dig out the finger foods Cook had provided, before everyone was settled. James growled at Mary's shy smile at his shorn head, glared at Mac, and frightened a bonneted matron away from their seats with his forbidding expression.

Not until the train was moving, with the children fed and sleepily listening to a story, could Mac jerk his head and command James away from curious ears. He counted on hauling the man out of his seat by the coat collar if he didn't follow, but, not unintelligent, Bea's tall "cousin" dragged himself up.

Locating an opening in the gentlemen's smoking

car, Mac waited for James to catch up with him. Without the wig, the footman appeared younger than Bea.

With his wife's face firmly in mind, Mac studied the handsome boy glaring back at him. Brown eyes, long jaw, high forehead, and that accursed red hair. On Bea, it was lovely. On this man . . .

"I suppose Squire Cavendish had red hair?" Mac asked coldly.

Leaning against the rattling wall, James shrugged. "Lots of people do."

All the vile emotions of the day crashed down upon Mac at once, and he didn't think twice about grabbing the younger man's coat, dragging his tall frame from the floor, and shaking him until his pretty teeth rattled. "I just left my wife defending her home from vicious rats, and I'm in no mood for games. The truth. *Now.*"

Unresisting, James lolled his head back and forth, and became a deadweight in Mac's grip. Disgusted, Mac flung him back against the wall.

Brushing off his lapels with abused dignity, James took his time replying. "It's none of your business." When Mac reached for him again, he hastily backed away. "It really isn't. I wouldn't hurt Bea if a thousand Mongols drove knives under my skin."

"That could be arranged," Mac replied grimly. He ground his teeth and clenched his jaw. "How much does my wife know?"

"Nothing," James said hastily. "I've been very careful. I told you, I wouldn't hurt her. She's earned every inch of that estate by enduring that addlepated old man all those years. Admittedly"—he held up his hands to fend Mac off—"the old man had a kind heart, but he also had a simple head. He seldom thought things through, didn't want to be distracted from his hounds. He paid my mother for my support, so he didn't owe us a farthing, but I told him I wanted to meet my half sister and see if the country would suit me, and he obliged. He had an appalling sense of humor to let me wear my disguise, and too much pride to let me work for anyone else."

Mac crossed his arms. "And what the hell did you think you'd accomplish by taking the position of servant in your father's household?" he asked. "Unless you inherited his disposition not to think things through," he finished maliciously.

James shrugged again. "Maybe I did. My mother is an actress, and I've supported myself the same way, but I was bored. I was curious to see what would have been mine if he'd bothered marrying her. If nothing else, I figured it would be good practice for the stage." His shoulders rose in a deprecating gesture. "He died so soon after my arrival, and Bea was so devastated, what else could I do but stay to help her?"

He didn't want to hear this, Mac thought. He really didn't. The six-foot baby had played the part of footman to visit the country and got stuck there. *Idiot!*

But then, what did that make him? Bea was devilishly easy to care about.

Mac stared out the window at the passing landscape, wishing he could see all the way back to Broadbury and Bea. How would she take the realization that her father had had an illicit affair and that her footman was actually her half brother?

He couldn't look backward. "Do you have a name?" he asked while groping for some sense in James's revelation.

The footman shrugged. "Matthew. I use my mother's name of Carstairs."

Matthew. Mac had as hard a time adjusting to the new name as to the new image of fop as relative. A Carstairs? The mind boggled. "Who's your mother?" he asked, figuring Bea would also demand an explanation one of these days.

"The black-sheep cousin of the Carstairses, cast out for her promiscuity. She is my mother and I love her, but I will be the first to admit that she is a shallow, vain woman who threw away her position to have as many men love her as she could find. I can understand what happened, I suppose. I'm four years younger than Bea. Her mother died when she was two. The squire was a grieving widower, susceptible to a pretty face. My mother was young and no doubt bored with the rural home where she'd been banished. I don't know what she was thinking, except of herself."

"And the squire had enough sense to realize she'd be no good mother to his daughter and send her off to London with a nice nest egg, which is probably all she wanted in the first place," Mac finished for him.

"Something like that, I imagine." James looked defiant. "What do you intend to do about it?"

"Hell, there isn't anything I *can* do about it. I'll be on a ship come morning, and you can do anything you damned well like. But so help me, if you hurt Bea . . ."

James rolled his eyes. "Aren't you listening? I'm her *brother*. I'm all the family she has besides Lady Taubee, and she's the one who encouraged me to stay. If I wanted to hurt anyone, I'd go after the Carstairses. I was just curious to see how the other half lives."

"And your reason for leaving her now?" Mac asked caustically.

"To tell her when you've sailed safely," James-Matthew answered blandly.

Bea clung to her bonnet as Digby raced the pony cart up to the train station, just as the train steamed away. She couldn't believe they'd come all this distance, only to watch the train carrying Mac and the children pull away. She was too stunned to weep.

If only she'd had the courage to go with him in the first place . . ."

"It's all right, dear. I'm sure there'll be another."
Mrs. Digby patted her arm.

Bea could only watch as the rackety cars clattered
past and out of sight. She searched every window in
hopes of seeing Mac, Buddy, anyone, but there was
too much smoke and steam, and the whole scene was
a blur before her eyes. She couldn't even raise an
interest in the view of her very first train. It was all
noise and smell and rumble—taking her family away.

The tears rolled then. Wiping inelegantly at the
moisture, she sat stiffly, waiting for Digby to tie up
the horse and make inquiries. She had only herself to
blame for letting them go without her.

She'd tried to make a marriage out of a business
arrangement, and had failed miserably. She'd tried to
make a family out of servants, and lost the only family
who mattered. She couldn't do anything right.

That wouldn't stop her from trying. It would have
been wonderful if she could have reached Mac before
he sailed, but she still had to find the earl. Stopping Mac
probably hadn't been within the realm of possibility
anyway. He was determined to take the children away,
and she supposed he must. His poor mother would
need them to fill the emptiness of her daughter's loss.
He was right to do this.

She had been wrong not to go with him. Mac had
said courage came from experience, but she had none.
Only now, she thought maybe courage came out of
love.

He had returned her estate to her name, taught her
to stand up for herself, given up his own time and
money to aid her. Maybe he did yell and get irritated,
but he'd taught her to read her father's ledgers, let
her see what she needed to know, even when she refused to believe it. Instead of frightening her into hiding behind closed doors as her father had, he had

encouraged her to come out and look around her. And she had failed him.

She wouldn't fail him now. The love he'd also taught her spilled recklessly from her heart, had driven her into the wild ride to the train station, and would keep her going forward.

She accepted the inevitable gracefully when Digby returned to report that the train might or might not return tomorrow evening, depending on track conditions.

"I'll hire a driver to take me into London," she said bravely. "You've done all you can, and I shall be forever grateful."

"The viscount's likely to have ridden straight to his father," Digby said sternly. "Horses travel faster than carriages, and he has a head start on you. Write a letter."

Write a letter. Once, letters had been enough. She had lived vicariously through words full of sound and fury, signifying nothing. Shakespeare had it right. Action was far better than words.

"No, I must see the earl myself. He has neglected Broadbury for far too long. He has neglected his grandchildren. No doubt he has neglected his son." She glanced around at the station and its environs. "Where would I go about hiring a driver?"

Digby sighed. "I could not live with myself if I let you go alone. It's late. We'll find an inn, and be off to London in the morning."

Bea listened to the blare of a mail-coach horn, and smiled. "No, I cannot impose on you. Take me to the coaching inn. I can find my way from there." She patted his freckled hand reassuringly, although there was nothing certain in her soul.

Digby looked horrified. "Impossible! Mr. MacTavish would have my head, and rightly so, should I let you do such a thing."

"But a mail coach will be in London by morning, and far more safely than we could travel," she pointed out.

"I'm not certain they travel at night, dear," Mrs. Digby said prosaically, forestalling further argument. "But it wouldn't hurt to ask. We need an inn anyway."

Bea didn't even know when coaches traveled, but she would learn. She would learn whatever it took to reach the earl. And then she would try to find Mac. That was probably another impossible dream, but she clung to it for all she was worth.

They took the cart to the nearby coaching inn, and while Mr. Digby went inside to make inquiries, Bea and Mrs. Digby availed themselves of the facility. Bea had never seen a public convenience before, and she truly didn't wish to see another again. She couldn't imagine how her aunt traveled if that was the state to which her comfort was reduced.

Wiping her hands daintily on a handkerchief as she stretched her legs in the rose garden beside the inn, she waited for Mrs. Digby to return. Everything was such a hustle and bustle here, she didn't know which way to look first. Her shyness prevented her from speaking to strangers, even if politeness hadn't required reticence. She could only watch and listen and learn and pray. She prayed a lot.

"Mrs. MacTavish," an aristocratic male voice called from just behind her.

Where had she heard that voice before? Nerves shattered by all she'd been through this day, she whirled to search the hedge. No one ought to know her here.

The Viscount Simmons and his hired man stepped from behind the nearest bush. "I believe your transportation is ready."

He did not smile when he said that. This was the man who had allowed his children to be abused, who'd drunk himself into signing them away, who wanted to heave Mac in prison so he could claim the allowance meant to keep his children. This was not a civilized gentleman with her best interests in mind.

Panicking, Bea started to run, but the burly guard blocked her way. She was taller. He was heavier. She turned to run in the opposite direction, but the ruffian grabbed her arms from behind so she could not scratch his eyes out.

Mac was right: men were stronger than women, even large women.

She screamed, and the viscount shoved his perfumed handkerchief into her mouth.

She didn't suppose they were taking her to see Mac.

Thirty-six

With weary pride, Mac watched as his gleaming new ship bobbed on the Thames. He'd had it built in England at a considerable expense to keep it secret from his father and to give him an edge over the other clipper designers in the States. Sails furled, fresh white paint shimmering in the sunshine, it merely waited for his command. He'd ordered *The Beatrice* painted in gold letters on its side just last week.

He could be sailing away on the morning tide. He should be brimming with excitement, so why did he feel as if this was the last place he wanted to be?

Despite their exhausting journey, Buddy was shouting in joy at the sight of the boats and the river. Mary looked nervous, and James-Matthew, disapproving. Once upon a time there had been only himself and his profits to think of. Now he had an entire army waiting for his command, and he wished he had Bea here to translate his irritation into polite words.

Oddly out of sorts, Mac ordered a rowboat to take them to the ship. He'd almost be happier if Simmons would show up so he could punch him and fling him into the Thames.

The nagging despondency didn't go away as he installed the children and Mary in his well-appointed cabin, and his new captain chattered about all the features Mac had personally designed. Beside them, James-Matthew sniffed his disapproval, but it wasn't the footman's opinion affecting Mac. It was his own.

He was deserting Bea. He'd left her in Overton's competent hands and would go ashore later to speak with his father's agent and the bank, but none of that was enough. Overton wouldn't teach her to set up new ledgers. The bank wouldn't help her to make decisions about the mill. And if she carried his child . . . he wouldn't know of it for months.

He couldn't leave her.

Mac stared at the bunk he'd hoped to share with his wife, and knew it was no place for Bea. She'd been right to stay behind. The tiny cabin wasn't suitable for the children either, but in that he had no choice. He would protect Marilee's children with his dying breath, and Virginia was the safest place for them. He just wished there had been some way of protecting them and keeping Bea by his side as well.

Mac propped his shoulder on the door frame and ignored the footman's pacing, the captain's chatter, and the noise of the children as they discovered the trunk of toys. He conjured up the image of Bea's worried expression as he'd told her farewell. At the time, he'd been methodically working his way down the prepared list of things he must do before sailing, but nowhere on that list had there been the right words for good-bye.

He'd *thanked* her.

God, he was the biggest lummox this side of the North Star. He should have hugged her, begged her, ordered her to come with him.

He should have told her he loved her.

The thought couldn't have hit him harder had they lowered the boom on his head.

He loved his beautiful, timid, courageous, marvelous wife. He wanted her in his bed every night, wanted her smile in the mornings, her eager questions in his days. He actually wanted to spend his time in the company of a woman, a lady, who smelled of lilacs and wore silks and kissed him until his head spun.

He didn't need ships and railroads for excitement. He had Bea.

She'd asked him for one good reason why she should leave the safety of the world she knew for the unknown of his, and he'd offered her nothing. How could he have been so blind? He'd left her thinking he'd married her for convenience. *Hell and damnation!*

He couldn't do that to her. He had full confidence his intelligent wife could stand up to a worm like Simmons, but he couldn't leave her thinking she wasn't worth all the love he possessed and more.

Buddy tugged on his trouser leg, and Mac glanced down to see the child waving a toy sailboat. "I'm sailing! I wanna show Mama Bea."

With tears building behind his eyes, Mac crouched down and hugged the boy. "So do I, laddie. I'll see what I can do." He couldn't leave them. He couldn't leave Bea.

He'd have to get rid of the viscount.

Standing again, dismissing the captain's ceaseless nattering, Mac started for the deck. "Send the cabin boy down to help with the children," he ordered. "Have the men help the nursemaid in any way she asks. I'm going ashore to see if a governess has been located." He strode off, leaving his captain with his jaw down.

James-Matthew eagerly fell into step with him as Mac traversed the deck in the direction of the rowboat. "If my duty is done here, I have errands to run in the city. What time will the ship sail? I'll see it off, and report to Bea as soon as it does."

"Balderdash," Mac said mockingly. "Unless you tell

me the truth, you'll stay here until I return. I'll not have you cavorting about the city, causing trouble."

"I can't stay here!" he cried in anguish. "I've things to do—"

"You'd best tell me what things, then." Mac signaled the ship's mate and pointed at Bea's irate half brother. "Keep this idler here until I give you leave otherwise." Bea would never forgive him if anything happened to the fool.

Mac climbed into the waiting rowboat while the seaman grabbed a screaming James. He'd rather the boy told him what he was about, but he didn't have time for games.

"The earl's supposed to have arrived in town by now!" James shouted as the rope on the boat creaked downward. "I can get an audience with him. Let me go with you."

Mac halted the boat's descent and considered the boy's anxious expression. Not a boy, actually. A man of twenty-four years who'd never had any responsibility of his own. Mac could sympathize.

Grimacing, he directed the seaman to release him. "I can get an audience without you," he grumbled as Bea's half brother all but dove headfirst into the boat.

"I'll be your witness," James gasped as the boat began its descent again. "I'll testify to your character, to the children's well-being, whatever you need."

Mac had been seriously contemplating returning to Bea to tell her all those things he'd forgotten to say, but the idea of confronting the earl had a definite appeal. The earl could stop his son. The man deserved to know that his grandchildren were safe. Maybe, just maybe, he could turn the man to his side. . . .

As they approached the shore, Mac frowned at the unusual amount of activity on the dock at this hour. He could swear there was a lady in an elaborately decorated feathered hat pacing back and forth. Perhaps she belonged to the elegant gentleman lounging against the lamppost, watching the ships on the river, although the lady appeared considerably older.

He was almost certain that was Cunningham waiting with his hands behind his back as the boat rowed closer. He hadn't summoned him. He didn't have time for this. He needed to see the earl—

"Lady Taubee!" James whispered in horror. "What is the old harridan doing here?"

Mac didn't know and didn't want to find out. Lady Taubee was not good news.

The footman uttered a curse and grabbed Mac's tall beaver hat to hide his bare head. "Baron Carstairs," he muttered, sinking low in the boat. "Why the devil is Carstairs here?"

"Why do I have the feeling I don't want to know?" Mac asked in resignation as the boat rowed closer, and the small crowd of London fashionables began to gather near the landing stairs. No one was supposed to know where he was. *Damn Cunningham.* Everyone in town would find the children at this rate. "How well do you know Carstairs?" he asked James suspiciously.

"No more than I know Simmons," James retorted. "They hang about backstage, looking for actresses."

Mac didn't want to hear about it.

Lord Hugo Carstairs looked mildly interested as he regarded the liveried footman in a beaver hat, but politely, he allowed Bea's aunt precedence as the rowboat docked.

"You wretch," Lady Taubee shouted. "You vile ingrate! You venal jackanapes! Had I thought for one moment you would desert my dearest niece and leave her—"

Carstairs stepped in to right the lady's slipping shawl and to block her parasol as Mac scrambled up the stairs. "Badly done, old boy," he admonished before Lady Taubee could continue her tirade. "No matter what the excuse, Miss Cavendish deserves better."

"Will someone tell me what the devil is going on? Cunningham? What are these people doing here?" Looming over all of them, Mac still felt outweighed and outnumbered.

"There seems to have been a mishap, sir," Cunningham replied calmly.

"Bea has been kidnapped!" Lady Taubee shouted, holding her hat in place against the strong wind coming off the river. "She has disappeared! I left her in your care and—"

"Mr. Digby believes there may be some connection with the Viscount Simmons," Carstairs intruded with a languid air covering a hint of steel. "You know something of this? Digby was kind enough to provide Mr. Cunningham's whereabouts so we might consult you on the matter."

The agent cleared his throat. "I have also received a missive from the viscount." All heads turned to stare at him. "He wishes to exchange the lady for his children."

Mac was aware of James freezing beside him, of Lady Taubee's furious exclamation, and his agent's curiosity, but the words *Bea has been kidnapped,* had hit him with the full force of a typhoon. He was halfway up the street and grabbing the reins of a promising stallion before he realized the others were racing after him, shouting.

"You'd best see Coventry first," Carstairs advised, catching the reins of the horse that Mac recognized from the blacksmith's in Broadbury.

"That was my intent," Mac said grimly. "If you have his direction, I'd be obliged." Surrendering the horse, he commandeered a waiting carriage by the simple expedient of jumping up past the idling coachman and grabbing the traces.

"That is my carriage, young man." Lady Taubee struck at Mac's knees with her parasol, but he shrugged off the pinprick while waiting for Carstairs's answer.

He growled as James leapt to the rumble seat but held a firm grip on the reins while the baron shouted up a street number.

"Cunningham, do you have the final paperwork on my ship?" Desperation ground at Mac's soul, but he'd trained himself to think logically at times like this. Fear and fury might be warring within him, but he understood the need for weapons.

His agent produced the packet from his coat pocket and handed it up. "All is in readiness and awaiting your word. Shall I accompany you?"

Mac stuck the papers inside his coat. "Have you had any luck in locating a governess who is willing to emigrate?"

"Two ladies have inquired upon your wife's recommendation," Cunningham said. "I thought you might wish to interview them."

"Normally I would, but if anything happens to me, that ship must sail. Bring both of them aboard if necessary, and await word."

Excellent agent that he was, Cunningham nodded and stepped back.

In a flutter of skirts and a rash of curses, Lady Taubee succeeded in climbing up the outside of the carriage. "You left Bea!" she ranted, smacking Mac with her parasol again.

"I have not left her," he shouted, snatching the parasol and heaving it overboard. "I have no intention of leaving her, and I would greatly appreciate it if you would be quiet and let me think." Flicking the reins, Mac sent the horses barreling down the street, leaving the lady to hang on as she would.

How could the viscount have kidnapped Bea? He'd

left her surrounded by servants. He didn't perceive Simmons as a particularly dangerous man so much as a desperate one. His precautions should have been adequate.

Mac glanced at the old woman clinging to the seat. "Why is Carstairs here?"

"Digby sent messengers to everyone in London." She regarded him with hauteur. "Carstairs came to me to see if it was a hoax. Smart young man. I should have chosen him instead of you."

"Carstairs had twenty-eight years to recognize Bea's worth and capture her interest, and he didn't." Mac dismissed her insult without further thought. Digby had sent the message. How had Digby let Bea be taken from the house?

The carriage careened wildly around a street corner, but Bea's aunt gamely clung to her seat and hat. "And you did, I suppose?" she called scornfully.

Torn from his thoughts, Mac stared at her before registering her question. "I married her, didn't I? You don't really think you forced me to do anything I didn't want to do?" He guided the horses around a tangle at an intersection, then whipped them faster. "I was afraid it wasn't the best thing for Bea, but if she agreed and you approved, I didn't intend to argue. I know value when I see it. There isn't another woman to match her in this world. If Simmons really has kidnapped her, she'll have him regretting it soon."

Lady Taubee stared at him as if he were deranged. "How can you say such a thing? My poor Bea will be terrified! I know she is priceless, but the poor dear is afraid of her own shadow."

Remembering how her "poor dear" had seduced him out of his decision to leave her bed, Mac grinned. "I hate to disagree with a lady, but Bea has the soul of a soldier. She's civil and obedient and willing to do as told until she's told to cross the line between right and wrong. The woman knows her own mind and is as stubborn as an old mule."

"Sir!" Indignant, Lady Taubee sat back. "That is no way to speak of my niece."

"Calling her timid isn't either." Mac hauled on the reins at the sight of Carstairs dismounting in front of a mansion far bigger than the one Marilee had called home. If this house was his, the Earl of Coventry had wealth and power to spare.

It had never crossed his mind that he might lose Bea.

It hadn't occurred to him that he might lose Marilee either.

Terror grinding at his already heaving gut, Mac leapt down the instant the carriage halted. Let James assist the harridan.

A powdered and liveried servant buffing the newly installed door knocker swung around in astonishment at Mac's abrupt dash up the stairs. The man's eyes widened as Mac grabbed him by the back of the coat and shoved him past the partially open door.

"Get the earl. Now!" Mac threw the man in the direction of the interior stairs.

The servant stumbled and hesitated. Lord Carstairs sauntered through the open doorway, swinging his walking stick and doffing his hat. "Is the earl receiving?" he asked in polite tones.

The servant looked relieved at this example of civility. "No, sir, he is not. He and"—the man looked nervously at Lady Taubee as she swept in—"and Lady Coventry are still abed."

"He married an actress," Lady Taubee hissed in loud tones that would have fared well in an opera house. "Old fool. Of course they're still abed."

Mac didn't have time to waste arguing. He started up the stairs two at a time. He'd find the earl without help.

"I say, old boy," Carstairs called to him, "that just isn't done."

"Someone intending to stop me?" Mac continued upward. He'd spent too long waiting for the old man to show up and inquire after his grandchildren. Well, he wasn't waiting any longer.

"MacTavish!" James-Matthew shouted up at him. "That's my mother up there. If you insult her, I'll have to call you out."

Every head in the foyer turned to stare at the garishly dressed footman as he entered, removing Mac's hat to reveal his shorn red hair. James-Matthew glared back.

"What the devil is all the racket?" a querulous voice called from the upper landing. "Constance, is that you I hear? Paula won't be up for hours. Go away."

Into the appalled silence that fell, Mac shouted up the stairs. "Coventry? I want my wife back, and I'll hang your son if he doesn't hand her over!"

Thirty-seven

"Can't a man have a minute's rest without being driven from his bed by every ragtail and gaggle in the kingdom?" the earl roared, stomping down the stairs in bedslippers and satin dressing robe. "Where the hell are my servants? What do the lot of you want? Constance, you're old enough to know better," he shouted, finding the one woman among them.

"Don't speak to me that way, Percy Ludlow Simmons, or I shall rip every gray hair from your soft head!" Constance called back, wielding her mangled hat like a sword. "Your wretch of a son has kidnapped my niece, and I'll have him dipped in boiling oil if he doesn't release her at once. We've known each other far too long for your blustering nonsense to fool me for one moment."

Mac interceded before the angry old man could launch into a harangue and the argument descend into name-calling. "Your son, sir, is threatening my wife."

The earl tightened the belt on his dressing robe, ran his fingers through his full head of graying hair, and, stomping off, led the gathering into his front parlor. A man of considerably less stature than any of the younger men in the room, he still commanded their attention with his presence.

"Why the devil should I believe you? This is preposterous. Leave the country for a few months and the whole place goes to rack and ruin. What do you want of me? If I had any control over my son, he'd not be the sot he is now."

Mac cut off a cacophony of replies with a chopping motion. "Yesterday at this hour, your son was in Broadbury, threatening my wife. Last night she disappeared. This morning my agent received a ransom note. My wife would not have gone with him willingly or quietly. Where could Simmons take her that they would not be noticed?"

"Landingham, of course." The earl shot him a look of disgust. "Not that any of this is at all likely. If we're talking about Constance's niece, I remember, she is not a small woman. Sebastian couldn't force her to go anywhere."

Mac had forgotten how small a world London society really was. Of course the earl knew Bea. His estates marched along hers somewhere to the north. He'd probably gone hunting with her father. "Your son hired a Runner. Bea has never learned the fine art of fisticuffs, but I have. You'd better hope *Sebastian* hasn't hurt her, or the next time you see him, he'll be in pieces."

Snatching his hat back from James, Mac strode for the door, his mind busily ticking off the various means of reaching Landingham. The earl didn't deserve to know where his grandchildren were. He hadn't even asked. And Mac damned well hadn't said.

Without asking permission, he caught the reins of Carstairs's magnificent mount. The animal reared in protest, but Mac held the leather until the horse knew who was in charge, then kicked it into a canter as shouts of outrage followed him into the street.

Holding her breath and biting her bottom lip, Bea worked at the final pin keeping the door hinge in place. No one had noticed the hinges' loosened condition when they'd served her a meal a little after noon, but should anyone attempt to open the locked door now, it would fall on his head. She'd rather it didn't fall on hers.

She had a hard time believing she was in this dreadful position. She lived a quiet, mousy life. Her first real venture into the world, and she got kidnapped. Quite preposterous, when one thought about it.

She supposed if one must be kidnapped, it was best to be taken by a viscount who brought one to a sprawling mansion, with fine linen sheets and hot baths and all the refinements. But she had no desire to stay here, particularly if the viscount had some idea of trading her for the children. She would not let him have them.

The last pin finally slid from its hinge under the persuasion of a little salad oil she'd demanded with last night's greens, accompanied by a judicious amount of butter from her luncheon roll. Holding the door in place, Bea leaned against it and listened for sounds from the corridor outside. As far as she had been able to tell, Landingham was all but deserted, although she supposed there must be servants in the kitchens. Her kidnappers thought her safely locked away in an empty wing of the mansion, where her screams wouldn't be heard. They didn't seem to grasp that she'd spent the better part of her life running a large household. One did not always move furniture for spring cleaning without first removing doors.

Hearing nothing, she eased the door off its hinges and opened it sufficiently to slip through. She wasn't under any illusion that they wouldn't notice if they checked on her. She had to escape before then.

She had never been inside Landingham. She hadn't a notion of how to find her way out. She'd tried watching as the Runner manhandled her up stairs and down hallways, but she'd lost count of doors somewhere along the way.

It occurred to her that she didn't want to be unarmed should she run into the blackguard again. Peeking into a bedchamber, she grabbed a walking stick and a brass candleholder. Next time she'd have more than her fingernails with which to dent him.

She located the main stairway easily enough. Hesitating at the top, she listened for voices, but the place was much too immense. She could take her chances and go down, or go back and try to locate the servants' stairs. She rather suspected the servants' stairs would be hidden behind paneling in a place like this.

Well, there was nothing to do but go forward.

Her luck ran out just as she caught sight of the spacious tiled foyer below. The front door swung open, and Viscount Simmons strolled in.

It wasn't as if she were small enough to shrink into the shadows, even if she didn't have billowing skirts and petticoats that spilled over several steps at once. If he looked up, he would see her. If she so much as moved, she'd draw his attention. And it was darned hard holding on to her rustling skirts with stick and candle in hand.

He looked up. She could have sworn she hadn't moved, so it must be his guilty conscience at work. Brazenly, Bea swept down the stairs as if she belonged there. She scarcely had any choice. The front doors were her best hope of freedom.

Her bold approach caught him by surprise. He didn't even start shouting for his hireling until she reached the bottom and approached him with weapons held high.

"I'm going home now," she told him calmly, although the statement was insensible enough to be hysterical, she reflected as the gentleman leapt into her path.

"Don't be foolish, woman. You can't go anywhere."
Rather than lay hands on her, the viscount blocked
the double doors.

Bea regarded him through narrowed eyes. She'd
learned men were far stronger than she'd thought, so
she wouldn't dismiss his padded frame too easily. His
cravat lay immaculately crisp and unwrinkled, and his
trousers were the picture of perfection. Not a hair
on his fashionably trimmed head seemed disturbed. A
kidnapper really ought to look more like a rogue.

This one smelled like the bottom of a malt barrel.
Bea had seen and heard men in their cups. She knew
to be wary, but she had to get past him.

"This is quite the most foolish thing I've ever heard
of, and I've tired of the game," she said. "I am going
home through you or around you. Your choice."

"Not until I have my children back." The viscount
crossed his arms over his chest.

"You had your chance with those children and you
mistreated and neglected them and now you've lost
them. Kidnapping me will not bring them back."
Hearing the sound of lumbering feet approaching
from the rear of the hall, Bea began to panic.

The viscount heard the steps as well, and relaxed
slightly. His mistake. He should never underestimate
the power of a woman. Bea swung the walking stick
with all her might, striking his knee with a satisfying
crack. He cursed and danced on one foot. Using his
unbalanced position for leverage, she shoved his
shoulder, toppling him sufficiently so she might jerk
open the front doors.

The pounding of heavy feet echoed on the tiles.

It was impossible to fly in acres of petticoats, but
she did her best. Clinging to her weapons, she lifted
as much fabric as she could grasp and ran full-length
down the wide front steps, the viscount stumbling to

his feet and cursing behind her, his hireling huffing and puffing in close pursuit.

If only she could see another person . . . She knew everyone in the shire. Surely they would report her presence, run to town, tell the curate, anything!

She screamed in frustration as she heard the heavy footsteps of the ex-Runner closing in. She thought Runners were supposed to uphold the law. *Damn the man.* She halted abruptly, turned, and whacked the stick as hard as she could across his jaw, then walloped him hard about the shoulders with the brass candleholder. The man howled in rage and grabbed for her. She dodged and ran for the drive.

The viscount raced at her from the side, and she stopped again to smack him hard enough to send his head spinning. She couldn't fight two of them at once. Grabbing her skirts as the viscount staggered, she ran harder, screaming her lungs out.

Mac couldn't believe his eyes as he raced the sweating horse up the drive and nearly galloped over a frantic, screaming Bea. Hauling on the reins, he lunged from the saddle almost before his mount halted, and enveloped Bea in both arms. She threw herself into his embrace with tears and muddled cries and grateful kisses. He couldn't make sense of her words, but he understood her tears and the sight of the two men pulling themselves to a standstill behind her. Both of them looked as if they'd been through a mill, and he squeezed Bea tighter.

"My turn at them, love. Stand back."

Fury pouring through him, Mac set his wife aside as the Runner approached with fists raised. Murder in mind, Mac disregarded his opponent's fists, and swung his boot violently upward instead. He needed the release of a solid strike more than he cared about the accuracy of his target or the method of his blow. He set his mouth in satisfaction as the point of his boot struck a soft muscle.

The Runner howled and bent to protect his valuables, and Mac countered with a swing of his fist to the side of a thick head. His opponent toppled like an overturned statue.

"Bea! My precious!" Lady Taubee screamed from the window as her carriage recklessly rounded the curve, and the driver attempted to haul the horses to a halt without trampling the combatants.

Mac looked up in time to see Bea vehemently swinging her walking stick at the viscount. Satisfied she had Simmons under control, Mac rounded on the Runner, who was trying to rise. It felt good to plow his fist into solid flesh.

Carstairs leapt from the carriage, leaving Lady Taubee to scream until someone lowered the steps. With eyebrows raised, the baron approached, idly dangling his walking stick while looking for a likely opponent. Mac ignored the baron as the Runner tackled his knees and toppled him into the dust. A kidney punch ended that presumption.

The earl's carriage rolled onto the lawn with the driver fighting the rearing horses to a standstill. James leapt from the rumble seat and raced toward the fray.

Figuring Bea might be tiring of holding back the viscount, Mac shoved away from the Runner, kicked him hard to keep him down, then, dodging Bea's swinging stick, plowed his fist into *Sebastian's* nose. A satisfying spurt of blood followed as the viscount sank to his knees.

"I've got him!" As the fallen Runner tried to rise, James-Matthew jumped on the man's chest and bounced up and down, slapping his jaw every time the man tried to move. "I've got him, I've got him!" he crowed in delight, until the Runner began to heave up his breakfast. James leapt aside and scrambled for safety.

"Someday remind me to teach you to fight like a man," Mac grumbled, standing belligerently over the viscount's crumpled form.

"Beatrice, my poor dear, are you all right?" Lady Taubee raced to take Bea into her comforting arms, nearly losing her towering hat in the process.

"My son is on the ground and you're asking if *she's* all right?" the earl asked wryly, sauntering toward his groaning heir and waiting for Mac to back away. "I'm thinking I should have stayed in France." As his son attempted to rise, the earl calmly planted his foot on the viscount's midsection, holding him down.

"Go back to France and your hedonistic pleasures," Mac replied coldly, brushing himself off and retreating so the approaching servants could tend the viscount. "Why concern yourself with the trivial matters of family and responsibility now?"

The earl scowled. "Why, you young jackanapes—"

Carstairs dug idly at the retching Runner with his walking stick. "Your son hired a bully to kidnap a lady. You might want to listen to Mr. MacTavish, my lord."

"I might wish to hear from my son," the earl stated firmly.

The viscount glared at all of them from his ignoble position flat on the ground. "If anyone is a kidnapper, *he* is," he said, indicating Mac. "He stole my children, and I want them back."

"You gave them away," Bea corrected, stepping away from her aunt. "They'd been mistreated so badly that Buddy had a broken arm and Pamela had nightmares. You're a pig and a selfish lout and you don't deserve those children any more than you deserved the wife you had."

"Buddy?" the earl asked in puzzlement as he removed his foot from his son and stepped away so the butler could help him to his feet.

Holding a handkerchief to his broken nose, the viscount turned his glare on Bea. "You know absolutely nothing! I loved my wife. The children are all I have left of her, and I want them back." He hiccuped and reached inside his coat for a flask. "She haunts me," he whimpered convincingly. "I cannot let them go." He wiped a bleary eye on his coatsleeve.

Mac screwed up his eyes and shook his head to see if cobwebs were blocking his hearing, but Lady Taubee was already comforting the elegant, weeping fool, and the earl was looking at Mac as if he were a murdering pirate. Carstairs had retreated in amusement and disbelief.

Mac lifted his head and found his wife staring with curiosity at an unwigged James. *Uh-oh.* The footman was looking both sheepish and determined, as if debating whether to reveal the truth. The last thing Mac wanted right now was to explain the indelicacies of the wretch's parentage. Maybe he could sail away and . . .

He wouldn't be another Simmons, dodging responsibility. He was bigger than that.

Far bigger, he decided with a grim smirk. Draping his arm over Bea's shoulder, Mac diverted "James" by introducing him to his other family. "Lord Carstairs, I believe Matthew here needs an introduction, since his mother . . ." Mac raised his eyebrows in the footman's direction, certain he had the story right. The boy nodded. "Anyway, it seems his mother is now married to the earl. Paula Carstairs? Ring any bells?" He'd be damned if he'd explain the nature of the boy's relationship to Bea in this crowd, but the lofty baron needed some starch taken out of him.

"Paula? My aunt? *His mother?*" The baron gaped in astonishment; then, fully taking in Matthew's livery, he almost staggered.

"Mac?" Bea whispered questioningly, looking for the entire story.

"Not now. There's more to be done." Taking a deep breath and leading her away from the shouting crowd, he whispered in her ear, "If I don't find time to tell you later, I love you. I wanted to tell you with roses in hand and a bed nearby, but I'm not making the mistake of letting it go unsaid a moment longer. I love you so much it tears me up when we're apart. All right?"

"Mac!" She gazed at him with as much astonishment as the baron was staring at his newfound cousin, but Mac didn't have time to explain. The shining light of surprise and adoration in her eyes gave him hope. "And how in hell did you manage to get kidnapped?" he asked in less gentle tones. He wouldn't let her off easily.

"Well, I was on my way to London to find you—" she started to explain.

"*You* were going to London . . . to find *me*?" He couldn't quite grasp that—Bea, leaving her home, for *him*?

"Why else would I go anywhere but to be with you?" she asked reasonably. "I was just beginning to learn the spirit of adventure when the viscount—"

"Don't even think of going anywhere without me from now on," he murmured as he planted a fast, fierce kiss on her mouth. Releasing her, he strode determinedly toward the man who held their future in his hands.

She'd been on her way to London . . . for him. *To hell with hope.* He felt damned cocky with certainty.

Pulling the ship's papers out of his pocket, Mac caught the earl by the shoulder and spun him around. The old man seemed too stunned and bewildered to protest the action.

Mac shoved the papers at him. "I'm full owner of

this clipper and its cargo. I want you to use it as collateral against the mortgage your bank holds on Bea's estate. I'll pay the interest on the loan when the cargo sells, and begin payment on principal when the fall crops come in."

"Mac, you can't do that!" Bea protested tearfully. "That's your future. You can't sink your money into a losing proposition. Even I know that much."

"It's not a losing proposition," he said firmly. "I'll recover my investment and more over time. My future is here, with you. A ship is no companion at all and makes for a damned cold bed partner."

Bea couldn't believe her ears. First he said he loved her, and then he said his future was with her? Where was the man who had arranged his marriage around his business? Had she wanted to hear those words so much that she'd just imagined them?

Mac ignored her questioning look in favor of pursuing his own goals. "I want Buddy and Pamela to stay with Bea and me," he continued resolutely. "Your son is a drunken sot and no fit father for them, and they love my wife. I will do my utmost to see that my niece and nephew are brought up as my sister would have done. If you cannot agree to that, I have it in my power to send them to Virginia, where you will be lucky to see them again—if that matters to you at all."

Now *that* was the man she knew, Bea thought. Mac stood tall, broad, and square-shouldered, his golden brown hair gleaming in the sun. With bloodstained shirt and torn cravat, he was more rumpled than a knight in shining armor, but he was stronger and braver than Lancelot. Bea dug her fingers into his arm. Mac was capable of striking down a whole round table of knights in defense of his sister's children. She thought perhaps she might have to step in and negotiate a truce. She could see where she might have some place in his life for the single purpose of soothing Mac and placating the people around him.

The earl still looked stunned and disbelieving as he gazed first at the papers in his hand, then at Mac, then over to his bruised and battered son, who was being mothered by Lady Taubee and bandaged by a maid. "Buddy?" he asked again.

"I'll be damned if I'll call him Percy," Mac answered grimly.

"Percy." The earl nodded in understanding, his expression clearing. "Always hated my name. Told the twit not to name him after me." He looked at Mac with more interest now. "You want to take on those two hellions? Have you lost your mind?"

"They're not hellions!" Bea protested. "They're wonderful, loving, intelligent children who've been unloved and unwanted for too long. Perhaps Buddy is a bit . . . creative . . . but there's nothing wrong with that."

"Creative." The earl snorted. "The brat can't be contained in the nursery for more than two minutes at a time. He'd make an excellent escape artist." He glared at her. "And you want to take in children who don't even belong to you? You must be as mad as he is."

"If I am, it's an honor." She smiled up at Mac, who still clenched his hands in fists. "I've never been told I'm mad before. Do you think that's been my problem all along?"

Her husband's lips twitched, but he continued watching the earl. "Aye, lass, and it's a bit fey you are to be taking on the likes of us, but it'll pass. And you willing or not, your lordship? I'm an American and a Scot and I'm not likely to be raising them with polished manners and hoity-toity airs. My father brought me up to work and earn my way, and that I have."

Lady Taubee heard this last, and she snorted in much the same manner as the earl had earlier. "Don't listen to his blather. His mother is Lady Jane Warwick, of the Gloucestershire Warwicks. A snobbier lot you'll never see. And for all his father is the younger son of a younger son and in the line of a whole succession of rebellious Americans, there's earldoms aplenty in that family as well. He knows his manners. He just doesn't use them."

Bea snickered and stood on tiptoe to press a kiss to the back of her husband's neck. He reddened and tried to stiffen his shoulders. Behind his back, she tickled him under the arm. He twitched and continued staring at the earl.

A whole line of earls and snobs had produced her rumpled, barking visionary of a husband. She kissed his neck again, and he reached back to swat her. Not that swatting her petticoats hampered her in any way. She wrapped her arms around his waist and leaned her cheek against his shoulder, and he relaxed, at last.

The earl patted the papers against his palm, glanced at his pleading son, and back again to Mac's determined expression. "You'll let my son see them? He's their father. He has that right."

"He surrendered that right—"

"Of course, if he is sober," Bea answered for him. Her daring no longer astonished her. It should be quite interesting to see if it had limits, though. "And if he stays sober and shows himself to be a willing and capable father, then of course we must all consider what is best for the children. But for now they need security, and they're happy with us."

The earl nodded and glared at his son. "You have a better argument?"

Looking ill and defeated, the viscount shook his head. "I don't know how to deal with them. I've hired nursemaids. . . ."

The earl turned back to Mac. "I won't interfere. I'd hoped your sister would steady the boy. I believe she tried. She was a good girl, a wonderful mother. I'd see her children raised as she was."

Tears welled in Bea's eyes as Mac thanked the earl and led her away. The children were theirs. Mac was hers. He loved her. She wasn't kidnapped anymore. It was all too much to take in at once. She didn't even look at James and Lord Carstairs. Or her aunt. She tried to grasp one little thing at a time.

"The children are still on the ship," Mac whispered in her ear. "Shall we go to London to fetch them?"

London. Oh, my heavens. London.

She couldn't remember answering coherently. She could only see the warm gleam in her husband's eyes as she looked up at him. She must have agreed for him to be looking at her like that. She'd agree to anything to keep him looking at her like that.

Her heart sang as they entered the waiting carriage.

Epilogue

"Shouldn't we retrieve the children first?" Bea asked anxiously as she gazed out the window of their luxurious London hotel room. She'd never seen so many amazing sights or eaten in so many strange places or talked to so many strangers as she had this day. Mac might as well have taken her to Virginia for all this resembled the England she knew. She could see gas lamps along the street below. Elegant carriages harnessed to prancing horses with bobbed tails traversed the cobblestones. She'd seen windows full of beautiful hats and gowns, and ladies garbed in trailing skirts followed by liveried servants more garish than James had ever been. And now she was standing in a hotel room adorned in velvet and silk with tasseled draperies and gilded French furniture and all she could do was gape.

"Cunningham left word that he'd hired two governesses and put them on board. They're fine. I think it's time I have a honeymoon alone with my wife."

"Oh." Bea swung around to gaze up at the husband she'd not thought to see again for months. His crumpled cravat had blood upon it, and he'd torn the seam of his best coat in his fight with the Runner. His hair hadn't been cut in weeks, and it fell forward over his wide forehead in an unruly swath. Her heart ached with so much love for him that she thought it might burst. A honeymoon!

She smiled slowly at all that could mean, and heat began to simmer in Mac's eyes as he read her expression. Heat and . . . mischief?

Untying her bonnet, he threw it on the nearest table and reached for the mantelet concealing the neckline of her gown. "I thought perhaps, after a long day like this, you might appreciate a hot bath."

A hot bath? Yes, that would probably be best, if she could think of anything other than the hands pushing aside her lace and reaching to unfasten her hooks. Close like this, Mac was just a bit . . . overwhelming. Bea breathed deeper to steady her beating heart as practiced fingers unhooked and unlaced and pushed her bodice down. She sank her fingers into his waistcoat and held on tight as she adjusted to the heat and strength of him. As he worked at her corset strings, she picked open his buttons and untied his crumpled cravat.

He kissed her hair and her ear and the back of her neck as he efficiently pushed her chemise and gown and petticoats to her feet and released her corset, leaving her in naught but her underchemise and stockings. Bea wasn't nearly as experienced and had done no more than loosen his shirt so it fell open across his broad torso. He growled deep in his throat when her hands slid over his bare chest.

"The bath," he muttered, catching her hands before she unfastened his trousers. "I've been told it is the most modern in the kingdom and that we will all have one like it someday."

Ah, her far-seeing husband was back, however briefly. If he could see a future in her crumbling estate, he could see futures in baths, she supposed. Without protest, she let him lead her to a connecting door on the far side of the richly carpeted room.

"Your bath, my lady." He opened the door on a pink marble chamber gleaming in lamplight. Bubbles and steam rose above an enormous tub sunk into the floor, with gold fixtures somewhat resembling the pump faucet at home, but with more knobs than Bea dared disturb. Thick towels lay across enameled chairs, and a bowl of scented soaps awaited her discretion.

"And we will all have this in the future?" Her eyes widened at the marvel of such a tub, and the things to which it could be put to use.

"I want one." Behind her, Mac threw off his waist-coat and shirt.

Bea glanced uncertainly in his direction, and almost melted at the sight of all those broad muscles playing beneath his burnished skin. Did he wish to go first? Or . . . ?

He dropped his trousers, answering that question. Bea lifted her gaze from the evidence of his desire to read his expression. The intensity of the heat she found there nearly melted her into the same steaming puddle as the bath.

"It's big enough for both of us. A little water sport for our honeymoon?" he suggested, reaching for her chemise. In a single swoop, he stripped her and carried her to the bath.

Bea thought she'd died and gone to heaven as she sank, naked, beneath the foaming bubbles with her equally naked husband. Both of them, in a bath, to-gether. Doing things that—

Bea gasped as Mac smeared her breast with soap, lifted her on top of him, and kissed her senseless. Wrapping her arms around his brawny shoulders, she returned his kiss, and sank greedily where he placed her.

They'd make water babies this way.

Feeling utterly weightless and mindless of anything

but all the places where Mac was touching her, Bea murmured, "I love you, I love you," to the tempo of his hands caressing her breasts, and his avid pace as he stroked inside, where she burned for him.

"I'm seeing the future, and it involves lots of baths and wide linen sheets and the woman I love more than life itself. Will you follow wherever I go?" he asked against her ear as his hands evoked sensations that rippled through her skin and into her center.

"Whither thou goest, I will follow," Bea agreed, without hesitation. She belonged in his hands, in his home, wherever that might be.

And then he took her where they both wanted to go right then.

"Papa," Buddy solemnly greeted the man waiting for them on the dock the next day. Holding his toy sailboat in his hands, the boy clung to the security of Mac's arms, and looked to Bea for reassurance.

Sebastian, Viscount Simmons looked sadly bruised and more than a little haunted in the bright sunshine as he greeted the family stepping onto the boards. He looked first to a stern-faced Mac. "I'm sober," he declared immediately. "I simply wanted to see them."

From Bea's arms, Bitsy crowed in delight at the sight of a seagull swooping to grab a fish head on the pier. "Mama, Mama," she chanted, before resorting to a gibberish only she understood. The sun glinted off wisps of her golden curls and angelic pink cheeks.

Looking at Mac and the children, Bea allowed love to pour through her and spill over to the poor man who had ripped her out of her protected world and into the real one. The viscount's was a harsh world, and it would be harsher still for being denied the cheer of the children. Before Mac could say something rude, she smiled forgivingly. "I think they must look a lot like their mother," she said, reminding both men of the bond they held in common.

The viscount nodded with tears in his eyes. Mac would say they were from the glare of the sun, but Bea preferred the charity of believing the man actually cared.

"My boat!" Buddy yelled defiantly. Before Mac could shift him to a safer position, he scrambled down his leg and raced to the edge of the dock.

Bea emitted a brief squeal of terror as she swung to catch him, but then she saw what Buddy had seen. From the river, Mac's beautiful clipper raised its sails to catch the morning tide and wind. The sun glinted off the snowy white canvas, and danced on the gold lettering bearing her name, and a thrill of excitement chased through her as she eased closer to her husband. He draped his arm around her and watched admiringly as the clipper sailed away.

"Will you always regret this?" she asked sadly, feeling how much he must ache to see this thing of beauty sail off to his family without him.

"Never," he assured her. "We have all our lives to chase the seas, should we wish. We can make the decision to do so together." With a grumble, he released her to reach for Buddy, who leaned over the dock to set his own small boat in the water like his uncle's.

Buddy's father caught him first, holding him nervously by the waist of his trousers so the boy could reach the water and set the boat free.

As Mac stepped back to hold her again, Bea leaned against his shoulder and let tears of joy run down her cheeks. Life's road took strange twists and turns, and someday Buddy would be a viscount and an earl, like his father and grandfather before him. She would try to teach him a little of the people who would rely on him, so that he could lead the way into the future that was still a sparkle in Mac's eyes.

"Do you think the earl will visit Broadbury a little more often now?" she asked wistfully, thinking of the leaking church and the neglected store fronts.

"Certainly, if only so that his new wife might show off her finery," Mac said with a grin, disengaging Pamela's grasping fingers from his crumpled cravat.

Bea leaned over to smooth it for him. "And James?" She stepped back to admire her husband's broad chest adorned by the gleaming white linen.

"Matthew," he corrected. "I don't think I wish to hear the family discussion on his existence. The earl had to have known he was marrying an actress, not a saint."

"You know, I never understood what would make a respectable woman do indecent things with a man, but I think I understand a little better now," she mused.

"Experience," he teased. "You didn't even know what indecent things were until I taught you."

"Umm," she murmured, steadfastly watching the ship sail out of sight as pink heated her cheeks. "Do you know, I think James . . . Matthew looks a good deal like the portrait of my father at that age. Isn't that extraordinary?"

Mac rolled his eyes and grabbed Bitsy before she fell trying to climb onto his shoulders. "Yes, quite extraordinary," he agreed with a measure of haste. "And now don't you think we should take our two new governesses back to town and introduce them to Broadbury?"

Bea smiled beautifully. "We can have a school now, and the Widow Black will have her sister to help her. The future looks bright to me."

"Aye, and it fair glitters with gold from here," Mac agreed huskily.

"Good, then we can ask Overton to teach James

Matthew about estate management too." Briskly, she strode down the dock toward the waiting carriages.

He hadn't known how to tell her about her half brother, but she knew, Mac realized. And she accepted James just as she had accepted children who weren't her own. She simply opened her heart and shared it with everyone, without judgment. *Definitely extraordinary.*

As Mac carried Bitsy, and the viscount gathered up a struggling Buddy, the two men exchanged understanding glances for the first time in their lives, forced into partnership by the impenetrable logic of women.

"It's beds they belong in," Mac muttered, stomping toward the street.

"It's beds that get us these." Simmons indicated his son as Buddy screeched, grabbed his hair, and tried to catch a seagull.

Mac grinned and watched the sway of his wife's skirts ahead. In a few months' time, she could be big with his child. That ought to slow her down.

"Yes," he agreed joyfully. "I'll have to build and name a ship for every child she gives me." A family of ships, definitely a plan for the future, he thought in satisfaction.